THE
BROKEN
LAND

OTHER BANTAM BOOKS BY IAN McDONALD

DESOLATION ROAD
EMPIRE DREAMS
KING OF MORNING, QUEEN OF DAY
OUT ON BLUE SIX
SPEAKING IN TONGUES

THE BROKEN LAND

IAN McDONALD

BANTAM BOOKS
NEW YORK·TORONTO·LONDON·SYDNEY·AUCKLAND

THE BROKEN LAND

A Bantam Spectra Book / October 1992

Published simultaneously in hardcover and trade paperback

BOOK DESIGN BY GRETCHEN ACHILLES

Library of Congress Cataloging-in-Publication Data

McDonald, Ian, 1960–
     The broken land / Ian McDonald.
        p.   cm.
     ISBN 0-553-08983-8 (hc)
     ISBN 0-553-37054-5 (pbk)
     I. Title.
     PR6063.C38B76   1992
     823'.914—dc20   92-7696
                                                        CIP

Published simultaneously in the United States and Canada

PRINTED IN THE UNITED STATES OF AMERICA

FFG   0 9 8 7 6 5 4 3 2 1

TO PATRICIA,
ALWAYS.

TIM AND ALLIE:
THE FLAGS ARE STILL THERE,
BUT WE AREN'T.

THE
BROKEN
LAND

THE
TOWNSHIP

GRANDFATHER WAS A TREE.

Father grew trux, in fifteen colors.

Mother could sing the double-helix song, sing it right into the hearts of living things and change them. *Around we go, and round.* . . .

A house ran amok in Fifteenth Street the day the soldiers of the Emperor Across the River came to Mathembe's township. The sound of the armored carriers in the streets of Chepsenyt frightened it. Split into its components it was a thing of little intelligence, easily frightened. One of the big dazzle-painted metal machines had lurched to a halt across the end of Fifteenth Street and the house had panicked. Civilians and soldiers and house units like long hexagonal centipedes, or wheels, or domes on soft-running plastic treads, or concertinas with legs: all running around in the street, the civilians trying to round up the house units, the soldiers trying to round up the civilians.

The Rajavs had wanted to have the house reassembled by night. Now it did not look like they would ever find all the components of their home again. Mathembe shooed away a big skittering thing like a walking umbrella that was making a dash for the trux pens. It would have alarmed the young organicals, sent them careering into each other, wheels spinning. The Rajavs were moving up to the Proclaimer end of town. Twelve generations had lived and died on Fifteenth Street; now they had packed their lives into five trux and disassembled their house into its components. They had been working since before the edge of the world dipped beneath the sun. Mathembe had been fascinated. She had never seen a house come apart before. Twelve generations, and now they were going. They did not care who knew the reason. Intimidated out of their own homes: Mr. Rajav shouted it in the streets for all to hear. Threatening letters, obscene notes, attempts to burn law-abiding citizens out of their own homes. The Ghost Boys. That was who were behind it. The Ghost Boys. Thugs, the lot of them. Louts.

It had not been much of a fire. A halfhearted bomb attack that had left a few scorch marks on the walls, soon cleaned off. Not even worth troubling the police in Timboroa over. Mathembe suspected her younger brother Hradu's involvement. He and Kajree Rajav had been friends until the Word of God had come from the tabernacle and Mr. Rajav had forbidden his son to keep company with idolatrous Confessors.

They would go to their own kind, the Rajavs; they would stay not one moment longer among those they had always thought of as friends, always treated as good neighbors, and who all along had wanted them out, wanted their home burned and them dead, wanted the skins of all the Proclaimers in Chepsenyt flayed and nailed to their front doors.

And now they were dashing about trying to round up the fleeing, panicked sections of their house.

The armored carrier turned. Its metal tracks squealed dreadfully on the ceramic cobbles. It came down Fifteenth Street. Mr. Rajav shouted at it to go back, go away, but the machine came on, so hard and pressing that the soft contours of the street barely seemed capable of containing it. Standing half out of a hatchway was a soldier in the black uniform of the Emperor Across the River. He was shouting but no one could hear what he was saying because of the people's voices and the din of the engine. No soldier likes to go unnoticed. He swung the big black heavy machine gun on its mount so that it pointed upward, fired. Five, ten, twenty shots. At the sound of the shots tearing the air apart the people fell silent and still. The pieces of dismembered house ran where they willed while the people listened to what the soldier had to say to them.

The Emperor Across the River required that all citizens of Chepsenyt township in the Prefecture of Timboroa present themselves at the town center. Forthwith.

All citizens?

All citizens. Forthwith.

The soldier was very young. He had the pale hair and skin of the people from across the river. The long pale hair was tied back in the military fashion and fastened with a clasp bearing the symbol of the Emperor: a hand with a heart in its palm. He spoke the Old Speech grammatically enough for one not born to it, though his cross-river accent sent the inflections staggering hither and yon. The hands that rested on the black heavy machine gun seemed to Mathembe too young and soft for such devices. Tinny trebly music came from the open cockpit.

Mr. Rajav, small and very very angry, stood before the hard metal face of the troop carrier and the soldier with the pale, soft hands.

"I am a loyal Proclaimer, a true subject of the Emperor; you cannot mean me, you cannot include me and my family with those of questionable loyalty." He licked his lips with a tiny dart of the tongue, left and right, so; looked from side to side, so, as he said the words "those of questionable loyalty."

"All citizens," the carrier commander said in his grammatically correct Old Speech. The carrier's engines blared into life. Black smoke puffed from exhaust ports. The vehicle came slowly down Fifteenth Street. Its squeaking tracks left ugly, regular scratches on the glass cobbles. Mr. Rajav stood before it, small and very very angry. So angry and proud he could not see what Mathembe could see: that the carrier was not going to stop. Ten meters five meters three meters; then it was as if Mr. Rajav had been touched with the illuminating wand of one of the Ykondé saints. He saw the advancing carrier for what it was, an unstoppable irresistible wall of metal. He jumped to one side as the machine brushed past him. The soldiers of the Emperor Across the

River within laughed. Mathembe could hear their laughter, and the loud dance music from their cockpit radio.

Mr. Rajav was white and trembling. The street value of his loyalty had shocked him. The house units ran wild and capering down Fifteenth Street toward the paddies and orchards.

The people gathered at the Founding Tree: Confessors and loyal Proclaimers. The Founding Tree was the heart and root of Chepsenyt township. From it had grown every house and garden and paddy, every shit beetle and gloglobe and ceramic cobble scratched by the tracks of the war machines of the Emperor Across the River. The tree had been planted uncounted thousands of years of dreaming ago when the Green Wave broke across the barren land and the Ahleles had gone striding out, covering whole prefectures in a single stride, calling out the heart names, the cell names, of every living thing and binding them to their service. The Founding Tree stood, as befitted its legendary stature (though there was nothing much to look at; you had to see it with the eyes of faith), in a large glass-cobbled square surrounded by half-dead half-bankrupt shops that sold nothing of any significance and cafés where the old people played their endless games of *fili* and got drunk and garrulous on bad wine.

Five armored carriers were parked around the edge of the square. A young trux nuzzled up to one, mistaking it for a syrup digester. Laughing, the soldiers drove the little mound of blue synthetic flesh away but it kept nuzzling back again. It was only content when one of the soldiers fed it a stick of chocolate. When all the people were gathered, Confessor and Proclaimer, an officer stepped forward. He was dressed in the black combat uniform of the Emperor's army. Beside him was a tall metal pole topped with a crossbar. The crossbar was wrapped in a cloth. When he was certain, quite certain, that every eye was fixed on him, the officer in black pulled a release cord. The wrapping came undone and fell to the ground.

A cry went up from the people in the porcelain square.

Fixed to a rack at the top of the pole were five heads.

They were long dead, those heads. Lips had shrunk away from gums. Eyes, hair had fallen out, the skin was shriveled and leathery. Long dead, but still alive. The organicals clutching greedily to their severed necks maintained them. They were alive though dead, and they would speak.

This is what the heads said.

The heads said they had been foolish and vain and proud in raising their hand against the righteous, fair, and good government of the Emperor Across the River. They said an eternity would not hold enough sorrow for how they had misled young men and women and incited them to insurrection against the Radiant Personage of the Emperor. They said forever would not be long enough to live out the guilt they felt for having caused the deaths of these fine young men and women. They asked the forgiveness of the people of Chepsenyt township. They begged the forgiveness of the Emperor Across the River. Most of all, they craved the forgiveness of those they had so vilely misled under the banner of the Warriors of Destiny.

When the heads had spoken, the officer in black took down the pole and wrapped the heads in their cloth. The soldiers woke themselves, woke the engines of their carriers, and one after the other drove away through the narrow streets and closes of Chepsenyt, tapping their fingers to the music of the cockpit radios.

"My God," Mathembe's father said at the table when the world had risen above the sun and the gloglobes hovering in the corner of the room had stirred and turned on their cool yellow light. "My God, it would almost make you want to join the Warriors of Destiny, it would."

Mathembe's mother gave her husband a look that warned against saying such things in front of Hradu. It was the impressionability of the young that had led so many into the Warriors of Destiny and to eternity as heads on poles. Impressionability, and the idealism of youth.

"Still," Mathembe's mother said, "they did not have to do that, not that with the heads; that was barbaric. Inhuman. They try to teach us that the way of the Empire is more civilized than the ways we have lived for four thousand years, and then they put heads on poles. They did not have to do that. They were wicked and stupid people"—this for Hradu, chewing his food absently, round-eyed with fascination: his parents talking *sedition*—"but they did not have to do that. It would have been enough to have sentenced them to servitude. Maybe for a long time, maybe twenty, maybe fifty years, but not to do that."

Mathembe rapped the back of Hradu's hand with her spoon for he had grown so enwrapped in the conversation that he had forgotten to chew and the food was dribbling from his mouth. She remembered the time when there had been a Public Absolving in Founding Tree Square. Her parents had not thought it a suitable spectacle for a young girl—it had been years before her puberty—but she had taken herself surreptitiously along and lost herself in the crowd. There had been the Town Procurator in his sash of office, and a State Executor who had come down from Timboroa on a government traix. It was clearly an event of some import: Chepsenyt's snack vendors and tea sellers had left their established pitches to patrol the edge of the crowd, scuffling as they vied for customers.

A reverent hush fell as victim and convict entered the square. The case was a celebrated one. The convict had been found guilty of rape and had been sentenced by the court at Timboroa to the organical service of his victim until such time as she forgave him. Mathembe's father remembered the case. He had been of the same generation as victim and culprit when the crime had taken place. He had known them both. Now, after fifteen years serving the woman he had raped, fifteen years working in her plantations and paddies as a gardener organical, the rapist was to be forgiven.

The Procurator read aloud the declaration of forgiveness. The woman assented. The State Executor went to the tall, spindly gardener organical, all legs and arms and fingers and eyes, and did something that Mathembe could not quite see because the crowd all pushed forward for a better look. She tried to press through, press through the tight-pressed bodies and the craning necks and the voices asking *What's going on what's happening can you see?* and when she pressed to the front she saw a ball of tangled floss, like a silken cocoon within which a dark, not-quite-human shape moved. The sun had crossed the sky; the vendors had traded their teas and wines and snacks. When Mathembe was quite sure that nothing was going to happen and was about to go home, the silk cocoon had torn, ripped, from top to bottom, and a man tumbled out onto the glass cobbles, naked and wrinkled and far, far more than fifteen years older than when he had been changed in that same square into an organical.

She remembered the way he had looked at his hands, as if they were friends he had not seen for many many years.

"Pray God you never get sentenced to serve a Proclaimer," a voice on her right hand had said. "They never forgive."

She thought about that naked man kneeling dumbfounded on the cobbles as her parents hid away the true extent of their outrage at the speaking heads for fear their children might see it. He might have been her father, that naked, kneeling man.

After the meal she went to visit her grandfather. He had been dead almost a year but still was not fully absorbed into the Ancestor Tree. Her grandmother (little more than a single sunlit memory of an old woman shaping birds from plasm and setting them humming and flapping around the conservatory) had been drawn into the Dreaming in less than half a year, so Mathembe's mother said. The old grandfather had always been a bad-tempered, stubborn, feisty spirit.

His death was widely believed to have been an act of political defiance when the New Namers came to Chepsenyt township in the early spring of the previous year. You would not have thought such gray, drab little people capable of the disruption they were to unleash upon Chepsenyt. You would not have thought as you saw them walking from street to street, house to house, pointing and writing things down in their recorders, that they would take away the names of everything, the ancient names, warm and familiar from hundreds of generations of usage, from the people's mouths and give them dry, lifeless streams of meaningless syllables in their place.

As part of the ongoing process of the cultural assimilation of Mathembe's land into the wider civilization of the Empire, New Speech, the language that the Emperor in his Jade City used for his lovemaking and his lawgiving, was to be given equal status with Old Speech. It was intended that, through proper education, Old Speech would become obsolete and be replaced by New Speech, thus tying the transfluvian provinces indissolubly into the greater life of the Empire. To this end, Inspectors, trained linguists all, were dispatched the length and breadth of the land to change the cumbersome phonemes of Old Speech into syllables that sat comfortably on the tongue of the Emperor and his governors.

The New Namers, those gray men and gray women, had come in their soft gray mechanical car with its Imperial crest and its pall of choking vapors and would hardly have been noticed in Chepsenyt save that where the car went spreading its black foul-smelling fumes the names of the houses and gardens and closes changed, only by a vowel here, a consonant there, a diphthong elsewhere, a glide vowel shifted, a glottal stop modulated to make them pronounceable to tongues conditioned to New Speech, until in the end, when the gray car drove away up the road to Timboroa, there was no township of Chepsenyt, no closes or gardens or streets or houses, only a pile of names that sounded like the names they had worn since the Green Wave broke across the land but which were totally without meaning. Nonsense names. Babblings.

The coming and going of the New Namers was one of the few events that united Confessors and Proclaimers. The new nameplates in curvilinear Imperial that went up on the road into Chepsenyt vanished the same night they were erected: the work, so the township gossips had it, of an unholy and unique alliance between the Confessor Ghost Boys and junior members of the Proclaimer Spirit Lodges. Advocate Kalimuni, the Filelis' neighbor and prominent in the Proclaimer community, wrote in his official capacity to the Prefect of Timboroa protesting on behalf of the loyal Proclaimers of Chepsenyt whose rights and cultural heritage as a distinct and unique grouping were being eroded without regard for five hundred years of history. Though fluent in both tongues—New Speech was the language of the law and the courts—Dr. Kalimuni wrote the letter in Old Speech. It was a very beautiful letter. Dr. Kalimuni was considered one of Chepsenyt's finest ideographers.

The advocate Kalimuni and Mathembe's grandfather had been firmest friends. Their friendship was of the kind that is nourished by the friends' total inability to agree upon a single point. Over their endless games of *fili* under the awning of the Teahouse of the Celestial Blossom, they had argued Proclaimerism versus Confessorism, Imperialism versus Nationalism, organic technology versus inorganic technology with such vehemence that Proprietor Murangeringi had been on the verge of calling the constabulary at Tetsenok to restore peace to the glass squares of Chepsenyt. They had once argued long into the star-filled night, long after the chairs had settled back into their sleeping configuration and the awning had retracted, over the color of a speed dog that sat across the square from them scratching at parasites. They argued in Old Speech, of course, for it was the language of dissent and laughter. Now even the word "speed dog" had been reduced to meaningless sounds.

As a Confessor, Mathembe's grandfather could not resort to the law and organs of government with the same facility as Proclaimer

Kalimuni. Nevertheless, he too played his part in the protest against the New Namers. He embarked upon a word boycott. He refused to call by name anything that had been renamed by the Emperor's linguists. A point, a nod, a shrug, a general indication of "that there" or "this here" or "yonder thing" was all he would permit himself. People were reduced to monosyllabic grunts. Family, friends of many years' standing: grunt. Whole districts of township, prefecture, nation, and world became a *thitherward* toss of the head. He spat them all out as if they were shit and ashes on his tongue.

Mathembe felt solidarity with him in his boycott. His silence was not as complete as hers, but it was a bond between them. They became eloquent in silence. Even at the end when it was obvious to all that his dying was upon him and the time to enter the Dreaming and the fellowship of his ancestors nigh, he had obdurately refused to allow words tainted by the hand of the Emperor Across the River to remain on his lips. He had summoned advocate Kalimuni (by grunt and general indication) and demanded that he draw up a will that made sure everyone received their dues without actually having to be mentioned by name. He became legendary: the township came to know him as the man who was starving himself to death on silence. Though, as he confided to Mathembe, "No one ever died for want of words in his mouth, or you'd be dead long ago, granddaughter of mine. No, you have it right. Never to speak at all: that is the highest, the noblest protest."

Unto the very end when the people from the House of Heads came with their ritual masks and valises of organic technology to lop off the head, connect it to its support systems, and transport it, closed-eyed and cyanotic, to the Grove of the Ancestors, he had refused to call Mathembe by name. Even when he had felt the dying break over him like a cold drowning wave and he had cried out for someone to help him, hold him, please, hold him—though he knew the journey into the Dreaming is one we must all make alone—he had called out, "Son of mine, daughter-in-law of mine, granddaughter of mine!"

After the head had been grafted into the Fileli family tree, many in the township came to congratulate it for having protested unto death. The head did not acknowledge their presence. The people went away, hushed and reverent. The head was obviously in deep communion with the ancestors in the Dreaming, the great network of roots and synapses that underpinned the physical landscape into which the individual consciousness of the dead passed.

The head was doing nothing of the sort. The head was maintaining in death the protest it had made in life. It would not accept the praise and platitudes of those who honored it for doing something they had not the integrity to do themselves. It closed its ears to their words. It would not even recognize Dr. Kalimuni when he came to visit his old friend. It was a bold thing for the advocate Kalimuni to do—if the shrine moderator learned that he had been to visit a pagan Ancestor Grove, he would have been Named and quite possibly shunned by his co-religionists. Proclaimers, when they died, were gathered straight into the person of God. Mathembe admired their confidence. The Dreaming might not be heaven, but it was a fairly safe bet on some form of immortality and required no undue exercise of faith.

The only visitor that earned a flicker of recognition was Mathembe. She established a fuller communication with her grandfather in death than she had ever been able to achieve in life. Her visits to the Ancestor Grove became daily affairs. When the forests fell silent in that space between evening and night and the gloglobes began to stir themselves into luminescence, she would slip through the forest gate into the perpetual penumbra beneath the great trees that stood in the Grove of the Ancestors. Twisted, gnarled trunks, knotted and carbuncled, extended upward twenty, thirty, forty meters before arching into a dense canopy of branches and red leaves. Dead ancestors cast dark shadows. Each knot, each gnarl and whorl on the trunks was a soul—a head ten, a hundred, a thousand years old that had been absorbed into the flesh of the tree. If some seemed like faces it was because they were faces: lips, nose, eyes of wood, bearded and haired with red leaves, a slow metamorphosis from flesh life to root life. In the deeper shadows between the root buttresses tiny lights glowed: vials of bioluminescents, placed there with bread and fruit and wine as an offering to the dreamers. Anticipations of oracles to be given, heart thanks for oracles received. The souls of the dead flying free through the neural matrix of the roots could access an incalculable wealth of information. Occasionally they might be cajoled into offering insight and wisdom on specific problems of the living. Occasionally. More often than not they preferred to remain incommunicado within the nirvana communion of the Dreaming, the ecstasy of being at once everything and nothing, everywhere and nowhere, simultaneous and instantaneous. The dead surrendered their existenceless existence grudgingly and resented demands to solve problems that would yield to the simple application of common sense. Small wonder the popular belief that the dead were a testy crew.

Mathembe moved between moss-carpeted root buttresses glowing in their dark recesses with a thousand tiny bioluminescent stars. Prayer wands, each bearing a paper petition impaled on the end, bent and whispered their messages to the souls of the dead as wind stirred the grove. You had to be careful of those long, thin wands in the twilight between the trees. Only the season before, an old woman coming to nag her dead husband on his selfishness in leaving her a widow had tripped, fallen, and needed a new left eye grown in by the medicals. No uncertain petition to leave on a prayer wand, a left eyeball. She had died the following season: prayer answered. Mathembe slipped between the swaying prayer wands. Half-dendrified heads rolled their eyes to watch her pass by. Framed by wooden lips forever half open, moss-green tongues shaped silent syllables.

Her grandfather's head was the lowest on the tree that had sent the souls of two hundred generations of Filelis into the Dreaming. The callus of wood immediately above him, which still bore a caricature of a face, was Mathembe's grandmother. Her absorption into the Dreaming had been swift and blessed: Mathembe's grandfather had told Mathembe that he had searched long for her along the roots and fibers of the matrix but always in vain. He wondered that she might have transferred her spirit onto one of the Saint-ships that on rare occasions entered planetary space and sent her mind flying out across the universe among the Daughter Worlds. It was a great sorrow to him that beyond the loneliness of death could be the loneliness of the Dreaming.

Mathembe came every day to tell her grandfather how his township was faring on its journey through history. Great things and small things, those things that make a history. How the township educators had been given language implants for New Speech which they were to distribute to every child of educable age and those adults who expressed an interest. How the shopkeepers and café owners had been ordered by law to display a picture of the Emperor Across the

River in the glory of his regalia in a prominent position in their establishments. How her mother feared that Hradu was falling under the unhealthy influence of a gang of boys some years his senior: not that they might bully him, as boys inevitably will, or sexually humiliate him, as boys inevitably will, but that they might lead him into the Ghost Boys, which had been a semi-respectable society in her and her husband's young days but now seemed little more than a direct artery into the Warriors of Destiny. How those men, and women too, who called themselves Warriors of Destiny had vowed to drive the soldiers of the Emperor Across the River back across that wide river of his, back to his Jade City, so that this land which had been so long a province might be a nation once again. All these things she told him, everything: the hows, the whys, the wherefores of the life of the living. She thought she understood something of the loneliness of the dead. She understood *separation*.

Mathembe clapped her hands. It was an abrupt, almost shocking sound in the holy peace of the grove. The heads of the recently departed awoke in consternation. When they saw that it was only that strange rude girl, they returned to their dreaming.

"Ignore them," her grandfather said. "Bores, the lot of them. Bores. And farts. Can't even get a good game of *fili* out of them, always slipping into the Dreaming and forgetting the moves. Not one of them the match of the advocate, and he a left-handed Proclaimer. So, granddaughter of mine, what has been happening in this wicked world of yours?"

She told him. She told him about the Rajav family and the house units running wild in the streets. She told him about the big metal troop carriers and the soldiers of the Emperor Across the River with their long pale hair tied back and the music that accompanied them as they drove to war. She told him about the shooting and the people gathered in Founding Tree Square to hear what the heads of the dead rebels had to say to them. She told him all this. Not with words. She had no use for words, for language. She told him with a speech deeper and more articulate than language. She told him with the speech of her entire body: with mime and dance and sly, brief facial expressions, with looks and glances and mummery, with posture and pose and poise. She told him in her language, the only language she would speak, that seemed so clumsy and open to misinterpretation when broken into its component names but which, when performed by a young woman in the dark of the evening shade beneath the ancestors of Chepsenyt, becomes far far more than its constituents. It becomes more expressive, more lucid, more liquid and graceful than any spoken language. Language that transcends speech and becomes a new kind of silence. Movement that transcends motion and becomes a new kind of stillness.

And Mathembe stopped.

Something had moved in the darkness between the Ancestor Trees. She scooped round cobbles from the ground. It was said by those who see politics at the bottom of their soup bowls that there was no part of the land where glass cobbles could not be found buried in the soil, thus proving the continuity of biotechnological civilization. Even the earth beneath your feet serves in the struggle for nationhood. Mathembe hefted the solid, round cobble in her hand. She could throw far, hard. She could throw farther than any of the boys who came calling for Hradu.

Again.

It moved. Soft rustling of disturbed vegetation. Closer now: movement, sound, and a smell to join them. She flared her nostrils, frowned at the smell of something so familiar she could not identify it in isolation.

These things, when they happen, happen suddenly. Suddenly, a flurry of movement; suddenly, a bustle of sound; suddenly, a face staring at her over the root buttresses of a tree not twenty meters from her. She cried out wordlessly.

The face was not a human face. It was a face of triangles: triangle eyes, downturned triangle mouth, twin triangular slots for nostrils, huge triangular flaps of ears to each side, all on a long thin triangular face marked with a stark black-and-white maze pattern.

Not a face. A mask.

She let fly her cobble with a yell of anger, but the mask was too fast for her. The mask's wearer crashed and leaped away through the roots and the prayer wands. Grandfather's head hurried it on its way with a stream of oaths and imprecations.

It had been no ordinary mask, such as a child might make for a crèche-group pageant. This mask she had seen before in one of the semi-religious festivals when the young men paraded the icons of the

Ykondé saints through the streets to the doors and windows of every Confessor household in Chepsenyt and had their piety rewarded with wine. It was a Ghost Boy *pneuma* mask. For all the strength of her arm that could outthrow every boy on Fifteenth Street, Mathembe no longer felt safe and private in the Grove of the Ancestors. Its spirit of darkness and contemplation had been violated by the aggressive, sexual spirit of the *pneuma* mask.

The masks themselves were not dangerous. Until you put them on they were bland, flaccid sheets of flesh; then their integral circuitry took up your dominant emotion and amplified it and molded the mask's shape and coloring into the expression of that emotion. Some models featured pheromone-generating glands. That would account for the unfamiliar-in-its-familiarity smell.

The masks themselves were not dangerous. The wearers of the masks could be, when the emotion-enhancing circuitry fed back that emotion to the wearer in a self-reinforcing loop. When the wearer was a Ghost Boy and could claim immunity, invulnerability, and infallibility for being in the possession of an angel, then the masks could be very dangerous indeed. How long had he been watching her? Days? Weeks? Her skin felt unclean, with the itching, crawling of many insects. She was angry, angry and impotent in her anger. She flung a second glass cobble with all her might out into the dark and the soft glowing of votive lights; and another, and another, and another. The violation of her privacy could not have been any greater if he had spied upon her cleaning herself during her period.

The next afternoon the boys came calling for Hradu to come out with them and do whatever it was boys did that involved much idle hanging around street corners. Mathembe drove them away with stones and sun-dried shit from the trux pens.

It is the holy day. In the darkness before the world tips its edge beneath the sun, old Jashar the cantor has climbed the one hundred and two steps of the tower. One hundred and two steps, each in total darkness. He thinks of each step as a prayer, the tower as a parable of his personal journey to God. One hundred and two steps, once a week, for fifty years. He must have climbed halfway to heaven by now. As the first red limb of the sun appears, he flexes his old muscles in the cold and swings the heavy wooden hammer against the metal gong with deceptive, long-practiced ease. As the dawn light comes spilling across the top of the forest that enfolds Chepsenyt like a mother's womb, his voice goes out with the boom of the gong, out across the rooftops and treetops of Chepsenyt. There are other, stronger singers in the congregation of the shrine but none have the unearthly plangency of Jashar. The voice of an angel—say it low. Proclaimerism does not admit angels, or saints, or holy men. Each Proclaimer is all the holy men, saints, and angels that is necessary. Each Proclaimer may ultimately, will ultimately, become God through oneness with him. The song of Jashar Cantor goes out across rooftops and forest. Out in the dawn light that grows in strength and definition with every passing moment are two dark shapes moving above the forest. Hunting. Jashar does not see them. He sings the goodness and holiness of God, and the light of this world is darkness to him compared to the greater light of God.

The helicopters turn, rise up. The helicopters tilt their noses downward and head away together, very fast, over the top of the forest.

In the houses at the high end of the township, the Proclaimers make themselves ready. They have been making themselves ready since before dawn. That is the Proclaimer way, to rise in the darkness and make themselves ready. The children are complaining that they are hungry. This, too, is the Proclaimer way, to fast from the preceding sunset until their return from the tabernacle. The way of the most pious, that is. Come on, children, hurry up, we are going to be late; oh, I suppose God won't notice one little biscuit. Go on. Don't tell your mother. Have you got your hat? Where's your hat? Neesa, have you seen Ajad's hat? Well, give it back to him at once. Right. Can we go now?

Out they come with their heads respectfully hatted, led down by voice and banging gong through the glass streets that wind between the houses to the tabernacle. In his house at the low end of town advocate Kalimuni unhooks his Book of Witnesses from behind his ears, removes the reader from his right temple, and rises to answer the voice and the banging banging gong. Hurry hurry, quick quick. Lajmee the warden is busy with water and soap, washing a crude sketch of a man from the doorpost of the tabernacle. He must have it all washed away before the congregation arrives and is defiled by looking upon the representation of a human. It is no defilement to the one who washes it away, it would seem. Confessor louts. Nothing better to do. I suppose they think they are so clever and funny, hah hah.

There is always one late one, always one running for the door as it is closing, clutching hat to head, dragging children one two three four behind. It is always the same one. Now the banging banging banging gong and the singing voice can cease and Jashar Cantor descend the one hundred and two steps. Now the people are assembled in the presence of God, cross-legged on the neatly swept court under God's heaven. The men take their Books of Witnesses from their cases, hook them behind their ears, or lay them on their laps if they are the very old family models, press the readers to their temples. They always close their eyes while waiting for the inspiration of God and so can never see what the women and children see, that they all sit in exactly the same way, left elbow propped on left thigh, left forefinger pressed contemplatively to lips.

The men wait for the inspiration of God as the Scriptures tumble through their frontal lobes. The children fidget and play visual games with the blue sky and the floaters in their eyes. They are thinking about lunch. The women poke them in their fidgeting, which is no way at all to stop someone from fidgeting. They are thinking about lunch too. And sex. And Mrs. Anjalati across the road, the things she gets up to. And new clothes for the children. And are they safe when they go down to the tabernacle for religious instruction, with all those Confessor children hanging around the way they do? A thousand and one thoughts. All in the silence under the presence of God.

They come suddenly, so fast they are on top of the noise of their own approach. There is just enough of a warning for everyone to look up as the two black helicopters storm overhead in a threshing of rotors. The sound of the engines booms in the confines of the tabernacle like a drum. The downwash from their blades sends the carefully swept dust swirling up in choking clouds and hats rolling every way.

Have they no respect? Those were helicopters of the Emperor. Fellow Proclaimers. You think so? I tell you, to those from across the river, there is no difference. They look at us and they look at the Confessors and all they see are meatmen. That is what they call us, you know, meatmen. But what business have they to be flying about on the holy day anyway? Security. Everything is equally holy and equally profane in the name of security. Anyway, they are not true

Proclaimers like we are true Proclaimers. They are Proclaimers in name only; their faith means nothing to them. Nominalism. It has not stood the test of fire and tribulation.

The presence of God is not a place you rush into apologizing that you are so busy, so much to do, sorry. You would rush like that into the presence of the Emperor in the Jade City, would you? Preparations must be made, disciplines, stillings and quietings. Peace. Stillness. Silence. Let the inner spaces expand and be filled with the presence of God, let the word of the Book of Witnesses wash over you until the hand of God illuminates one particular canto and impels you to share it with your brothers and sisters. Silence. Stillness, peace. A presence touches you, a vast singing space through which shafts of golden light move, ineffably, inexorably.

Oh, what is that *now*?

Voices. In animated, excited conversation. Men's voices, women's voices, the high, thrilled voices of children. Why do they have to stop right outside? And why, when their voices are so loud, can you not make out a single word they are saying, so you have to strain all the more to listen and in the end what you are listening to is not the voice of God at all but the voices from outside? Silver laughter of women. Deeper, brazen laughter of men. Music, from radios. Hands clapping feet tapping, women singing along with the songs they seem to have been born knowing. The slap of children's running feet on the glass cobbles, the sharper, more self-conscious voices of the teenagers. Wheels: trux, drawing up outside. You ready? We're ready. You got? We got.

God burn you all, damn Confessors, for your idolatry, for your superstition, for your obdurate refusal to embrace true religion, for your rebellious spirits, for your feckless ways, for your manifold offenses toward God's Elect, but most of all, most unforgivably of all, for being able to laugh and talk and tap your fingers and feet to music while we Proclaimers are here in the tabernacle keeping silence, waiting for God to speak.

There was to be a trux hunt. Mathembe's father and some of the other growers in the township had arranged it. At any time there was a considerable population of feral trux wild in the forests around Chepsenyt. Some were cullings that had escaped and against the odds reached maturity, some those that had developed a spark of willfulness in their rudimentary brains and broken free from their conditioning, some the descendants of trux that had gone feral generations before. Whatever their pedigree or lack thereof, the wild trux were valued by the growers for their hybrid vigor and the genetic strength life in the wild conferred: attributes useful to the often overrefined domestic strains.

There had been complaints from among the poorer landowners that wild trux already rampant in the common foraging lands in the forest fringes were beginning to encroach upon their gardens and plantations. Trux were catholic and enthusiastic converters of vegetation to muscular energy. Feral populations totally defoliated entire tracts of forest in a matter of days, and legends abounded of plagues of trux reducing townships to famine level, devouring gardens, trees, houses, people, anything in their paths. Mathembe's father had always treated such tales with professional contempt. "Look," he had said, taking a young Mathembe and a younger Hradu down to the pens. "They metabolize complex sugars. There is no conceivable way a trux could eat a human being. They eat fruit, plants, and mech syrup. We would probably poison them. Anyway, they haven't any teeth."

Teeth or no, even a small family group could leave the smaller landholders of Chepsenyt destitute, forced to borrow heavily from the commercial gene banks or live hand to mouth from the common foraging. They had approached Mr. Fileli, who had approached the other truxers, and over wine and cakes (more wine, much more wine than cakes) in a street café they had arranged the hunt. It was not until the morning of the hunt as the people were gathering with their bottles of wine and flasks of maté and picnic lunches that they remembered this was the Proclaimer holy day and that Nasmir Jhirabha, one of the most important truxers in Timboroa Prefecture, would not be able to come. Holy Day or no, Nasmir Jhirabha came, in his boots and jacket of many pockets and broad, grinning, bearded face, radio staff clenched in his great left fist. Doubtless he would be Named before the congregation. God could wait. Trux could not.

First to go out would be the runners. To be a runner was an honor only bestowed upon the youngest and fittest. Their task was to run up beside the trux and slap a dazzler on it. Each runner was equipped with a belt pouch of these devices, organic circuits that, correctly placed, overloaded the trux's rudimentary nervous system with hallucinations and forced it to an introspective, dazed halt. Even in the dense understory of the forest, trux were capable of a surprising turn of speed when startled. It was something to brag about, if you were a boy and wanted to impress a girl, or even another boy, that you had run down a trux.

The truxers themselves, and the older, less spry members of their retinues, followed more sedately behind with docility circuits to brand and control their dazzled trux. Last of all came the very oldest and very youngest, laying out the great common picnic in clearings deep in the forest that had been hallowed for this purpose since the time of the Green Wave.

It had been a long time since there had been a trux hunt in Chepsenyt. That time Mathembe had wanted to go with her father but he had told her she was too small; she must go with her grandfather and grandmother in red trux to help with the food. She had seen the runners go loping and whooping and whistling into the forest and wished she could have gone with them. *Next time,* her father had promised. *When you are bigger.* Now was the next time. She had the belt pouch of dazzlers. She had her radio on a thong about her neck. She had her running shoes laced tight and close on her feet. She went to stand with the other young men and women who had been chosen to be runners. The young men were playing about, trying to smack each other on the head with their dazzlers. The organic circuitry could deal synesthetic shocks if they hit right: the smell of blue and the color of cold and the sound of light. There were slaps and yells and laughter. Nasmir Jhirabha shouted at them to stop messing about. The boys jeered him because he was a Proclaimer. When the young men saw Mathembe in her running shoes and tights and belt pouch and radio around her neck they laughed.

Oh yes, and how are you going to tell them where to go when you find a trux? Not bothering to add, *If you find a trux.*

Mathembe shrugged eloquently, dismissively raised the second object on a thong around her neck to her lips. It was a clay ocarina in the shape of a fat bird. She played a trill of notes and the boys did not laugh then because what she played was exactly the sound that the forest made at the place where two enormous fan trees rose from a grove of wild brownmeat. On her ocarina she could imitate the music of any part of the forest, and anyone listening on a radio staff who knew the forest would know within meters where to find the trux.

Mathembe's father and the other truxers were looking around them to see if there were any more still to come, which was the cue for the runners to stir themselves and jostle for the best exits. As always, the young men pushed themselves to the front under the eternal, erroneous impression that they were more deserving than the young women. The truxers conferred among themselves. Heads nodded. Nasmir Jhirabha bellowed out, "All right then. Let's be off!"

Whooping and jeering and calling out wild ebullient meaningless syllables, the runners went striking out through the paddy fields and forest gardens, leaping and ducking and weaving between the bulbous sacs of the wine fermentors and the spindle trees with their encircling clouds of bobbin flies on long silk threads. Gardener organicals fled from the breaking wave of ululating, wildly colored young bodies, went down waving sticklike manipulator arms. The young men and women of Chepsenyt hurdled over them, onward, into the greater forest beyond.

Mathembe ran alone. She chose to do so. The boys were tedious with their constant competing to outman each other. The girls took a more relaxed pace but their constant chattering about the boys was no less tedious. It was easy for Mathembe to thread herself between the trees and isolate herself as the perimeter of runners expanded. She was always happiest to run alone. It was not that she feared the company of others, as many solitaries do; their friendship or otherwise was irrelevant to her. She was content to have many acquaintances at the expense of true friends. Solitude was her sacrament. The presence of others stifled her naïve spirituality. In solitude with the greater congregation of the forest, she passed into a spiritual grace of self-loss where, for brief numinous moments, she became aware of herself as a tiny, transient, lightning flicker of consciousness moving with incomprehensible speed through the colossal, slow sentience of the trees. She had run out of herself into the selflessness of the forest. She felt that if she could only give her consciousness some final microscopic push, a subtle boundary would be crossed and she would perceive it all: the runners spreading out through the trees, the truxers and their retinues behind them, the old people laughing and dancing to the radio and making preparations in the forest clearings, the wild trux moving in the deeper fastnesses.

Is this what it is like to be dead? Is this the Dreaming, is this the consciousness of the roots of the trees?

She had passed from the edgelands, where human biotectured life and primal vegetation coexisted, into the deep forest. Tieve trees rose sheer, thirty forty fifty meters from the forest floor, before breaking into an impenetrable canopy of dark leaves. No ray of light penetrated to the forest floor; Mathembe ran in an almost nocturnal darkness over the interlocking hexagonal tiles of lichen. Here a parasitic fungus had colonized a tieve's root buttresses, and bioluminescent spheres as large as herself cast a green glow; there land corals had established themselves and built fantastic intricate spires and towers and crests tens of meters high. She avoided a tangled holdfast of roots and lines; cables draped with moss ran up into the darkness and anchored clutches of gently swaying photosynthetic balloons. Beneath the tendrils with which they filtered aerial bacteria were clusters of balloonlings like ripe fruit, soon to be released to drift across the roof of the forest until they might find a place to strike anchor-hold. From the canopy came a continual symphony of voices: chitterings, twitterings, boomings, risings and fallings, glissandos, arpeggios, sonorous bellings and chimings. The creatures that inhabited the understory went about their businesses in darkness and silence. Mathembe ran on. She felt she could run through this dark, singing place until the world ended. She had given up her Mathembeness and had been given a new identity, a new nature, a new spirit. The Proclaimer doctrine that people might beyond the edge of time unite with God and so become him shone in a new light. To give up the lesser to become the greater: she understood that. But how dearly the lesser clings to the little it calls its own.

She had long forgotten all about trux, or dazzlers, or radio.

Some perceptions come to you slowly, piecemeal. A gradual accumulation of quanta of data until between one moment and the next you *know*. A certain deeper darkness within the darkness of the deep forest. A certain regularity within the greater irregularity of whistles and whoops and distant calls. A certain pattern in the patternlessness that mimics your own, and you are aware that you are not alone. There is another, running with you, pacing you step for step, never falling behind, never drawing ahead, out there among the trees. You stop, you try to listen over the panting of your lungs and the hammer beats of your heart. Nothing to hear but the sound of the forest murmuring its great incoherent mantra to itself. You start to run again. You look to your side, just a glance: do you see something move, just that quantum of thought out of synchronization with you? Something? Someone?

You run on but it is not the same now. It is not the high and holy passion, it is not a divine fire. It has been sullied. Stained. Like the Kapsabet man whose wife is raped by bandits. He loves her none the less, he loves her more than ever, but it is not the same.

Once you have seen it, once you have connected those happenings and made the invisible visible, it cannot hide itself from you.

Tieve trees stood close and tall, shoulder to shoulder in a tight stand. Mathembe's shoes skidded on the damp leaves that covered the hexagons of lichen in the clearing as she slid to a stop. She crouched behind a root buttress, the clay beak of the little ocarina bird raised to her lips. She did not know how far she had come, whether she was within the range of the little radio organical around her neck.

The something came flickering and weaving out of the shadows between the trees, zig by zag, closer. Moving into and out of cover. A small birdlike cry escaped her lips as the figure appeared like a vision of an angel before her. The alienness of the mask, the triangular *pneuma* mask with its sharp angles and pointedness, startled her. She touched her lips to the mouthpiece of the ocarina. The boy's voice, barely broken, and laboring, sounded incongruous behind the thrusting, assertive mask.

"I am sorry. I did not mean to frighten you. I will take it off if you like." Then, remembering there would be no answers to any of his questions: "Would you like that?"

A nod.

The boy's face, barely of age and flushed from his exertions, came out from behind the angular aggression of the mask. He set the thing down by the tieve roots. Separated from the animating psyche, the features softened and ran; the mouth became a round hole gaping at the light beyond the leaf canopy. Insubstantial tendrils of sexual experiment and wondering and wanting went curling and coiling between the long nude trunks of the trees.

"You are so hard to get to talk to," the boy said, a somethingteen of no particular significance Mathembe vaguely recognized as one of those boys who lolled at the outermost tables in the cafés or toyed with tryx on the empty lot at the end of Twelfth Street. "All I wanted to do was get to talk to you. I thought the trux hunt would be a good time. I have never run so hard in my life. I thought I was going to die." He laughed, punched his chest with his fist, invited her to laugh too. Mathembe laughed, silently. "This is a nice place, isn't it?"

Mathembe realized the boy was afraid of her. It filled her with an evil pleasure, that realization.

"A nice place," he said, looking around. "You like places like this, don't you? I like places like this too: this is a really nice place for me. The Ancestors; that is a nice place too. I go there a lot, to be on my own. I have seen you there; you go there a lot too. I suppose you find it a good place to think and feel and be alone. I need that a lot, to think and feel and be alone; I suppose you do too. You know, some of the others, they think you are odd, funny; they say things about you: well, I do not want to repeat them because they are not nice; they are not nice, the others, they are stupid, but I, well, I think you are sort of nice—I have seen you in the Ancestor Grove and I think *Here is someone I could like who thinks like me* and I do not mind that you don't talk, that is all right, you have your reasons for that, I am sure, and I would not ask you to, honest, I would not want to make you do anything you would not want to; so: do you think it would be all right, hm? would you mind, would you like to, would you, can I, do you mind if I, just one little . . ." and all the time the pheromones were curling and coiling from the *pneuma* mask and he was coming toward her one step at a time, one small step at a time, and he was opening his mouth and she was opening her mouth and when she stabbed her tongue into his mouth he was shocked, he had not expected this, not like this, had something gone wrong? and then she was lifting up her shirt to let him touch her breasts and his head was going round he was going to die oh God oh God oh God oh God oh God, reaching out to touch, gently, fearfully, dreadfully, those breasts, those big flat nipples, oh God oh God oh God he had never imagined, never dreamed.

And next he knew he was reeling in a sudden explosion of hallucination, of angels that tasted of rust and yellow and blue music and boxes that sounded vaguely of folding and unfolding and refolding endlessly out of each other to fall *what what what?* in the leaf litter on top of the melting, sagging *pneuma* mask.

Mathembe tucked the dazzler back into her belt pouch, tucked her shirt back into her tights, pouted her lips at him, and ran off through the trees, playing a mocking, defiant, laughing music on her ocarina.

Reeling, humiliated, still not certain what had happened, the boy felt a vile stickiness on his chest. Exploring fingers pulled away a cloying, stinking mass of synthetic flesh. The *pneuma* mask lay smashed beneath him, exuding a malodorous yellow pus from its wounds.

The old people and the children are waiting with food and wine in a deep-wood clearing. Some of the children find it a little alarming to be so entirely surrounded by trees. The trees, they say, are looking at them. That, say the old men with the plastic wine flagons, is entirely possible. With that certain *so*, roll of the eyes. Look at the lay of the land, the way the trees grow in such a regular way: story and legend have it that there was once a township here where you are now standing. A town full of people and their lives. Now, there are only trees. If there are faces in the trees, they are the faces of those long-ago people, looking out from thousands of years of dreaming.

And the children, properly alarmed now, roll their eyes, *so*, and ask, *What happened to it?*

And the evil old men with the plastic wine bottles who have nothing better to do with their time than alarm children say, *God destroyed it. Like that. Rubbed out. Because* and here they grin maliciously *of all the nasty, horrible little children who would not believe what their elders told them.*

Then the old women scold the old men and tell them to get a move on and be useful and stop frightening the children, *Honest, kids, it is all just stories, just made up, not a word of truth in it,* but the seed has been sown and cannot be taken back.

Mathembe's father was pleased. Ten trux, corralled behind a neural-shock net, branded with his circuitry and purring with artificially induced contentment. The young men were disconsolate. For all their whooping and cheering and leaping, not one trux. The young women were pleased. Between them they had run down and dazzled thirty-three trux that day. Mathembe's father had bought them all drinks, they passed the wine bottles around and let the wine run down their chins and long, slender throats in mockery of the boys. Mr. Fileli passed the bottle to his daughter. "Ten trux!" he shouted, more than a little drunk. Mathembe smiled for him but she had seen in the edge of her vision the boy who had touched her breasts sliding out from the trees into the rear of the celebration.

"Ten trux!" Mathembe's father said to Nasmir Jhirabha, waving the wine bottle as a taunt between friends.

"Mine are not all back yet," said Nasmir Jhirabha. "I have still one runner team out. We will see what they have when they come back."

What they had when they came back was not wild trux.

Even before they had entered the clearing Mathembe could tell from the way they came crashing and whistling back through the woods that what they had found was not trux. They came bursting into the clearing, glazed with sweat and excitement, shouting, "Look what we found, look what we found, look, look!"

What they had brought back from the forest was a young man and a young woman. Their hair was long and disheveled, they smelled of human filth and damp forest, they looked cold and tired and undernourished and hunted, their clothes were the color of mud and mold, stained with the juices and dyes of the forest, but everyone could see quite clearly the patches on their shoulders that carried the device of a trefoil knot.

The symbol of the Warriors of Destiny.

"Look what we found, look, look!" the leader of the runners shouted again. The people of Chepsenyt murmured uneasily at this apparition at their feast. Mathembe's father looked for Nasmir Jhirabha but the big Proclaimer had taken himself apart, pretending busyness with his trux in their corral.

"They're Warriors of Destiny," the leader said proudly, which the people did not want to hear, for until the words were said they could have pretended that they were not. "Warriors of Destiny. They are on the run. They have been on the run for weeks. Those helicopters that came today were looking for them. They have been in the forest for weeks. Weeks."

Again the people murmured uneasily. Then a man pushed to the front: Mr. Kakamega, a tryx grower. He was fortysomething but still not married. Because of his business, the boys of the township hung around him, and he around them. He was well known for his political opinions and never afraid to offer them unsolicited. He stepped forward and thrust wine bottles into the hands of the woman Warrior of Destiny.

"Fine welcome Chepsenyt gives to strangers!" he shouted. "What a fine, welcoming town, that has not a mouthful of meat or a spit of wine to wash it down with for wanderers lost in the forest. Chepsenyt of the welcomes. Well, you are welcome. I make you welcome." He brought the young man and the young woman to the sheet spread out on the ground and bade them sit beside him and gave them food and drink. They ate as ones who have not seen food for months. They ate warily, each mouthful taken with a dart of the eyes here, there, watching. The people returned to their groups of family and friends and tried to eat and drink again. Someone turned on a radio, but it was not the same. Like the evil, invisible parasitic fly that the vintners say turns wine in the fermentory to vinegar, the day had turned sour in their mouths.

Only the most extraordinary of circumstances would bring Kimilili and Kiminini the policepersons roaring up the road from Tetsenok in their regulation shorts, boots, gloves, and helmets astride their regulation Timboroa Prefecture tryx. They were not twins; the two big women were not even related, or even particularly alike physically, apart from a shared bigness. The people of the cluster of townships they policed named them Kimilili and Kiminini because, faced with two women in regulation shorts, boots, gloves, and helmets, roaring about the countryside on huge regulation powertryx, they had inevitably concluded that they must be lovers. Another enduring legend that sprang up more or less simultaneously in the townships of their patrol was that the big clunky three-wheeled tryx they rode were actually two young men who had dared once to make passes at them. Kimilili and Kiminini, knowing good public relations when they heard it, did nothing to quash these rumors. Mostly they contented themselves to verbally harass pedestrians from a street café table in Tetsenok where they were stationed, only emerging from myth to reality on their annual visits to the townships to check up on organical licensing and royalty statements. It must have been something quite out of the ordinary to have called them away from shouting insults at passing jeepney drivers to a piss hole like Chepsenyt township.

The problem when an entire township is under suspicion is where to start questioning.

True to their legend, they parked their tryx in Founding Tree Square, straightened their regulation shorts boots gloves helmets, rested right hands *so* on shock sticks, and marched between the evil old men sipping tea and pondering *fili* moves at their shady tables into the café and up to the bar. Two pairs of gloved hands flat on the counter.

"Of course, being a loyal subject of the Empire and a law-abiding citizen, you would naturally report to the authorities the occurrence of any disloyal or seditious activity in your neighborhood."

"Of course," said the proprietor, topping off two cups of *raqi*.

"As we thought." Two smiles appeared beneath the reflecting data-display visors.

Because no one could ever accuse them of a lack of thoroughness in pursuing their investigations, Kimilili and Kiminini asked the same questions at every café in Founding Tree Square. Then, because it was getting on for lunchtime, they asked the kekab hawker grilling skewers of whitemeat over a radiant element on the corner of First Street. They asked the pastry vendor on the corner of Second Street and First Circular. They asked at the hot nut stall outside the town commerce. Satisfied of the unquestioned loyalty of the citizens of Chepsenyt township, they were crossing Founding Tree Square to their dozing tryx when a boy old enough to know better was heard to whisper to his friends, to impress them with his daring, "It's the dyke bikes."

Quick as a knife, Kiminini had him over the handle bars while Kimilili had his pants down and the end of her shock stick pressed to his perineum.

"We do not like disrespect."

"We do not like rudeness."

"It creates a common, unpleasant atmosphere."

"It breeds disrespect for the law."

"We do not like rude people. We especially do not like rude boys."

The boy squirmed and whimpered as the blunt end of the shock stick pressed harder.

"You see this tryx?"

"Mighty fine organical, isn't it?"

"Well, this was once a little boy."

"Just like you."

"He was a rude little boy."

"Worse, he was rude to us."

"Now he is getting used to the idea of having my ass in his face every day for the next fifty years."

"You like the idea of having my ass in your face?"

"I think he does."

"I think he does too."

The stick pressed harder, harder. The boy cried out but the big women held him firmly. People were gathering at a discreet distance.

"However, we are feeling merciful."

"Instead, we are going to ask you a question."

"And if you answer it truthfully, we might let you go."

"But if you lie, I am going to pull the trigger on my shock stick."

"It is up high."

"Very high. High as it will go."

"So, once they clean the shit and piss off the walls . . ."

"You can kiss goodbye to any thoughts you might have had of things to do with that pathetic object."

"You see, we have heard rumors."

"Reports."

"Things folk have been saying about this shit pit of a township."

"And we have been sent to find out if they are true or not. So . . ."

"Question is . . ."

"Is anyone harboring Warriors of Destiny?"

The boy glanced at his friends, at the people gathered at a discreet distance.

"No," he said.

"Oh, I am not certain if I believe that."

"Nor am I."

"You sure, boy?"

"I'm sure."

The shock stick withdrew and rammed painfully home.

"Still sure?"

"Yes! Yes!"

"I am still not totally convinced."

"Nor am I. Maybe I should shock him."

"Maybe you should. So. One final time, and if we do not like your answer, we will blow your ass all over this square. You are sure no one in this township is harboring two escaped Warriors of Destiny?"

"Yes!" the boy howled. "Yes, yes, yes! God, yes, I am sure!"

The shock stick withdrew.

"Thank you."

"Now pull your pants up you little bastard and get out of my sight."

As the boy fled back to his friends, sobbing and clutching at the waistband of his shorts, a true hero now for not having told his township's deepest darkest secret under torture, Kimilili and Kiminini woke their tryx and rode back to their office in Tetsenok to report to Timboroa that they were satisfied that the tipoff that two Warriors of Destiny had found refuge in Chepsenyt was false.

When she heard the news, Mathembe's mother wrote it out in a note and gave it to Mathembe to take to her father, who was out on the Bad Year Hill. It had been his forty-second birthday three weeks before, the most unfortunate age a man can be. He had been lucky on the trux hunt but did not wish to press the saints twice, so, while stoutly maintaining that it was all a load of superstitious balls, nevertheless obtained the requisite forty-two small items of value and went out along the forest paths to the shrine of Kilimam Bé, patroness of a man's middle years. Confessorism was a hard belief to systematize: fifteen saints-major, six hundred and thirty saints-minor, and thirty-eight thousand nine hundred and twelve angels, all busy on their divine businesses, were difficult to pin down to any one place at any one time, any one solid doctrinal statement; responsibilities and fields of influence overlapped; petty rivalries and jealousies between the exalted could have disastrous results if your prayer and supplications were addressed to the wrong spiritual being. And over all, within all, lurked the intangible, invisible congregation of the dead, millions upon millions of disembodied consciousnesses spinning their way to heaven through the neural matrix of the Dreaming. *Worship the divine essence in all things* was the final rendering down of Confessorism, so that it was at heart the identical twin of Proclaimerism, to which it claimed to be implacably opposed. As these things tend to be.

The Bad Year Hill was an ancient earthwork in a clearing some couple of kilometers by forest paths from Chepsenyt. Legend had it that it predated the Green Wave and was the burial chamber of prehistoric automobiles possessed of evil spirits that had killed their owners. No one had ever been sufficiently inclined to excavate and investigate the truth of the legend; Mathembe's people regarded all mechanical contrivances as in some way harboring the darkness of Nyakabindi, the evil under the sea. At the top of the small hill was the shrine to the saint—unlike many of the deep-wood shrines of the Ykondé saints, it was well cared for. The reason for its upkeep were the four flights of steps that led up the hill to the shrine, of twenty-seven, forty-two, sixty-six, and seventy-eight steps respectively, one step for each of the misfortunate years of a life. The tradition was that the one seeking to avert the danger inherent in the year climb the appropriate staircase, place an object of value on each of the steps, and finally clap hands three times before the shrine to attract the attention of the saint, light a biolamp, and impale a supplication for good fortune and prosperity on a prayer wand. While in a township of Chepsenyt's size there might not be many people of the dangerous age at any time, the ages of nineteen, twenty-three, thirty-one, thirty-five, forty, forty-six, fifty-two, fifty-three, sixty-three, sixty-nine, seventy-two, seventy-nine, eighty, ninety-one, and one hundred and twelve were reckoned to be years of minor danger, averted by an offering to the shrine keeper, so the Bad Year Hill was always kept wealthy, healthy, and holy.

Mathembe found her father on the next to last step. Beneath him were assorted breadapples, paper cups of rice, holy medals, almost-expended telecomm cards, unused bus tickets, cans of beer, pairs of socks, old shoes, numbering forty. Too young for living dangerously, Mathembe ran up the wide steps. Her father opened the message, read it carefully.

"The bastards. They have hobbled Nasmir Jhirabha's trux," he said. "All of them. Not one has escaped. The bastards."

The note fell from his fingers and became the forty-first object on the Bad Year Hill and he went straightaway to apologize to Nasmir Jhirabha on behalf of his fellow townsfolk.

The forty-second step remained bare.

"It is not your fault," said Nasmir Jhirabha to Mathembe's father. "You have no part in it, you have no need to apologize. Your hands are clean."

"But those whose hands are not clean are Confessors, and I must apologize for my own people," Mathembe's father said.

Nasmir Jhirabha looked at Mathembe's father in that way that people do who have walked past a certain house every day of their lives without seeing it. Until this moment.

"They did a thorough job," Mathembe's father said to his wife as she sat in the conservatory shaping balls of plasm into little singing creatures and setting them scurrying about the floor. "With blades. Some he can heal, but it will mean missing the Timboroa Solstice Auctions and he cannot afford to do that."

"Ghost Boys."

"Who else? As if Nasmir Jhirabha would have called in those two buffoons that think of themselves as policepersons. He knows how it is here. Chepsenyt is not that kind of place."

"Someone did if he did not," said Hradu. Mathembe shot him a glare that dared him, just dared him to say one word more.

"Chepsenyt is becoming that kind of place," said Mathembe's mother as the little wheeled creatures hurried around her feet, and Mathembe wondered how she could mime maimed and mutilated trux to her grandfather.

That night the helicopters came.

You are asleep in your bed. No, you think you are asleep in your bed. You are in that half-awake, half-aware state when even the familiarities of your own room are strange and unfamiliar. Awake or dreaming? You cannot be certain. You had dreamed of a great thrashing blade moving in space, carving slices off the edge of the world as it moves along its orbit; the sound of its thrashing fills the universe, the thrash of destruction, and you rush to the window to look out and see the street full of people running as the great blade comes down out of the sky. All around you is a great beating noise, and you do not know whether it has come from the dream inside your head into the outside or from the outside into your head.

The thrashing sound fills your room, fills the air, fills up the spaces in your lungs and between the joints of your bones with its beating beating beating. There is a light in the room, a curious light from an angle you have never seen a light come from before, casting shadows angular and frightening because of their unfamiliarity. A hard white light that seems to hiss, it is so bright. The shadows it casts look sharp enough to cut, cut through the dream, cut the dream to flying, tattered shreds.

Awake. This is no dream.

The street was full of people. People with hastily pulled-on clothes flapping and flying in the downwash of the helicopter blades; the helicopter blades beating and beating and beating, shredding the whole world with their cutting. The long dry dust of the spring heat was driven up by the blades. It choked the people, blinded them, set them coughing and blinking. The people shaded their eyes with their hands to try to look past the searchlights that cast long, sharp, unwavering shadows to see the helicopters. Voices boomed from loudspeakers, distorted with overamplification but still audible above the beating of the helicopter engines.

Out, out, everybody out. That was what they were saying. *Out into the streets, everybody, out. Young or old or man or woman. Confessor or Proclaimer, out, now.*

Mathembe pulled on hasty day clothes. She collided with her mother and Hradu in the door. She saw the expression on her mother's face. Hradu looked scared. Her mother's look was something of an altogether greater order of magnitude.

The searchlight beam played across the people who lived in Fifteenth Street. It seemed to burn in Mathembe's face, to burn into her soul and find and accuse there darknesses she had not known existed. She stood judged by the light. Then the helicopter swung its beam up and away, and all the others with it. The helicopters turned in midair. The beams played across their fuselages as they maneuvered through the air: black painted metal with curious protrusions and protuberances. Organicals grafted clumsily to Imperial technology. The heart-in-hand crest of the man in the Jade City was momentarily illuminated. The helicopters dipped their noses and went in for landings in the paddies and orchards around Chepsenyt.

Someone among the people gathered in Fifteenth Street swore, gently, the names of all the Ykondé saints. "The militia," he said.

Organicals grafted to Imperial machinery.

Mathembe remembered her mother teaching her plasm lore: always roll your apprentice pieces and experiments back into balls of synthetic life again. "You can't let them escape," she had said. "They go wild and fierce, loose in the environment. There is nothing wilder and fiercer than one of your own gone feral."

The beating of the helicopter engines died away. There was a new sound in the cobbled streets, the sound of running feet. Soldiers in the black of the Emperor Across the River and the brown of the Prefecture police. A company of soldiers came into Fifteenth Street and formed a line opposite the people. They looked fat and stupid and unfit. They looked like boys who have been let play with guns.

Struggling with the tie of his sleeping gown, Dr. Kalimuni stamped up to the nearest meat-faced soldier. He was very angry. Mathembe had thought she had seen him angry before when she or Hradu had committed some minor misdemeanor that involved him or his home. That had not been anger.

"What is the meaning of this?" he demanded in a voice like winter. "What do you think you are doing, waking the dead and pulling honest people out of their beds? Well? Where is your commanding officer? I will not waste my breath on men in the ranks. Bring me your officer."

The meat-faced militiaman stared past Dr. Kalimuni. An officer in a black-and-brown uniform with the shoulder flashes of the Timboroa Prefecture Local Defense Regiment stepped forward. This soldier did not look fat or stupid or unfit. He was lean and small and supernaturally calm. Clearly, Dr. Kalimuni could not read his small but perilous madness, for he marched up to the officer, saying, "I am an advocate, I know the law, and I know there are proper procedures to be followed. Proper procedures! Show me your authorization. Where is your authorization? Show it to me."

Without ever taking his eyes off Dr. Kalimuni, the officer gave a quiet order to his men. The fat meat-faced soldiers elbowed past the people standing in the street. Two went to each house and began to search.

"This is an outrage," said Dr. Kalimuni, but his fury was burned up and turned to ash. The black-and-brown officer whispered something to him no one else in Fifteenth Street could hear. The advocate went very pale and quiet. The black-and-brown officer remained impassive as a stone.

The *beep beep* of his communicator was only a small noise, but to the people in Fifteenth Street it was like needles through their ears.

The officer listened, impassive as a stone, then spoke. Shortly. Tersely. The doors of all the houses on Fifteenth Street opened and the soldiers came bulling and blustering out. Some were carrying bottles of wine they had liberated from the cellars of the treacherous in the name of the Emperor Across the River. One was munching a sandwich he had made from bread and whitemeat and pickles. They came through the people. The people dared to look at them as they pressed through. The militiamen unslung their weapons and, holding them like clubs, pushed the people up Fifteenth Street to its junction with Third Circular. As they came to the junction Mathembe could see people being pushed down the other streets by the militia into a rough circle around the intersection.

There under the plastic-weapon muzzles of a group of militiamen stood Mr. Kakamega and the two young Warriors of Destiny.

"Stay where you are, all of you," said the black-and-brown militia officer. From the brown-and-black ranks behind the encircled people came the hard plastic rattle of weapons being turned the right way around.

The officer gave an order.

Three soldiers unclipped tools from their battle packs and started to dig three holes outside Mr. Kakamega's house. The prisoners struggled but the soldiers held them firm. The young man began to cry. The young woman swore and cursed imaginatively. The shovelers dug up spadefuls of ceramic cobbles and chocolate-black earth. The shovels dug and dug. Under the guns of their militia, the people watched the shovels dig. The sobbing of the young man grew fainter and less coherent, a burble of fear. A small pool of liquid had formed on the cobbles at his feet. Mathembe closed her eyes. It was a shameful thing to see a man piss himself. The people watched and the shovels dug and dug and dug and when the holes were deep enough the officer gave a new order. The prisoners were stripped naked and their arms and legs tied with wire. The wire was twisted tight with pliers so that it cut deeply into the flesh. The soldiers wrestled them toward the holes. The young woman fought, trying to kick and punch and bite. Blood seeped from where the wire had cut her skin. The soldiers would always be stronger. The diggers buried the three prisoners thigh deep in the chocolate-black soil.

Then the black-and-brown officer addressed the people. The

young man and woman were members of a proscribed organization: terrorists, rebels against the rightful rule of the Emperor Across the River. They were guilty of countless crimes against the Emperor, acts of sedition sabotage and murder. The tryx grower Kakamega was guilty of aiding and abetting enemies of the Empire in their crimes and thus warranted the same punishment due any enemy of the Emperor.

"Sergeant, execute sentence," said the officer.

The sergeant opened a canister with a red biohazard symbol on it. He removed three round black seeds. Round and black and pitted, like the heads of long-dead ancestors. He wore gloves and moved cautiously, careful not to let the seeds touch his flesh.

He showed them to each of the prisoners.

The young man begged and moaned.

The young woman sneered and shouted slogans.

Mr. Kakamega the tryx grower said nothing.

The officer's face was impassive and cold as a great stone.

The seeds sprouted the instant they touched the soil. Within seconds they had put out roots and shoots. Within one minute they had encased the prisoners to the waist in vines. Within five minutes they were wrapped head to toe in growth and their legs were turning to wood.

The black-and-brown officer made the people watch until the prisoners' cries had ceased and the first branches were reaching out of their mouths and eye sockets. When there was nothing left of the young man and the young woman and Mr. Kakamega the tryx grower but three small trees bound in wire, he gave everyone five minutes to return to their homes and collect what they could. Five minutes, not one instant more.

I am certain this is a question you have asked yourself. You lie awake in your bed at night next to the one you love and you wonder. If something were to happen to your home, if the soldiers were to come and order you into the street and you have five minutes, what would you take? Things of fiscal value or things of sentiment? Documents or photographs? Have you a plan, everything in one place where you can put your hand on it right away and lift it and run into the street with it should that night of dread ever fall? Or would you lift happenstance, piecemeal, guided by the heart, and so find yourself on the street with an ornamental dog and your favorite recipe book and beloved old jacket in your arms and the chair in which you made love *that night* wrestled somehow, superhumanly, out the door and lying at your feet?

Five minutes.

Think about it. Count one-one-thousand two-one-thousand three-one-thousand and when you get to three-hundred-one-thousand you are out of time, time is no more, whatever doom it is you have imagined has arrived.

Now it was the turn of the brown-and-black militiamen to watch. They watched the people carrying their piles of bedding and sewing machines and cabinets of crockery generations old and icons of saints and loved ones and files of memory circuits and old, fond-remembered love masks and racks of seedlings and copies of patent licenses into the streets. Five minutes or no, the militiamen still had to go in and drag out a few who could not decide between this painting and that jar of preserved eggs, this bracelet and that wallet of document circuits and policies.

When everyone was out and standing by their heaps of salvage, the officer spoke into his communicator. At his word the helicopters that had been lying beating to themselves in the mud of the paddies rose up, all at once, and took up positions over the rooftops.

The downwash of their blades whipped the leaves of the three trees outside Kakamega the tryx grower's house.

The officer thumbed a button on his communicator and his voice was relayed through loudspeakers mounted on the helicopters. His voice spoke through the beating blades. It said that disloyalty was a terrible crime. Among Confessors, it was no more than could be expected, but to find it among Proclaimers was incredible. Intolerable. And the incredible, intolerable disloyalty was this: that, despite the warnings of the government on the radio and on the wall posters, despite the warnings of the two local policepersons and the visit of the heads of the traitors, it had still been brought to his attention that Chepsenyt township was harboring Warriors of Destiny. If the whole town was guilty then of harboring enemies of the Empire, the whole town would be punished.

He nodded. The barest, most imperceptible of nods. But enough for the eyes behind the image-amplifying visors in the helicopters. The ugly, misshapen, swollen bulbs of clumsily grafted organicals opened and threw fire across Chepsenyt. The houses exploded into flames.

The helicopters moved slowly, deliberately, along the numbered streets and circulars, pausing over each rooftop to bring their weapons to bear and send the house raving up in a ball of fire. The helicopters burned the houses of the Confessors and the houses of the Proclaimers. All were alike to the Emperor Across the River. And because all were alike to the Emperor Across the River, the helicopters burned the house of the man who had telecommed the authorities at Timboroa and informed on Mr. Kakamega.

Clutching their hastily gathered belongings, the people tried to flee but wherever they turned there were helicopters moving slowly, deliberately, throwing fire from their weapons. The houses of Chepsenyt, a thousand years a-growing, went up in a great cry of conflagration. Crazed by fire, central nervous networks destroyed, some of the houses split into their component units and stampeded, near mindless, through the streets. People went down beneath the millipede feet or the fat bulbous tires or the plastic caterpillar tracks; children stood screaming, screaming, as the flames went up all around them while parent fought parent in the mass of shouting, hurrying bodies to try to reach them.

When they had finished with the houses, the helicopters moved out over the paddies and orchards with the same slow deliberateness. The gun crews behind their data visors slowly, deliberately, took aim and sent trees orchards power plants up in ecstasies of burning.

The trux in their pens behind the Fileli house were on fire. Mr. Fileli grew them in fifteen colors but now they were all the color of fire. Confined, they revved and spun their wheels and rammed into each other, blinded by heat and pain. Mr. Fileli shouted instructions over their wailing keens of agony but his wife and children knew what to do without need for orders. Mathembe was already swinging back the gate as her father and mother darted between the onrushing, blazing organicals. Her mother had the control rod. There. In the middle of the rush, one red trux was not on fire. Mrs. Fileli darted with the control rod, connected with the socket, and swung herself up onto its pallet. She fought the panicked organical out of the stampede to a stand outside the collapsing ruins of the Fileli home. Mathembe and Hradu piled what small possessions they had managed to rescue onto the pallet while Mr. Fileli stood like one vouchsafed a vision of God, staring at the runnels of blazing molten synthetic flesh that ran over the cobbles down from the Proclaimer end of the township.

"Come on, man, what are you standing staring at?" his wife shouted. "Over. Finished. Done. Get a move on."

He heaved boxes of photographs and canisters of the plasm from which his wife made her toys up to Hradu on the trux but it was plain to any who could spare a glance that the eyes of his heart were fixed backward, at his blazing, melting trux. In fifteen colors.

The exodus was forming up, family groups piling whatever they could on any available means of conveyance: trux, tryx, drays, jeepneys, handcarts. Some had all their worldly goods balanced on house units. Some had all their worldly goods piled onto their backs. All were moving very slowly, very painfully, toward the Timboroa road.

"Let's go," said Mrs. Fileli, twisting the control rod nervously in her fingers. The streets were almost deserted now, but for the spirits of burning. Even the soldiers had withdrawn to their pickup points.

"No!" Hradu shouted. "Mathembe is not here."

"Where the hell is she?" Mr. Fileli said.

In the act of loading the trux, Mathembe had noticed a change of pitch in the beating beating of the blades and, looking up, had seen the helicopters moving. Away from the paddies and orchards. Toward the Ancestor Grove.

What is one more scream in the greater screaming of Chepsenyt dying? She ran like a runner in a trux hunt, ducking and weaving and darting between the burning homes and the families and the piled possessions. She ran, glancing up at the helicopters that moved with deliberate slowness above her. Her lungs were raw from smoke and exertion. The helicopters kept pace with her, one small running mote in the devastation below. She kicked open the forest gate. No thought for the dangers of prayer wands, no thought for unseen root holes. The helicopters took up station overhead. Wooden lips sunk deep into the Dreaming whispered to the runner. Votive biolights formed intimate constellations among the buttresses. The helicopters spread out to cover the Grove of the Ancestors with a canopy of engine noise.

Mathembe ran.

In the blister mounts, weapons rolled to bear, like eyeballs in sockets.

Mathembe ran.

She could see him. Eyes closed in repose, serene in the root dreaming. *Wake up wake up wake up!* But she did not have the words. She hooked her fingers into the holdfast that grafted him into the Ancestor Tree, heaved. Heaved. Heaved. All the while silently shouting *Wake up wake up wake up!* She glanced, panic-stricken, at the sky.

She could not see the stars for helicopters.

She braced her feet against the trunk, heaved. Heaved. Heaved. Heaved until her fingers felt they would rip. Heaved until her arms felt they would tear from her shoulders. Until her eyes and heart and lungs would burst. Until she felt she would pull the world from its orbit. Past the limits of her strength and will, she heaved.

And the head came free with a terrible tearing roaring mandrake shriek. Her grandfather's eyes opened wide in horror, his mouth gaped. She feared she had torn the head free but left the spirit disembodied within the matrix. No time, no time, for doubt. She went bounding back over the roots and prayer wands with the head—living, dead, dreaming—under her arm.

And the helicopters opened fire and the Ancestor Trees exploded in pillars of flame. From deep in the Dreaming, the fifty thousand ancestors of Chepsenyt woke in fire and screamed as the trees came crashing down in showers of sparks and ash and Mathembe with the head wrapped in her shirt went leaping and darting between the falling, screaming ancestors. Burning flakes of ash settled on her skin and hair; she did not feel them; all she knew was the need to run and jump and dodge: that and the forest gate thirty, twenty, ten meters in front of her.

She came running up Fifteenth Street like a minor demon from the Nyakabindi mystery play, a thing of flame and smoke with a head under its arm. Mathembe's mother goaded the trux to its best speed, Mathembe's father reached to scoop his daughter up onto the pallet. The trux turned and sped away up Fifteenth Street through the collapsing embers of Chepsenyt township. Behind it the fifty thousand ancestors came crashing down on top of one another in sparks and flame. At the corner of First Circular the trux passed three small trees that, by the grace of God, had escaped the burning. The enduring legacy of Chepsenyt township.

The black helicopters came in low for one final pass over their achievement, landed to pick up the troops, and clattered off somewhere to the north.

THE ROAD

RAIN. RAIN. RAIN. RAIN.

Falling over the forest that stretches farther than the imagination can hold. Falling on the treetops, the treetops all huddled and pressed together. Falling all across the world. The rain. See it fall. Here it comes. Falling on the forest, on the road through the forest, the white road that cuts through the close-pressing trees, like a long white scar from a long knife, long healed over but irredeemably scarred. Falling on the people moving along that road, black on white, falling on the men and the women and the children, falling on their bundles and bags and boxes, falling on the trux and tryx and drays and jeepneys and handcarts, on the packs on their backs as they file along the white road. Falling from the low gray clouds curdled and coiled low above their heads. The low gray clouds caught and tore on the tops of the tallest forest trees and dropped their burden of rain.

It had begun in the night, the rain, in the hours close to dawn, where all desperate and treacherous things are born. The wind had changed quarter and brought the warm rain clouds out

of the south. The smell of wet ashes had hung over the people as they walked through the rain toward the morning. The world tipped its edge beneath the sun but the rain had not relented. It plastered your hair to your head, your clothes to your body, it saturated your books and clothes and quilts and documents and ornaments, it saturated you until you no longer cared that you were saturated; you had forgotten it was possible to feel any other way than the clothes rubbing against your legs and the rain running down your face, down your neck.

The universe was filled with the stink of smoke and rain.

In the night the refugees had been spun out by the road into a file kilometers long. Those with organical transport led; those who bore their lives on their backs or in handcarts went to the rear. With every hour of rain along that white road, the community of Chepsenyt attenuated further, to the very limits of cohesion. Mathembe's family were within the first few hundred meters. With morning it had become apparent that the trux had not escaped unscathed. An area of skin the size of a conversation table was scorched and blistered and leaked pale yellow ichor. Given time, rest, and food it would make a complete recovery, Mr. Fileli said, but time, rest, and food were precisely those commodities that were in shortest supply. Its syrup sac was full, but when that was digested, there was no more. It could metabolize human food if necessary, but at a lower level of activity. Mathembe's father did not need to elaborate the mathematics of supply and consumption to his children. The contagious panic of the fire had damaged the trux's mind. It would stop dead for tens of minutes at a time, or accelerate alarmingly, or veer at nothing, threatening to send the carefully stacked possessions on its pallet sliding to the ground. Mathembe's mother sat astride the hump, working under her sheet-plastic rain cape to synthesize new control circuitry using some of her biobase plasm. Hradu rode on the pallet with his mother. He was wet and snappy from lack of sleep; that was what he said but Mathembe, who *knew* him, knew he was lying for the sake of them all. This was no time to talk of loss, and shock, and dislocation. Hradu tried to sleep against a heap of quilts protected from the rain under a plastic sheet, but the drum of drops on plastic and the erratic veerings of the trux made sleep impossible. Mathembe's father walked beside the trux, examining and tending and stroking it with the singlemindedness of the man who has lost every thing but one. He talked to it, cleared wet leaves from its slow-turning plastic tires, inspected its wound with manic regularity, encouraged it to go on, go on, keep going, keep going, good organical brave organical faithful organical.

At the rear was Mathembe. She had never thought a road could be so long. She had never thought there could be so much rain in a cloud. She had never thought a head could be so heavy. A lifetime of memories is weighty indeed. While her parents had shouted at her for being stupid reckless idiotic dangerous she had rooted out the old tree pot among the salvage and planted the head in it. She had glared at them for their shouting—she had not yet learned to distinguish the shouts of love from the shouts of anger, or that they may be both at the same time—jumped down, and walked a deliberate defiant twelve paces behind the trux. Then it had begun to rain and the pot had filled up with rainwater and become even heavier and the rooticles and nodules clumped around her grandfather's neck had moved and flexed and greedily sucked up all the water.

Through the night and into the morning, and through the morning, as she had walked her twelve paces behind, her grandfather's head had rolled and lolled and drooled and gibbered nonsense so that Mathembe's fears of the night, that she had pulled the head but left the spirit spinning in the Dreaming, returned redoubled to her. The head yawned and gurgled in its throat; its eyes opened and closed and rolled up; from its synthesizers came long garbled monologues and eloquently obscene croaking flapping noises.

"Mother-O, father-O, where have I put my hand-i-O, will the shrine keeper know will the prayer caller know will Makananee and Makahanee and Makadidié know oh-loo-loo-loo liddle-ay-ay here they come can't you see them? feet the size of houses coming down plod plod better run better hide, here they come, the Ahleles, striding across the land, whee! whole kilometers gone at a single bite did I say bite? stride, that was what I meant to say, stride-eye-eye-eyed; look at that would you look at that, cannot even rely on the holy ones to have good manners these days, I mean, they are just ripping up great handfuls of trees and soil and plants and plastering them onto their bodies; look out, oh, too late, not loud enough, never did really like them anyway, there go Makananee and Makahanee and Makadidié, scooped up by big big *big* fingers and pressed into the body with the rest of them, where are they going, where are they *going*? Don't you *know*? down to

the South Sea, of course, to do battle with the evil things that live
there. Good advice, good advice, who wants some good advice, who
will heed some good advice, that is more the question; hey you, yes,
you, what are you doing with that dwelling-room unit, it is not
supposed to do that, you are not supposed to do that with it, you know,
you want some good advice? here's good advice, never trust anyone
who lives too near the sea. That is true as I am standing here. Devils
in them, that's what. Unclean spirits dissolve in water; you never taken
a bath, you filthy beast? when you get clean where does all the dirt go,
into the water that's right; a little water in my unclean spirit, no thank
you waiter I like my *raqi* like I like my women: pure and strong and
unadulterated. Do you know, do you know that Silali and I did it all
the time, everywhere, even before we were married—especially before
we were married—in the house, on the back of a trux, in the orchard
under the trees, in the deep dark ghostly forest, in the Grove of the
Ancestors with them all watching, weren't they jealous! up to the waist
in mud and water in the paddy fields, anywhere, any time at all; well,
lookee here, what do I eye-spy, my good friend the Proclaimer
Kalimuni. The Proclaimer Kalimuni, who I promised I wasn't going to
talk to, except that is another promise blown to piss and buggery; so,
what are you doing here, Proclaimer Kalimuni who I promised not to
talk to except that I am talking to you, what are you doing by the side
of the road in the pissing pissing rain, you, hey you, you who have
hold of me, put me down, stop I say, I want to talk to my good friend
the Proclaimer Kalimuni."

Dr. Kalimuni sat cross-legged on the moss by the side of the road.
Soaked by rain, splashed by wheels and feet, he sat with his Book of
Witnesses in his lap, hands comfortably relaxed over his knees, readers
fixed to his temples. Up above the rain it was noon, the hour of
contemplation. Other Proclaimers might neglect their duty to God but
duty was duty irrespective of circumstances. In all things, God was to
be contemplated and imitated. Rain ran down the advocate Kalimuni's
face. His eyes were closed, his lips formed speechless syllables and
mantras. The Word of God unscrolled across his frontal lobes.

Mathembe set down the raucous, confused head on the shoulder
beside Dr. Kalimuni. She sat and covered herself as best she could
with her transparent plastic sheet.

"Kalimuni!" shouted the head, by degrees returning to sentiency, as if after an epic drunk. "Kalimuni, what is going on? What is happening, Kalimuni? Kalimuni!" it shouted. "Kalimuni!" it roared.

Not a flicker of recognition disturbed Advocate Kalimuni's face. Not a twitch of an eye, not the tightening of a muscle, not even the slightest falter in the unending chain of prayer.

"Kalimuni!"

Mathembe put her hand over the roaring, drunkard's mouth. Yelped in pain. The head had bitten her. The long procession passed slowly by. Parents, brother, and red trux were already indistinguishable within the curtains of rain that drew themselves across the straight white road.

Dr. Kalimuni opened his eyes, disconnected the readers, and coiled them back into his book.

"My dear Mr. Fileli! And Mathembe too. How good to see you both, how kind of you to have stopped. Thank you for joining me in my meditations; it may seem a trifle incongruous under our present circumstances, but one must cling to one's daily disciplines and familiarities."

"Kalimuni!" roared the head so that Mathembe feared that it might burn out its speech synthesizer circuits. "I know I promised never to speak to you again, but I would break a promise for you I would not break for anyone else. I can trust you, even if you are a left-handed Proclaimer: just what the hell is going on?"

And while Dr. Kalimuni told the story of the night the helicopters came, the refugees passed. Mathembe watched them come along the road, through the curtains of rain. Some glanced over. Some stared. Some looked disapprovingly. Some spoke among themselves in a muttering way. Some just passed. Along the straight white road came five young men. Mathembe did not know them but she knew what they looked like. They looked like single men, the unmarried, unpartnered ones who are the most dangerous segment of any society. They looked like Ghost Boys who have grown too big and too old but still cannot give up the gang and the running with the pack.

They sat down in the pouring rain across the road. Their fingers searched in the dark red moss for small irritating things to throw but there was nothing to be found so they threw names instead.

"Hey lawyer."

"Hey Proclaimer."

"What you been reading in that book of yours?"

"You been reading how it is to be a good Proclaimer?"

"You been reading up on how to be like God, be just like God, be real good, just like God?"

"Real good, like doing your duty to God's appointed Emperor and God's righteous soldiers?"

"That is real real good, Proclaimer."

"Maybe it would look real real good to God, maybe it would make you his bright-eyed biddy child, if you were to tell God's good soldiers where the evil, wicked, sinful Warriors of Destiny are hiding out?"

"Enough of that. Leave the man alone. I will not have my friend talked to by the likes of you in that way!" shouted the head. Mathembe curled her fingers around a clump of moss, ready to tear it up and stuff it into her grandfather's foolish mouth to silence any greater reckless-ness he might spew.

The five young men hooted with laughter, plucked stalks of fungus from between the white cobbles of the road.

"Your fine friend," said the big dull one who is always the leader of groups like that. "Well, maybe we have been looking in the wrong place for our traitor. You know, there is one thing makes me sicker than a traitor Proclaimer, and that is a traitor Confessor. Proclaimers, well, you cannot expect any better from them. Confessors, your own kind, that really sticks in my craw."

"Do not be so stupid," said Dr. Kalimuni with a directness that took Mathembe's breath away. "My house burned as well as yours. All my lawbooks: gone, in one single moment. All those years and years: gone, in one single moment. I did not inform the militia, neither did Mr. Fileli; how could he? He is dead. Now, if you would please leave us in peace and go on about your business."

"Damn smart-mouth Proclaimer," said the big dull one in the stung, embarrassed way a person talks who has been made to look very very stupid. Mathembe clutched her grandfather to her, wished that words could be put back into mouths again, chewed, swallowed. The big dull man came swaggering across the road, pushing through the line of people moving along the straight white cobbles. His jaw jutted, daring a fist.

Mathembe clenched a fist of her own, tested its weight, assessed her strength. A kick to the balls would be much more effective. The four friends were two steps behind the swaggering one, pushing the slow-moving weary wet people aside.

"Damn smart-mouth Proclaimer," he said again, as if they were words well worth repeating. He stared at Dr. Kalimuni. Dr. Kalimuni stood up. He dusted spores and moss from his saturated clothes. Dr. Kalimuni stared back. He was not a tall man, not as tall or broad as even the least of the five troublemakers, but he stared and stared and stared and there was something behind his stare cold and inflexible and indomitable. He stared the leader down, and the young man snatched his eyes away and was beaten, he and his overgrown Ghost Boy friends. They went on their way, up the straight white road through the forest, throwing names back behind them until their voices were obliterated by the rhythm of the rain. Grandfather Fileli swore back while they could still hear him.

"Please do not, Mr. Fileli," said Dr. Kalimuni. "It is over. Let it be."

A second form of order had imposed itself upon the refugees, over and above the order of social mobility. It was an order of religion. The kilometers-long many-legged beast that was Chepsenyt had precipitated by a process of inner tension and attraction into long chains of Confessor families punctuated by compact groups of Proclaimers. The scientists say there are five fundamental forces in the quantum world. There are also five fundamental forces in the atomic sea of human interactions: kinship, friendship, likeness, difference, and suspicion.

The rain rained and the road was a straight white division through the many-colored forest into evening. Dr. Kalimuni had saved from the fire a moribund jeepney Mathembe had never suspected he owned. As he drove Mathembe, the head, and his few possessions past the stolidly moving files of people, a wind came down from the north and tore the flat low gray clouds apart. The smell of wet ashes that had hung over the people all day was lifted up and carried away. A thin sepia light spread along the white road from someplace far beyond towering purple and yellow clouds. Dr. Kalimuni's jeepney splashed through the puddles. The head was asleep, snoring odiously through its vocalizer. As he drove, Dr. Kalimuni listened to the early evening news on the radio: the Voice of the Empire, broadcasting from the very heart of the Imperial capital. Mathembe's New Speech was rudimentary; what she could not understand, Dr. Kalimuni gladly translated.

* * *

Another soldier has died in a military hospital in Ol Tok last night, bringing to six the total killed in a Warriors of Destiny attack on an army patrol in Ukerewe Prefecture. Five other soldiers remain in critical condition. A military sweep is being made through Ukerewe but it is feared that the terrorist unit has disbanded and fled into neighboring Timboroa, where the local militia, acting on intelligence received, is conducting a security operation.

Protesters once again are marching in the Imperial capital demanding that the Empire withdraw from its transfluvian provinces. Among the demonstrators driven from the Eight-Fold Gates of the Jade City are relatives of soldiers recently killed while serving across the river.

Delegates to the Imperial Council from the main constitutional transfluvian nationalist party are pressing for an early statement from the Jade City on the formulation of legislation for limited self-government in the provinces. Meanwhile, representatives from the predominantly Proclaimer northern prefectures are lobbying support from Imperial councilors for an amendment that would exclude the nine northern prefectures from any proposed legislation.

Imperial legate Mr. V. J. S. Randra, on an official tour of neighboring nations, has come under criticism on account of the conduct of Imperial forces in combating terrorism in the transfluvian provinces, which, it is claimed, have involved widespread violations and abuses of human rights. Legate Randra expressed concern over evidence that the chief terrorist organization active in the provinces, the Warriors of Destiny, may have obtained modern inorganic weaponry and explosives that can be directly traced back to that country.

Meanwhile, legal moves to have Garsen Kitii, the president of Ourselves Alone, the Warriors of Destiny's political mouthpiece, extradited from the Heptarchy to face terror charges, collapsed when the judge refused the application on the grounds that Mr. Kitii must be considered a political refugee.

At eighteen twenty-two Imperial Standard Time, the first Saint-ship from the Daughter Worlds in six years will transit into orbit around the planet. It is hoped that the ship will remain in the planetary vicinity for upward of three months.

As Dr. Kalimuni translated effortlessly, adding his own small comments, asides, or elucidations, Mathembe was made devastatingly aware what a small and parochial world she had been forced to inhabit by her lack of New Speech. Her people had always listened to the local stations, the music channels, the ones that dealt with farm prices and weather forecasts and small-town interests in the language of the small towns: Old Speech. They would no more have tuned their radios to the Voice of the Empire than they would have considered signing on board a Saint-ship and traveling across the universe in an instant of time. What had the things of the wider world to do with Chepsenyt township and its small needs? In Chepsenyt, Confessor was Confessor and Proclaimer was Proclaimer and these things were not to be questioned any more than that the world would dip its edge beneath the sun and the rain would come on Papa Tiiti's Day were to be questioned.

Dr. Kalimuni's translation of the radio news revealed a depth, a complexity, an ambiguity in the essential structure of the world. Mathembe was not certain she felt securely anchored in a world that, examined closely, revealed its stark light and shadows to be shifting patterns of uncertain photons. Uncertain, insecure, but exhilarating. She felt angry, shortchanged by history, to have grown up a Confessor and a Nationalist without ever understanding why the equation between the two was assumed, fixed and immutable; without ever understanding what those two components of her society meant. Confessors were Confessors and Nationalists, and Proclaimers were Proclaimers and Imperialists, because that was how they were: no questioning, no doubting, no need for understanding. Her father, her mother, her brother, her grandfather's head snoring in her lap: they seemed lit from an entirely new quadrant of the sky that cast new planes and shadows, revealed darknesses, uglinesses, blindnesses, ignorances that deeply shocked her. She could not be part of that consensus of ignorance. Out there, beyond the edge of her world, were humans who looked and smelled and thought like her who could move entire Saint-ships, tens of kilometers across, instantaneously through trans-stellar space—how would they regard the deliberate refusal to think, the comfortable drawing in of the borders of the world like a quilt on a winter's night, the acceptance that things were as they were because they were? The world was big, the world was complex, the world was painful and rough-edged, but it was the way the world was. Grandfather lolled in sleep, the old man who had died rather than speak foreign words. Those dangerous, dangerous words that might have challenged the straight-edged geometry of his universe and curved it round, that might have cut newer, deeper roads through this thinking: he had refused them because, like a child spitting out medicine, he could not think beyond the taste in his mouth. Dr. Kalimuni tapped his fingers to some rhythmic, vigorous piece of ensemble music. Mathembe saw a man who was what he was because it was what he had chosen to be: a Proclaimer who was a Proclaimer, an Imperialist, because he had considered the questions intimately and had moored his life to what he considered the most steadfast answers.

I do not agree with your answers, Mathembe said in her heart, *but until I have asked the questions, I cannot say why I disagree and what answers I consider to be better.*

The sky was clear now and had darkened at its zenith to indigo. Dr. Kalimuni switched on the biolights on his jeepney. The people moving along the road were a river of bobbing lights moving through the night forest: some carried votive lamps, others had tethered gloglobes to their vehicles. Ahead, the lights spread into a wide, still pool: some obstruction, some incident, something against which the people had piled up. Dr. Kalimuni steered his jeepney through a throng that grew denser with every new arrival, a bank of people and organicals so dense Dr. Kalimuni had to tether the jeepney to a tree, pocket the control circuitry, and try to press a way through as best he could for Mathembe and the heavy pot to follow.

Voices. Many voices. Angry voices. Always voices, but you never make out the words.

"Excuse me, excuse me, excuse me," said Dr. Kalimuni, pressing between the still-damp bodies. "I am a lawyer, I may be able to help. Let me through, please." Solidity, stability in the confusion: Mathembe had seen the wounded red trux. She seized Dr. Kalimuni, tugged at him, pulled at him: *This way, this way.* The trux was parked with several others and an array of more improbable vehicles in the very foremost rank. A bright and unwavering light from immediately in front illuminated the scene. Father and Mother stood on the pallet.

Mathembe had to punch her father's leg several times before he pulled her up beside them.

"And my friend Kalimuni too," insisted the head. The advocate came up beside them onto the pallet.

Now Mathembe could see the nature of the obstruction against which the people had broken. Where the orchards and paddies of a township gave way to primal forest, a roadblock had been set up. Trux and agricultural organicals stood in a line across the road; their headlamps cast the harsh, unwavering light. Men stood in rows, shadows within shadows, atop and before their vehicles. Legs apart, hands apart, the way men stand when they feel the confidence a weapon imparts.

"You cannot come in," said a loud voice distorted by amplification circuitry. "We will not permit you to enter this township." Mathembe could not see which of the shadow men had spoken. The angry people of Chepsenyt howled and bayed. The amplified voice shouted them down. "Go away. You cannot settle here. If we let you come in you will not leave again and we cannot feed you all."

"Cannot? Will not!" came back a single voice from the Chepsenyt side. "Tired, wet, hungry, homeless, and in the name of decency you will not even give us one night's shelter!"

The reckless young men of Chepsenyt, who are always to be found at the front of any such crowd, had adopted that same stance as the men blocking the road into the township. But it is not the same if you do not have a weapon in your hands to give you confidence. A new voice came over the amplifier.

"We do not permit rebels in our township!" The men hefted their weapons, the angular shadows moved.

"We are not rebels!" answered a third voice. "We have lost everything. Everything. Houses, trees, everything. Burned. There is no more Chepsenyt."

"Soldiers burn your township and you tell us you are not rebels? You will have nothing from us."

A new voice spoke now, from the rear of the crowd. Mathembe turned with all the others to see who was speaking: a small man from the Proclaimer end of town, balanced perilously on the hump of a trux, shouting through cupped hands.

"Bajeer Rajtamanee, is that you? Bajeer Rajtamanee? It is me!

Me!" The small man beat himself on the chest with his hands. "Me!"

"Dhav Jhiringi?" came the amplified soulless voice.

"Dhav Jhiringi!" the small man replied, again beating himself on the chest, like some Jantic crazy-priest beating himself naked through the streets and not the sober cast-in-the-image-of-God Proclaimer that he was. "And Rana. And Yasni. And Basda, and Sheerjha. We're all here."

"All here?" asked the booming amplified voice but the absolute authority, the solidity, had gone out of it.

"All here!" the little man shouted back into the wall of light. "All of us Proclaimers, we're all here!" A new theme rose within the sound of the mob, the voices of the Proclaimers proclaiming themselves over the anger.

"They burned your houses too?" the voice asked. "We had not heard that. We thought it was just, you know . . . them."

"Everything, they burned them all," the little man said, and the Proclaimers gave a great murmur of assent. The rigid, angular shadows of the men blocking the road moved into new configurations. The impatient young men of Chepsenyt, with the impatient fists and empty, impatient stomachs, started forward to rush the barricade. The black silhouetted weapons snapped around.

"We did not know that," said the big voice that did not sound quite so big now. "That makes it different. All different. We did not know it was Proclaimers too. You can come in."

The angry young men's passion burst in a howl of outrage. The man with the amplifier shouted over the top of them.

"It is our township; we let in who we like and we keep out who we like. If we say they can come in, they can come in. If we say you stay outside, you stay outside."

There is a certain sound the plastic of a weapon muzzle makes when it is snapped down into the palm of the hand in readiness to fire. There is no other sound quite like it. Little Mr. Jhiringi led, balanced on the hump of his trux, as the families with their smoke-smelling possessions moved through the unmoving Confessors toward the wall of light that had opened a blackness at its heart to admit them. Family by family, the Proclaimers came forward under the guns of their fellow Proclaimers and entered into the township. The angry young men shouted abuse at them, and their women, and their children, clutching their holy-day hats to their breasts, and the not so young, and the aged men and women. The ranks of the people of Chepsenyt thinned as the Proclaimers moved through and out until all had passed into the embrace of their brothers in the closed township. All but Dr. Kalimuni, standing beside Mathembe on the pallet of the Fileli family trux. All the decency, all the righteousness to which he had aspired had been annihilated by the blatancy of the act of discrimination. He climbed down from the trux and walked away through the people toward the trees of the forest's edge. As the two wings of light rejoined into a wall once more, the people broke apart into families and kinships and drifted away to prepare for night under the trees. Some few remained to shout and throw stones, but it was clear the township folk would hold the roadblock until the last Confessors had gone on their way.

It was not long until the argument started. A great fire had been built, a good place for arguments to collect, around which all the people were supposed to gather to decide what was to be done. Where there are people trying to decide what is to be done there will always be arguments. The louts, no-goods, and Ghost Boys wanted to attack the township, at once, in force, burn it, loot it, let Proclaimer blood run over the cobbles. Others favored sneak raids into the paddy gardens: such a long perimeter could not be completely secured. Still others counseled caution and advised no rash or foolish action; there were women and children and old people in their midst. But the roaring boys must have their honor and their glory: what kind of creeping venereal disease were the people of Chepsenyt that they would sit on their hands and rock back and forth like old witless incontinent fools rather than act in the name of their ancestors, what sort of penisless boys? Caution. Care. Consider. What sort of words were those? Voices were raised, tempers and tongues grew hot by the light of the fire, firelight shone on thirsty, sweaty faces shouting at each other, and in a very few sentences the discussion had cast off its covering of *What is to be done?* and stood naked in the fire's heat as *Who is in control here?*

Curled up against the still-warm, yielding side of the trux, Mathembe listened to the voices growing louder. The spirit of argument was an infection. Soon it would infect her own family: the head first, or perhaps Hradu; her father next. Her mother would fight the hardest to maintain peace and order and sense in the face of disaster, but even to fight is a symptom of the disease and she too would succumb.

Mathembe slipped out from under her quilt and took herself away, far away, away from the voices, into the trees. When she could no longer hear the sound of the voices, she lay down and looked up through the branches at the stars. If she lay long enough and still enough, she might convince herself that she could feel the world turning in space with her pinned to it by a spear of gravity. Thousands upon thousands of kilometers per hour, rushing through space with a terrifying roar of vacuum, like the rush and boom of her blood through the spaces of her body.

She had been shown a great world, a complex and vital world programmed by whirring, interlocking wheels of thought and language, dizzyingly splendid and powerful. She had seen that same day another world where everything was reducible ultimately to one question and one question only: Confessor or Proclaimer? It ran like a fault line through every action, every thought; it struck against the glittering belief machines of the wider world and cleaved them into two totally separate entities: black or white, left-handed or right-handed, Confessor or Proclaimer? For us or against us?

The paucity of it appalled her: that, in all things, that which is not demonstrably of us, for us, by us, is against us. No middle ground, no spectrum of possibilities, just light and light's opposite.

Please God, must I be like them?

A star moved in heaven. The answer to a prayer? Against all the laws of celestial mechanics, it came up from the south side of the sky: a single green star. It moved over Mathembe lying under the tieve trees looking up to heaven and stopped. And Mathembe gave a cry of fear and wonder and awe as light flooded the forest. The light of morning shone from a clear blue sky: daylight, sunlight. Birds rose in a storm of wings from their roosts, animals and organicals gave voice to their terror in a chorus of whistlings, chimings, yelpings. Day-in-night lit up the forest for ten long seconds and was gone. The birds flapped blindly through the canopy; the forest chorus died away voice by voice by voice.

Mathembe had been too young to properly understand her parents' explanations of what was happening when last a Saint-ship had transited *ur*-space, lighting up the night half of the world with the daylight of another planet streaming through the portal in reality. But the memory was indelible.

Three new stars formed an ephemeral constellation over the night forest. The small green star fell back beneath the horizon. The huge soft red moon and the small brilliant white star hung unrivaled in the sky. Mathembe called to mind images from the education circuits: the vast carrier body, a sphere of biotechnology eighty kilometers across orbited by the two-kilometer-diameter silver metal ball of the command body, within which resided the spirits of the crew. Her grandfather had always suspected that the spirit of his beloved Silali had shipped aboard a Saint-ship and been taken forever beyond the reach of his love, through the timelessness and spacelessness of *ur*-space to the dazzling Daughter Worlds.

The education brainplants had noted a theory that the Saint-ships were the highly evolved humanity of an incredibly advanced Daughter World. Begging the question: *Which is the man, then, and which the woman?*

In the morning, there was the sound of mothers mourning.

Five of the young men had attempted a raid on the closed township under cover of darkness. They had gone running and ducking along the embankments and footways between the paddy fields. By fits, and starts, and slow stealthy glides, they had come to within meters of the patrols that sent their biolight beams swinging out across the flooded fields. They had twist knives in their belts, those brave five, soft pieces of plastic that realigned their molecules into wicked little blades when you twisted them. They were not interested in stealing food. They wanted to see blood spill in the dark waters of the paddy fields, blood for the honor of Chepsenyt. And then the night had turned to day. They were exposed and naked as children. The Proclaimers had opened up with their weapons. In those ten long seconds when they had been cut apart, the Proclaimers had come whooping and splashing after them through the waterlogged fields as they dragged themselves away. None had escaped uninjured. Some had gunshot wounds or burns from lasers. Others displayed the characteristic wounds of bioweapons, or paralyzed limbs where neurotoxin darts had struck. One young man, a head-to-toe mass of fungal infections, was not expected to live. When Mathembe heard the wailing of the women go up around the embers of the council fire, she knew that the headmasters had come with their monomolecular loops and valises of organicals.

The mothers of the wounded pushed the mother of the dead young man around the encampment in a handcart. She sat cross-legged with her son's head cradled in her lap. Mathembe recognized the head. It was the head of the stupid young man who had taunted Dr. Kalimuni. Tears streaked the white clay mourning the woman had daubed on her face. The proper funeral masks were ashes in Chep-senyt.

In their anger, the five mothers succeeded where their sons had failed. They succeeded in breaking the solidarity of the refugees. The mother of the dead young man declared that her son would not enter the Dreaming among the hoi polloi of the municipal interfaces, but in the company of his ancestors. His own ancestors. His own tree. In his own Ancestor Grove. Nowhere else. No matter that the Ancestor Trees were fallen and burned. No matter that Chepsenyt was still-smoldering ashes. They would go back, the five of them, back to their own place. Had they not seeds and cells and house units? Could they not grow a new Chepsenyt from the old? They could, verily; they would, and if they did not have sufficient genetic material, they would use their own bodies; see if they did not. Who would come with them? Who had the pride to pick themselves up and dust themselves down and piss on the humiliation of the Proclaimers and the Emperor's militia and go back to regrow Chepsenyt as it should always have been, a Confessor town for a Confessor people?

Mathembe's grandfather had always been easily stirred by wine-bottle rhetoric. He would have had the trux woken and turned around back down the straight white road without one further thought. When Mathembe's father refused because it was decided that they would go on to Timboroa and there take the train for Ol Tok, where there were relatives and more opportunity for trux growers, it was for setting out on its own, see if it would not, if it had legs, if it had transport, if it had been anything but a helpless dead head.

"Listen to them now," said Mathembe's father. "Listen to them. 'For the sake of my son's sacrifice, for the sake of his glorious act of defiance against the Proclaimers, for the honor of his head, go back.'

What kind of talk is that? You want to go back to a town where people talk about thugs as if they were the Ykondé saints?"

But the people were irrevocably divided. Those who had chosen to follow the head and its mother gathered up and left before noon. Those who remained were less than a third of the refugees who had fled from Chepsenyt. Of those, some elected to remain where they were in hope that the Proclaimers might relent if they were faced with fewer and more reasonable refugees. Some others took themselves through the forest to places and parts unknown. Others melted family by family into the trees to make what life they could under the canopy of leaves: forest dwellers, semi-civilized nomads on the edge of society. Small groupings of them had occasionally passed through Chepsenyt to trade deep-wood genetic material. Mathembe's mother had bought samples of birds and animals to work into her toys. Mathembe had never been comfortable with the sight of her mother pouring thimbles of wine for the small, naked, pale-skinned urchins crowding her conservatory.

In the end, twenty families remained to continue together to the railhead at Timboroa and thereafter seek their separate fortunes. Twenty families and Dr. Kalimuni.

Scavenging for wild bladdermilks and brownmeat, Mathembe found the advocate sitting disconsolately under the same tree where he had parked the jeepney the previous night. Of the jeepney there was no trace, but all his worldly goods were gathered into a close circle around him. It was unusual to find Dr. Kalimuni, most self-possessed of men, discomfited.

"Oh, dear child, dear child, dear dear child," said Dr. Kalimuni. "Such is the price of integrity. I refuse to be party to blatant sectarianism, yet I return here to find my poor few things scattered and smashed. Hither and yon. Hither and yon! Deliberate destruction. And my poor jeepney. . . ." From behind his back he produced a plastic strut-bone. Scraps of synthetic flesh clung to the bone; the hard ceramic plastic showed signs of teeth. "Animals! No, that is to demean animals, who are without conception of good or ill. Worse than animals, to do such a thing!" Both Proclaimers and Confessors agreed that to eat the flesh of organicals was a detestable thing. Only out of great hunger, or great barbarism, could it be contemplated. But never countenanced. "It had been my intent to travel to Timboroa and there take train and country bus to Jadamborazo, where my brother holds a medical practice. However, what had been merely taxing has been rendered nigh impossible. My dear girl, for the sake of the neighborliness between myself and your family, nay, friendship—I do not think it is too strong a word—would it be possible for me to travel with you?"

The twenty families were ready to move within the hour. The ragged procession of trux, tryx, jeepneys, and staggering, stumbling house units worked its way around the closed township at a respectable unthreatening distance.

"See, we go on our way. Peacefully. Quietly. Law-abidingly!" shouted Mr. Fileli, then muttered under his breath, "Piss on this township and all in it." The Proclaimers on their barricades watched. When a house unit lost its footing on the paddy causeways and slipped into the water, they did not raise a hand to help. Those hands were too full with weapons. Mathembe helped save what was savable from the muddy water but the house unit drowned. The flailing of its skinny legs grew weaker and weaker until they failed and lay floating in a neat trefoil on the surface.

It was a beautiful day. The forest sang with flyers and fritillaries and glyders; the great stands of tieve trees had given way to a many-colored reef of fans and tines and pillars among which clutches of balloons grew so densely as almost to form a second sky.

Mathembe did not care. She was experiencing a new sensation: a feeling in a center of her being, not quite a pain, not quite not a pain. At times it peaked into an almost physical nausea. At times it left her feeling weak and light-headed so that the long white road and the forest and the balloons in the blue sky spun end for end, over and over.

When you are born into an economy of abundance where your every need may be gratified immediately by the act of reaching out and plucking from tree, shrub, or organical, you never learn to save against adversity. The economics of scarcity are meaningless in the midst of boundless self-sufficiency. The sensation of *hunger*, chronic gnawing hunger, is as alien as the far side of the moon.

Dr. Kalimuni and the head were arguing. Dr. Kalimuni had been lent a small handcart which could be towed behind the trux. The advocate sat facing backward, toward Chepsenyt, amid his possessions. The head rode beside him. Arguing for them was the dimension of their friendship: if ever there was a subject they could not share with each other in argument, their friendship would have been shattered by the rock of mistrust. The head was asking Dr. Kalimuni how a Proclaimer could profess loyalty to an Empire that burned the houses of Proclaimers and Confessors with equal disregard.

"Meatmen," it spat out. "You and me both. That is all we are to them in their gleaming metal cities. Meatmen! You bow to an Emperor who holds you beneath contempt?"

"No sir, no no," said Dr. Kalimuni. "Even if it were so, I would still be loyal. Is a prayer dog disloyal to its master because the master is a human and it a contemptible organical?"

"You think you are a dog? Then you are agreeing with me: that we are held in contempt by the Emperor. But we are not dogs. We are humans."

"You miss my point entirely. Entirely!" proclaimed Dr. Kalimuni, and they fell to it again so that Mathembe, newfound faith in a complex, subtle world doubt-shaken, signed to Hradu to come with her to forage along the roadside. Meat plants and bladdermilks and many of the older staples might be found in degraded, feral forms in the wild, either escaped or deliberately released in defiance of the Patent Laws. The yield from this unfamiliar forest was disappointing: less than enough, when divided among the family, to drive away the hunger pains.

The refugee column moved along the road to Timboroa. Other roads now joined the main road, roads that led off at intriguing angles through the forest until perspective diminished them to invisibility. Traffic was abroad on the highway: local homesteaders in trux-hauled wooden carts; children and ugly women openly staring; the occasional country bus roaring past, horns blaring rudely at the refugees, twelve big wheels churning up the dust that had arisen in the heat of the day from the mud of yesterday.

Immediately ahead of the Filelis was Murea Mithika and her much younger husband. Murea Mithika had run a daily country bus service on a circular route through Chepsenyt, Tetsenok, and Olmarok, once a week making the overnight run to Timboroa. Her bus, her pride, her joy, her life (a fact to which her much younger husband was learning to accommodate himself as a precept of marriage) had burned in its garage in Chepsenyt; they walked behind a moribund tryx towing a handcart laden with plastic bags and holdalls. When a country bus announced its advent in a plume of flying dust, horns blaring *Get out of my road into the ditch where you belong*, Murea Mithika would wave forlornly. She knew all the drivers on the Timboroa runs. The buses bowled past in one continuous shout of horns and she stood, rocked and blinded in the slipstream, hand still raised in salutation, just another footslogger.

Many and various were the buses that ran between the townships and the larger centers, but none so magnificent as Murea Mithika's. Mathembe's father had helped design the curving horns and tusks around the power compartment: its wheels were taller than the tallest man in Chepsenyt, its organoplastic hide was mottled and striped in tones of silver, mauve, and pink. Every passenger seat on the trailer was fitted with personal radios and converted into cots for overnight runs. There was a shithouse and a shrine to the angel Yemlenekidé, and one of her ancestors (with his consent, of course) had been fitted as onboard oracle and relief driver. The grandest bus on the Timboroa road. Gone, and without it the drivers bowling along to Timboroa could no longer recognize Murea Mithika.

Kombétet barely deserved the grace of a name. It was so unworthy a place it had escaped the tongues of the Emperor's New Namers and so retained its full and original Old Speech meaning. Kombétet, translated, meant "The Place of the Piss." It came into existence at the point of absolute bladder distension of the average bus traveler on the way to Timboroa. One day a traveler of a more entreprenurial slant, while pleasurefully watering the ground, saw the word OPPORTUNITY writ across the heavens in shining ideograms. He returned with family and organicals, dug a row of pits, brought in a batch of shit beetles and biogas bacteria, put up partitions, and charged five enns a go. Five generations had taken a comfortable living from the excreta of the desperate. It was not very long before the vendors and peddlers came to spread their plastic tarpaulins on the ground, pile up their pyramids of fruit and meat and sticks of traveler's chocolate, erect their grills and braziers, and open for business. Seemingly within minutes of Kombétet's invention there were wine sellers loping up to the country buses, plastic flagons swinging from shoulder yokes, and tea girls clinking their bowls together and shouting out their prices. Fifty families, including that of the founding Father of the Toilets, now drew their livings from the buses; homesteads and gardens lay scattered throughout the surrounding forest on both sides of the road. It is always a certain sign of respectability when imitations appear; Kombétet now had a rival in the form of the so-called New Kombétet, which had sprung up one night on the other side of the road to milk the outbound traffic. Though little more than a private syrup digester and a few piles of dubious radio cockles and bootleg magazine circuits, rivalry between New and Old Kombétets was intense. Old Kombétet did not even acknowledge the existence of its bastard offspring as a separate entity and thus refused to accept the title "old." There was only one Kombétet and a few ragged-assed freebooters. New Kombétet, with all the patriotic fervor of a place that has recently discovered it has an identity and a nationality, had applied to Timboroa Prefecture for permission to grow a full-scale hostelry, café, bar, shop, and service area for the buses.

War between the two Kombétets across the straight white road seemed unavoidable.

Old Kombétet, *the* Kombétet, depending on which side of the road you were driving along, was changing over to the night shift when the dying red trux pulled off the road into the laager of refugee vehicles. Flights of tethered gloglobes, bobbing in the darkening air, were lighting up one by one; the day vendors were returning with bulging belt pouches to their homesteads in the forest while the night vendors—wives, husbands, children, parents of the day vendors—took up their places cross-legged and infinitely suspicious on the ground behind their wares. Biogas generators kicked into rhythmic, thumping life; neon tubes bent into Old Speech ideograms flickered fitful cerises and electric blues. Imported Imperial technology. Mathembe stared at the neons, reached out a blue-lit finger to touch the cold glow. She had wandered in search of food while her parents and the other refugees haggled with Kombétet's proprietors over the price of a night's stay. She went up and down the rows of hawkers squatting on their groundsheets with their whitemeat and brownmeat and redmeat and fruit and spices heaped in front of them. She knelt down and lifted a breadapple.

"That will be five," said the hawker.

Mathembe shook her head.

"Oh, all right then, have it your own way. Three."

Mathembe shook her head again.

"All right all right all right. Two."

A third time Mathembe shook her head. She replaced the breadapple on its pile and cupped her hands in the way that says *Give. Please*.

"What do you think I am, a bloody charity?" said the hawker. "Get out of here, go on, get!"

Country buses were pulled up on the side of the road, the country people wandering up and down the aisles of plenty, thoughtlessly eating from bags of hot pastries and stuffed glazed fruits as they picked up cockle radios and argued over a copy of a bestseller book circuit. Mathembe went among them, between them, hands held out to them, saying *It is the hunger only the hunger, otherwise I would not be embarrassing you or humiliating myself: please, and I will go away*.

Such eloquent hands. But the country bus people could not read the eloquence of her hands. They saw a gawky township urchin with a snub nose and filthy clothes, begging. They understood *begging* as little as Mathembe had once comprehended *hunger*. She went along the sides of the buses where the wine sellers and tea girls were passing bowls up to the passengers for small change and bartered knickknacks—a pair of earrings, a well-read magazine plug, a stick of makeup. She lifted her hands to the people behind the windows, people from Tetsenok and Olmarok and Kapsabet and Garsabit and Timboroa who had lived all their lives throned in plenty and had never see anyone *beg* before.

She held up her hands to a small boy in a window seat next to his mother. His mother was otherwise occupied with a man across the aisle who seemed to be engaged in flirtation purely to while away a long and tedious journey. In an instant of contact, Mathembe and the boy were caught up in a fragment of audacious conspiracy.

Give the hands said.

The little boy unhooked the cockle from his ear, lowered it out of the louver window.

Mathembe shook her head.

The little boy picked up the book in his lap, held it up for Mathembe to see, reader leads dangling.

Mathembe shook her head. *Give*, said the hands. And *hungry*.

The little boy delved his hand into the plastic bag on the empty seat between him and his beflattered mother, produced some fondant-stuffed sweet meat wrapped in rice paper. He was not a thin little boy, this little boy. Looking sidelong to make sure his mother's attention was fully engaged by the unctuous man, he held the sweet up to the window.

Mathembe nodded her head.

The plump little boy looked incredulous.

Mathembe nodded her head. *Yes.*

The boy dropped the sweet through the louver slot. *Quick.* Quick: Mathembe's hands darted to catch and jam it into her mouth. *Sugar sweet chewy food good food.*

The blow sent her reeling against the side of the bus, into the dust among the feet of the wine sellers and tea girls. The sugary sweet chewy morsel flew from her mouth. Mathembe was on her feet in a sharp flicker of movement: hand drawn back to stab at throat, eyes; foot ready to kick.

"My saints. Hit *me*, would you, you little bitch?" said her mother.

Mathembe crouched, growling and furious.

"This is what we are come to, is it? Fighting for the drippings from other people's tables?" Her foot twisted the sugary sweet chewy thing into the dust. Mathembe gestured savagely at her stomach.

"We're all hungry. But we do not beg. We still have some pride. I am disgusted. Disgusted." She walked away, upright and handsome and righteous. Mathembe followed, angry and humiliated. The wine sellers and tea girls clicked their bowls together, *click click click click click.* The altercation had woken the boy's mother from the suave man's spell. Now she was shouting at her son and trying to cuff him around the head.

"They would not take our cards," Mathembe's father said. "They had doubts about whether they were backed by solid biological specie." Mathembe could imagine the dubious expressions on the faces, highlighted by the card-reader screens. "For God's sake! They will let us stay, though. Just one night."

"What did it cost?" Mathembe's mother asked.

"What did it not cost?" Mathembe's father nodded toward the slumbering trux where the belongings were being picked and picked and picked over again by the fingers of the entrepreneurs of Kombétet. They took the quilt under which Mathembe had slept all the days of her life in the room through which the birds flew in the morning. She slept that night under plastic sheeting huddled for warmth against the trux while the quilt's new owner, ignorant of its freight of history, took it home to his shack among the trees and did it to his fat woman under it all night in that way she did not like.

In the gray morning Mathembe squatted under her plastic sheet in line with the other refugees, cup held out while the traders came around with their pots dolloping out scoops of breadapple mush.

"Thank God, no blasphemy intended," said Dr. Kalimuni, politely refusing the slop, "it is the holy day today."

Hradu screwed his face up at the beige mush in his plastic cup. Mathembe wiggled her empty cup at him in the way that says *If you do not want it, I will have it*. She caught her mother's judging eye. Hradu gulped down his breakfast with much grimacing. The buses came and went in a haze of dust and early morning mist; the sun was a distended belly of indefinite illumination. The people of Chepsenyt moved through the shadowless light with an exaggerated slowness, a lifeless lifting and setting, loading and preparing, like a labor of ghosts.

Before even an hour's walk was done, Mathembe was hungry again.

"It would not be so bad if one made a regular practice of fasting," said Dr. Kalimuni, marching along prim and fresh and upright. "There is a lot of sense in the old disciplines." Mathembe scowled at him and took Hradu off into the forest to scavenge. The forest beyond Kombétet was more similar to that which stood around Chepsenyt than the weird, anarchic growth of the previous day's march. The dark vault of these woods held aloft by many many thousand slender columns was intimate and welcoming. Forest dwellers are never far removed from the womb. In woods like these there would be many pickings. Within minutes Mathembe had filled her belt pouch with translucent pearls of bladdermilk and was savoring the sweet drip of nectar from dew plants on her tongue. Hradu waved, calling Mathembe to the clump of feral whitemeat he had discovered in a damp crevice of a root buttress. Mathembe picked one of the wrinkled brown cylinders, peeled back the outer skin to reveal the white, phallic flesh inside. Brother and sister gorged themselves and crammed what little they could not eat into their belt pouches.

From her earliest remembering and before, in that pre-remembering time when she had made the binding decision that speech was a waste of time and energy, Mathembe had felt Hradu's welfare to be incumbent upon her. As a male he was capable of staggering stupidity, especially in the name of vanity, but he was not beyond redemption. His physical, mental, educational, and spiritual development was her concern—perhaps handed to her personally in the womb by the saints. She regarded with horror the prospect that he might, purely by neglect of conscious choices, grow into another unthinking, unquestioning, undemanding, useless lad-about-town like the ones who had once hung around outside Mr. Kakamega's tryx shop. She was not yet certain what she wanted him to be, but she was certain what she did *not* want him to be. How she could go from the latter state to the former she had no idea whatsoever.

If, through the voice of Dr. Kalimuni's radio, she had been brought to an abrupt appreciation of a wider, brighter, subtler world than the one into which she had been squeezed from her mother's womb, it should be even more possible for Hradu, with his better understanding of New Speech, the tongue in which the real world iterated itself. It was not that she thought of her parents as inadequate; it was that their lives were lived on one side of a perceptual gulf and she and Hradu and all her generation played upon the other.

In her contemplations, the course of her scavengings and probings through the wood had diverged from Hradu's. She was alone beneath the trees. A sudden cry broke the silence: a cry, and a crashing, and the sound of feet, fast feet, on soft forest litter. A figure came dashing through the darkness beneath the trees: Hradu. A second figure bore down in pursuit, larger, faster. Mathembe flew headlong to the aid of her brother.

And suddenly there were dark figures everywhere, out of every root and trunk and fungus stand and coral cluster. Mathembe wheeled and ran and the dark figures came leaping and running after. Whoops and shouts filled the vault beneath the canopy, and laughter that spurred Mathembe to run harder, faster. She had never suffered anyone to laugh at her.

Run, you are the runner, you are the one begged your father, next time, next time, I want to be a runner, I am fast, I am quick, I can dart and weave, there is not a branch can snag me not a patch of moss can make me slip; run, it is the trux hunt only you are the hunted, the trux

*running out of tricks darting and weaving with the runners closing in
behind them, glance back, quick, just a glance, they are coming they
are coming whooping and jeering and laughing pretending it is like a
big game, laughing, where is Hradu? nowhere to be seen, you are alone
now, yourself, alone, running, getting away, getting away, pulling
away with every step, you are fast, you always were fast, you were the
best runner, the strongest runner, the fastest runner, no one can catch
you, no one is as fleet and quick and nimble as you and you laugh at
your cleverness and quickness and nimbleness and brilliance and talent
at outrunning them and suddenly it is there rearing up before you, the
dark figure. Looming up above you cannot stop cannot dodge feet slip,
you are falling, brought down like a forest tree falling. . . . .*

The woman Mathembe did not like did not like Mathembe either. She
was small and tightly muscled and had a dominating overbearing way,
but it was not that Mathembe did not like. She reminded Mathembe
of Kiminini and Kimilili and she thought she knew why but it was not
for that that Mathembe did not like her. She was the leader of the
group, which explained, if not excused her manner, but it was not for
that either that Mathembe did not like her.

Mathembe did not like her because she called Mathembe *girlie*.

After her belt pouches had been searched, the small woman
questioned Mathembe for half an hour about what the *girlie* was doing
in the woods, where the *girlie* had come from, where the *girlie* was
going and with whom, and how, and why, and, receiving not even the
slightest acknowledgment of her sentience, had concluded that the
girlie was either deaf, a cretin, or terminally stubborn. Any of which
Mathembe was more than content for the small muscular woman to
believe about her.

"She does not speak," said Hradu.

"She cannot speak?"

"She will not speak."

Hradu could speak. Hradu was more than willing to speak: no
threats, no bribes necessary; it was more than honor to be thought to
hold information useful to an Active Service Unit of the Warriors of
Destiny.

When noon had passed and shadows began to emerge out of the forest
onto the roadside, Mathembe's family had begged the caravan to stop

and wait for their missing children. The shadows had filled up the straight white road, the evening mist had come up, and, though Timboroa was no more than an hour's walk distant, the people had consented to spend one last night under the naked sky. When Mathembe and Hradu stepped out of the darkness into the biolights, their mother and father had been filled with that uniquely parental emotion of exultation and fury. Then the figures came stepping behind them out of the forest into the pale yellow light and Mr. and Mrs. Fileli and everyone in the roadside camp was very quiet. And still. And fearful.

The small woman addressed them. At the bottom of an unnumbered page in the unwritten Handbook of Irregular Forces is the unbreakable law that states that Active Service Unit commanders must always be long-winded. An unspoken subclause expands further that Active Service Unit commanders must always announce at great length who they are, who they command, and what they stand for. Especially when it is patently obvious to those foregathered who they are and what they stand for. Here then is a précis of what the unit commander said. They were the Warriors of Destiny. They were the remnants of the First Ukerewe Brigade that the Imperial Forces of Occupation had been sweeping through the forests of Timboroa for these past weeks. The Imperial Forces of Oppression had outflanked and encircled them and were preparing to close the trap and destroy them. Their only hope of escape was to insinuate themselves among travelers along the road and pass through the roadblocks and checkpoints to Timboroa, where they could once again dissolve into a network of cells and agents. They had hoped to hijack some country bus—"hijack" of course was not the word the small woman used; a refugee column was even better.

"Our township burned for you, and you want us to smuggle you through checkpoints?" The challenging voice belonged to the father of the Ghost Boy who had tried to seduce Mathembe in the deep woods. His son squatted at his feet, in the dust of the Timboroa Road. The small woman's deputy, a tall thin man who smelled strongly, as many of the Warriors did, of something nose-wrinkling but not entirely unpleasant, stared with frank astonishment at the man who had spoken.

"Your country means nothing to you? This land that has fed and nurtured and loved you for a hundred generations, and when she stirs in her chains, cries out in agony against a thousand years of oppression and injustice and violence against her, you turn your backs and walk away? It was not us burned your township. It was the soldiers of the Imperial aggressor burned it."

"It was the Timboroa Prefecture militia burned it," said Dr. Kalimuni with breathtaking daring. "Men who speak Old Speech as well as you, men with a hundred ancestors in the Dreaming, like you; men who call this country home and love it, like you."

"Proclaimers," spat the tall thin man. "Proclaimers!" As if the name, that one word, could somehow trump, could somehow repudiate and annihilate any word that might be spoken in its defense. Proud and idiotic, Dr. Kalimuni prepared to debate law and history but the small woman ended the argument.

"We will not presume upon your political sensibilities, which have clearly been blunted and dulled by recent events. How many days have you been on the road? Two? Three? You will not have found much in the way of picking in the forests around here. Piss-poor prefecture, Timboroa." She held up Mathembe's pouch, poured her day's collecting onto the earth, and ground it to pulp beneath her boot. "Piss poor." Grinning, she thrust her hand into her battle pack and raised it high for all to see. Fresh, soft whitemeat oozed between her fingers.

It was the trux hunters' picnic again, in the clearing in the forest, a table spread under heaven. There were meats of all colors, red and brown and even yellow; fruits and barks and grains and milk, even prepackaged vacuum-sealed bags of military rations: boil them in water, cut them open quick quick (hot! hot!), pass them along the line one spoonful each from the bag, tasting of that funny taste you cannot quite place but tastes the way the Warriors of Destiny smell; never mind, hot and good and flavorful and much. There was wine. Someone filled up Mathembe's grandfather's pot and as the organicals drank it up he became silly and verbose. Someone found a radio and poked it into life. A strange modulating music made everyone fall silent and listen in wonder, an eerie many-layered sound that defied comprehension: the sound, one Warrior said, of the Saint-ship high in orbit singing to itself. Then the radio retuned to another station and bright jangling music about love and hurt and leaving burst forth. A

spirit of dogged enjoyment passed between the refugees, a well-this-
is-how-it-is-so-we-might-as-well-enjoy-ourselves-ness.

Dr. Kalimuni did not eat. Though the time of fasting had ended
with his noonday meditations, the food remained untouched on the
leaf in front of him. Dr. Kalimuni himself sat tranquil and upright in
the way someone does when he has committed himself to an
irrevocable action. The Warrior of Destiny who sat opposite Dr.
Kalimuni had noticed the advocate was not eating. He pushed the food
toward the Proclaimer.

"Go on, eat."

Dr. Kalimuni swiveled his eyes toward heaven for one second,
then returned to his contemplation.

"Go on, you must be hungry, eat something."

"I will not eat the food of rebels and murderers," said Dr.
Kalimuni smoothly.

"Eat it," said the Warrior. "Eat it." He picked up the leaf, pushed
it toward Dr. Kalimuni. "Eat it. Eat it!" He pushed the food into Dr.
Kalimuni's face, screwed the leaf around and around to force the food
into his mouth. "Eat it!" he screamed. There was a click. The muzzle
of his weapon was at Dr. Kalimuni's chin. "Eat . . . it."

The food ran in gobbets and runnels down the advocate's chin.
Dr. Kalimuni did not move. Dr. Kalimuni did not say a word. The
Warrior held the weapon to his jaw, and held it, and held it, and then
it trembled, then it wavered a little, then the Warrior jammed it back
into his holster and got up and stalked off.

"Hah hah you look pretty stupid with that shit running down your
face!" the Warrior shouted, but he knew and Dr. Kalimuni knew and
Mathembe who had sat beside the Warrior knew and everyone knew
that the Proclaimer had defeated him.

The party spirit, fragile at best, was dissolved away in an instant.
Mathembe ate, they all ate, but the food tasted like ashes in their
mouths.

One morning, not so many years ago for the memory to have
become semi-legendary, mythologized and idealized, Mathembe had
rushed in to her mother in her conservatory to proudly show her the
chocolate-brown smear in the crotch of her panties. Mathembe's
mother had gone out to make the appropriate visits, and the next
morning Mathembe had been woken by a sound like some new and

wonderful bird calling outside her window. And when she had gone to look she had seen that, yes, there was a new and wonderful bird, three of them in fact, dancing and preening and scratching on the cobbles beneath her window. Great birds, magical birds, with wings like rainbows and long floating feathers that shone in the early sun as they danced and cried and stamped. Her mother had come then and led her out into the street to watch the dancers, for dancers they were, in the wonderful bird costumes traditional to Womaning Day, and at the prearranged signal the musicians came out from behind the trees and outhouses and struck up on their guitars and drums and keyboards and the dancers danced all leaping all diving all whirling in a dazzle of sound and brilliant flashing feathers and Mathembe had clapped her hands, face radiant that all this, all this could be for her merely because of a discharge in her panties; and then one of the dancers had leaped higher than any of the others and the wind caught his costume and blew it up around him so that she could see underneath it, and what was underneath was an old naked wrinkled man with skin like leather that has been in the paddy fields a year and a huge shriveled dangling penis and flat flaccid thighs and bony ridged feet, not any old man but *the* old man, the one all the girls knew about because he was a dirty filthy perverted old creature who tried to chat with you and give you things and touch you and show you dirty pictures of girls just like you doing it with men older and viler even than he.

Then the bird feathers had closed and concealed the ugliness that moved and operated beneath them.

Mathembe found him rather attractive. For a boy, no, not quite; a man, no, not quite. Tall, but not too. Dark, but not too. Shy, but not too. Smiling, but not too. He had the sunlit aspect of those who live long and close to idealism. Mathembe had never seen this quality in any of the men of Chepsenyt, and it attracted her like an angel to the light. He liked to walk beside her, and she beside him. It did not matter to him that she would not speak, would only smile, rarely, and shyly. They shared silence. It did not matter to her that underneath the folds of his coat was a black Imperial automatic and clips.

The small woman had infiltrated one of her command into each family group but had left it to the individual discretions of the families to devise a story that would convince the soldiers at the checkpoint.

Mathembe's father and mother had been far from convinced. The young man might pass as a cousin from Kapsabet whose identification had been lost in the fire. To add conviction, Mr. Fileli buried his own smartcard in Grandfather's bowl beneath the rooticles. *See? Neither of us has any identification, officer.*

With the muzzles of the guns never far, breakfast had also tasted like ashes.

Convoys of armored black carriers came pounding past, along the road, many many vehicles going out from Timboroa to close the net around the fugitives. Dread rooted Mathembe to the roadside, apprehension.

"Act natural," said the young Warrior.

That is a thing easily said, thought Mathembe as the column of armored vehicles rolled past, down the straight white road.

Timboroa: the Town in the Valley Where God Touched Earth in Old Speech; in New Speech, four syllables, four chunks of sound, *Tim . . . bo . . . ro . . . a.* God pushed back up through his crack in the sky by the New Namers. You came upon the town suddenly; the main road did not follow the valley route between river and rail tracks but ran straight across a plateau to the valley edge. Centuries of travelers had been surprised to find the road seemingly ending sheer before them in the blue sky and the city beneath their feet, winding to left and right along the contours of its valley. You seemed to be standing on the rooftops of the uppermost houses; you might think you could go down into Timboroa by stepping from roof to roof to roof, as if descending a giant staircase.

The soldiers had set up their checkpoint at the place where the forest ended and the road fell away in loops and swags through the gardens and houses to the town. Five carriers. Black. Soldiers with daytime television game shows beamed from the heart of the Empire on their heads-up data visors. And ten thousand watts of music power in each cochlea. Helicopters moved, black and chattering like unclean insects, through the gulf in which Timboroa lay.

The soldiers were polite, as polite as they could be in a language they only knew through teaching implants. It was good public relations to be polite, to say *sir* and *madam* and pick up small children and set them on their armored carriers, and to cluck and wink at babies. Family by family, please. Orderly line. No jostling. May I see some form of identification? Where are you going? Where have you come from? Have you any knowledge of any terrorist activities? Thank you. Family by family, please. Orderly line. No jostling.

"You.

"Yes, you. What is your name?

"Yes, you. I am talking to you. What is your name?"

The tall thin officer, Mathembe realized with a shock, was talking to *her*. Suddenly she was more frightened than she had ever been before in her life. So sudden, so mighty, it was like a kick to her womb.

"What is the matter, have you lost your tongue?" the officer said in his brainplant-taught Old Speech.

"She cannot speak," said Mathembe's mother.

"Is this correct?" the officer asked Mathembe by means to a trick question, though not much of a trick question.

Mathembe nodded.

"I do not suppose you have any means of identification?" said the officer. His officer-class Old Speech was just good enough to permit minor sarcasm.

Mathembe shook her head.

The officer flicked her through with a wave of his forefinger. As she walked between the blunt metal prows of the armored carriers she felt as if the back of her body had turned to glass and all her sins were clogged up inside like shit for all to see. The soldiers with their weapons stood to either side; she walked between them expecting at any moment the voice of Dr. Kalimuni to crack out like a bullet declaring that here, here, were the treacherous murderous Warriors of Destiny.

Mathembe's father stepped up to the officer.

"I do not suppose you have any means of identification either?"

"My smartcard burned in the fire, sir."

"A convenient fire, that."

"I do not think you would call your home, your work, all your possessions burning *convenient*, sir."

The officer flicked him through.

Next came the young Warrior of Destiny.

The tall thin officer sniffed.

"You are?"

"Yesip Fileli, sir. A cousin. Visiting from Kapsabet."

"I see. Identification?"

"The fire."

"Of course."

The thin officer sniffed again. It was not a runny-nose sniff, it was the sniff of someone trying to scent something.

"Kapsabet?"

"In Timboroa Prefecture, sir."

"I am aware of the geography of this country. I could not place the accent."

"Many foreigners have difficulty in appreciating the subtleties of our accents."

Mathembe gasped at the audacity. The officer smiled. And sniffed again.

"Kapsabet. In Timboroa Prefecture. Odd you should say that. My last posting was down in Elemborasha Prefecture, down in the south, near the sea. Have you ever been there, in the southern prefectures? Near the sea?"

"The only place I have ever been, outside of Timboroa here, is Chepsenyt."

"Well, I find that most curious. When I was down in Elemborasha, I was stationed among the yatoké growers. When they dry the pods in the sun, I tell you, the smell, it gets everywhere. Three months after I was reposted, people would still say to me, 'You were in Elemborasha, weren't you, in the yatoké country?' There are still traces of it on my uniform."

The officer sniffed again, more carefully, more systematically, down the lapels of the Warrior's coat, up the sleeves, along the collar line.

"You see, what I cannot reconcile is how a man from Kapsabet in Timboroa Prefecture, who has never been farther than Timboroa and Chepsenyt, happens to smell of sun-dried yatoké pods." The officer twitched back the young Warrior's coat, and the black plastic of the Empire-made weapon was laid naked. Before the young man could move his hand even a fraction of a thought toward the webbing holster, the soldiers had leveled their weapons and flicked off safety catches in a rattle of movement.

There was no flickering game show on the heads-up visors. There was no treble pulse of ten thousand watts of music power from the ear cockles.

The young Warrior shot his hands up into the air, pleading disbelief. The officer shouted in New Speech. The soldiers moved through the stunned refugees, pressing the muzzles of their black guns between husbands and wives, fathers and daughters, sons and mothers, brothers and sisters. The men were pushed to one side of the road and the women and children to the other. In the confusion Mathembe's father pushed the head in its pot into Mathembe's hands before the black muzzles pressed pressed pressed him away from his family. Those boys who did not reach the Imperial heart-in-hand crest on the officer's uniform were spared. Those taller were taken. Mathembe saw the silly, clumsy Ghost Boy who had tried to touch her breasts fail the thin officer's test and be taken. By a short centimeter, Hradu was spared. Mathembe's father was taken. Dr. Kalimuni the Proclaimer was taken. Fingers interlocked behind heads, the men were marched away behind the parked carriers and made to squat in rows on the moss shoulder. As the men were taken, one of the Warriors of Destiny glanced at the small, domineering woman who stood undetected with the rest of Chepsenyt's women and young. One glance, one small, sour glance. But it was enough for an observant soldier. He started toward the gathered women. The small woman moved toward the far edge of the crowd. The soldier shouted something in New Speech, came pushing forward. The small woman broke and ran.

The soldier shouted in Old Speech for her to stop. The small woman went leaping down the slope, through the gardens of Timboroa, more falling than running, slipping and sliding with great leaps, down between the trees. Again the soldier shouted for her to stop. The woman plunged on. Mathembe found herself cheering the small woman on: Go on, go on, do it, do it, the houses are only a few hundred meters beneath you, then the streets, the alleys, the closes, they will never find you there. This, even though the small woman had called her *girlie*. A third time the soldier shouted for her to stop, stop in the name of the Emperor Across the River. On hurtled the small woman, on on. The thin officer gave an order in New Speech. A soldier knelt down by the stones that marked the edge of the road. He took careful aim with his weapon.

He fired.

The sound of the weapon was not as loud or as final as Mathembe had expected. The soldier had fired a target seeker. The small woman was within meters of the nearest house. The streaking missile caught her in mid-leap. In the middle of her back, it caught her. The blast splattered her lungs and bones and small flat breasts over the wall of the house. The small woman waved her hands in a final spastic jig and died.

Two soldiers were dispatched to locate the body, carefully picking their way down the slope. Mathembe could see them shaking their heads by the way the sun shone from their visors. The tall thin officer seemed very angry for some reason. Flicking orders from his fingers, he had the soldiers pack the men of Chepsenyt into the backs of the troop carriers. Two black helicopters came hovering in and landed. The officer and the pilot of one of the helicopters talked; then the officer jumped up into his command carrier, flicked his finger one final commanding flick, and drove away.

The women and children, with their trux and jeepneys and remnants of lives, remained at the side of the Timboroa road. After a time the helicopters took off in dust and noise and, bending low over the wailing women, flew into the west.

THE
CITY

IN OL TOK THE ADVERTISEMENTS BATTLE IN THE 3 A.M. BOULEVARDS while the sleeping streets sweat and cry out in city heat.

In Ol Tok a head will hear the confession of your darkest sins, or pray for your deliverance, or answer the deepest questions of your soul for a drop of *raqi* on its rooticles, or a couple of enns in its mouth that it will spit with wondrous skill into a saucer full of coins, or a kiss, or a small sexual favor.

In Ol Tok the city is at war with itself. New strong suburbs push up through old, long-grown, half-dead districts, sending out shoots and tendrils and rhizomes that are sewers and water pipes and conduits and ducts and power lines and telecomm channels, pushing the old boros—so ancient and massive with millennia of growth that the streets have been crushed down into tortuous alleyways (even crawlways) and the individual buildings fused into ossified hives of warped biotecture—cell by cell, centimeter by centimeter, into the river.

In Ol Tok nostalgia rises like cool mist from the river that is wider than the heart can see, a mist that runs like silver thread

through the street cafés and bars and restaurants, and when you ask your waiter or chanteuse *What is it?* he or she will say *Do you not recognize it? It is your soul.*

In Ol Tok demons stalk the night: very small demons, discarded domestic organicals, stray organs, lost or abandoned toys or plasmals all fused together into elegantly obscene hybrids, seeking heat, seeking blood, seeking completion, seeking new hosts, seeking new elements to incorporate into themselves.

In Ol Tok there are too many vehicles for the streets (the streets themselves are constantly redefining themselves as new buildings spring up and push their old out of their way) so that conveyances mechanical/organical/human-powered with license plates ending in even numbers and those ending in odd numbers are only allowed to drive on alternate days.

Once ten thousand thousand angels watched over Ol Tok. In the heat of high summer, in the stale airless streets, people would look up at the sudden touch of a cool river breeze on their faces and say *Ten thousand thousand beating wings.* The angels have all been driven away by helicopters. There is never an hour of the day or the night when there is not a helicopter of the Emperor airborne above some part of the city, watching, as the angels did before them, for the sin of human hearts. There is never a day when the clapping of blades, near or distant, does not form the constant rhythm of life.

Ol Tok is the open mouth of a dead beggar in the gutter of Keekorok Boulevard, stained green from eating organical flesh.

Ol Tok is fish and spices and breadapples grilled over radiant elements or pans of charcoal made from ancient lignified houses.

Ol Tok is the song of the riverboats, out in the offing, inbound with cargoes of fabric, spices, organochemicals, consumer electronics.

Ol Tok is the smell of water deep and full, the smell that satisfies like no other because it is the smell of our deepest memories of our racial womb.

Ol Tok is ten thousand pilgrims slipping off their clothes to wash and pour the turd-ridden water of the river over their heads as the edge of the world passes beneath the sun.

Ol Tok is the woman who only exists from the breasts up plugged into a cartload of organical support systems clapping her hands for alms on the corner of Gandhatta Avenue.

Ol Tok is trans-stellar merchants in their soft-running Imperial automobiles, whirring softly along the riverfront Corniche to meetings in floating restaurants or select cafés.

Ol Tok is five million bicycles.

Ol Tok is ten million radios playing at once.

Ol Tok is twelve million umbrellas.

Ol Tok is the cry of Jashar Cantor and his banging banging gong sounding out from ten thousand prayer towers; Ol Tok is a million prayer hats bobbing through the streets in a sudden spring downpour.

Ol Tok is roof gardens and dark, dank courtyards crammed with towering piles of shit digesters and reprocessers and biogas plants.

Ol Tok is sprawling suburban villas set among their private terraces and orchards on the city's celebrated forty hills.

Ol Tok is whole districts afloat upon the sacred waters, uncountable generations of watercraft fused together into one continuous mass where a family's proudest boast is that in twenty generations no member has ever set foot upon hard land.

Ol Tok is the song of the longshoreman in dawnlight, the never-ending song, ten thousand years in singing.

Ol Tok is the fishergirls diving in the twilight from their bamboo perches, the shine of their skin as they burst wet and shouting from the waters with some deep-river fish on their hunting spear.

Ol Tok is the taste of a whore's mouth behind the Proclaimer tombs along Rajjit Prospect and its invitation to die, with these gathered faithful, your own little private death.

Ol Tok is the moonlit smoothness of the inner thigh in the warm lagoons on the terraces high upon the forty hills.

Ol Tok is a woman and a girl and a young boy, dragging a travois made from plastic girders through the thronging streets. The woman is tall and upright but does not yet understand that Ol Tok cares nothing for her pride, will casually annihilate her into the anonymity of its freight of lives. Yet she leans into the webbing harness with a determination that leaves some impression upon the cyclists and jeepney drivers and wine peddlers and pilgrims and shoppers and trans-stellar bankers and fortune tellers and policepersons. For one moment, they think, *What a proud woman.*

The girl is likewise tall, sent shooting into uncomfortable prominence by the sudden thrust of hormones and desires. In her spirit she is stripped naked, flayed by the countryperson's agoraphobic dread that every eye is on her, every head turned toward her, every mouth commenting upon her: *Look at her, that girl, she is from the country, you know, you can tell, you can always tell; look at her; what is that she is carrying, a head?* The fact that she is pretty in the way that is *interesting* rather than *beautiful* only compounds her crushing self-consciousness.

The boy is too young to understand pride but old enough to know humiliation. Bent almost double, he drags along under his enormous pack. The pack could be ten, twenty times as great and heavy, he would not care as long as it hides him entirely from the contempt of the pressing pressing people. He hates his mother for the way she strides along so proud and upright, dragging the contemptible travois with its cargo of cheap things and few. He hates his sister for carrying so blatant and immodest an object as his grandfather's head. The curiosity of strangers is like thorns in his eyes. Someone will pay for this humiliation, he swears, some small day.

Mathembe had watched the axes fall: long axes, glittering in the light that fell into the plaza outside Timboroa station, on the ends of long slender poles. Axes falling and rising, smeared with green gore.

The ticket clerk had refused her mother's smartcard. *No credit*, she had said, this sexless toad of a woman, smelling of her own warm fat. *Not drawn on the Chepsenyt gene pool. Next, please.*

Once, her mother would have argued. Argued until the end of the world. Once. Before the carriers had driven away, leaving scratch marks on the straight white road. Once. Before her spirit went into retreat.

But sometimes, when the spirit is in retreat, the mind is thrown into a remote, thoughtless capability to act and achieve with seemingly instantaneous intelligence. In the plaza outside the station, bustling with travelers and flower sellers and magazine vendors, she had ordered Hradu and Mathembe to unload the trux while she went to find a meat buyer.

The price was enough for three tickets on the night train. Hard class. No meals.

The trux had died halfway across the plaza. The meat buyers fetched a squad of men and with their poleaxes had cut it up, there, outside Timboroa station. The axes had risen and fallen in the noon light, lopping the organical into chunks of quivering synthetic flesh. Other men had loaded the meat onto a trailer. It would be taken away and broken down into cellular base from which new organicals might be made. The axes rose and fell, splitting the plastic carapace of the brain pan, cleaving the soft organic circuitry.

The last concrete moment in Mathembe's life had been the meat buyers' trailer, driving away across Station Plaza with a thin trickle of yellow ichor leaking onto the cobbles. Everything after was like a play of shadow puppets on a house wall: the night train, cleaving the forest apart with its sharp steel line and the cone of its headlights; the hallucinatory half dreams of a night spent hard class, propped against the window, without meals; the arrival by dawn's early light in the cacophony and vibrancy of a big-city railway station, the army check at the end of the platform—the soldiers polite, expressionless as they scrutinized identities—the head that hailed her, laughing vilely, on a street corner from atop a transparent column of pulsing organicals with an invitation to a good tonguing: so much tissue and translucency, artifacts of light and movement, without texture or substance. Her spirit demanded a response, some response: anger, hatred, defiance, resentment, pain; found only a blank expressionlessness. Impassivity.

Mathembe's Uncle Faradje lived in a pile of aged, sagging houses on a narrow sunless street called Lantern Lane that was only a few hundred meters but entire social universes away from broad, bright Keekorok Boulevard. Over the millennia the houses of Lantern Lane had grown over and into each other so that Faradje's apartment, ostensibly on the third floor, rambled vertically from fifth to second and intertwined intimately with a number of other apartments on the same level. The rooms at the back overlooked a courtyard full of partly digested garbage thrown in by residents of the adjoining apartments. Foot had not been set in that courtyard for decades; local legend had it that any trespasser would be instantly eaten alive by the weirdly mutated garbage digesters that roved and reproduced down there. From the aromatic detritus grew a tangle of heating ducts and water pipes and the knuckled fist of a gloglobe holdfast. The rooms that fronted Lantern Lane were dominated by an immense holographic advertisement for imported beer mounted on the tenement opposite. A fair-faced flaxen-haired Imperial beauty traced dewdrops down the side of a beer bottle, licked her lips, slipped the open top into her mouth, and swigged the amber nectar down while leering lasciviously through Faradje's grubby windows. The hologram was poorly tuned; the windows and balconies of the apartments opposite and the lives that moved within them showed through the ghostly image: a parable, for those who must seek parables, of humanity living and working and having their being within the spiritual totality of God. Much like God, the Five Hearts Beer girl oversaw every thought and word and deed in Lantern Lane, shone her light into the deepest recesses of the apartments. Between her and the gloglobes above the back courtyard, Faradje had not bought a domestic light unit since moving into the tenement.

The radio burbled constantly in its alcove in the living room. Day and night, night and day.

Faradje was Something in city government. He had long ago maneuvered himself into a comfortable administrational nest that provided him with sufficient authority to garner respect yet was totally devoid of any responsibility whatsoever. He could have afforded much better than Lantern Lane—sinecures as a rule pay well—but comfort was the polestar to which his life was hitched. Those small efforts he did make were dedicated solely to pulling times and circumstances into a tight, cozy bundle within the warm confines of which he would one day blissfully die. The arrival of his sister, her two children, and her father-in-law's head was a major disruption to his well-trodden routines. The events that had brought them to his front door were so drastic, so far removed from the orbit of his days, that he could scarcely bring himself to believe them. That such things could happen to his own sister . . . this could not be how the world truly turned. He shied away from the pain of others. He had done so all his fat life.

The head was the source of greatest discomfort to Faradje. Urbanites have an aversion to anything remotely raw and gross. The heads of Ol Tok dreamed eternity away in niches in the great walled mazes of the cemeteries or occasionally performed useful social duties on the streets. The heads of Ol Tok never turned up in the middle of the living room rug, slurping and belching offensively in a potful of organicals. It was obvious from word one that Faradje and the head would never peacefully coexist. While Mathembe and Hradu were going around quietly exploring their new home, moving carefully, unobtrusively, making as little intrusion as possible into the life of their new patron, the opening shots in what was to become a blood feud were being fired. Faradje and the head agreed upon every point, social moral spiritual material political; the congruence of their opinions only made it the more obvious that they could not stand each other.

Mathembe lay on her mattress by the open window. She could not sleep. In Chepsenyt there had been sounds. Here were *noises*. Voices. Feet. Radios. Vehicles moving along Keekorok Boulevard at the end of Lantern Lane. The personal private sounds of people in the other apartments intimately entwined with Faradje's. In the far distance, almost at the edge of hearing, the hard, flat noise of shots fired. Above it all, behind it all, the beating, beating, constant beating of helicopters in the high night air. Like God, like a prayer, the face of the Five Hearts Beer girl searched Mathembe as she lay in white sleep. The dew-wet finger, the soft lips, the caressing tongue, asked of her, *Mathembe Fileli, you have had home, life, memories, father— everything you have ever held precious—taken from you. Why will you not cry for them, why will you not feel for them, why do you lie like a stone, like a dull and stupid stone, why will you not give them even one tear?*

In the morning she went with her mother, guided by Faradje's written instructions, to Rag Market and sold what remained of Chepsenyt from two plastic bags on the ground. It did not fetch much. After all the stock had been sold to the recyclers, Mathembe's mother went up and down the aisles of dealers and buyers trying to sell her flesh-sculpture kit in its folding leather case. She had held it back from the recyclers. It was hers. It was precious, the only thing apart from her children, her seed, she could call her own. The dealers and buyers of Rag Market pursed their lips and shrugged their shoulders and shook their heads. When a pitying stallholder offered small change, Mathembe grabbed the leather case from his hand.

Pride, she said in the set of her face and shoulders while the children of the tenements and barrios ran around them, brandishing their plastic toy ray pistols that, overnight, had become fashionable with the arrival of the Saint-ship from another world.

The money earned from one market was gone within minutes at another. The concept of "*a place to buy food*" was quite alien to people accustomed to their every need satisfied within arm's reach. Faradje was outraged at the four small bags of provisions Mathembe and her mother brought back from Food Market.

"You do not have to do that. I have plenty, more than enough to meet my needs."

His sister gave him the high look of pride she had relearned in Rag Market from her daughter.

"Pride buys no rice," said Faradje. "How much did that cost you?"

She would not answer. Mathembe it was who shrugged the expressive shrug that says *everything*.

Mathembe did not know what had put the seed in her heart, but that night, when the only sounds were the prayer of the radio to the listening world and the distant beating of the helicopters, she slipped out of her bed, crept to the balcony that overlooked Lantern Lane. She knelt before the Five Hearts Beer girl: *Here I am to offer myself to you, strange and jealous new god of the boulevards, I come before you with nothing, for everything has been taken from me. What will you give me in return for me?*

Did the eyes gleam her-ward? The finger raise in blessing?

Tears: that was the first gift the Five Hearts Beer girl gave her. All the rage, all the darkness, all the desperation, all the shattering, all the hurting was released as the Five Hearts Beer girl brought tumbling down the walls of impassivity and numbness. Mathembe cried silently, exultantly, into the morning and was born again. Pass beneath the waters, be born again. And the Five Hearts Beer girl had a second gift to bestow: a seal, a thumbprint of ice-cold beer on her forehead that admitted her to the world of the boulevards and avenues, the dark damp closes and alleyways, the plazas and intimate squares, the markets and commerces and business districts. Baptized. A believer. A member, a sister, one-of-us. To the born again, nothing is strange and alien, for everything is new, to be absorbed and appreciated with the open-spiritedness of a child defining its own world.

The city was hers, and she was the city's now.

His name, he said was . . .

She did not need to hear his name. It would be some Proclaimer clatter of syllables.

He was a . . .

She did not need him to tell her what it was he did. She knew

from the way he stood, polite polite, when she entered the family room
after a day running, walking, breathing, touching, tasting this bright
toy of a city her new god had given her, and found her mother and
Faradje sitting with their hands folded in that particular way you fold
your hands when you meet one of *their* profession. She knew from the
vague unctuousness of his smile, she knew from the rustle of his
clothing, she knew from the whisper of his skin speaking against itself,
she knew from the affected unaffectedness of his greeting to her. She
knew from his smell, the smell she had smelled even in the street lobby
that had ruffled the hairs on the back of her neck and made her growl
softly in her throat. That smell alone would have been proof enough:
a *lawyer* in the apartment.

"You will have to excuse her, Mr. Sharjah. She does not speak."

"I am sorry to hear that," said Mr. Sharjah, mistaking, as did
everyone who heard the explanation, "does not" for "cannot." He
smiled at Mathembe. The smile was a declaration of war between
them. Hate at first sight is no less remarkable than love at first sight,
and considerably more common. Mathembe would rather have slowly
slit her eyeballs with razor blades than let her family be placed in the
confidence of this man. It was not that he was a lawyer, nor that he was
a Proclaimer, though he unconsciously twisted a Spirit Lodge ring on
his left middle finger. It was a chemical thing, a clashing of
pheromones. She understood now how Faradje and her grandfather
(banished to the kitchen sink, where they hoped the chuckle of
running water over his rooticles would prevent from him hearing, and
thus commenting upon, whatever the Proclaimer might have to say)
could have taken such an instant animosity to each other.

"I have been approached by your mother to attempt to locate your
father," said Advocate Sharjah, perched *so* on Faradje's best chair. "I
understand the, ah, sense of loss? you must be experiencing, the
emotional trauma, the dislocation. Of course, I cannot for one instant
begin to personally comprehend the suffering you have endured. Any
expression I might make would be glib to the point of insensitivity. Best
if I were merely to repeat to you what I have already told your mother
and uncle: that I believe, firmly believe, that your father is well and
sound, in all likelihood held in some regional detention center." Mr.
Sharjah moistened his lips with a reptile-quick flick of the tongue.
"Despite our best efforts, it is increasingly difficult to keep politics out

of our individual lives. I would not presume to judge your political inclinations; however, with the worsening situation there are bound to be, certain to be, abuses of the rule of law and gross miscarriages of justice. The innocent suffer alike with the guilty. The chaotic state of the civil government does not assist matters; the left hand does not know what the right is doing." A wry Proclaimer smile and a dry Proclaimer joke that was not lost on anyone in Faradje's dirty, evil-smelling room. "The local militias seem to be acting independently of regional control, often—how shall we put it?—acting on long-established sectarian instincts. Of course, I have no need to remind you of this, forgive me."

"My husband was arrested by regular army," said Mathembe's mother. "Not the militia."

"Of course, of course. Nevertheless, in all likelihood he and the others from your township have been passed to the local authorities; the army does not have its own detention facilities. No, I think my investigations will have to begin at the Timboroa Regional Detention Center." He slapped his hands on his thin thighs, neatly but decisively, exactly as intended. "Of course, I cannot make the promise that I will be able to locate your husband quickly, and the authorities must be convinced that he was a coerced party in the alleged offense. But I shall certainly try with all my might and main." The advocate Sharjah stood up, bowed punctiliously to each and all. "Leave this matter with me, Mrs. Fileli. I promise you it shall receive my most assiduous attention."

Mathembe was instructed to open the door for the advocate and show him to the street. As she waited with him for the jeepney to arrive she made certain he saw her look. All lawyers are body-literate: so much of the truth that is sought in the courtroom is not spoken aloud. She knew he would understand she was saying: *I do not trust you, you who when he says "not quickly" means "not cheaply," when he says "difficult" means "expensive": that is my mother, her life has been shaken and beaten in ways you could not even begin to comprehend; she has known enough hurt for any five lifetimes, and if you add to that hurt by raising her hopes and crushing them like insects, I promise I shall make you scream for it, do you hear me, Lawyer Sharjah?*

But he had turned away from her and she did not see his face again until the moment he bent down to enter the jeepney cab, when, as the driver was saying, "We will have to make a detour, sir; incident of some kind over on Yohimbi Opango Street," the light in Lantern Lane caught his face and Mathembe saw in the glitter in his eyes and teeth that he had indeed understood her, understood her every last word, and that he was saying, in the silent speech of his own heart, *Think what you will of me, it is no matter, but whatever you think of me, would you have your mother shoulder the burden of finding your father alone?*

If, as its residents contend, the decaying biotectural pile of Gangerabili is the dark navel from which Ol Tok grew, then Flesh Market is the womb in which Gangerabili was conceived. A drop of angel seed dripped into the mouth of one of the Nyakabindi demons in the sea and was conceived and gestated and squeezed out of the River Mother onto the hard land. One hundred and twenty thousand people dwell within Gangerabili in darkness so complete it is a proud boast among the roaring boys never to have seen light of day, under such a pressing mass of moribund biotecture that whole generations have never known what it is to stand upright, in a constant breath damp warmed by one hundred and twenty thousand crushing lives to blood heat.

They love it. They would not live anywhere else. The intimate proximity of their living and loving and crying and dying breeds not a knife-edged irritability but a buoyant, vibrant spirit of community, of being grafted into a many-branched many-rooted tree of kinship. Ten thousand brothers. Ten thousand sisters. One hundred thousand grandmothers.

Flesh Market is a parasite with thrusting hooks and claws: Gangerabili distilled. The only light in the darkness is from bioluminescents, faltering neons, television screens, smudge fires; its labyrinthine twining so utterly inscrutable that, but for an urchin to guide you for a handful of enns, you might wander forever a soul damned; its air stale, fetid, every breath exhaled by a dozen lungs before yours, musky with flesh perfumes and glandular secretions. Yet all around is laughter and music and bright flashing tempers like blades and no small quota of alley wisdom: bright lives burning with such intensity that your own seems wan and lackluster in comparison.

Anything wrought by the hand of God can be bought for the flicker of a smartcard in Flesh Market.

Mathembe found her pitch on the third attempt. She had been driven from her first, close by the Tombalbayé Street entrance, by the proprietor of an oraculum; Mathembe's grandfather had been unwelcome competition to his stable of heads rooted deep into the Dreaming matrix. The second, on the junction of two thronged thoroughfares bright with holograms and biolights, had been in the possession of a troupe of beggars. In Flesh Market, the bizarrerie and imagination of deformity was rewarded with smartcards; begging attained the status of a performing art. The beggars had borne down upon her, some in small wheeled carts, some attached to organical or mechanical transport. Mathembe had fled. Her final pitch was beside a small street shrine to Saint Zanzan Bé, Patron of the Crossing Ways, whose bailiwick included aspects as diverse as telecommunications, banking, premarital love, social work, harbors, railway stations, airports, and forest paths. The shrine, poorly maintained, with only the faintest rattle of enns in the offerings box, stood across a litter-strewn alley from a stand-up café. The fat, slightly wobbling proprietor, known as A Dose of Worms, watched the thin dark-haired girl, skin sun-darkened—she would soon lose that in the gloom, he thought—set down a head on the dusty cobbles, look around her nervously, and open a small leather case. Her activities were marginally more interesting than the television, which shone blue and unregarded on a high shelf above the tables.

Mathembe had been taught the skill but it had never become the art with which her mother had sung the double-helix song into the heart of things in the cool cool cool of the Fifteenth Street conservatory. Self-conscious and terminally awkward, Mathembe took the lump of undifferentiated plasm in her hands, turned it over and over, feeling for the fissures and grooves. With a twist, the ball fell apart into two identical pieces of synthetic flesh. She lifted one up, breathed life into it, pressed it to her lips, shaped it with the silent words of her tongue and mouth, turning it over and over and over in her fingers, breaking it along its crease lines into units, stretching and pulling and shaping and molding those units with her fingers, with the silent words of life on her lips, fusing, re-forming, building, creating, until before her face in the open palms of her hands lay a tiny, delicate, diaphanous flying creature, like a minuscule helicopter spun from silk, all eyes and legs and whirring rotors.

Behind his counter, A Dose of Worms was grudgingly impressed.

Mathembe threw the flying creature into the air, sent it whirring and buzzing around the heads of the people moving along the alley. Some looked, some batted it away from their faces, most walked on unnoticing. Mathembe called the flying thing back to her hand. Across the alley, A Dose of Worms shrugged sympathetically and poked at grilling things. By noon—however noon might be reckoned in Gangerabili—Mathembe's original ball of plasm had replicated twenty-five times. Small cuddly, feathery, big-eyed blinking cooing things clung to her jacket; skittering, skirling things ran in carefully defined orbits around her bare feet, and flying, hovering, buzzing things roosted in her hair.

Not a single one had sold.

"Give it up, granddaughter of mine," the head said. "It is a good idea but it is not working."

Mathembe kicked its pot, nodded. A child stood on the bank of the river of people—its parents had paused for a moment to stroke and sniff at a fur grower's stall close by—a girl: seven, eight, well dressed, well fed, pale-skinned pale-haired. A young Imperial. Mathembe crouched, offered a tiny pink-furred mewling something in the palm of her right hand.

"Buy a toy?" the head whispered. "Only eighty enns." Mathembe gestured for the child to take it. The little girl touched it apprehensively, expecting fangs in the fur, claws in the cuddliness. The creature blinked its huge neotenous eyes at her. The little girl shrieked in delight. Her parents came to see what was so pleasing to their daughter. The little girl held the toy up to them. It waved its stubby arms and legs, mewled again.

The head opened its mouth to spiel. Mathembe nudged the pot with her elbow.

"How much?" the man said. A Tourist Talk pay-by-the-day brainplant was looped behind his ear.

"Eighty enns," the head said. Still kneeling, Mathembe reached out the card reader on its thong around her neck. Readouts glowed, transactions transacted. Only when the tourist family were beyond eye and earshot did Mathembe permit herself a small leap and an air punch of victory. A Dose of Worms nodded, smiled. A girl was sent over from the Tipsi Café with two bowls of small eats. Solidarity.

"They will not be so happy when it falls apart in three weeks," said the head. Mathembe, fingers greasy with meat slivers, gestured in the way that says to those who have eyes to see, *She will have lost interest long before then*. Mathembe sold five toys that day. In celebration she bought a flask of *raqi* from A Dose of Worms and literally watered her grandfather's rooticles.

"You want me going back to your mother pissed and legless?" the head complained, unconvincingly.

There is a shrug, if you can master it, that says exactly: *You have been legless for years anyway*.

Mathembe's mother was furious, a cold silent fury that burned hotter than any mere display of temper. *It is for you, the money, for the advocate Sharjah*, Mathembe tried to say. *I will not let him accuse me of not doing my part to get my father back*. But her mother would not hear, would not touch the money. She could not tell Mathembe, but she feared that her silent daughter had earned it by the selling of her own private flesh on the streets of Ol Tok. Mathembe left the card reader and the small leather case on the floor and went up to her shared room to sulk. Later, much later, her mother came to her. The small leather case of plasmals was open in her hands. She took out a globe of dormant life. And she showed Mathembe how to do things, make things, shape things, sing things like she had never dreamed.

The walk that says *I am making it* is not a learned thing. Not a thing that thrusts its roots through the skin behind your ear into your brain to go chasing harum-scarum through your frontal lobes while you sleep. It is an infection that spreads through your body cell by cell, muscle by muscle, joint by joint: a divine humility so that at no time can you ever be sure enough of yourself to say *Yesterday I was not making it, but today I am*. It is a gradual infusion of confidence into the bones and blood.

By the end of her first week in Flesh Market there were enough tips, tithes, and tradables in her belt pouch to barter for a set of tiny ceramic bells to decorate her favorite black skin boots. In the upper room that was filled with the light of Our Lady of the Dewdrop Beer Bottle she turned and twisted and clicked her fingers to the never-ceasing music from the radio, and the tiny holy bells rang and sang.

She gained a place: *Hey you, yes you, you no-good damn goondah tramp bum, take your custom melanomas off out of here someplace else, this pitch is spoken for.*

She gained a name: *Go to the Bell girl, cannot miss her, corner of Belladonna and Shine, right, and across from the Tipsi Café: she got bells on her boots never speaks, just jingles maybe something funny up there (tap tap finger to temple tappity-tap) but she got real magic real magic in those fingers of hers: the Bell girl, that is how we all know her.*

She became fashionable: *The jewelry, dear heart? Down Flesh Market of course. Where have you been hiding yourself? Used to be disgusting. Used to be. Low. Common. Vulgar. Indescribably vulgar. These days, quite the place to go. See this? Look, see, it is alive. Is that not quite the most extraordinary thing? Of course they do not last very long but, well, that can be a positive advantage. I mean to say, one has to stay abreast of fashion.*

She was perfectly placed to exploit the new fad when it hit. It had been an occasion for national rejoicing when an Ol Tok lifeware designer won the commission to create a body for the captain of the visiting Saint-ship to occupy while visiting the world. A shrewd reader of the commercial tides, he had opted for a percentage royalty on derivative material rather than a flat-rate payment. No sooner had the captain stepped from the tank in his ruggedly handsome (but-not-too) indeterminately-colored-so-as-to-cause-no-offense-to-any-racial-group well-muscled-but-*sensitive*, with-it body than a torrent of Ship Captain posters, Ship Captain masks, Ship Captain jewelry, Ship Caption book covers, Ship Captain personal computers, Ship Captain personal vibrators, Ship Captain cups mugs wineglasses coolflasks, Ship Captain T-shirts, Ship Captain jackets, I-♥-the-Ship-Captain stickers for any conceivable surface to which a sticker might adhere, Ship Captain moving tattoos, Ship Captain slouch hats, Ship Captain toiletries, Ship Captain boxed individual dinners, Ship Captain underwear, Ship Captain wunder-gum, Ship Captain–brand rice beer came thundering from the Free Trade Zones and Special Economic Regions. Within one month the designer retired to his new bel-aire mansion on a hilltop overlooking the river that was as wide as the sea, obscenely rich. Within one month of his moving in among the neo-gentry the bel-aire mansion burned. The Proclaimer youths of Fijjad Hills were choosy about their neighbors.

And down in the guts of Gangerabili, across the alleyway from A

Dose of Worms's stand-up café, Mathembe Fileli rode to no small measure of wealth and success on the crest of the wave of fad and fashion. She could not replicate the balls of plasm fast enough to meet the demand for her Ship Captain toys and homunculi. Of course, they would fall apart and dissolve into evil-smelling slime in some hard-to-find corner of the house in three weeks, but by then the fad among Ol Tok's crucial women to have a micro Ship Captain waving at their society friends from deep in their cleavage would be unutterably passé. In two frenetic weeks Mathembe made the equivalent of two months' takings. Enough to contribute to Advocate Sharjah's own personal strivings to the height of Fijjad Hills, where, because he knew the handshakes and wore the right ring, he could rest assured that his bel-aire mansion would not burn down in a single night.

So the Five Hearts Beer girl honored her compact with Mathembe.

The new gods are the most eager to explore their powers and limitations.

The new gods are the most jealous of their divinity.

The most powerful are always the least trustworthy.

THE STORY OF MATHEMBE
AND THE NATIONALIST PRISONERS OF WAR

This is the story of how what is freely, freely given may be freely, freely taken. To tell it adequately, we must go back to a time before Mathembe and her family came to the house of Faradje on Lantern Lane. We must go back to the time of the hunger strike.

To tell of the hunger strike adequately, we must go back to a time before the heads of the rebels (or the heads of the heroes; such discriminations are always a matter of opinion) even came to Chepsenyt, to the dispute over the Emperor's portrait.

To tell the reason for the dispute over the Emperor's portrait we would need to go back a thousand years or more to the time when the Empire decided to stabilize its recently annexed still-rebellious transfluvian province by colonizing it with loyal, hard-working, peace-loving, right-worshiping Imperial citizens.

But this is the story of Mathembe and the Nationalist Prisoners of War, not the story of Empire and Province, Proclaimer and Confessor;

you can read that story in any good history. This space is properly Mathembe's, and if we shift the focus from her to her background it is only to place a frame around her life and times.

If you saw a portrait of the Emperor you would not be greatly impressed. You would see an old and very small man, eyes sunk deep in folds of skin despite rejuvenation treatments, dressed in a simple white silk robe of state and holding a decorated inscribed fan. Your first thought would be that he looks more like a monkey dressed up in human clothes, like you see in advertisements on television, but you would immediately suppress that thought because, monkey or no, man or no, he is ultimately an *emperor*, graced with the mandate of God. Even though this Emperor in his lifetime has seen his Empire dwindle from a quarter of the planet to a cluster of small free-trade zones and a single province to which, because it is the last, he clings all the more tenaciously.

The Emperor is pictured sitting in a garden. The artist has attempted to convey a sense of serenity and tranquillity radiating from the August Personage: the still center that holds an unraveling commonwealth together. Symbols of that tranquillity and serenity abound throughout the portrait for those who have eyes to see. The artist—though, in strictest interpretation Proclaimerism the representation of the human form is an offense against God—has been as kind as his artistic integrity will allow to the wrinkle-shrouded eyes, the wizened monkey face.

However, it is not the portrait's qualities as a work of art that are at issue; it is that it is the representation of the Divinely Ordained Presence. More importantly, that, by Imperial Decree 9,936,332, the Imperial likeness must be displayed in all places of public intercourse, commercial, social, recreational, political. Including the council chamber of the Ol Tok Metropolitan Council, where the councilors, before embarking upon their vital deliberations, were required to stand and bow respectfully to the little extension of the Imperial Personage beaming out from the Garden of Contemplation in the Jade City across the bustling, polluted land, across the river wide as the sea, into the council chamber of Ol Tok.

When the Ourselves Alone councilors, under the leadership of Adé Janderambelé, refused to stand and bow respectfully to the Image Divine, they found themselves immediately suspended from public office by V. J. Shrih-Ghandda, appointed governor of Ol Tok Prefecture by the express command of the Jade City. The dozen or more pro-Imperial parties and the Proclaimer population as a political generalization chorused approval. The law, after all, was the law, despite the religious conscience clauses many members of the more fundamentalist parties invoked to keep themselves from bowing down to dull-eyed icons. The suspended councilors were undaunted; indeed, they soared to greater prominence on the crest of a wave of defiance that swept the Confessor populace. In full regalia of office, they presented themselves in attendance at the various committees and bodies on which they had been elected to serve only to find themselves politely but strictly barred entrance by the masked public servants of the Governor. Protests that democracy—a word that has always served so faithfully those who would wield it in their personal interests—was being ground thin in the wheels of sectarian machinations were met by the Proclaimer councilors standing side by side across the council chamber doors, holding up the Imperial likeness while pointing to an Imperial heart-in-hand flag draped across the door lintel. "Tread on it, would ye? Tread on it?" the councilors were asked.

The Mandate Divine, to those who had eyes to observe the embarrassing debacle of symbols and emblems, seemed wistful for his gardens and bridges and gay summer pavilions.

There were protests. Of course.

There were demonstrations. Of course.

There were corpses. Of course.

Though denied access to official information channels, the barred councilors issued calls for a city-wide campaign of civil disobedience, which spread with the speed and enthusiasm of a venereal disease through the Confessor boros. From Gangerabili and Mittita and Drug Market and Soul Market and Cemetery Hills, from the sampan cities and pontoon townships of Kaléhé and Waterside, from suburban Kilimatindé and Ladywell unrolling like a richly patterned carpet of gardens and swimming pools toward the indeterminate south, portraits of the Emperor—now a little bemused and perhaps nostalgic among his geneform trees—were turned to the wall. In shops, schools, markets, newsstands, cafés, restaurants, sports clubs, football grounds, dance halls, drinking clubs, television halls, shebeens, suburban

railway stations, shrines, and oraculums, the cardboard rear of the Emperor faced the world.

In the history of democracy—that word again—there can seldom have been as unrepresentational a piece of legislation as the cram-read Ol Tok Council bylaw declaring it a punishable offense to show public disrespect to the image, likeness, or name of the Emperor. The measure was passed by eighty-eight votes, two more than a quorum. To manage even that, three councilors had to be brought back from holidays in sunnier, happier parts of the planet, and one rushed, still connected to organical support systems, from the Saint Lia-Mulea House of Healing. One hundred and seventy-six suspended Ourselves Alone councilors took no part in either debate or vote.

The Ol Tok police, as ever the shit-end agents of political masturbation, after only three days of snap raids and inspections, declared the law unenforceable: the prefecture Prosecutor's Office broke down under the mudslide of unprocessed information and refused to handle any further prosecutions. The Confessors crowed and farted. Adé Janderamé and his Ourselves Alone councilors were chaired and cheered through the boulevards of Ghiambeni into Keekorok and all the way along the riverfront Corniche that is fifteen kilometers long. Victory! was the toast at the lagoon-side parties in laid-back Kilimatindé.

Gnawed by the tapeworm of humiliation, the Imperial councilors found refuge in an obscure clause of the Councilors' Oath of Office (sworn in the name of the nice little monkey-man in the garden to truly and faithfully represent the people of Ol Tok's one hundred and sixteen boros, with which Ourselves Alone had never found quarrel) declaring that any councilor who willfully failed to carry out his sworn and elected duties was liable to prosecution and fine.

Summonses were issued.

Those summoned refused to attend the hearings.

One hundred and seventy-eight Ourselves Alone councilors were fined. One hundred and fifty enns, the price of one of Mathembe's Ship Captain dolls, the maximum the court could impose.

Seventy-five Ourselves Alone councilors refused to pay the fine. And, against all popular belief, seventy-five Ourselves Alone councilors were sentenced to organical imprisonment until such time as they agreed to respect the law and pay the nominal fine.

There were riots.

There were deaths.

There were more young, beautiful heads in the niches of Cemetery Hills' meandering walls where the prostitutes called and fluted by batflight.

The seventy-five semi-dendrified prisoners stood in a small enclosed yard at the rear of the rambling Law House. Within a week, fifty had repented, ordered the necessary transactions made from their credit banks, and been returned wholly to flesh.

At the beginning of the second week Adé Janderambelé announced that he and his twenty-four colleagues would neither eat nor drink nor take any form of sustenance until the court orders against them were quashed and all suspended councilors were fully reinstated.

Two days later, Mathembe and her family arrived on the night train—hard class, no meals—from Timboroa.

It is now Day 46 of the hunger strike. Here comes Mathembe in her shorts and black skin boots with ringing singing bells and seal-up jacket with the big colorful logos of international corporations from countries she cannot even place on the globe, with her hair cut one centimeter all over because of the heat and the insects and the thousand parasites of Flesh Market, and her belt pouches full of plasmals.

She could tell they were trouble by the way they moved through the crowd, like an overlarge turd forcing itself from constricted bowels. She saw them enter A Dose of Worms's café where her grandfather spent his days now the business was established, drinking *raqi*, cheating at *fili*, and shouting ill-informed comments at the television news. The exact details of what business the trouble boys transacted there were invisible to Mathembe. A teenager was holding up a furry pink cuddle-thing in front of her and inquiring *How much?*

Then it was her turn. She had never seen such a pair of thoroughgoing hoods in her life. Hair shaved to within a millimeter of nonexistence and patterned with obscene ideograms. Matching jackets. Tight tight shorts. Stomping thick-soled boots. Live furs draped across the right shoulders, thonging around wrists. Thick, square faces.

Her father had grown more intelligent-looking trux.

"Would you care to make a contribution to the Nationalist

Prisoners of War Fund?" Trux Number One. A card reader flickered gray digits at her.

"Support the hunger strikers." Trux Number Two. Oddly high voices. Mathembe shrugged, smiled. Furry pink cuddle-thing had been that day's only sale.

"Come on, where is your loyalty? Support the prisoners of war." Trux Number One smiled.

Mathembe frowned.

"Minimum suggested donation, three hundred enns." Trux Number Two coughed solicitously, glanced downward. The toe of his thick-soled boot was resting lightly, but firmly enough to prevent escape, on a small crawling reptile toy.

"Really, you should consider it not so much a donation as an investment," said Trux Number One as his partner bore slowly down and burst the little writhing creature into a splatter of green flesh and ichor.

Three hundred enns. Two days' takings. Money she had saved for the advocate Sharjah. Trux Number One stuck a little green sticker on the end of Mathembe's ugly-cutesy nose and swaggered, laughing, with his partner to the next entrepreneur. The sticker read I ♥ THE NATIONALIST PRISONERS OF WAR.

No one that evening seemed much surprised when, at the meal table, Mathembe made a sudden gesture with her fist jabbing out from her heart that said, unmistakably, *extortion*. Her grandfather esteemed it an honor to have been considered worthy of paying protection to Ourselves Alone. The struggle had to fund itself somehow. Uncle Faradje shrugged. Uncle Faradje's sole defense against an inimical world was a shrug. Her mother sympathized when Mathembe explained that she would not be able to give any money that week but was oddly resigned. Hradu, as usual, was not there at table with them: out running with his boyfriends, playing football in the global gutter, spraying political slogans on the universal wall. As they sat eating their evening food with their fingers the radio said that the hunger strike was in its forty-sixth day and the condition of some of the protesting councilors was giving cause for concern.

One summer in Chepsenyt there had been a plague of vampire moths. Great soft whirring things, with wings like rich carpets, and equally soft and thick. Despite the heat of the summer nights, Mrs.

Fileli had ordered all the windows shuttered and firmly barred at dusk each evening. No one was to go out unless protected by several layers of net and veil.

"One bite will not harm you. It will sting a little, and no one likes the thought of some soft-winged thing drinking your blood, but it will not do any great harm," was the advice she gave a wide-eyed Mathembe. "But even that once is too much. Because once they get the taste of blood, they will come back, again and again and again, until you are bled white."

Their shoulders were as broad. Their smiles were as synthetic. Their shorts were as tight. Their request was identical.

Suggested minimum donation . . .

She did not have three hundred enns.

How much did she have?

Seventy-seven enns. A jingle, a jangle of change. Look. See? Here it is, all on the reader. Here are the digits. You cannot make them lie no matter how dearly you wish it.

Seventy-seven enns would be an acceptable donation.

They took the jingle-jangle of small change.

Three times. In as many weeks.

Hunger strike, Day 60.

The advent of authority always advertised itself in Flesh Market long before its physical arrival. A murmur in the crowd. A turning of heads *that* way. A slow but noticeable osmosis of population the *other* way. A certain contagious nervousness, a certain exaggeration of normality into abnormality. A Dose of Worms dusting off the portrait of the old old Emperor he kept behind beer crates back of the bar and hanging the Divine Presence on the wall.

Beams of white light played through the fetid darkness of the alleys. Two policepersons. No fat, pathetic Kimininis and Kimililis: these were young, serious, professional. Dedicated to law. Three soldiers with battle packs and weapons formed their escort. The light beams were from shoulder-mounted spotlights. They were checking: Something. Mathembe felt fear in the pit of her womb like an intimation of death. They stopped at A Dose of Worms's counter. He wiped glasses while they checked papers. A Dose of Worms caught Mathembe across the alley's eye, flicked his eyes: *Go*.

Then the searchlights turned upon her. The disclosing light of God from which no secrets are hid, no desires concealed.

"Have you any means of identification?"

She proffered the card reader. Spirals of genetic material bonded to the polymers tagged each device unique to its owner. The taller, fatter policeperson inserted it into some official device that made noises.

"Thank you Miz Fileli. That will be all. Oh. I almost forgot. Can I see your public trader's license?"

It was as if she had been struck from behind with something unimaginably huge, unimaginably heavy. Like a planet. Her lungs forgot to breathe. Her heart forgot to beat. Her brain throbbed like a Proclaimer prayer gong. She fumbled in her belt pouch, offered a tattered scrap of paper. It was a tram timetable from Gangerabili to Keekorok. A diversion, nothing more.

The taller, fatter policeperson opened the scrap. As the frown materialized on his serious *professional* face, Mathembe bolted.

In the forests around Chepsenyt she had run out of her Mathembeness into the intimate consideration of God, but she never ran then as she ran now. With the Ukerewe Active Service Unit bounding and cackling and whooping after her soul she had outrun even God, but she never ran from them as she ran from the soldiers through the warren of Flesh Market.

Shouts from behind: "Stop . . . that girl. Stop that girl. Stop her."

The people parted before her; she could see the faces, frozen by the relativity of her movement, the small, sly smile, the tilt of the eyes.

And the soldiers came after.

Dodging through stalls hung with slowly flexing fatworms. Jumping over plastic sheets laid out with rare organs. Ducking under bookstands, around sex circuit booths. Pushing through racks of oracle heads, waking them from dreams of paradise.

And the soldiers came after.

She ran, panting with fear, with exertion, with the knowledge that, like that small woman, that small muscular woman who had run her down in the forests near Timboroa, who had called her *girlie*, she could never outrun a bullet or a target-seeking missile. Would it hurt tremendously? Would there be no pain at all? Would it be fast? Would it be slow? Would she be allowed to see her spine and lungs and small flat breasts fountaining outward in a spray of bone and meat and blood?

She turned into an alleyway so narrow that the overhanging walls of biotecture met overhead. An arm snagged her. A square crop-headed bully-boy face grinned at her.

"Now, daughter, seeing your, shall we say, predicament, was it not a wise thing that you made sure your insurance was paid up?"

The hand stroked her cheek. The bully-boy face pouted, a moue of mock regret. The hand released her.

"Get. Go. Run. Leave this to the big boys." The big fat hand pushed her away. Army boots splashed over piss and ichor-soaked cobbles: close, closing. Mathembe looked around her. The grinning boy was gone but the street was filled with cries, Ghost Boy howlings, the thunder of hands drumming on walls. She ran on. Behind her, made loud, immense by the acoustic architecture of inner Ganger-abili, weapon fire: the hard flat sounds of bioweapons in ambush. Here the houses grew so close that she had to turn on her side to squeeze between. A forsaken spot to die, squeezed between two warm, throbbing walls of biotecture. Finally the two walls sealed into one. Escape was a triangular slit where wall met cobbles.

Sobbing with fear and exhaustion, Mathembe pulled herself through on her belly by the tips of her fingers. She could no longer hear the bootfalls behind her. She could no longer hear anything but the beating of her own heart that seemed to have set the whole billion-ton cancer of Gangerabili throbbing in resonance. She pulled herself forward, pulled herself forward along the dark tunnel through the heart of the dying boro until the slit opened into a crack into a crawlway and finally into a narrow, twining canyon of an alleyway that went up sheer to a vaulted roof studded with windows kilometers above her head.

Radio news. Hunger strike, Day 60. A joint army-police patrol engaged on a routine search for illicit street traders in the Ganger-abili/Flesh Market district is reported missing after giving pursuit to a suspect.

No trace of the three soldiers was ever found. Not so much as the bulb from a shoulder-mounted searchlight.

It was a week before Mathembe could go back to the tunnels. She pleaded sickness: many and arcane viruses were continually abroad in the tunnels. In the privacy of her room, in the sanctum of her heart, she raged at the Five Hearts Beer girl. *I do not wish to be part of it, I do not wish to be drawn into it, how dare they presume to do this for me, who wants nothing to do with them?*

No God has ever recognized a mortal's right to rage at them. When she did return, smoldering with a diffuse, directionlessness rage, Mathembe found A Dose of Worms looking at her in a new way, the way that says to those with Mathembe-eyes *Now you are one of us indeed*.

That was the look the fat meatboys wore when next they came swinging along the alley. Smiles expanded to continental plates of designer enamel as they pushed away Mathembe's proffered card reader.

"No further contributions are required, thank you," said the one who seemed to have been given both boys' share of words. "Consider it a public relations investment."

He put a green ♥ sticker on Mathembe's nose and, as she tore it off, slapped one on her ass. Laughing, swinging along, off they went, designer butts moving under those tight tight shorts, broad body-shop shoulders rolling under live-fur drapes. And Mathembe stood as if she had been held down by the big, beautiful, smiling boys and slowly, pleasurefully, politically raped.

And that is the story of Mathembe and the Nationalist Prisoners of War.

The firing had kept her awake all night, and as she lay learning to distinguish the sporadic shots of the Warriors of Destiny from the brutal staccato answers of the soldiers' heavy weapons, she became aware that, first Hradu in his bed on the shadow side of the room, and then her mother in the room upstairs, and then Faradje, and then the head whirling like a demon bat through the Dreaming, and finally every other soul in Lantern Lane, was breathing in exact synchronization with her. Heavy armor thundered on Keekorok and in the morning, as Mathembe's ceramic bells joined the morning throng, there were three new trees on the corner of Keekorok and Mama Ngee outside the fire-blackened shell of a newsstand. Small trees, small and twisted; you would hardly notice them, busy on your way to another day, another enn. But they stopped the jingle of Mathembe's bells, stopped them dead. People pressed around her on their way to another day, another enn, while she stared, stared, stared at the trees twisted in a slow, vegetable agony while images so terrible she had put them to sleep the instant she conceived them rose from their roost in a storm of wings.

We are still, join us in our stillness; we four, for a moment, forever.

Thrusting, blind branches push from Mr. Kakamega the tryx grower's eye sockets.

The small woman goes bouncing down the slope, slipping and sliding toward the rooftops of Timboroa. And the missile comes after. The missile comes after. The missile . . .

The wind blows across the bare, stretched vocal cords of the head of the traitors.

Blazing trux run through the streets of her memories. The three trees hold her like a stone in the great soul river of people passing unconcerned along Keekorok Boulevard while they ask her the one question she has never dared ask herself.

Do you really believe he is still alive?

Existence, the Jantic mystagogues teach, is not a precipitous teeter along the mountain ridge of God's will, fearful of the abyss of self-loss on either side; existence is a valley hemmed in by high mountains through which many paths wend. Life, which is more than existence—that, both Confessor and Proclaimer would agree—is a pilgrimage through the valley of the will of God, steered and guided by certain landmarks. Events, people, places, relationships; births, marriages, deaths; parents, friends, lovers; houses, universities, prisons: we migrate, we navigate, we peregrinate toward around through them.

Or . . . is it that life is a river breaking in eddies of circumstance around the clashing rocks of reality?

Or . . . is it that life is a spatiotemporal continuum and people, places, circumstances the stellar masses to which we are gravitationally bound?

Whatever the answers, if answers there be, the question Mathembe was forced to confront on Keekorok Boulevard turned her life path inevitably toward the Bujumbura Ballpark.

Troubled times had spread its reputation far beyond the district in

which it stood, beyond the city, beyond even the land: it cast a
monolithic shadow across an entire planet's conscience.

Mathembe arrived as the banks of floodlights were being switched
on, panel by panel of hot white light. The tiled plaza before the
stadium, where in the days of Sporting Bujumbura's glory a thousand
and one ticket touts, fast-food hawkers, wine sellers, and street
entertainers had plied their trade, now seemed in the fading light like
a suburb of Khirr, the Proclaimer hell. Flickering trash light, a loose
constellation of a hundred and more smudge fires. Tattered banners
moved in the smoke from the fires: angry words, slashed and torn.
Faces gathered beneath them, demon-lit. Somewhere a bass drum
beat. Somewhere bells and finger cymbals chimed counterpoint.
Somewhere voices chanted. Names. Endless mantras of names.

Bodies crowded past her, carried her toward the bright shining
gate and the parked troop carriers. The Emperor's men were black
silhouettes against the floodlight glare within. Someone collided with
Mathembe. She turned, glimpsed a hooded face. A white face. A
twisted, melted face, as if cast in clay and pulled by fingers. *Demon!*
Mathembe fled. Gasping, she fought through the people toward the
tram. The shaking did not cease until she was within two stops of
Gangerabili.

One of her most powerful Chepsenyt memories had been
touched. She was too young, her mother had said, it was not a book
for children, but she would not be told and one night when Mother
and Father were out wining with friends in Founding Tree Square,
wetting the head of a newborn child, she had taken the book of
religious stories down from its alcove, hooked the reader behind her
ears, and pressed the contacts to her temples. It had taken tranquilizers
to get her to sleep that night, a lunar month before she could sleep
without waking from nightmares of the Nyakabindi, the evil that dwelt
in the volcanic mid-ocean ridges of the southern sea.

On the tram the spell of the drum and the fitful firelight and the
pull of the pure white light was broken. The face that had confronted
her had not been that of a demon, but a funeral mask. Their
malformed, eyeless gaze had surveyed her childhood from their hooks
on the memory-room wall. She had worn one when her grandfather
had passed stubbornly into the Dreaming. Their circuitry stimulated
memories of the dead, reassured the wearer with a twilit glow of

remembrance. The mask outside the stadium had been reengineered to project overpowering loss and rage at the face-to-face range at which Mathembe had encountered it. The psychic shock chilled her still.

Mathembe remembered an urban legend she had been told by her grandfather, the kind of story you are told by someone who knows somebody who knows the actual people involved or was there when it happened.

Versions of this story can be found in every township and big city boro. Accordingly, every township and urban boro claims it as its own. In every version, the central character is an old woman whose beloved husband passed into the Dreaming after many many many years of devotion and love. Distraught, the old woman dons a mourning mask but at the end of the appropriate period she declines to remove it and place it back on its hook on the wall. The memories, she says, are too precious, she cannot let them go, not yet; let her stay with them for just a little while. So she keeps the mask on and days pass into weeks pass into months, and every time her family and friends suggest she take the mask off she says *Give me just a little more time with him, just a little more, I am old and memories are all I have.* But the day comes when the remembered face is not so clear, the remembered voice less distinct, and she says *Yes, I can now pick up my own life, what remains of it, and carry it forward, I will remove the funeral mask.* But when she comes to lift it off it will not come. It will not move. It has bonded itself to her flesh, become one with her. She cannot take it off even if she wishes. She goes to her family, her friends, the doctors and healers and specialists and holy people, but they cannot pull it off, cut it off, science it off, pray it off either. She becomes known as the Lady of the Mask. She stops going out. She stops seeing people. She shuts herself up in her house and only leaves at night when the sight of her funeral mask in the dark streets frightens small children and love couples. She disappears from the life of the community. She becomes legend. It is only when the people begin to grow suspicious that there has been no movement, no light, no radio in the house for too long that some brave women and men break down the door. They find the woman dead on the floor, with the mask on her face. They go to her and find that it lifts off, clear away, as if it had never been there at all.

And is that it? Is that the end of the story?

No, this is. This is the end of the story. The rider. The kicker.

The sting. When they take the mask off, even the bravest of the brave men and women go pale. The face beneath the mask is not the face of the old woman. *It is the face of her long-dead husband*.

These mythic voices that rule our days and our long dark nights.

That was a legend. This is a proverb, likewise common to all people in all times, yet each considers it unique: *Before you ask the question, do you want to know the answer?*

In the night, some vagrant soul in need of a blessing had left a can of beer as an offering in the shrine to Zanzan Bé. Some less pious soul had drunk the rice beer, crushed the plastic can, and left it balanced disrespectfully on the saint's head. A swirl of warm wind spun off from some small chaotic disturbance far and deep under Gangerabili knocked the can from its perch and sent it rattling over the cobbles in front of Mathembe's pitch.

The Five Hearts Beer girl on the can regarded Mathembe Fileli. Knowing a message from God when she saw one, Mathembe picked it up, tried to decipher the New Speech copy on the back.

> Five Hearts.
> Heart of Good Times.
> Heart of Cordiality.
> Heart of Generosity.
> Heart of Friendship and Fellowship.
> Heart of Courageousness.

The can clattered on over the cobbles, onward into the deeps of Flesh Market. A Dose of Worms looked up from his hot-shop counter and saw that Mathembe-Across-the-Alley was gone.

Her apprehension increased with every step she drew closer to Bujumbura Ballpark. She unfolded the note she had scrawled and read it, refolded it, put it in her pouch, took it out, unfolded it, read it, folded it again, put it back in her pouch again, took it out again, unfolded it again, reread it. . . .

Have you seen my father?
His name is Kolé Fileli.

Daylight in the great tiled plaza multiplied the distances between the shapes and forces of the previous night, no longer close, no longer threatening. Beneath the ripped, spray-painted banners the protesters maintained their vigils. The sectists kept up their continuous chanting of the names of the disappeared. Beneath the hooded robes, the funeral masks abroad on Bujumbura Plaza were mere masks, nothing more, masks that could be taken off and laid to rest. By some trick of perspective, the circling walls of the stadium appeared to be reaching for Mathembe to draw her into the open gates and the armored vehicles that guarded them.

Apprehension. The roll of paper grew damp in the sweat and heat of her hand.

The soldiers did not even spare her a look as she passed between them into the tunnel. Along the arched passage were lined those guilty of small misdemeanors against the Emperor. Mathembe stared unashamedly at a half-woman, naked flesh from the waist up, gnarled trunk firmly rooted in the concrete from the waist down.

"Why don't you just piss off, you stupid little bitch?" the half-woman growled at her. Stung, it was a moment before Mathembe thought to unfold her slip of paper. She approached a personable-looking young man with muscles that made you want to lick them. A hand gripped her arm. A funeral mask drew close to her face.

"Leave them alone. They will pick your pockets as soon as look at you. Bribe the guards, they can shorten the sentence. Especially do not go near that one, he is a real bastard. He will inform on you, pretend you are an accomplice of his, accuse you of anything just for the fun of seeing someone else in his place. That girl there, see?" The masked figure—man, saint, spirit?—pointed to a girl of Mathembe's age with beautiful cascading black hair. "He got her five weeks, and all she did was say to him she felt solidarity with him. Leave them alone, do you hear?" Tears ran down the face of the girl with beautiful hair, down her beautiful crescent-moon breasts, down the rough, scarred wood of her trunk.

Mathembe came into the afternoon sunlight of the stadium.

She opened her hand and let the slip of paper fall to the ground.

Row upon row, row upon row, row upon row, the man-trees filled the ballpark. Thousands . . . thousands. She had expected tens, dozens, maybe a few hundred. But thousands . . . thousands. Mathembe descended the steps between the tiers of seating into the amphitheater. Branches covered her, shaded her. She went along the first row, bewildered, benumbed by the sameness of the trees. Trunks.

Branches. Twigs. Trunks, branches, twigs. Trunks branches twigs. Trunksbranchestwigs. The outstretched hands of the condemned wheeled above her, mercy mercy Mathembe Fileli mercy mercy child have mercy. She ran faster. Faster.

This person kneeling on the neat carpet moss, arms lifted in supplication? imploring? futile rage? That person, arms wrapped around a knotted trunk, rubbing cheek against rough bark until blood flowed; this untidy pile of biolights, beer bottles, and chocolate; that child sitting in the fork of two branches kicking its heels; these icons and spirit medals, those coins and dead smartcards hammered into the trunk; those branches painted with the colors of an imaginary nation, black silver and green. On and on and on, up and down the rows so many so many too many trying to take them all in, all those trees twigs trunks branches hooded people weeping masks all whirling and blurring into a relativistic smear of impressions so many so many too many how could you know how would you tell she might have passed it, it might have been the first tree of the very first row but how would she ever know, how did any of them know, should she go back and search through them one at a time, a whole day if need be over each tree to pick some memory of identity from bark and branch and leaf? But there were so many so many too many and any one of them might be, might have been . . .

Her father.

Falling. Falling. Forward. Too many. Too many.

Mathembe rolls into a tight fetal huddle. The trees lift their branches over her. Benediction. The masks and the robes push push past.

She hears footsteps.

She hears a rustle of folding fabric.

She hears the air displaced by a body bending near hers.

She hears breath intaken, the moist click of lips parting in the instant before words are spoken.

"Are you all right? . . .

"Are you looking for someone? . . .

"Of course you are looking for someone. We are all looking for someone. Else why would any sane soul be here? . . .

"Your first time? I was like that my first time here. First time here; listen to the man. You would think I was like one of those old dark dog-women who have been coming here every day for twelve, thirteen months until they are as twisted and gnarled and root-rotten as the trees. Probably more so. No, I have come nine times. This is my ninth visit."

Mathembe looked up to see what it was that so high-handedly had interrupted her anguish. He knelt between her and the sun. Long, soft waves of hair fell continually into his eyes and were pushed futilely away with large, useless hands.

"Stones."

He stood up, offered a large, useless hand to help Mathembe up from the turf.

"You have to look for the stones. Sometimes if they know they are going to be executed they will pick up a pebble or a loose cobble or something and write their names on it. They hold on to this stone while the guards strip them and wire them in the changing rooms below. Then they take them out of the team tunnel to the planting site and, while the guards are digging them in, they try to drop the stone so some record of their identity remains. You can find them hidden among the roots if you look: the names of the disappeared. Come. See."

In the crook of a tree branch was white glass cobble. Black charcoal cursive, much eroded by wind and rain, a name. A history. An identity. *I Am. I Was. Remember Me.*

"Sometimes they do not drop it in time and the stone remains embedded. It will not work on stone, you see. Nor teeth. Did you know that? At the center of every man-tree are two rows of teeth; intact, perfect, entombed in the wood. There is an image in that, but I do not know exactly what to do with it. If I can even do justice to it."

Mathembe judged him to be maybe ten, maybe twelve years her senior, yet in his manner, his way of speaking, of using his large, useless hands, was a naïve unworldliness that seemed almost childish.

"I see it as an allegory. But then she used to say I saw everything as an allegory. An allegory frightening in its implications: if the teeth are intact, might not the spirit be also? Trapped inside. Entombed in wood, blind, deaf, dumb, insensible. Alive and aware and conscious, but unable to get out. And we would never know. How could we know? How could they communicate anything to us? Stop it, Ghavra, you are frightening yourself. Overactive imagination. She used to tell me that all the time, I have an overactive imagination. I am sorry, did I frighten you too? I am sorry. Well, goodbye. I hope and I do not hope you find what you are looking for. This place engenders mixed blessings like that."

They parted, moving in opposite directions along opposite rows. Mathembe searched for white stones with a name on them until the sky grew dark and the banks of floodlights came on panel by panel, pouring white light down into Bujumbura Ballpark.

He was there the next day, passing up a row as Mathembe was passing down. After that she did not see him for three more days. By then she was conscious that she was searching not just for white stones but for his shadow in her peripheral vision. The fifth day she met him at the tram stop and was surprised by the thrill she felt when he remembered her. That day they worked together under the high, distant beating of helicopter rotors, along the ranks of condemned prisoners.

Ghavra. A Proclaimer name. Ghavra was a poet. Not any poet, but a jangada poet. Not any jangada poet, but a *political* jangada poet. Not any political jangada poet, but a *Proclaimer* jangada poet. Mathembe knew of jangada poets from Faradje's radio. Mathembe knew of jangada poets from Faradje's reaction to Faradje's radio. The first soft slap of drums, the slink of guitars, the plink of thumb pianos and, with an uncharacteristic blaze of anger, he would be out of his sagging chair, retuning the station. "Damned ocarinas!" he would swear. Never having heard more than two bars of introduction, Mathembe could not say if the accusation was justified or not.

Jangada: blank verse ecstatically improvised to music. The river-shanty people conceived it from poverty and want, gave birth to it down in the boondocks among the drums and surdus and tablas with which the longshoremen accompanied their never-ending song, found in the rhythm of the angels and the hallucinatory poetry a communal apotheosis. But it was in the hands of middle-class dilettantes—the usurpers and perverters of all such clay-footed media—that it gained the same kind of raw intellectual respectability that Ghost Boy graffiti on municipal trams and trux had earned a season, a year, before. Jangada was in grave danger of becoming a fashion. Any growing thing that loses its roots withers: a truth the strolling *wajangada* moving from street café to street café along the Corniche and Riverside Drive, flattering the tourists in verse for small change, small beer, seemed either to have forgotten or conveniently misplaced. The advent of political jangada claimed to have come to liberate the music from the grip of the bourgeoisie and restore it to its noble plebian origins as the song of the oppressed. These new *wajangada* performed by biolumi-nescence and trash light on street corners, at tram-drivers' cafés and longshoremen's bars, and the river-shanty people scratched their heads and shrugged their shoulders *so* at what fine words like *nation* and *liberty* and *martyrdom* and *the cause* had to do with them.

Faradje reserved his most biting invective for *political* jangada. He saw hearts-and-bones nationalism, the essential naïve political heart of the people, bowdlerized, bastardized, and sanitized for their protection by namby-pamby, arty-farty, and probably sexually deviated intellectuals. The notion of a *Proclaimer* political jangada poet was as far beyond his comprehension as the metaphysical underpinnings of *ur*-space.

Mathembe saw no contradiction. A man could be a jangada poet, and a nationalist, and a Proclaimer, and a daily searcher for white stones among the roots and branches of Bujumbura Ballpark: the true world, the world she had glimpsed that time with Dr. Kalimuni, was a big house, with shelter for many under its eaves. In the enervating heat of an Ol Tok high summer, they worked their ways along the aisles of the trees. In the shade of the branches, he told her about the one for whom he was searching. She had worked for an organization called the Glass House. Had she heard of it? No. Not many had. Had she then heard of the National Cultural League? She had: a vague gossamer umbrella, beautifully colored, beneath which an uncomfort-able alliance of painters, writers, artists, musicians, university profes-sors, eccentric widows with too many pets, serious students, and well-intentioned but clueless foreigners congregated with the common aim of promoting the uniqueness of their national heritage. It rated scant credibility in the tunnels of Flesh Market, did the National Cultural League. The Glass House was a semi-autonomous bud of the League, a project of young activists committed to iterating Nationalist thought through contemporary street arts, transforming them into potent tools of political expression. Before the Glass House, Ghavra had been just another poet publishing an anemic volume of verse every few years or so, hopelessly abstracted, touching nothing, changing nothing. Then one night as he lay on his bed wrestling with his artistic impotence, voices had gathered in the square below his window. He had rushed to the balcony to see what was happening, and the wild wild words and soaring chordal dance of jangada had struck him like a physical blow. Everything changed, changed utterly: terribly, beautifully. He had given his spirit to this consuming, passionate new poetry and almost without thought had been swept along by dancing feet into a heady whirl of music, hallucination, and politics. The tide had inevitably carried him to the Glass House even as the Glass House pushed toward the explosive popularity of the new music. And there had met her. She had been a local organizer. Slowly, shyly, they had fallen in love. They had lived together in an apartment on Kimathi Street for a season and a half, a timeless pre-creation Dreamtime in which their similarities and disparities had ignited each other with such brilliance that those who drew close to them were dazzled.

And then she was evaporated.

"That is the word," he said. "Evaporated. You are not arrested, you are not interned, you are not *helping the police with their inquiries*; you are evaporated. They have given the verb a new transitive form. Not a word. Not a sign. Not a trace. No letters, no communiqués, no legal representation. Official silence, neither confirmation nor denial. Evaporated.

"One evening she did not come back from the Glass House. That was all. I waited, and I waited, and I waited, and she never came. No one saw anything, no one knew anything. Evaporated."

Later, when he was able, he asked Mathembe his first and only direct question. It was: "And you?"

Mathembe found a piece of paper and the pencil stub she kept for adding up things in her belt pouch, wrote one word: *Father*. Ghavra nodded and never again was Mathembe's wordlessness questioned. They searched on but neither found what they were looking for. At the tram stop he said to her, "You know who I am, but I do not know who you are."

Mathembe she wrote in her fat, ugly ideograms, like spoiled children. She pressed the note into his hand and ran madly for her tram, bells ringing.

When she was little more than an apple, her grandfather, with the mandatory grandfatherly glee for the distasteful, had shown Mathembe one of the bandanna-colored slugs that were such a pest in Chepsenyt's garden orchards. The story went that they were the descendants of scraps of bioplasm lost down the backs of chairs, in corners, under beds: rolled and shaped by the rough hands of evolution. Mathembe had grimaced as her grandfather had lifted the gross, gaudy thing, long as his hand, muscular and vital as an extra organ, and held it for her perusal. A forefinger was raised to the corner of his eye, a single tear squeezed onto fingertip. He brought the single tear toward the slug's waving tricorn of horns. The horns retracted with un-sluglike speed; the whole ghastly blob oozed away from the finger.

"Salt in the tears," her grandfather had said. "They cannot tolerate salt. If you cry on them, they dissolve and die."

She was a slug, a slow-moving, conspicuous, cumbersome slug, her horns reaching out, questing, testing. *Do you feel as I feel? Am I silly and stupid? Is it real? Should this be right?* Stinging, salty questions. *Do not rain tears on me, because I might dissolve.* She had desired her world opened up, unpeeled like fruit, but not this way. Lady of the Holographic Mercies, not this way.

When business was slow, slow as a slug, or when the wind from deep under the quarter stirred her spirituality, Mathembe would tend the shrine next door. She scooped up incense ash and tidied away burned-out cones. She piled dead dark bioluminescents into a recycle sack and polished the rare metals. She swept up the litter and evicted any vagrant parasitic organs that crept in during the night to feed off the biolights. She removed out-of-date prayers from their wands, made sure there was a supply of paper slips and something with which to write on them. She never saw anyone make use of her provisions for the spirit, but the fact that every day there was something to do at the shrine testified that it was being used. The small disciplines became a walk of faith for Mathembe: faith not in Zanzan Bé and his attendant sub-saints and angels but her own personal celestial patroness. When she became familiar enough with the nature of faith to know that Zanzan Bé would not mind—as a Ykondé saint (the highest spiritual state achievable by humans short of divinity) he was incapable of jealousy—she built a small sub-shrine for the Five Hearts Beer girl out of interlocking sections of plasm. The stuff multiplied faster than she could sell it. Over the weeks the shrine grew into an elaborate, disturbing pagoda of smooth black plastic skin stretched over bulging ribs and bone buttresses, of phallic knobs, puckered lips, and throbbing organs that dwarfed the original shrine and turned the attention of the passersby. Mathembe decked her shrine with biolights, candles, and whatever ornaments she found clinging to her sticky fingers as she moved through the streets of Ol Tok.

There are moments, only moments, when the sun penetrates the juttings and pilings of Gangerabili into the streets of Flesh Market; moments when rays of dusty sunlight strike like lasers laying open to the light places long lain in darkness, illuminating hidden inviting doorways, entrances to whole undiscovered realms of personal geography. Placeless places, timeless moments.

The light is warm, dusty as an old kiss on her cheek. She stands before the shrine, closes her eyes, claps her hands three times. Behind her the people throng through the streaming light, sun-warmed, illuminated, casting new, curious shadows. To her they are no more substantial than those curious shadows. The sound of their feet, their voices, their music, their commerce and passage is silence to her. Three times three she claps her hands. Brings palms together.

You have helped me make it, help me keep making it.

My mother. There is something not right with her. I do not know what it is; no one but her knows what it is and she will not say. Help me help her when she does not want to be helped.

My brother. Keep him safe, keep him out of the fingers of stupid little boys, let not his stupidity be compounded, stupidity upon stupidity; keep him safe.

My father . . .

The biolight is placed in its niche. The warmth of her fingers stimulates it into activity. As the beam of sunlight falters, regains a final quantum of strength before the terminal fade into the penumbra, the shrine glows, a captive constellation. A thousand lights. A thousand prayers.

The moment dissolves. The spirit passes. Time and space reassert themselves.

She bowed, turned. And he was there. Leaning against the wall of the Tipsi Café, arms folded.

She was furious. She was humiliated. She felt like a vile, bandanna-colored slug.

A light glowed in the fingers of his left hand. A cold green light.

He came to her side. He bowed, clapped his hands, three times three. He placed the biolight on the tabernacle.

"We cannot ask things of our God, as you can of yours," he said. The humiliation, the self-consciousness, was burned away like low river mist. Suddenly everything was good. She wanted to give him things, buy him things, show him things, share things with him. She pushed him into the Tipsi Café, waved at the bottles racked behind A Dose of Worms. On the television high on its perch an international sports team was being presented to the Emperor in his Jade City. Grandfather's head was muttering and protesting at a tableful of fellow political bums.

"You are welcome to my café to have whatever you wish any time you want, girlie," said A Dose of Worms. "If you come without your friend here."

Mathembe banged her fist on the counter.

"As I said, you are welcome any time, but without your friend here."

Again, first hammered counter, palm opened, upward: *Why?*

"Tell him, next time he wants to pray at one of our shrines, to one of our saints, to put the light on with his *right* hand."

Mathembe bared her teeth and with one gesture swept small eats glasses tea bowls to the floor.

He caught up with her in a small cobbled plaza deep within the inner labyrinth where many ways met around an overgrown public drinking fountain, much graffitied by the lovers that met there.

"I am used to it. It only stings for a moment and it is gone."

But I am ashamed she tried to say to him, but he was blind to her.

"If I am angry, it is not for myself, not on account of any insult to myself. I am a poet, insults are the stuff of my sinews. No, I am angry because of the sheer, bloody, stupid ignorance. A thousand years of ignorance."

Ashamed, she said. *And angry. My own people*. He did not hear.

"Ignorance. That is the true enemy. Not Proclaimers, not Confessors, not the Emperor nor the Warriors of Destiny. Ignorance— the ignorance we have been kept in, kept ourselves in, wallowed in—so that we could never get our heads above hating each other to see the real issues. Ignorance. Left hand. Right hand. Shit."

He took a pen from a pocket. With his left hand, his Proclaimer hand, he wrote among the so-and-so loves so-and-so and the scribbled telecomm codes the words *Ourselves Alone: our day will come.* He tossed the thick pen in the air, caught it with his right hand, the Confessor hand, wrote beside the first message: *What we have we hold. A Proclaimer land for a Proclaimer people.*

They walked on through the lanes and alleys of the slum, through the pressing people, the eternal people. Where a single vertical shaft struck down through Gangerabili's many levels to illuminate a quiet corner of a busy concourse they stopped. They stood close, embedded in light. She wanted to speak. For the first time, there were words worth her saying. He looked up into the light, squinting, striving for one shard of perfect sky. Mathembe took a tiny jewellike winged creature from her toy pouch, ran a pin through its belly, fastened it to Ghavra's left cuff.

His reaction was one of shock. Rapidly suppressed shock. But shock. He studied the squirming toy with barely disguised revulsion.

"This is the thing I can never come to understand. A place I can approach but never enter, and because I cannot enter, I am forced to confront my own ignorance. The way you people handle life, so ruthlessly so carelessly.

"I think I am so clever, I am told I am so clever, so tolerant and understanding, I am an artist, able to sympathize and empathize with any and every point of view, be all things to all men in the name of Nationalism, and then I look down and I see a beautiful living thing pinned and writhing on my sleeve and the old Proclaimer in me kicks. I see your gift, and somewhere Spirit Lodge drums beat and banners wave."

His fingers moved to pull the pin. The creature fluttered its gossamer wings and he shrank back as if a demon were drinking from his veins.

"I come from a very straight, very staunch Proclaimer family, up in the far North, in Simsharra Prefecture. My township was Faharj, under the breath of the great north woods themselves. The farther from the river, the louder they beat the drums; that is a Proclaimer saying. They beat them loud in Faharj, and long. They would have beat them all day, if they could, though there was no Confessor within a day's drive to hear them. Tabernacle every holy day, daily instruction every day after school from the shrine keeper, nothing but New Speech and the radio tuned to the Voice of the Empire. Do not play with Confessors, they are dirty, nasty, they tell lies and kick you when you are hurting where it will hurt most and then steal your smartcard; that was what my parents taught me. Dear, dear people. I loved them dearly. Can you understand how?

"So, when I met my first Confessor, I did not even recognize him. No talons. No green face, no fumes pouring from his nostrils, no red hair, no blue eyes, no cloven feet."

They moved to a small trough fed with water from a pair of ossified jaws. Water plants released a pleasing perfume. They sat on the rim. Mathembe trailed fingers in the cool cool water.

"Education was highly esteemed among my people. The old kind, what they call Proclaimer learning. Not sticking circuitry into your skull and having your head filled full of facts while you sleep. Learning; understanding, knowing what to do with those facts, what they mean; *thinking*. 'Learn' they said, my parents. 'Education is the great gift of God.' But they never understood the essential paradox, that by insisting upon the holiness of learning, *thinking*, they led me ultimately to reject every other value they held so dear.

"Or, perhaps not." Again, his fingers approached the impaled organical. They could not touch it. "They were strict-interpretation Radanta sect. You probably do not understand what that means. In Radanta, life is the essence and image of God, who is the source and center of all sentience and being, its master, controller, and ultimate shaper. To take life, genetic material which is the source and seed of life, and manipulate it, adapt it to serve the purpose of man, is, in their theology, a sin of monumental pride. Faharj was a predominantly Radanta township; my people tried to lead lives that respected and reverenced life. Biotechnology was anathema. Outlawed. A social obscenity.

"To socially ostracize biotechnology was an oddity even among northern Proclaimers. My parents saw it rather that those other Proclaimer sects had compromised and adulterated the revealing science of God and fallen irredeemably from grace. They were farmers—it is kind of a necessity among the Radanta; they do not permit themselves biotectured food. They cultivated the soil the way they did ten thousand years ago in the Gray Age, opening the earth with metal plows hauled by machines, sowing: plain, simple staples;

no meat plants, no milk plants, no wineries. Everything plain, raw, simple. Dirty. They killed and ate animals.

"I was born and grew up in a dead house of bricks and stones and sheet plastic on a dead street of stone and concrete. Dead houses lit and powered by electricity made from running water and moving air, not biogas, not solar plants. Where we went in the world we walked or rode big, clanking bicycles. If we had far to go, to relatives in another town, we would go in metal trailers towed by metal tractors. I went about the world clad in cloth spun and woven by machines, not skimmed from the surface of vats of bacteria.

"When I sickened, I was given chemicals. No healing viruses to restore my inner man to harmony. And if I died in my sickness, I would have been buried in the earth, standing upright before the presence of God. No root dream of an afterlife for me, only a sad, slow rotting into the cold, pressing earth. The Dreaming was the unforgivable blasphemy, that man should deny the God-given gift of mortality and death. But as a Radantist, I would go joyfully to my grave, filled with faith and hope."

Mathembe shivered, the cold wind of mortality abroad in the lanes of Gangerabili. A death that was death: brittle lives suspended over an abyss with nothing to hold them, nothing to catch them should they be shattered and fall sparkling into the dark. She thought of Dr. Kalimuni, how brave he had been against the weapons of the Warriors of Destiny. Now that she saw the darkness that overshadowed his life and the life of every Proclaimer, she caught the true measure of that bravery.

"Can you understand how a thing may be rich in its simplicity? It is only now, after years of self-humiliation and loathing, of despising my parents' faith, that I have come to treasure my childhood. It is an indissoluble part of me, I cannot wish it away; therefore I shall rejoice in it, take joy from it, even if, at the time, I wished to escape from it without one second's delay. I was an educated fool, clever enough to see the shortcomings of my life and world but without the wisdom to appreciate them. My first act of rebellion was when my father and mother wanted to induct me into a Spirit Lodge—the Seed of Tears Society; I was born under the aspect of the Ninth House—and I refused. There had never been such a scandal. Prayer callers were summoned, shrine keepers, elders, moderators; they all took turns to talk to me: very slowly, very loudly, as if my problem were deafness, not rebellion. I said the lodges were bitter, narrow, and intolerant: hatred of Confessors masquerading as religious virtue; I would not relent, I would not join. My mother stopped up her ears with wax so she would not have to hear such blasphemies: my father has not spoken to me since, not one word. Of course, I was Named before the congregation—my infamy spread even to the corrupt Proclaimers, as I had been taught to think of them. Had I been a Confessor, I might have been better treated. Only my mother and the official delegations from the shrine would speak to me. I was not being formally Shunned, they told me: I failed to appreciate the honor. I wished then they would have; if I was a sinner, then let my sins abound, let them multiply; but I realize now the elders drew short of Shunning not for me but for the sake of my family.

"I am sure the whole town sighed with relief when I left for the university to curse myself with education. I am glad that none of them ever sought to make contact with me there; the repercussions for my mother and father of a good Proclaimer boy abandoning the faith of his fathers and, in his darkness and doubt, turning to the evils of Nationalism would have been terrible indeed. The Lodges are powerful and vengeful. The burden of sin must be placed somewhere, and they are not particular where they put it.

"Now you know. I am a Proclaimer and a Nationalist. So why, in the name of that Nationalism, do I find myself playing advocate for Proclaimerism? Perhaps it is that I disprove the formula that equates Confessor with Nationalist and Proclaimer with Imperialist. Perhaps because a thousand years of Proclaimer presence in this land, Proclaimer thought, Proclaimer faith, Proclaimer society and language and music and art and literature and culture, cannot be written off and dismissed as an aberration of history. Proclaimerism is part of this land: the land has taken it, as it has taken everything else, and changed it, and shaped it, and molded it into something uniquely its own. The faith of my fathers is not the faith of the fathers across the river. This is as much my land as your land, as much my land as the Warriors of Destiny's, or the Ourselves Alone councilors starving in a courtyard somewhere: my land and I love it, all of it, not part of it, not corners of it, not partially. Confessors and Proclaimers.

"I am sorry. I am sorry. I get excited. And loud. And embarrassing." He spread his big, useless hands.

No, Mathembe said. *Be embarrassing, be loud, show me this greater nation of yours.* But the spirits, having flown, would not return in that place, at that time, again. His fingers finally reached the now-quiet toy, touched the synthetic flesh.

"Oh, we think we are so sophisticated, so astute in our political smartness, and then a little scrap of flesh, a toy, something alive one day, dead the next, and it is Ghost Boys and Spirit Lodges again. Always more to unlearn than learn. Thank you." He stroked the gift; it fluttered translucent wings. "This is more than a toy, this is a test, a trial. An understanding machine."

No it is not, Mathembe said. *It is a toy. A nothing. A few grams of bioplasm, plastic flesh sung into life by me, for you, as a gift. No more.*

"Come," he said. "You have shown me where and how you work; now I must show you where and how I work."

The Glass House filled most of a small but bright plaza in Tsirinana. By design or by accident, some biotectural anomaly had caused the slumping slag pile of a dying house block to blister out into huge transparent bubbles, like clusters of ripe fruit, each many times human height. Walls had been pierced, connections made, floors and decks laid, power and telecomm conduits run all over like a nervous system, furnishings and office equipment moved in along with the requisite personnel. People in glass houses need to look busy.

One final detail. At some time while the Glass House was being blown, a photochemical reaction had turned the polymer pink. Quite pink.

"After a while you stop noticing it," Ghavra said as pink light fell on pink desks, pink chairs, pink terminals, pink papers pink posters pink pamphlets. Mathembe watched the people with pink smiles on their pink teeth as they hurried past Ghavra busy busy on their busynesses in the name of Art and Nationalism.

"All acts are, can be, political acts if they are conceived as such and informed by a set of culturally sound values," Ghavra said, but the words did not convince Mathembe. She sensed that they did not convince Ghavra either, and more: that the Glass House's groundbreaking work in making every act from wine-drinking to street ball to graffiti a political act had left him isolated, one Proclaimer political jangada poet, an oddity, an anachronism, an embarrassment, like the too-old child who still plays with the four-year-olds. When Ghavra suggested they leave she was glad for them both. While they walked he talked about how once you knew the signs you found infections of Imperial culture in every part of life, but Mathembe did not take in a word. She had become aware of a curious optical phenomenon. At first she had thought it was a trick of the light in an unfamiliar quarter, but no, everywhere she turned her head, there it was: posters, billboards, scraps of paper in the gutter, the white cobbles beneath her feet, laundry billowing from the balconies above her, even the white cumuli passing ponderously above her, all were tinged with a slight but definite *greenness*. Ghavra noticed her attempts to rub the green out of her eyes.

"Negative afterimages." Uneducated Mathembe did not understand. "It used to baffle me too until it was explained to me. The pink light, you see. The eye adjusts, and then when it is back on the street, everything is shifted that little bit in compensation. It passes."

It was three days before the last photon of green was gone from Mathembe's vision and white was plain and sacred white again.

That was the where. This is the how.
Bad day.
No luck.
No money.
Bad temper.
Empty bowl.
Empty card reader.
No sale.
Hands in pockets.
Kicking boots against wall. Kick. Kick.
Bored. Cross. Poor.

And the previous night the advocate Sharjah had come with his correct smile, *so*, and his soothing words, *so*, about how he was certain, *certain*, that news would be forthcoming very soon, and the best possible news imaginable, and Mathembe had not the courage to tell her mother, sitting there like some storm-blasted bird, hands on knees, terribly, frighteningly, inexplicably sick, mortal, fallible, that in her faithlessness she had been to Bujumbura Ballpark ten, fifteen, twenty times; her mother had looked so sick, so desperately sick, and the advocate's words had been so soothing, so healing to her, that she could not drive such a needle of pain into her heart, however truthful. *We all must make an effort for the advocate Sharjah*, her mother had said, and here she was today bored cross poor.

Beggars would do better. Better off eyeless handless legless earless mouthless everythingless. No one half-scared, half-thrilled tourist penetrating into darkest Gangerabili, not one wrinkle-nosed socialite, not one boyfriend/girlfriend buying for girlfriend/boyfriend.

Nothing.

Whisper the words of unlocking, roll them back into a ball, stuff the ball into your pouch, and tomorrow is another day.

And then he came. Smiling. Cocky. Arms folded, leaning against the posters for concerts and rallies and sales. Smiling. Cocky. Damn him.

"Come," he said. But she was still angry.

"Come," he said again and reached his hand across the alley to her.

"Come," a third time and she took the offered hand and something like a small shock of excitement ran from his fingers into hers, and while she was still trying to puzzle out what it was, he had pulled her away from the dull dirty dispiriting day *come* through the alleys between the stalls and booths and the vendors calling and the blaring banal radios and the blue television tubes *come* out into the air under the open sky, breaking into a run now *come come* blinking in the unaccustomed light, early evening light falling in planes and shafts across Ol Tok *come* hunting now, running with a clear sense of call, of purpose, of direction, two bright motes of life and movement weaving their own course along crowded sidewalks between street café tables around newsstands dodging policepersons army patrols great growling troop carriers darting across boulevards gnashing with traffic *come come come* the spirit was kindled within her seizing her up in a vertigo of excitement and anticipation of the miraculous *come come come* through streets broad and streets narrow where the air tasted of deep deep waters, cool cool river, away from the familiar districts and boros, linked hands a conduit of energy between them *come come* the fast-settling night of these southern skies was pouring through the streets, behind their heels the city broke into lights, district by district, boro by boro, but they outraced light itself and she laughed aloud giddy with the brilliance of her passage *come* and with the first stars penetrating the indigo, musk- and river-water-scented skies, they burst out of the stifling embrace of alleyways onto the Corniche and the river was wide as the sea before them, dappled with the riding lights of riverboats, silvered with starlight reflections.

There they waited for them, the musicians, the *wajangada*, women with drums slung at their waists from black green and silver sashes; men bent over guitars, tuning, testing, frowning with concentration, people with metal piston rings from the engines of dead Empire-built automobiles and ten-centimeter steel nails to strike them with; people with tambourines and maracas and wooden claves and surdus and congas and tablas and things you beat and things you scraped and things you ran your finger along and out poured a cascade of sound like the flight of angels.

"Jangada!" shouted Ghavra, and his face was exultant.

"Jangada!" shouted the people and, hands still joined, Ghavra presented Mathembe (suddenly shy, suddenly self-conscious) and shouted, "My friend, Mathembe here, has always wondered what jangada is about. Tonight, I propose we show her."

"Mathembe," said the guitarists and the drummers and the beaters and scrapers in a roll of voices like thunder across the river. "Mathembe." A drum struck up, the simple two-four rhythm of a tabla. Ghavra stood legs apart, head back, fingers locked behind his head. His foot tapped to the rhythm. The musicians moved into a semicircle behind him, standing, squatting, kneeling according to their instruments.

The voice of the single drum called. And the people came to its calling. From their tenements and housing projects, from the houses on the heights and the river bluffs, from their pontoon towns and houseboats; pilgrims from the river steps swathed in white, shoulders ritually bare, water dripping from their hair; teenagers ruminating wunder-gum and dressed in shorts, T-shirts, and jackets with the Ship Captain printed on the back; serious young men and women with Ourselves Alone badges and Warriors of Destiny scarves around their necks and I ♥ THE NATIONALIST PRISONERS OF WAR stickers on their lapels; mothers with infants jiggling their little ones up and down in time to the drum *dance dance little one*, fathers with flagons of wine and stolid you-will-not-get-me-dancing faces, and silly old men and women prancing with each other, in and out, over and under, roaring with laughter, too old for silly pride.

Jangada!

Then out of the night came the song of a single guitar, a simple theme but subtle, counterpointed by a second guitar, and then between the end of one beat and the beginning of the next in came the bass and rhythm and it lifted you up so high it took your breath away, so wonderful you wished they would go back and do it again because next time it might just make you cry with wonder.

Jangada: the people dance; the musicians bend and sweat and flash knowledgeable brilliant smiles at each other. *Jangada*: all is rhythm and movement, a dozen tempos pulling in a dozen different directions creating a fabric of continuity that exists only because of their tension; all is movement, all is dancing. One point of stillness only: Ghavra, the Proclaimer, standing still, legs apart, hands clasped behind neck, head back, looking in the dark sky so full of stars and saints. Upon what spirits might a Proclaimer, cursed to live, scared of dying, call?

But whatever their names, they hear his call and answer him. Slowly, very slowly, he folds himself down into a tight curled ball, tight as a fist before the blow is struck. Mathembe wants to go to him, *Is this part of it, is that meant to happen?* It must be, because the musicians are playing and the people are dancing and waving their flagons of wine and their green black and silver scarves. Is it only Mathembe who can see that he is suffering? She must go to him, she cannot hold back any longer, and as the decision is made, Ghavra straightens up. As he is half uncurled, a wail breaks free from him like no sound Mathembe has ever heard before, like the wail God might make if he were to call his faithful Proclaimers to prayer across the depths of space. The wail grows greater, louder, as he draws himself upright; jangada on the radio was never like this, jangada on the radio never released the ancient animal sleeping curled beneath the brain, jangada on the radio never shook you with its ancient primal fears. The musicians stop, waiting, sensing, counting time. The wail breaks into a torrent of language and the players scoop up the rhythm with drums and guitars and in an instant it is Mathembe who is lifted up on the stream of improvisation. *This, this, is indeed how it is meant to happen.*

They are about a river, Ghavra's words, and because they are about a river, they are like a river: a river which is many things, cool cool waters deeper than remembering, a spiritual state, a pilgrimage, the flood of history across time, the never-ending song of language, the iteration of the universe to itself through the tongues of men, associations, allusions tumbling over each other in the splash and run of his words. The expression on his face—pain, rapture, confusion, pride—is the apologia of his faith: that all men can—indeed, this one man may have—become God. *True* his face says. *True.* Words and music flow together and run onward into the night, trux and automobiles are stopping along the Corniche, everything shifting everything flowing everything changing like pilgrims lifting handfuls of holy water from the river that runs away through their fingers the moment they claim hold of it. No man can own a river, only borrow it and let it flow on.

So high. So holy.

Too high. Too holy, Mathembe realizes. Uncertainty fills the dance; the people pause, stop, stare. What is he saying? What does it mean? What has this to do with our lives, our hopes, our land? Step by step, the dance dies, killed by incomprehension. But Mathembe wills him on, on. *Burn on, burn on, Ghavra; they would lime and cage you, make you sing their songs; do you not realize this is why they look at you with suspicion in the Glass House, this is the insincerity behind their plastic pink smiles? The angel that inspires you will not submit to their rule, and they would leave their greasy fingerprints on the insides of its perfect thighs. You are no Proclaimer political jangada poet, you are greater than that.*

A voice cried out. A teenage girl, hair plaited into greased ropes, Ship Captain–jacketed, pointed at the sky.

"Look! Look!"

The musicians hesitated, lost the beat, fell apart into mismatched rhythms.

"The sky! The sky!"

And Ghavra, in mid-flight, failed. Big, useless hands clawed the air for the fleeing words.

"Look! The sky!"

An entire constellation was on the move. Lights drifted from their ordained positions and fell away toward the horizon. Beams flickered across heaven and were answered by beams lancing up from beyond the westward edge of the planet. The soft red moon and the hard silver star of the Saint-ship hung at the zenith.

And it was day. A new sun shone at the noontime. Alien light fell across the night half of the planet. Birds rose from the river with a collective cry and thunder of wings, wheeled, squawling, above the Corniche, while the nocturnal voice of the city was unnaturally hushed. The people gazed wondering at the light of another sun a quarter of a universe away.

And it was night.

The soft red moon and the hard silver star were gone.

The girl with the plaited hair, in the Ship Captain jacket, was crying.

Here is another Old Speech word for you to learn. You have already mastered *wajangada*: "the jangada people." Now we will say together the word *wakinéma*. Say it like this: wah . . . kee . . . *neh* . . . ma. Try it on your tongue, roll it around, try it for size and shape. *Wakinéma*. Is it comfortable? Does it sit well on your lips? That is good. Perhaps you might try now, having learned a little Old Speech, to guess what it means? *Wa*, people, a plural personal prefix used to transform a noun into a vocation; *kinéma*, a noun, derived from an ancient word for motion. *Wakinéma*: the moving-picture people.

Wakinéma: it ran like the rumor of a new season along the cobbles, up the tangles of conduits and pipes, from balcony to balcony, a disease of excitement that passed mouth to mouth to mouth.

Wakinéma. Where? Here? Lantern Lane?

Wakinéma. Yes. Here. Lantern Lane. Soon. How soon? Next month? Next week? Two days. Two *days*?

Wakinéma. What will they be showing? I do not know. But it will be good. It will be great.

Wakinéma. Tonight! Tonight tonight tonight. This is the night, this is the place, we are the people. Got chairs? Yes. Got beer? Yes. Got things to eat? Yes. Got friends, family, all coming? Yes.

No liberating messiah at the head of ten thousand armored trux, no palanquin manhandled through the streets enshrining the relics of a saint was ever greeted with the unforced enthusiasm with which the children of Lantern Lane celebrated the arrival of the *wakinéma*. Their trux were tired and listless, the flesh buyers' poleaxes long overdue; the fine paintwork on their wooden trailers, once bold, once gaudy, was now faded and scabbed. The *wakinéma* themselves were greasy-haired, parasite-ridden, and dirty but the eye of faith has no regard for such things. The children followed them around in small adoring flocks as they rigged guy wires for the big screen, ran out public address systems, and readied the projector gantry.

Wakinéma! Tonight! Tonight!

Mathembe heard them at their work as she squatted on her heels by her mother's bedroom door. It was a pose she had learned from Flesh Market, that squat: the pose of waiting. Enduring. Vigil-keeping.

The burden of mystery of her mother's recurrent illness had been handed to Mathembe. It was not a burden she was unwilling to assume, had she been consulted. Her anger was the automatic assumption of her family's men that sorrow must always be borne on a woman's shoulders. For a while it had been the concern of them all, that first time when Mrs. Fileli had fallen sick and deteriorated with terrifying rapidity and they had all taken their turns waiting by the bedroom door not daring to ask the question: *Will she die?* Healers, medicals, spirit prayers, herbalists, layers-on of hands; all had come and Mrs. Fileli, lying in her bed, fingers clutching at the thin sheet like the spirit of famine on a prosperous land, had said *Send them away, send them away, I will not speak to them, I will not see them, the only one I will see is the advocate Sharjah, I will be all right, I do not need them, believe me, send them away; is that the advocate I hear?* and as the sound of the labored breathing filled the apartment, the healers medicals spirit prayers herbalists layers-on of hands had shaken their heads and said in low murmuring voices *Mrs. Fileli refuses to see us but maybe if you were to give her this little vial, this little prayer ticket, this little prescription, this little sachet of tisane, this little verse of holy writ . . .*

Then, one morning, she was gone. Gone a whole day. Pushing aside political principles, Faradje was on the verge of telecomming the local police when a jeepney arrived in a blare of horns and radios, and clattering up the street stairs came a smiling bright cheerful woman who looked in every way like Mrs. Fileli except that she was not ghastly, luminous, rotting in the bed from which no one had ever truly believed she would rise again.

"Yes?" said Mathembe's mother. When asked how she felt she replied testily that she felt fine. Fine. Why should she not? "I think, maybe, it would be good for us all to go out tonight as a family for dinner. We do not get out enough, together, as a family. I saw a little place today, not too expensive, down in the Vintners' Quarter. . . ."

She was the only one in the cheap small restaurant on Winetavern Street who enjoyed her dinner—and the dinners of those who found themselves without an appetite. "You not eating that? Give it here. I have a hunger on me like a forest fire. I do not know why I should be so ravenous, but I am. Pass the hot sauce."

The next day she took son, daughter, brother, and father-in-law to the Water Gardens. Troupes of musicians perched precariously on gondolas paused to serenade them in their canal-side pavilion while Mrs. Fileli took tea and everyone else's share of sweet and dainty eats. She rose to throw a handful of change to the musicians, suddenly tottered. She fell in a clatter of chairs china change.

"Leave me alone leave me alone leave me alone!" She swore at the hands that moved to help. "I am all right, I tell you. There is nothing the matter with me."

Within three days she had retreated to her bed again. Faradje dispatched Mathembe and Hradu with a sizable sum of money down to Drug Market to shop among the vials of cut-and-mix bacteria, the quasi-legal viruses, the precious medicaments from the genetic arks of the primal forests—known as the Footstep Forests, for myth had it they sprang from the footsteps of the Ahleles—for something, *something* that might help. Costly treatments. Many days' wages. Mathembe found the empty vials on the back balcony. Sprinkled as a libation upon the shit digesters.

"Is that the advocate Sharjah?" her mother would cry at the slightest rattle of the street door. "Bring him up bring him up bring him in."

Then, in the night, she was gone. Again.

Mathembe grasped the sharp blade of responsibility alone. Hers had been the duty of watching and warding by night—though why a watch should be kept no one could say, unless for death coming up the street stairs, and that no one could deny entry. Hard days selling under Gangerabili, hard nights squatting by the door: if her eyes had closed, she would have sworn it could not have been for more than an instant. And the bed was empty.

The transformation was no less disturbing for happening a second time. No family dinner this time. No family outing to the pleasure punts and pavilions of the Water Gardens. But suddenly there was money for an educator for Hradu, who had until then successfully evaded the fingers of responsibility and seemed set on becoming another ignorant Confessor lout waiting on the street corner for eternity to arrive. Having thoroughly checked the credentials of all the private tutors on Water Street, Mrs. Fileli signed Hradu up for courses that would lead to diplomas and certificates. Without diplomas and certificates, one was so much toilet tissue in this eat-your-own-fingers world.

"I have been to see the advocate Sharjah," she announced at the evening meal around the table, under which resided a trux rear stabilizer unit that everyone suspected but no one was prepared to accuse Hradu of minding for his Ghost Boy friends. Some great and secret project a-growing in a vat in a disused warehouse over in Ladywell. Under any other circumstances Mathembe would have made the investigation of it her prime concern. Under any other circumstances. "Great news. He has found a contact in the Timboroa Regional Detention Center, the sister-in-law of a cousin of his who is engaged to be partnered to one of the governors of the center. He is certain, quite certain, that news will be forthcoming any week now of the whereabouts of your father. Is not that great news?"

Great news. Great great news.

She pretended for a week there was nothing wrong with her before the pains, the headaches, the nagging weakness and shivering forced her to her bed again while the sun poured through the window and the smell and sweat of sickness grew unbearable in the airless room. Outside the wakinéma put up their screen and rigged their sound system and had the small boys of the district stuff totally unnecessary flyers in every pigeonhole.

An hour before the edge of the world covered the sun, Lantern Lane was swarming. Distant relatives trammed in from Gobéte and Ashkamurthi Hill. Chairs were prodded into a sullen waddle only to dump themselves exactly behind the fat woman with the largest and most bouffant coiffure in the street. Small kids were wrapped up in quilts and robes and told that if they promised to go straight *straight* to bed the moment the final credits rolled—no quibbles, no arguments—they could come and watch. Householders nervously tested the stamina of dubious balconies. Hot snack and wine concessionaires materialized out of the dirt and litter and dried peeled house skin in dark doorways. The smell of celluloid. The whines and feed-back wails from the geriatric sound system. Old people complained they would not be able to hear over the traffic noise of the boulevard and they would get piles sitting out there in the cool cool cool of the evening and they could not see past the fat woman with the dreadful bouffant hair and if there was any sex, any flesh, any rubbing of *parts*, or *bits*, they were not watching that and lurched off to the toilet causing whole waves of spectators to be displaced from their seats. Children screamed for the sake of listening to their own echoes, threw sweets at each other, farted, sang *Why are we waiting, whai-ai are we waiting?* A cheer went up when the technicians—a greasy-haired bunch of permanent adolescents—found the controls to the Five Hearts Beer girl and vanished her, a god unremembered, into limbo. A louder cheer as the projector stuttered to life and the screen lit with an advertisement for Five Hearts Beer.

In the shadows of a dead doorway Mathembe waited, a glitter of eyes. The general hullaballoo died down. The Full Supporting program was starting. Halfway through the first reel the street door opened. Wrapped in a smother of coats despite the naked heat of the summer night, Mathembe's mother ventured onto Lantern Lane, slipping between the tenements and the rows of silver-lit, delighted spectators. A flicker of shadow; Mathembe was behind her. She had guessed right. While Faradje, Hradu, the head gaped at the billowing screen, filled with vast images like half-remembered angels, she had made her move. Mathembe folded herself into a Credit Union doorway while Mrs. Fileli waited for a tram. The big street emphasized her fragility. Mathembe wanted to go to her, lift her, carry her home to bed and family and love. The tram arrived. Mrs. Fileli took a window seat. Mathembe broke cover, followed on foot. One stop. Two stops. Three stops. Eight stops. Nine stops. Ten stops. Mrs. Fileli disembarked, crossed to another line. Mathembe pretended she could read the pro-Imperial flyers pasted to a street light pillar. A tram came swinging into the stop, spraying sparks from the catenary wires. Like most of her fellow countrypeople, Mathembe was afraid of electricity. It was the essence of demons wrung out by the mills of the Emperor and tamed just enough to be useful but never enough to be totally trustworthy. Mrs. Fileli took the rear seat, swaddled in her coats and wraps. Sweat trickled down Mathembe's sides as she ran after. Stop by stop, spark by spark, the tram drew nearer to Karasvathi.

Every part of a city has its dark counterpart. As Lantern Lane was to adjacent Keekorok Boulevard, as Gangerabili was to the Corniche sweeping up to the garden parties of Fijjad Hills, so Karasvathi was to Drug Market: its evil Siamese twin.

What a man might seek among Karasvathi's tortuous walkways and footpaths was no one's business but his own. A shadow in her hooded sleeveless top and black tights, Mathembe followed her mother through a dark maze of decaying, moribund biotecture where nothing ran straight and nothing ran true, where no line was steady, no perpendicular vertical. The lowest stories of Karasvathi's buildings had been so compressed by the burden of millennia of biotecture that the inhabitants—a cowled, furtive race into which Mrs. Fileli, cowled, furtive, blended almost invisibly—came and went through knee-high doors under sagging lintels from passages no more than crawlways. Carved wooden shingles decorated the bowed-out walls. A syringe. A brainplant. A head. An elegantly curved wooden phallus. A pair of scales. A five-lobed leaf. Mathembe's mother ducked into a long dark passage beneath the sign of a snake-haired woman's head. Doors led off the passage. All closed. All shut. Somewhere close by a deep-voiced musical instrument beat like a heart.

Door one: a flight of shallow steps jogging off into Karasvathi's interior darkness, rising gently in defiance of planetary curvature until perspective dwindled it to nothing.

Door two: blank wall.

Door three: a penetrating couple. The woman looked pityingly at Mathembe as she ground her hips: *around we go, and round.*

Door four: something huge and lunging and barking.

Door five: a dead beggar encrusted with ossified parasitic organicals.

Door six: a shop. The head of a snake-haired woman was painted on the floor. Gloglobes floated in the corners. By the left-hand wall an old naked man lay with his back turned to the room. His head was wreathed in pulsing green tendrils, an umbilical looped from his anus through the floor. Against the right wall sat an enormous young man staring enraptured at his left big toe. He was naked except for a pair of shorts with yellow chevrons down each side. Mathembe had never seen such muscles. They were like geological features. The bioboy's forehead was studded with terminals. Biocircuitry coiled back over each ear and clung with small curved claws to the nape of his neck.

In the far wall was a door.

Beyond the door was the machine.

It stood like a man, the machine. It was black. On shoulders, hips, thighs, forehead, gray readouts flick-flickered.

She had heard of these machines, whispers of them, murmurs of them running like vermin through the alleys of Gangerabili. *They make all the promises, the guarantees, that it will not hurt you harm you have no aftereffects no side effects no bad reactions. And you take the money. The money is good. The money needs to be good. And they inject you with the stuff: memory viruses, drug antibodies, things they sell out of the backseats of automobiles on the Corniche that you take once and next thing you know they are pulling your body out of the gutter for the organ runners to cut up. But they never tell, you see. They never tell you because if they told you no one would do it. The fevers.* The sickness that got worse and worse every day until you felt—more, you *knew*, that you were dying—though how could you die when in your bloodstream were circulating enough black-market antigens to immunize an entire prefecture? The hallucinations. The sure and certain knowledge that God was peeling your body apart with his fingers, worrying out the very marrow of your soul with his ceramic claws. The terrible terrible things. And then, the appointment down behind the door with the medusa head in Karasvathi. The appointment with the machine. The machine that sucked away your blood.

Clamped inside the machine was a naked woman. To wrists, shoulders, breasts, groin, inner thighs, ankles were hooked black snake things, fangs embedded in the flesh. Plastic tubes ran from the heads of the snake organicals over the head of the man machine, where they were tied in a bundle, down to the molecular filters. The blood flowed over the tiered rafts of gills like water from a fortunate fountain where you throw a coin to ensure safe return, or joy in love. At each stage the filters leached out the valuable viruses that had seeded and multiplied in the woman's bloodstream. The blood dripped from a single needle into a dialyzer and was recirculated through the body to absorb more tailored viruses.

In the embrace of the biting snake heads, Mathembe's mother opened her eyes, beheld her daughter. In that instant Mathembe would have overturned filter stacks, smashed pumps, processors, crushed gray Imperial logic circuits, but the eyes flicked toward the half-open door in the wall behind her. Mathembe peeped through the crack. In a bright conservatory two men sat at tea. On the low table between them was a pot, a water flask, and three vials of sparkling silver somethings. One of the two men was small, rodenty, no more than one would expect at such a trade in such a district. The other was the advocate Sharjah. He smiled and sipped his tea polite polite as, fired by an anger darker and quieter than she had ever suspected her spirit could harbor, Mathembe ripped her mother free from the sucking machine.

Blood dripped from the dead, gaping fang mouths onto the floor.

Blood seeped from the parallel puncture wounds in her mother's wrists, shoulders, throat, breasts, groin, inner thighs, ankles.

Mathembe wrapped her mother in a sheet draped over a chair, thought a moment toward loot and plunder. Thought again. Escape was all. The door to the outer room opened. The giant youth stood grinning. Blue bioluminescence pulsed along the circuitry that encircled his cropped skull. He rested hands on the door frame: *You shall not pass.* Mathembe glanced behind her. In the conservatory doorway stood the rodenty man with a control unit in his hand. The advocate Sharjah stood behind him with an expression on his face that was part shame and part sorrow, though neither for the proper reason. Mathembe glanced back to the huge, artificially grinning bioboy. And focused all her dark anger, her passion, her strength into one crushing kick to the balls.

He went down like a toppling tieve tree. Mathembe and her mother were over him and out into the night before even thought could catch them. By the left-hand wall the old man dreamed out whatever dreams the tendrils gave him. But the deep, slapping bass instrument had stopped playing.

The next morning a letter dictated by Faradje in his best civil service New Speech was sent by express byx messenger to the offices of the advocate Sharjah on Sorrowful Street informing the advocate Sharjah that his services were dispensed with forthwith, that all monies paid into his accounts would be returned immediately and without question, and explaining that, even as he was reading this note, a handwritten transcript of his unlawful practices was being delivered by Mathembe Fileli to the Department of the Fellowship of Advocates on Samtanavya Place.

The note to the advocate Sharjah was returned that evening by another byx messenger. Seemingly, that very morning the advocate Sharjah had paid off his staff, emptied out the company accounts, locked the office, and disappeared.

"Understand, kid," the head tried to explain, "no one is seduced all at once. Even when you are being conned out of your life earnings, you know you are being conned, but you also know there is nothing you can do about it. At any time you may say no, but at no time are you capable of saying it. Do you understand?"

Mathembe shook her head.

"Lot to learn about love, granddaughter of mine."

The boy came tap-tapping at the window in the heat of the heart of an Ol Tok summer night. Thunder growled like night dogs around the gutters; rain punished Ol Tok for its thousand thousand sins.

Tap tap tappy-tap.

"Hradu."

Lightning convulsed the city. Far off among the Proclaimer hills, thunder answered.

"Hradu."

He crouched on the balcony, fingernails scratching the window. Naked but for a pair of tights hand-decorated with Ykondé symbols in felt marker. Boots laced twice around the ankles. Twin deformities on his back, like amputated wings, were *pneuma* masks slung across his shoulders.

"Hradu. Wake up. Tonight. It is ready."

Hradu needed no waking.

"Tonight, Hradu. Tonight. Get dressed."

He reached for day clothes. The boy smiled, teeth bright by lightning and hologram shine.

"No, Hradu." He stepped into the room, picked up a pair of Mathembe's shorts. "We are the Tiati Omuwera Chapter. We serve the Saint Nyaja Korotindilal herself. She says to us, 'I am the one who protects you, I am the one keeps you safe. If I will you to be invulnerable you may run naked upon the blades of your enemies and none shall harm you; if I will you to die not all the armor of the Emperor himself shall save you.' Some will go naked tonight in love for the Saint Nyaja Korotindilal. But for you, these will be enough."

The boy already had one leg over the balcony. Rain streamed down his thin body. He held out a *pneuma* mask.

"Take it. Wear it. Once you put it on, they cannot stop you. You are under the guidance of the saints." The boy slipped on his own mask, swung out over Lantern Lane like a figurehead, arm stretched out behind him, gripping the railing.

"Look, Hradu. See?"

It filled Lantern Lane like a cancer. Black, wet with rain, highlighted by the oily sheen of its own organic secretions. Blue lightning, many clouds away, glistened along its ribs and spines. The tenements seemed to shy away from it, a gothic pile of black biotech half as tall as Faradje's balcony. The Ghost Boys stood waiting, rain streaming from their upturned masked faces onto the cobbles. The same violent stance, feet apart, hands relaxed, ready. Some wore shorts, some tights, some had decorated their bodies with spray paint and marker, some were naked.

"Born from the tank. Now, see how your stabilizer unit plays its part! Come, Hradu, come. Tonight!"

And they were gone.

Thunder shook Keekorok like hunted vermin. And Mathembe was awake, eyes wide, staring. Something incomplete. Something gone. Some vital component in her world disconnected.

Hradu.

In a soundless cry she was at the window. She saw the Ghost Boys vault up the flanks of the black battletrux to take positions in cupolas and howdahs. Hands reached down, dragged Hradu into a cockpit rimmed with long ivory tusks. Lantern Lane trembled as the battletrux flexed walls of muscle. Wheels ground over the cobbles.

By the time she hit the street it was an echo of many wheels and Ghost Boy laughter.

Mathembe looked up at the Five Hearts Beer girl, backlit by pulses of lightning. One look may be a prayer. She ran into the lightning. Hunting. On the corner of Toloitich Way she paused to finger-comb her rain-soaked hair back across her head. In a lightning-lit doorway a man and a woman were dancing close to the music of guitars and drums from the radio, dancing in the heat and sweat of the night. The woman wore shorts that cut tight into her crotch, a halter top, and high heels; the man overalls, jacket, and suave hat. Jeepneys splashed past, rain sheeting from the drivers' plastic rain capes and coolie hats. The black boots ran on, bells ringing.

The eyes of the prostitutes smoking in the rain under café umbrellas along Red Fort watched the girl with the silver bells pass by. Huddled in dark doors, teenage wunder-gum junkies, faces identical with numb anonymity from overabuse, saw a dark figure run through their slomo dreams but did not comprehend. Divinely lit by a videowall advertisement for a cross-river banking combine, a naked Jantic eremite, fat and pale as the slugs of Mathembe's childhood, squatted in the contemplation posture called Two Trees. Seeing Mathembe he raised himself on his hands; smiling beatifically, he squeezed out a seemingly endless turd.

Onward.

Wild neon, chrome and glass and loud loud music. Lights glaring, belching evil smoke from its triple exhausts, the streamlined tailfin lowrider pulled alongside to curb-crawl Mathembe along Penyanamama Street: Proclaimer cocks down from the hills above the Corniche, tuft-hunting along the boulevards in their imported Imperial oil-eater. They crowed and clucked and called lewd invitations and comments about the size of her breasts, all-too visible through her rain-soaked T-shirt. Mathembe ran faster. The automobile went up a gear. Mathembe slowed to a walk. The automobile slowed to a crawl. Mathembe stopped. The automobile stopped. Mathembe saw her face reflected in the ten million raindrops that clung to its streamlines. She backed away from the car, hands outspread in beseeching, one cautious ringing step at a time.

Howling and jeering, the boys waved their genitals out of the open windows, then revved off into the rain and the lightning with a squeal of tires and laughter.

Onward.

Coming out of an off-boulevard lane onto the Bourse, Mathembe ran into an army foot patrol. She and the wet, fair-haired soldiers saw each other in the same blink.

It was the tunnels under Gangerabili, and the policeperson demanding to see her public vending license.

Mathembe stopped. Mathembe turned around. Mathembe began to walk away.

" 'Ere, girlie, w'ere you fink you're goin'?"

The distance between them stretched. The short shaved hairs at the back of her neck tingled as if stroked by a lover's fingers.

" 'Ere, girlie, you stop when we bloody tell you to stop, roit?"

A side street beckoned.

"Oi, you, girlie, you bloody well stop or we bloody well blow you away, roit, girlie? Oi! Nah where she gone?"

Up. Hand over hand, panting, sweating, shivering with wet and fear, up a tangle of pipes and conduits and vines that clogged the alley mouth, up onto the roof, where she huddled knees pressed to chest in the warm acid rain, listening to the voice of the soldiers.

"Aw, leave the silly bitch. We got beddah fings a do."

God, God, she prayed in the rain and the summer thunder, *please what have I done, why can I not hold things together? All I want is to be strong. Please do not let me fail with Hradu the way I failed with my mother.*

But that is one prayer no god will answer, for gods do not appreciate human strength.

The summer storm cleared to the west. A pale gray morning settled upon Ol Tok. The rain passed. The night ended. Mathembe on her rooftop woke not realizing she had slept. She unfolded cold, rain-rusted limbs, leaned over the parapet to take in the miraculous new morning. Close eyes. Breathe in, breathe out, one two three times. She would find him. The city was vast, but she would save him from the terminal folly of the Ghost Boys. The thunder-washed air was clean as virtue, cool and sharp as wine.

The pink people pushing pink papers on pink desks managed successfully to ignore Mathembe Fileli squatting on her heels in the lobby for half a morning. When it became embarrassingly obvious that that dirty, sulky urchin was going to sit there messing up the great work of Nationalism until people stopped ignoring her, some sub-sub-assistant was dispatched to take care of her. The clean, well-clothed young woman took the slip of paper with ill-concealed distaste. The calligraphy was execrable.

"Just one moment please." A ruffle through files. "There you are." Mathembe scrawled the address on her left forearm with a marker she had stolen from a stationer's stand on Yotananda Drive.

Semi-dressed, less awake, Ghavra's astonishment at finding Mathembe behind the two-fisted hammering on his door was complex and many-layered. She pushed past him into his apartment. Ghavra closed the door to the sleeping room, directed Mathembe into his underused kitchen. Jangada poets, *political* jangada poets, *Proclaimer* political jangada poets, eat out a lot. He let Mathembe storm out her anger in the room that smelled of burned spices, walk the spirits out of her.

HRADU, Mathembe wrote in her big, silly ideograms on his white tabletop.

"What about him?"

HELP HIM.

"What do you mean, help him?"

GHOST BOYS.

"Is he involved with a chapter?"

She wagged her head, *Yes, no, sort of.*

"Is he missing from home?"

Yes.

"Gone off with them?"

Yes.

"What do you think it is I can do?"

YOU NATIONALIST. KNOW PEOPLE. CONTACTS. POWER.

"Mathembe, Mathembe, what am I? A poet who loves his country. Who listens to poets who love their country? Power? Contacts? The Ghost Boys are the law now. They are the power in this city. Not a poet. Not a Proclaimer poet."

GLASS HOUSE.

"Finished, Mathembe. Obsolete. Bypassed. The people do not want poetry. The people do not want art. The people do not want literature, they do not want a national culture. The people do not even know they have a national culture. The people want to sit in cafés and swill wine and listen to the radio and call themselves an independent nation. That is what the people want."

Mathembe circled her brother's name, three times.

"It has no power, Mathembe. That power belongs to Ourselves Alone now and the Warriors of Destiny. They hold the hearts and the minds and the spirits. They might have the power to control the Ghost Boys. The Glass House? A gaggle of old farts and young intellectuals who have catastrophically lost touch with the surface of the planet. Go to Ourselves Alone. The Glass House cannot help you. I cannot help you."

The kitchen door opened. A woman entered. She was wrapped in a silk house robe. She moved in the silky, smooth way of people who are naked beneath luxurious fabric.

"Ghavra? Love? I heard voices."

"It is all right. Eleya, this is the kid I was telling you about. Mathembe Fileli. Mathembe, Eleya. You know. I told you about her, at the Ballpark?" His eyes shone with naked love. "Mathembe, she came back! They released her! Oh, God, they released her!"

Mathembe did not hear his words. She saw only the woman: beautiful, tall, clean, full of words and cleverness and skill and talent, beautiful beautiful eyes beautiful beautiful skin beautiful beautiful hair beautiful beautiful hands that minutes before had been touching Ghavra and even now could not keep away from him, resting lightly on his shoulder.

Beautiful beautiful people. Beautiful beautiful smiles.

Mathembe mashed the point of her stolen pen into a mess of splayed black fiber. She threw over the table. She cleared shelves of spice jars herb jars glass tea canisters with a single sweep of her arm.

She ran on. She ran unable to stop for if she did stop she would never move again, pressed into the earth by the gravity of emotions she could handle only at long distance, as if they were hazardous biological waste. She had loved him. He had made her feel like something wild, like something dying and something coming to life. He had never known. In his monolithic self-obsession, he had never suspected. She ran on but she could not outrun the feelings, the feelings that had no one name to describe them but were simultaneously rage and betrayal and humiliation and desire and wanting to kill and wanting to die.

The heat and sweat of the summer night found her in a doorway in a dirty part of town. The last tram had long since crackled into its barn. The last café folded its last table and its umbrella trees closed shut for the night. The first rounds of the nocturnal killing were small, abrupt asterisks of violence punctuating the night. The line between depression and redemption is as fine as that which marks the end of night from the beginning of morning.

"Lonely? Depressed? Despairing?"

Mathembe wheeled; an angel had called her name. Angel indeed: a glowing face hovered above the sidewalk, tied by a flickering thread of laser to a rooftop projector.

"Fulfillment can be yours, joy and peace, yours, through the power of the Lord Siyaya Siyananga." The holographic face filled into a homunculus, a child, naked but for a bejeweled G-string, odiously obese, seated cross-legged on the air. A many-tiered crown rotated above his head; his left forefinger, held upright in blessing, was encircled by a halo; his right hand, palm up, held an everchanging diversity of spherical objects: heads, stars, planets, apples, Saint-ships, eyeballs, universes, plasmals. His soothing voice spoke from a talk bubble fluttering on leather wings above his shoulder. The lip synch was poor.

"The Interactive Holographic Advertising regulations require Primal Light Missions to inform you before any evangelism takes place that this simulacrum may be terminated at any time by saying the words 'Away Avaunt.'"

Mathembe growled.

"Very well. Hear, you downtrodden, you despairing, you poor, you sick, you lame and halt, you oppressed, you mourning, you defeated, you depressed: hear good news: LORD! SIYA! IS! HERE!" Explosions of pastel ideograms accompanied the great pronouncement, fading like tiny novas as Mathembe walked away down Koinange Street. The hovering avatar accompanied her.

"Hear now the marvelous truth of Lord Siyaya Siyananga!

"Untold billennia ago, in the universe that precedes ours that is called ya-Shu, dwelt a race known only as the High and Shining Ones, beings of such loveliness, such nobility, that were we to behold one in even the ten-thousandth part of his glory we would worship him as god. Such were their powers that they might have outlived the universal death, but great was their wisdom, greater than any wisdom that calls itself wise. They chose rather to pass from life, die with their universe in the glorious fire of the retrobloc. Yet, that their knowledge and power might not pass utterly from being, they caused certain artifacts of power—rings, and beacons within which the light of ya-Shu was captured—to be contained within caskets of timelessness and thus escape the destruction. For they understood that even as they had conquered wickedness in their universe and attained perfection, yet evil would arise and needs be defeated by creatures of puissance and goodness. Untold billennia the rings and beacons of power fell through space. Forever they might have fallen, but for the will of the High and Shining Ones, who caused one such ring and beacon to come to earth upon a world so incredibly remote that to begin to describe it would overrun my program parameters."

Mathembe lashed out at the hovering image. But who can strike an angel, even a holographic evangelist of Primal Light Missions?

"A simple peasant was he, our Lord, when as a boy he found the glorious artifacts, and having been judged by them time out of mind to be pure in heart, mouth, and deed, noble and upright in etiquette, was finally permitted to don the ring. Wonder! Glory! Transcendence! Power! For such was the purpose of the High and Shining Ones that whosoever was worthy of the ring might, by its power, draw upon the light of ya-Shu that was contained within the mystic beacons and, whatsoever he willed, so it would be instantly created. More: to him would be given knowledge of all things, the power to traverse from world to world with but a single step, and the possession of power and wisdom incalculable. In one instant, one glorious instant, a humble man became as the High and Shining Ones themselves.

"LORD!
"SIYAYA!
"SIYANANGA!

"Homage to Lord Siya!
"Praise to Lord Siya!
"Glory to Lord Siya: all-knowing, all-powerful, swift to rescue,

sure to redeem: Destroyer of Evil, Master of Earthly Passions, Conqueror of Sin and Failure, Guardian of Right, Defender of the Oppressed: if you but put your trust in him, he will come to you and by his power lead you on his path of purity and holiness.

"LORD!
"SIYAYA!
"SIYANANGA!"

Hands seized the talk bubble before it could flutter away. Leathery wings beat; Mathembe twisted the thing between her hands. Bones snapped, struts splintered. Organical ichor ran between her fingers onto the cobbles. The child avatar's lips moved, wordless as her own. Mathembe grinned, made an obscene gesture to Lord Siyaya Siyananga, all-knowing, all-powerful, Destroyer of Evil, Master of Earthly Passions, Guardian of Right.

Blue laser light struck dazzling to earth. A second hologram resolved itself before Mathembe: a towering Proclaimer patriarch, the Witness Rajee Rann, tall as a tenement, feet the size of municipal service organicals planted in the gutters of Koinange Street.

"Know ye God!" boomed the Witness Rajee Rann. Helicopters clattered overhead, distant and irrelevant as interstellar battlecruisers. "Know ye God, that ye may be transfigured into his likeness and attain oneness with him." A tremor shook the huge simulacrum like a lapse of faith. The guidance sensors had registered the activity of a dissenting hologram and brought a sub-routine into play.

"Blasphemer!" roared the Witness Rajee Rann. A hooked sword appeared in his left hand, striking down from heaven at the Lord Siyaya Siyananga. Primal Light Missions responded with fuzzballs of light from its avatar's right hand, where lay the power ring of the High and Shining Ones. In a flicker of clashing holograms, Mathembe Fileli slipped away. She had heard sirens dopplering along Ol Tok's sweaty boulevards, gathering at some indeterminate point into a hard knot of sound. With a clapping of rotors that drowned momentarily the acrimonious feuding of the two gods, the helicopters came about in a sweeping arc above Koinange West. As they passed over Mathembe— low, hard, fast—she broke into a run. Something in the street had called her name. The winking navigation lights guided her.

The end of the boulevard was solid vehicles and flashing lights. The helicopters that had guided Mathembe to this place hovered at rooftop height, searchlights stabbing down into the street. People had gathered. People will always gather where there are sirens and flashing lights. Unseen, untouchable as a spirit, Mathembe passed through them. The great black battletrux lay on its side against the parapet of a small municipal fountain. Ichor bled from ten, twenty, fifty bullet holes. The cobbles shone slick with it under the focused beams of helicopter light. The bodies lay on the wet boulevard. Some were attended by medicals. Some were unattended. Some were covered with sheets.

Mathembe walked on, a ghost.

Two silhouettes knelt by a dark mound. Whispers exchanged. A valise opened. The monomolecule plastic of a loop was a line of light. One of the kneeling figures grunted with brief exertion. A click, audible even over the thunder of helicopter engines. The second kneeling figure lifted the head by the hair. Two new figures pushed the headless meat into a plastic bag.

Mathembe walked on.

She found him sitting against the side of an ambulance wrapped in a thermoplastic blanket. She touched two fingers to his arm, made a small bird whistle. He looked. He recognized. He smiled. She struck him across the face. Hard. Very hard. As hard as she could strike, with all the anger and worry and fear and concern and guilt in her spirit. And in the same second she pulled him to her, embraced him, pushed his face into her shoulder, *cry now, cry*, rocked him rocked him. Rocked him.

A policeperson stood against the light from the sky. His lips moved. Mathembe frowned.

"Bloody useless racket," he shouted. "Is this one yours?"

A nod.

"Is he hurt?"

A shake. A shrug.

"I suppose you might as well get him out of here back home. It has been a bloody mess. A bloody mess."

A questioning frown.

"Stupid bloody idiots, tearing up the boulevards. Stupid bloody kids. What makes them want to go out tearing the place to pieces playing like kings of the street? Why the hell did they not stop when they saw the checkpoint? What else could they do but shoot when they saw it was not going to stop, bloody black bastard of a thing. Like something from the bottom of the South Sea, that bloody thing. Bloody mess. What a bloody mess. God knows how many dead: three? four? five? The older ones, that is who I blame. Put the kids up to it. Bare-ass naked as the day they first spoke, some of them. Can you understand that? Beyond me. A bloody mess, that is all I know it is. Bloody mess.

"Go on. Out of here. Out of my sight. I will pretend I never saw you."

She locked herself with Hradu in the uppermost bedroom. Mother banged on the door. Faradje banged on the door. Friends, neighbors banged on the door. A Dose of Worms was summoned to bang on the door. Grandfather's head shouted outside the door. Mathembe ignored them all.

First, the shock and shivering.

Second, the pleading: "Let me out, let me out, Mathembe, please."

Third, the impatience: "If you do not let me out so help me God I will . . ."

Fourth, the playacting: "I am sick, can you not see? I need help."

Fifth, the stubbornness: "If you are not going to say anything, then I am not going to say anything, and then we shall see who can go the longer without saying anything."

Sixth: the sullen silence.

Through them all, the shivering and the pleading and the impatience and the playacting and the stubbornness and the silence, Mathembe sat, Mathembe stared, Mathembe waited.

And after the silence, words.

"I am not going to excuse myself, I am not going to explain myself, I am not going to say I am sorry, not to you, because it has nothing to do with you, you bitch sitting there, always sitting there never speaking never saying a word just watching, just what is wrong in your head, just what went wrong with you in the womb, eh? Just what do you think gives you the right to say what Hradu does and what Hradu does not do, who told you you were to be my conscience, my guide, my mother? You are not my mother, understand? This is not your life, this is my life, my own; who said you could choose it for me? You do not know anything about me, not one thing. You have this idea about who I am and what I am like and how I should be and do you know what? You do not know a thing. Not a thing. You are always too busy, when are you ever here? out down in Flesh Market all the time or seeing that Proclaimer boyfriend of yours—oh, I know all about him, the Boys know all about him, lucky for you he is one of us—Ma is still getting over that thing with that lawyer, Faradje is a bum, a tit-grabbing bum, and Grandfather, he thinks he knows it all but all he does is sit around getting pissed on your money pretending he is the great Nationalist, the hero, the one who died rather than speak a word of New Speech even if he speaks it as good as the Emperor in his Jade City. At least I am doing something, not just words words words; everyone has words, all those words, and what do they do? Nothing at all, that is what they do.

"All those words about what we are going to do about Pa, all those words we wasted on the bastard Sharjah. Every one of those words was paid for in blood, in Ma's blood, and what did they do? No, I have had enough words, words about Ma, words about Pa. I do not know if he is alive or if he is dead, where he is, when he will come back to us; I have stopped thinking about that because it is all just words words words and none of them will bring him any closer or tell us if he is still alive.

"Do you not understand? If I go out with the Boys, if I stone troops, if I throw fire bombs, if I beat the shit out of Proclaimers, if I run roadblocks, if I get shot at, I am doing it for him. I am paying them back, for all the things we do not know about him, for every drop of Ma's blood, I am paying them back, I am putting right the wrong things in my own way. So, it is not your way, it is not how you would want to do it, but it is the only way I know, and you know? it makes me feel good. It is my war now, my own battle. You do not have the right, no one has the right, to take it from me. I have thought about it, I have decided, it is mine. It is between me and him and no one else."

A hundred things she should have said came welling up like blood from a wound in Mathembe's mind, each glib, each trite, each sanctimonious and hypocritical, so that for once she was glad of her gift of silence for she was shamed by her brother. And now that it was quiet and safe, came the knocking at the door and her mother's voice saying, "I think you should both come out now. There is something on the radio I think you should hear."

Hunger strike. Day 88. Nineteen twenty-seven in the evening. A news flash beamed into every ear cockle, splattered across every videowall and hologram, every municipal tram-stop television. *We are interrupting this broadcast to report the death earlier this evening of Ol Tok Councilor Adé Janderambelé on the eighty-eighth day of his hunger strike.*

And the streets and the avenues and the big bright boulevards that had been full of people hurrying on their way to cafés or restaurants with flowers and bottles of wine and boxes of imported sweet eats fall silent and immobile in shock.

They could not let it happen, how could they have let it happen? they could not let someone starve himself to death in any kind of decent civilized country. But they have. He did. Up on their hills, by their biolit poolsides, on the terraces of their country clubs, at their dinner parties and supper clubs, the Proclaimers crowed.

For a night and a day the Confessors in their ghettoes and endlessly unrolling suburbs, in their hives and tenements, in their Flesh Market and Drug Market, on their boulevards and avenues, in their doorways and tunnels kept silence. Shock. Anger. Twin spirits, joined at hip and heart, with empty, giggling brain pans.

The soldiers of the Emperor Across the River *intensified their presence.* Those were the words the Voice of the Empire beaming from the heart of the Jade City used for troop transports on every street corner; for roadblocks on every routeway between Confessor and Proclaimer boros; for helicopters beating beating beating the sky to blood above Ol Tok, enough helicopters to lift the whole city bodily into heaven and the nearer presence of the saints; for young men spread-eagled against walls while policepersons checked their smart-cards, for soldiers with sin-black data visors smashing into homes to evaporate your daughter your son your husband your wife your lover: *intensified presence.*

A night and a day of silence. And then, as if a great word had been spoken, the Confessors rose up. Anger emptied itself into violence, an unfocused expression of communal fury: Proclaimer shops looted, Proclaimer houses burned, Imperial offices stormed and torched, municipal transport smashed and set alight, trux and jeepneys maimed and slaughtered, streets barricaded with rotting flesh.

The *intensified presence* of the Emperor Across the River awoke from its dark entries and dim street corners and roared in the heat of the night. Troop carriers slewed to a halt across Ol Tok's luminous boulevards where a day and a night before people had gone with their flowers and wine and expensive sweet eats. Soldiers in bioweapon-proof riot armor armed with shock staves filed into cordons and containments. A spark was struck. A keynote sounded. The streets exploded. The directionless, unfocused rage had target and purpose now.

The people hurled themselves upon the soldiers, men and women, old and young. Understand: rage is not a thing bound by age and sex; rage is strong, rage is hot, rage is ever young. And foolish. Armed with whatever their hands found—glass cobbles, chunks of paving brick, pieces of ripped-away biotecture, smashed café furniture, blistered ceramics, fused plastic slag—they broke upon the black soldiers of the Emperor. Hands tore. Hands smashed. Hands hacked and gouged. Hands beat beat beat themselves bloody.

And the soldiers drove them back.

Again the people broke upon the adamant black edge of the Empire.

And the soldiers drove them back.

A third time the people hurled themselves upon the soldiers, like the waves of the Elder Sea where the dark things drown. They pressed and they pressed but the soldiers held them, the soldiers held them, the soldiers held them, like the land holds against the sea.

From their attics, from their fire escapes, from rooftops and tenement windows, the Warriors of Destiny saw the moment and opened fire.

Where are the Warriors? the people had asked. *Our Warriors, where are our boys?* Every soldier that fell, a neat bullet hole punched cleanly through plastic riot shield and plastic bioweapon-proof body armor, was their answer. Fifty thousand voices thundered approval. Fifty thousand fists punched air. They were committed now. No more wavering, no more indecision. The lines were drawn, war declared. Smiling, the Warriors of Destiny reloaded for their second volley. The soldiers began to be afraid. Their resolve wavered. Their advance failed. Leaving their fallen black on the shining boulevards, they withdrew to the cover of their troop transports. Charges ricocheted from their armored machines: Ghost Boy–grown battle viruses and poisons found no purchase on Imperial foundry plate. The young men, the loud bragging young men who are always at the head of any trouble, danced and jeered and lobbed fire bombs that fell in a gout of liquid flame among the dead. The mob shouted glee at every transport that backed away out of the flames.

Come on come on come on all you fine soldiers, taunted the young men. *All you fine brave soldiers hiding behind your machines, come out come out come out.*

Then a new sound was heard in the boulevards: drums. Drums drums drums. Crashing louder, louder even than the sound of the fluttering, useless helicopters, shaking the city by its throat, *Step in time with us. With us.* The people hesitated, drew back. For they had seen the banners, and the proud marching men, and the glint of neon from the beating drums. The Proclaimers. Come down from their hills and suburbs and country clubs and supper parties, ordered up beneath the banners of the Spirit Lodges, marching to the beat of their man-skin drums to the aid of their Empire when their Emperor had most need of them. Loyal and true. The banners hung limply in the thick heat of the night. Drums beating beating beating, the Proclaimers formed up behind the beaten soldiers of the Emperor. When you know there is someone at your back, that you are not naked and alone in a thousand kilometers of alien and hostile land, that puts fiber in your muscles, stiffness in your back, fire in your heart and hands. You are a soldier of the Emperor, that is what you are. You are not a mudman, you do not need mudmen to tell you that.

The fine, brave soldiers came. Out from behind their transports they came firing. Firing and firing and firing their weapons. And the mob screamed and the mob broke and the mob ran and the mob that was no mob now but only people, an atomic sea of fleeing individuals, tried to hide but the soldiers kept coming, firing and firing and firing. They had been made to look shameful, and no soldier will tolerate to be humiliated by mudmen.

The mudmen went down before them.

Behind the advancing lines of troop carriers came the Proclaimers, drum skins bloody from beating hands, banners leaning in red pursuit. In their attics and rooftops, the Warriors of Destiny let off a rattle of fire; soldiers went down, banners waved and keeled. Laser sights weaved across the skyline of Ol Tok; then the heavy turret-mounted weapons gave answer and the Warriors of Destiny had no reply. The people fled before the soldiers, but they were soldiers, men who are given orders and obey orders: their black-uniformed officers called a halt to their advance and they stopped to take prisoners capture weapons aid the wounded and the maimed. But the Proclaimers poured on, running now, scooping up discarded clubs, spears, blades. They had the scent of it now. One thousand years of passion is not restrained by the command *Halt!*

They stayed by the radio deep into the morning in the apartment on Lantern Lane, never straying more than necessity demanded from the receiver with its always reasonable, always right Voice of the Empire. They feared they might not be included in a solidifying moment of history.

Widespread civil disturbances are still being reported in districts of Ol Tok. Large-scale looting and destruction of property are continuing, though crowds of demonstrators are being dispersed by police and army. Disturbances have also been reported in Oldonok and Kuwera, and many rural prefecture roads have been blocked by armed vigilantes. Police barracks and army outposts have been attacked.

"It is the Rising, the Rising!" shouted the head. "At last, at last, the people have risen!"

"Shut up, you old fool," said Mathembe's mother.

In the cities and towns, Proclaimer communities have been arming themselves and sealing off entire districts in expectation of attack by Confessor mobs, though as yet there have been reports of only minor sectarian skirmishes. Communications with outlying regions have been badly disrupted. In Ol Tok security forces have come under fire from units of the Warriors of Destiny and have returned fire. A number of arrests have been made. Army and police casualties are described as minimal. An assault on civil service headquarters has been repelled.

"More the pity," said Faradje. The apartment trembled as a helicopter thundered over at rooftop height. The sound of many vehicles, many engines, many track links passing down Keekorok Boulevard reverberated in Lantern Lane's crevices and acoustic crannies. Faradje lifted the tiny organical to his ear. Frowned. Stared in naked disbelief at the device in his hands. Went out onto the balcony, raised the little radio above his head. Threw it down with all his strength. The radio burst on the cobbles in a mess of sap and circuitry.

"I will not have lies in my house," he said. "I will not have lies. This is not a house of lies. They said Bujumbura Ballpark was burning. They said we had done it. We had set light to them, to our own."

With the radio dead the people in the apartment now had only the sound of the street from which to piece together the thing that was happening to their city. Snap and crack of gunfire. Clatter of forged steel tracks. Heavy stammer of automatic weapon fire, frighteningly close and sudden. Shouting voices, voices as devoid of words as Mathembe's. Far removed: rataplan of drums drums drums, engines, radios, the flat, remote blare of overamplified voices. Close, intimate: a soul swearing elegiacally, almost in religious ecstasy. Universal, omnipresent: the beating wings of the Emperor's war helicopters.

And then a new sound. A startling sound. The sound of the harsh, incongruous syllables of the men from across the river.

It was a stupid thing to do, to rush to the balcony to see what the voices of the Emperor were doing down in Lantern Lane. But what is one more stupidity in the vaster and nobler stupidity that was engulfing the city? They saw that every other balcony was filled with stupid, curious people just like themselves.

There were two soldiers down there. Somehow, God only knew how, they had come blundering in on unarmored tryx. Reconnoitering. Cut off from their squad. Messengers. Lost. Sightseeing. War sacramentalizes our stupidities. But they must have realized they were far from home, for they looked up and saw the eyes watching them from Lantern Lane's many many balconies. And if that were not certainty enough, the hands convinced them. One hand first, slapping balcony railing: *slap sla-sla-slap*. The rhythm passed from balcony to balcony, hand to hand. *Slap sla-sla-slap.* The hands beat, the eyes looked down into the sounding drum that was Lantern Lane. The doors opened. The men stood in the open doorways. The men knew and the soldiers knew and every hand beating every railing *slap sla-sla-slap* knew.

They were the mob's now.

The soldiers tried to kick their tryx into motion but the *slap sla-sla-slap* had spooked the organicals. They revved. They whined. They ran in mindless circles. The soldiers swore horribly but could not control their mounts.

The men stepped out of their open doorways. The soldiers were encircled. One of the soldiers was screaming into his helmet microphone, but the *slap sla-sla-slap, slap sla-sla-slap* screamed louder. Louder. Faster. Louder louder. Faster faster. Louderlouder fasterfaster.

And stopped.

The first stone was thrown. A soldier fell from his tryx, clutching his face. The stone had shattered his data visor, driven spears of plastic into his eyes. Blood squeezed from between his fingers. The blood excited the mob. The holy silence broke in a purr of delight. The men rushed in upon the soldiers.

Mathembe shrieked, reached forward as Hradu swung himself over the balcony, went hand over hand down the ducting and pipework to join the mob. She was half over the railing to drag him back from the brink of irrevocable action. Faradje's hand on her collar stayed her.

"Leave him. Leave him. They will tear apart anyone who tries to stop them. They do not care who. There is nothing you can do. Come inside. We do not want to see this."

Mathembe snatched free from Faradje's gentle grip. She would stay. She would see.

Lantern Lane was a sea of heads and hands and fists raised against heaven, highlighted by the smile of the Five Hearts Beer girl.

What do you think of this, Lady of the Boulevards? Sacrifice enough for you?

A shot split the night.

The mob quivered.

A second shot. The mob fell back, growling, surly. One soldier remained standing. He waved his weapon in the face of the mob. He was shouting, New Speech, his mother tongue. All that could be understood was the fear in his voice, and that required no translator. His helmet had been lost. His hair shone golden blond in the hologram light. So young. Screaming still in his incomprehensible New Speech, he dragged his friend across the greasy cobbles to the door of a dead and derelict tenement house. Fear gave him a strength the mob respected.

The synthetic flesh of the two tryx had been stamped into the cobbles. Ceramoplastic bones had been torn out for use as weapons.

The screaming blond soldier blew in the door with a pulse of his weapon. He dragged his friend inside. From her place above the crowd Mathembe could not tell if his comrade was alive or dead. The surface tension was pierced. The mob rushed into the empty space. Some charged the doorway and were driven back by fire from the soldier's weapon. Some dragged shattered limbs, some sat clutching their faces, some lay hands raised in the air, some lay unmoving in strange, unnatural postures.

Stones bones bottles cobbles rained against the dead house. The mob fell upon the house, beat it with their fists. We . . . are . . . coming . . . to . . . kill . . . you. . . . We . . . are . . . coming . . . to . . . kill . . . you. . . . We . . . are . . . coming . . . to . . . kill . . . you.

Then someone struck fire.

The people sighed a huge, wondering sigh, drew back from the holy fire. The fire was passed from hand to hand, split into many fires. The young men, the fire bearers, lifted their flames high for the people to see and threw them down at the base of the house. The flames flickered doubtfully. Some guttered low. Some guttered out. A wind from across the river blew into Lantern Lane. The wind gave heart to the flames, carried them up the bulging sides of the dead house. Ancient tinder-dry lignoplastic blistered, popped, exploded into flame. Fire raced up the face of the tenement. Again, the mob sighed its huge, wondering sigh. Mathembe caught sight of Hradu's face, there in the front row, upturned with the others, lit red by the flames.

The long, licking flames sent final flickers of sentience through the long-cold neural pathways of the house. Fire. Pain. Burning. It woke. It screamed, every window and entry opened wide. Out of the mouth of that terminal scream came the soldier. Leaping out in a graceful dive. Arms outstretched, like the falling saints of the Ykondé pantheon. He fell toward the waiting mob.

He seemed to take a very long time to fall.

The mob raised its fists and stones and bones and Mathembe could not look any more.

We are strong.

We are strong.

We are the people. The people.

We shall stand by ourselves. Alone.

The house was one great flame now. Sparks poured up into the night. By the fire's red light the people passed from hand to hand to hand the things they had scavenged from the soldier. Scraps of cloth. Boots. Bootlaces. Wallet. Photographs of lovers. Shards of shattered helmet. The heart-in-hand badge of the aged aged Emperor. The black weapon. Glowing red flakes settled on the men's hair and hands and clothing as they paraded the looted things above their heads like icons in a festival. They did not notice. Glowing red flakes of ash settled on the roofs and balconies of their homes. They did not notice. The burning house collapsed in coals and molten plastics.

It was over. It was broken.

The men saw what they held in their hands and were ashamed. They tried to put them down, put them away, but their hands would not let them. The bones, the scraps, the wallet, the photographs clung to their hands. As the strong wind from across the river swirled and eddied, they looked at their hands. They did not see, no one saw, the flames running under the windows along the edge of the roofs, the flames leaping from rooftop to rooftop to rooftop, leaping like Nyakabindi demon dancers across the narrow canyon of Lantern Lane.

Then one man felt a falling flake of ash stroke his face and burn him. He looked up. The wind blew, hard, and the entire street was on fire.

"My God my God my God!" he shouted. "There are people in those houses!"

A blue lightning flash, a huge blast. Lantern Lane shook. Mathembe rocked on her unsteady perch. Ribbons of plastic membrane rained down into the street. The tethered gloglobes had detonated. A dying globe collapsed in flames onto the roof of Faradje's tenement house. Mathembe leapt back into the apartment as a curtain of fire fell on the balcony.

"Down, down," Mathembe's mother shouted, and she was again the brilliant, competent woman Mathembe had always known. The fire had reignited her spirit. "Down. Downstairs."

Faradje stood like a fool in paradise in the living room, arms spread wide wanting to take every scrap of his comfortable life with him, unable to make the cruelest of choices, to play the five-minute game. His sister seized his fat arm, propelled him down the stairs. Smoke filled the evil-smelling room; Mrs. Fileli snatched up the head. Without a backward look she was down the stairs and pushing Faradje through the gently falling drops of blazing plastic. Mathembe, in the street, among the wheeling, bellowing people and the soft snow of ash, took the head. The Five Hearts Beer girl was haloed in flames. Cool cool moisture dewed the sacramental bottle. *I have done my best, sole and faithful worshiper.* Now is Götterdämmerung. With a final wink and a smile, the tanks of laser coolant exploded spectacularly. Shards of hologram fell sparkling into Lantern Lane as wild lasers raked the street, uncontrolled, sinful. Where laser struck god-shard, an image of the Five Hearts Beer girl was impressed indelibly into the glass cobbles.

Hradu? Mathembe asked with her body. Her mother shrugged, a terrible, careless, abandoning shrug. Mother, daughter, uncle, head fled with the tail end of refugees between monumental pillars of fire onto Keekorok Boulevard. In a gout of flame and sparks, Faradje's tenement block folded in onto itself.

An entire boro was burning. The evacuees backed across Keekorok Boulevard. Though the heat was infernal, they were tied there by the fascination of fire. Sirens became audible over the roar and suck of destruction. Personnel carriers came pounding down Keekorok Boulevard, slammed to a halt at threatening angles. Troops poured out—black troops, with flames reflected in their night visors. They formed a cordon line down the smoke-filled boulevard. The wide street was littered with the detritus of riot.

The people were afraid. Much afraid. The fire had only been destruction; the soldiers of the Emperor were fear itself. Not even God could tell what they might do in their anger. The soldiers moved into position between the people and the fire. An officer struggled to make himself heard over the burning.

"You cannot stay here," he shouted. "It is not safe. Move on back down the boulevard."

"Those are our houses!" someone answered him.

"Were our houses," someone close by muttered.

"It is not safe to remain here," the officer said again. "We have orders to evacuate all the way out to Red Hill. Please. Go now, before it is too late and we are all cut off."

A burning building on the end of Lantern Lane toppled into Keekorok Boulevard. Without waiting for the soldiers, the people drew back toward Ogundelé Plaza and River Way.

"Pray the wind does not change," said a man next to Mathembe who had lived with his sick wife in the apartment next to Faradje. Mathembe watched the flames leaping greedily to catch the stars and burn them. Helicopters passed overhead: always, always, helicopters. There was an explosion, hard, flat. And another. And another. Close by. Four. Five. Six. A woman started to scream and would not stop.

"They are blowing up the houses!" cried a young woman. "They are blasting a firebreak with air-to-surface missiles!"

"No, it is biogas plants going up," said a fat woman, shiny with smoke and sweat. A seventh blast shattered Keekorok Boulevard. A spinning object arced high through the air, trailing flames, fell to earth somewhere close to Kiyoyo Avenue.

"They have evacuated as far as Kijembe," said a girl who had saved only the cockle radio in her ear.

Then Mathembe felt a breeze stroke her face, her hand, ruffle her hair.

"Oh dear God dear God dear God!" a woman shouted for all of them. Down toward Ladywell, the flames were bending low across Keekorok Boulevard to touch the banks and cafés and insurance houses and set them burning.

"Stay exactly where you are!" shouted the officer, but Mathembe could hear the uncertainty in his voice, the hesitation that is fatal to authority. "The situation is under control. There is no cause for panic. The situation is under control. We will withdrew in an orderly and systematic fashion toward Ogundelé Plaza."

Perhaps if he had not said "The situation is under control" the people would not have panicked. But it is to those words that the fear in the voice most attaches itself, and the fear ran faster than even the flames running along the rooftops of Keekorok Boulevard. Each smelled the fire, imagined their flesh crackling and searing and charring and burning, their souls going up in white heat. The people broke and ran. Civilians, soldiers, Confessors, Proclaimers. The confused, brave officer was trampled down. Community no more. Discipline no more. Morality no more. The sole good is one's self.

But the fire outran them. The First Keekorok Savings Factor and Credit Union crashed into the street. Penned in by flame on three sides, the people tore their way through the tangle of narrow streets to the west of Keekorok. Bodies surged through the closes and entries, filled them with their rising tide as behind them the red glow in the sky grew wider, taller. Mathembe, her mother, her uncle, the head were carried along in the flood of fear. Mathembe saw her mother's face, her mother's arm outstretched, saw the bodies press between, saw her mother carried away from her, swept away into a different stream, down a different street, along different closes and courses.

Alone.

On. On. Do not look up to see if the flames are outracing you from rooftop to rooftop. Do not look up to see the glow in the sky spread until half the night is on fire. Do not look up when you hear the shatter of blades overhead so low that you would cry out in fear had you breath, had you life, had you energy to do anything but run. Do not look up. Look down. Your enemies are not the flames. Your enemies are your fellow humans. Look down. Watch your feet, for if you trip, if you fall, they will crush you without a thought. Look down, look carefully, watch their feet: a gun, a smashed drum, a broken mask, a toppled newsstand, a cracked crystal column leaking organical ichor—no head to be seen—a tattered shop awning, cartridge cases, a torn shirt: a body, oh God a body you cannot avoid it, you hurdle over it you cannot avoid looking at the face, you know it you know it, it is it is . . .

No. You only thought you knew it.

It had not been him.

It had not been Ghavra, the Proclaimer political jangada poet.

On. On.

But you had wished, for an instant, that it had been him. It would have been worthy punishment for a faithless Proclaimer political jangada poet. And then you are sorry. Ghavra, wherever you are, whatever you are fighting with, be alive.

Then, stillness: no movement in the packed mass of bodies. Voices: New Speech. A smell: within, above, beyond the smell of smoke and fire, a deep womb-water smell, the river. A sound: within, beyond, above the sirens and the thunder of burning, the threshing of riverboats. A vision: lights moving in the offing, massive rafts of barges and lighters, like entire floating cities, maneuvering out there in the flame-lit water. Shapes moving: riverboats? shuttleboats? ferries?

Hair matting under your feet, not cobbles.

Water, not buildings all close around you.

Fear to your left: *Where are we going, where are we going?*

Fear to your right: *They are taking us off on ferries, out to the riverboats.*

Fear in front of you: *The radio says the Warriors are still fighting; there are uprisings now in every prefecture in the land.*

Fear behind you: *Where can we go now? Where will they take us if the whole land is rising up against the Emperor? Across the river? Are we to be hostages for our land?*

"Let us off, let us off!" the head cradled in Mathembe's arms shouted. "We cannot go onto a riverboat, we have people back there." But it was just another voice among the ten thousand pushing down the river steps toward the flame-red waters. Fat, awkward ferries moved in toward the shore, ran their boarding ramps up against the holy steps where the pilgrims washed their sins away. Beyond those nearer craft, out in the deep-water channel, ferries were off-loading earlier cargoes of refugees onto the barges and floats and lighters, all lit red, green, gold with riding lights. The evacuees swept toward the boarding ramps, up onto the boats, faces lit red, gold, green by the great burning behind them. Even as the ferry captains pulled up their ramps, pulled away from the sacred steps, engine muscles groaning at the burden of lives, a few souls clung to ropes, plastic trux-tire buffers, waded chest deep into the flame-red water toward reaching hands.

Mathembe struggled to escape the inexorable press of bodies onto the boats, pushed back toward the Corniche. A soldier stopped her on the river steps.

"Sorry," he said. His Old Speech was atrocious.

"Her mother my daughter her brother my grandson her uncle," the head jabbered, crazy and incoherent with the spirit of panic.

"Sorry," said the soldier. "None go back there. God knows how many dead: fire, fighting. God knows. Must to go on ferryboat."

The red, green, gold light in Mathembe's eyes read *desperation*.

"Make to river, all of you," said the soldier. "Be all right. Find again when all is over. Go. Now." The soldier gently pushed Mathembe into a column of people moving up and onto a ferry. The soldier was a year at most older than she was. His long hair, clasped with the hand of the Emperor, was the color of the sun.

A man with a gene-shape bird toy in a cage helped Mathembe to the side of the boat. Mathembe balanced the head carefully on the rail. He balanced his bird in its cage beside her head. One by one the boats retracted their ramps. Paddlewheels trod water; the boats moved into the deep water where the big commercial ships waited.

The ferryboat turned, swept Mathembe with her grandfather across an awesome panorama. The city was one great flame now, lit sporadically by detonations and rocked by bursts of weapon fire. Bourse and Corniche were all heads, hands, faces. Then the current caught the ferry, turned it into the deep flow. The paddlewheel thrashed and Mathembe was carried away, out into the black night and the dark water and the waiting nation of barges and lighters and dispossession. Helicopters, jeweled clusters of navigation lights in the black velvet night, roared low overhead, headed east toward the burning city.

THE
RIVER

THREE NAMES.

On the day that the Captain's second grandson was born a school of deep-river dolphins was sighted, an auspicious omen meaning that here, waving its minuscule hands, screwing up its minuscule eyes, was one whose blood was mingled with river water deep and clear, indissolubly bound by the soul to the flow of the water. On the day that Two—to which his family name of Number-Two-Grandson-of-the-Fifty-ninth-Captain was abbreviated—was given his crew name Feeder-of-Heads (Feeder, thereafter), a raft island, an occasional agglomerate of hybrid biotech, was spotted. On the raft island grew seven fan trees. In each of the seven fan trees perched seven birds. Around each of the seven birds that perched on the seven trees floated seven shimmering bubbles. That was the best of all possible signs, according to the old people on the aft deck, more than halfway both geographically and spiritually to the Well of Spirits, though none was able to calculate whether the seven times seven times seven portended favor in love, fortune in business, length of years, multiplicity of descendants, or enormous genitalia.

Number-Two-Grandson-of-the-Fifty-ninth-Captain Feeder-of-Heads received his third and last name (unless by some catastrophe of succession he became Captain), his state name, Undersecretary to the President, three days before the exodus from Ol Tok.

Three names, one name.

Unchunkolo was the third by direct descent to bear the name on the river. Sister ships, birthed at the once-in-a-generation Great Meetings, bore other names; their gene lines were not pure, unsullied. Only *Unchunkolo III* could trace her ancestry to that first *Unchunkolo* that had carried settlers from the Empire shore across the waters to new lands a thousand years ago. Now, with three hundred years of river water beneath her blunt bows, the time was drawing near for *Unchunkolo* to pass seed and matronymic to another.

Unchunkolo. No definite article. Never *the Unchunkolo.* Tell me this, when you go up to town on the country bus to trade, to buy a little, sell a little, deal a little, drink a little wine and tea, do you say, today I am going to *the* Timboroa, *the* Cucuyonbayé, *the* Lapsanjabet? When you meet a woman in the cool of the shade trees by the light of the moon, when you tell your friends the next day what you did there and where and how often, do you say, Tonight I will take *the* Jhelé out dancing; tonight I will sing to *the* Lititta by the light of the moon with a small guitar; today in the cool of the shade trees I shall ask *the* Luwayo to be my partner? *Unchunkolo.* No definite article.

In her three centuries she has grown with the twelve generations that have lived and reproduced and died within her body, putting out new decks and ramps, shooting up derricks and gantries, cupolas and pergolas and gazebos, bridges and davits and companionways, growing accommodation pods, agricultural blisters, sending out domes and arches of plastic flesh. And all that time the great muscle machine that is her beating heart has turned that big stern wheel, pushing rafts of lighters and barges and pontoons loaded with organochemical processors, meatplants, live-fur tanks, consumer electronics, mass market shoes, pulp timber, from port to port all along the river. Before that beating heart falls still and her family that is her crew abandon her to the current that will take her down to Elder Sea and the forgetting, she will have pushed an entire planet's weight of merchandise up and down that big river.

Three names, one name.

No name.

The river is like God. As you draw closer to it, the names fade; as you pass into it, all names are dissolved into its waters. You hinterland people horizoned all your lives by land, who have never known the scent of deep waters or felt the pull of the flow in your spirits, you mining-town and mill-town people have names for it. Names like Lualaba and Ganjacee and Tubinreya. Many names, many tongues, all of them the same: Mother of Waters. And you teeming millions to whom the throb of ferryboat engines among islands, the sight of great rafts of timber or baled waterweeds or organochemical plants like small floating cities are as familiar as the color of your children's hair; you who take your livelihood, your eating and drinking and washing from it and return every night to your homes along the riverain coast, it is more than Mother of Waters. It is *the River*. No more. No less.

But to you river people, you who are bound by the waters of your wombs to it all your lives, you captains, you engineers, you clansfolk, you lifters and loaders and crane operators, you fisherpeople, you sweet brown diving girls, you ferrymen, you pilots and navigators, it is not even *the River*. It is something deeper and more reverential than that. You call it *she*.

She is looking kind today.

I think *she* is going to blow up bad today.

I had a load far down; you know, where *she* runs out into the sea.

She.

Before Empire and Province, *she* was.

Before Proclaimer and Confessor, *she* was.

Before the Daughter Worlds, before the stars themselves were reached and let go again, as a child will abandon an outgrown toy, *she* was.

Before Green Wave, before Gray Age, before organical and mechanical, before the great technological breakthrough that enabled the human nervous system to directly manipulate DNA, *she* was.

Before all science, before all knowledge, before all history, before all legend, *she* was.

Before the word, *she* was. Before the name. Before man. Before ice, before fire, before earth and sky, *she* was.

While *Unchunkolo* and her nineteen sisters were still shrouded in the night fog that rose from the river, Two was up out of his hammock and about his business. His bed on the rear deck, close by the Well of Spirits where his ancestors dreamed eternity away, had become markedly less comfortable since First Mate had bought a new *red* automobile on the Empire side of the river and, suddenly stuck for storage, had suspended the thing from a derrick above Two's dreaming head. One does not sleep well with a ton of Imperial steel creaking and swaying overhead. And these days of days, Two needed his sleep. With the refugee crisis, he had risen to temporary prominence in *Unchunkolo*'s political system.

He woke with a grumble and a shiver. Work to do. The camera crews were coming. You heard them before you saw them: the drone of organical outboards in the mist. Then you saw the prickle of light from their riding lights; then, moments later, the long gray shadows darting, knifing out of the rolls of cold-water fog. Pirogues, outriggers, each with its complement of soundpersons tapping meters and checking power packs, and camerapersons bitching about light levels and the bilgewater that was *ruining* their five-hundred-a-pair All Terrain Boots, and reporters applying bags under their eyes and a little judicious grime so that half a planet of viewing public would be convinced they were sharing the living hell of the thousands of refugees stranded in mid-channel by a ghastly comedy of political fudging and not, in fact, fresh from steak-and-wine breakfasts in the Riverside Hotel.

As Junior Undersecretary to the President, Two had been given the job of liaising with the news teams. Onshore it would have fallen to External Affairs, and his Cousin Lifter, a girl a year older than Two, into her body in no small manner and making it no secret that she wished to be equally into Two's, would have been Ship's Liaison. But here the reporters came to the ship, so it was Internal Affairs. External Affairs claimed to retain control of the language brainplants, which invariably meant an official visit from Junior Undersecretary to Foreign Minister Lifter and some minutes of minor sexual harassment.

A pirogue drew along *Unchunkolo*'s monolithic flank, engine idling, eating water with a voracious gobble of hydrocarbons and froth. The news team came trepidaciously up the access ramps. The wide-mouthed woman with the very clean hair who was the chief correspondent seemed to find the notion of living flesh and hair matting under her feet repugnant.

"In the name of the Captain and crew of the Mercantile Para-State of *Unchunkolo the Third*, you are most welcome aboard," said Two in the half-dozen languages he had memorized. Straight New Speech. Good. All riverboat folk were born bilingual. "I am here to assist you in every possible way. If there is anything you require, I shall do my best to arrange it for you."

Requirements were: One toilet. A drink—oh God!—of *some-thing*. A fistful of analgesics. And none of those endorphin-secreting mold patches, either. Something to eat; the food in the hotel is *shit*, dear, shit. And they wouldn't happen to have an omnidirectional high-impedance microphone, would they?

Bloody savages.

The cameraperson wanted shots of the *meat* fighting when the black marketeers came. Which they did an hour or so after the camera crews; they were more chary of their boats in the fog, they could not afford the insurance. Looks good, women fighting for food. Gets the sympathy glands going. Maybe we could go down to the pointy end—what do you call it, the bow? yes, there—so lead on, no we do not want shots of mothers with babies, dear thing, we are inundated, positively inundated with shots of mothers with babies, and, well, frankly, dear thing, it does not work any more. Gets anesthetized to it eventually, does your Joe Television. Burns? Burns, darling. Where? Body and chest, that all right? Yes, that would be all right. We will get back to you in a minute, yes, just a minute. If you'll sign this release form. Facial burns? Can we use facial burns? No? Sorry, can't use facial burns. Oh, now, this is good. This is very good. Yes, come on, lovely lighting, lovely God-shot with the sun breaking through the fog banks. Wonderful. Just hold it, excuse me, you people, could you just hold that pose, just stay where you are one moment longer?

No, we cannot hold, we will not hold, why should we hold for you smelling of steak-and-wine breakfast in the Riverside Hotel? No, here come the traders, cutting in in their dinghies and outriggers, the traders standing up and smiling and holding up cartons of baby milk and fresh flopping fish expiring their last in the clearing fog of early morning and fresh green mangoes and plastic-wrapped slabs of brownmeat and whitemeat and breadapple, vials of glittering viruses protruding from between their fingers; why should we hold it for you? to hell with you piss on you shit on you if I hold for you I will miss my place at the rail someone will get there before me with their radio or watch or family ornaments or piece of jewelry or clothes or boots or handkerchiefs or antique tea sets or holy medals or anything and everything that might be negotiable.

But the cameras moved through them regardless, catching the reaching hands and the imploring faces and the traders standing in their boats weighing and judging and valuing and transacting or not transacting and the correspondent saying she had never seen human need and suffering on such a scale before nor such a display of naked human greed and avarice as the traders who came out in their boats every morning to take away the people's lives little by little and that the twenty riverboats held off the Imperial coast by gunboats could only be days, days away from a major human catastrophe and the cameraperson was shouting *Hold it hold it, you got to see this, this is classic, classic television* and a woman too distraught to display any emotion but desperate bewilderment was holding out her baby to the traders, legs walking upon the water, *Take it take it, I do not want anything in return only take it away from this please* and the traders were shaking their heads and grinning, *No profit no gain no trade not negotiable not transactable no deal no sale no value no worth.*

Then the strong ones came. They pushed the weak ones, the women, the children, the old, and the young; they pushed them aside. Those who had not learned their proper place in the order of things, who dared to raise a fist in defiance, they were smashed down. Men beat other men with that straight-armed blow brought straight down on the head that is so terrifying to see because it is so unlike the glamorous gorgeous violence of television or *wakinéma*, that is the violent heart of man exposed. And women too were fighting now, in the way women fight that is based on the idea of thrusting fingers up to the knuckles in your enemy's eye sockets.

Good good great great classic television classic television naked human drama at its finest.

The Televisual Uncertainty Principle: The act of turning a

television camera upon something changes its very nature. The act of *watching*—in your family room in your café on your ionospheric cruiser on the stratoscraper videowall on your wrist in the depths of the forest—makes it different. Without the cameraperson and the soundperson and the correspondent, there is no suffering.

It had been different, then. Before the cameras. There had been a quiet dignity among the people crowded onto *Unchunkolo*'s barges and lighters as she slipped downstream on the flame-colored waters, a sense of solidarity: families had helped each other make shelters out of plastic sheeting and empty containers and plastic chemical drums; hoarded food was brought out and shared; those with radios had stood them on upturned plastic drums for added resonance; and all had gathered around to listen to the cool, calm, utterly unbelievable Voice of the Empire reading reports of an entire land dragged by one misfired shot into a piecemeal, directionless uprising. This was not the dream of the heroes. This was not the great rising by the moon. This was Ghost Boys attacking fortified army posts armed only with the spirits of the Ancestors. This was Kiminini and Kimilili smoked out of their police station, hamstrung and dragged to bloody pulp behind their tryx around and around and around Tetsenok Square. This was Proclaimer districts sacked and burned. This was Imperialists turned out of their beds, lined up against some café wall, and shot through the left eye. This was Warriors of Destiny and Imperial forces in pitched battle on the burning streets of Ol Tok. This was as vicious as two drunken women fighting in an alleyway. This was as cruel as a father raping his daughter. There was no beauty in this. There was no nobility in this. This was war.

In the night as *Unchunkolo* drifted past the burning shore, she and her sisters from Ol Tok were joined by small flotillas putting out from each of the right-bank ports they passed, loaded to the waterline with the fearful and the hopeful and the just damned tired. The captains conferred by the satellites that went tumbling high high above the fighting land: Yembé, the major port of Kulubayé Prefecture, lay sixty kilometers to the south. There perhaps they might find haven. Sixty-three ships, more riverboats than had ever been gathered in stream at one time, ran south with the flow to Yembé. Gunboats met them under the dawn sky: low, black Imperial cutters, built low and fast, like speed dogs. Yembé was closed. Yembé had been seized by the rebels and was now under siege by Imperial forces.

Yembé was a plague city.

Warriors and Imperials were fighting it out street by street with biological weapons and isolation suits.

On their bridges, the captains activated teleconferencing facilities never used within living memory.

Where?

Where the riverboat people had ever gone when the flow was hard against them. South. Into the Thousand Islands.

Now even the Thousand Islands and what they had found there was far behind, churned up into white wake, and Two sat on a mooring bollard where *Unchunkolo*'s thick plastic lips nuzzled against the steel and wood of the barges watching the reaching hands and the pressing bodies and the darting, invasive cameras.

The woman correspondent with the bobbed fair hair wanted an interview. Could the riverboat boy translate?

Yes, the Junior Undersecretary to the President could.

Bloody savages.

You. Yes, you. We would like to talk to you. Tell him we would like to talk to him. Ask him how long he has been here.

He has been here since the night of the fire. In Ol Tok. Three weeks.

And is he alone, or does he have family with him?

He has a wife and five children. His youngest child—the name translates as Thankfully-the-Last—is very sick.

And has he had any food from the relief agencies?

The last meal he had was two days ago. He has bartered for food with the boat traders. He has not heard of any supplies, any relief agencies. He asks, Is this a joke? If it is, he apologizes for not appreciating the humor.

Could you ask him if he or his family have received any medical treatment?

He says that the healers come every day at noon: the foreign doctors—he thinks they are from the United Republics. No, he has not had any treatment from them, though his children are receiving viral treatment for diarrhea and dehydration. It is from drinking river water, he says. The healers are very good but they have limited medical

supplies. That is why he has not gone himself; he thinks they should
be kept for those who need them more.

What would he say if we were to tell him that international relief
could be here by nightfall?

He would say thank you very much, but he does not need
international relief. He does not need powdered milk and foodplants
with A *Gift from the People of the United Republics* on them, he does
not need teams of international healers from the Heptarchy; all he
needs for himself and his family is for the Empire to withdraw its
gunboats and open its ports to its own citizens.

Has he heard reports that the rebellion in his home province has
been largely put down and that a general call to dump arms and
surrender is likely?

He says that if rumors were meat there would be none hungry on
these boats.

Okay, thank you. Thank him, will you? Oh, geez, almost forgot.
Here's twenty. Should get him something from the boat traders,
something for his little girl, what does he call her, Thank-God-It's-
Over? So, how much of this can we use, then?

Not sure. Five, maybe ten percent? I hate when they get cynical.
Makes them look like ungrateful bastards.

Still, the children were good.

The children were beaut. Well, if I can talk the Captain of this
shitbucket into letting us use the satellite link, I will get this edited
down and wire it. More would be better, though. Yes! Yes, yes, you
there, yes, you with the burns . . .

The river was wide at Yembé, twenty kilometers wide, wide
enough for a whole fleet to ghost past on the edge of the horizon out
of the sight of the quarantine flags and the pyres of smoke going up in
steady parallel columns. Helicopters shadowed the fleet, dirty, irritating insects, probing and sniffing with an angry drone of engines. The
ships pressed on. On the barges the refugees gathered by moonlight
and listened to the voices of the radios. They had radios, then. The
Voice of the Empire, always calm, always collected, always cool and
right and reasonable, told them of immense victories and utter routs,
of anarchy punished and order restored and the bright name of the
Emperor carried like a banner into the vile dens of lawlessness and
rebellion.

No one believed a word of it. But they listened, because lies are more comforting than silence.

All night they ran with their cargo down the current. With morning came the Thousand Islands. South of Yembé the river broke, as if confused by its sudden loss of impetus, into a labyrinth of forested islands and shifting sandbars. No maps existed of the shoals and shallows of the Thousand Islands. Every winter flood rearranged entire geographies: whole islands, thickly forested, often inhabited, could be eroded away in a single season; dreams, hopes, dreads carried down in a thin film of silt to the delta, where the cities on the edge of Elder Sea stood upon strata of sedimented memory. On this stretch of the run south the navigator's art came into its own; her skill at interpreting the sonar map of the riverbed perhaps the difference between a cargo delivered as per contract and an entire season spent stranded on a sandbar waiting for the level to rise with the winter rains. River legend had it that many inhabited islands were the remains of ships and crews that had run aground; the ships' organical systems colonized the bleak sandbars and eventually dissolved into plastic ribs and spars, draped with weed and creeper, while the crews' descendants sported in sybaritic barbarism within the dark enfolding forest.

The Thousand Islands, and the rain. The barges were a patchwork of colored plastic sheeting where the refugees had rigged makeshift shelters from discarded cargo coverings. The slow, heavy rain was a drum-beat roar on the stretched plastic, the river alive with falling drops. *Unchunkolo* pushed through the gray veils of rain, seeking out true channels. High walls of vegetation drew close enough, it seemed, to touch. Dark-trunked trees leaned over the deep-water channel, rain beat on leaves. Soon, very soon, the leaves must close overhead altogether and condemn *Unchunkolo* and her sisters to eternal wanderings in this labyrinth of channels and islands. The refugees, unnerved by the cry of *Unchunkolo*'s echo-location system, huddled by families and friends beneath their plastic sheets, watched the tall, rain-wet trunks of the trees slip past: fearful, threatened, exiled to an implacably alien place. The great convoy of ships pushed their clutch of barges and lighters through the falling rain toward the heart of the Thousand Islands, synapses twitching the huge slabs of engine muscle to dead slow ahead.

In riverain culture the islands were the traditional place of refuge and sanctuary. History became lost in the pattern of shoals and bars; questions tangled in the web of channels. Two's family were a pragmatic people; their credit rating would not permit the ferrying of a nation's dispossessed up and down river indefinitely. *Unchunkolo* doubled the tail of a long teardrop-shaped island into the main channel, and its crew saw that they were not the only ones to have thought of space and time to think among the Thousand Islands.

When Two had first seen the fleet that set out from dying Yembé, he had thought he had seen every riverboat there could be. Now he was confronted with the paucity of his imagination. Hundreds, each with its family of barges, lighters, and pontoons glittering with a thousand rain-jeweled plastic shelters. *Unchunkolo* ghosted between the outer pickets of the riverboat navy, the threshing of her big wheel echoing eerily from the walls of hanging vegetation. In the deep-water channel the ships were moored so close their attendant craft formed an unbroken surface over the water. The Captain in her chair gave a sign. *Unchunkolo's* beating heart stopped; auxiliary thrusters churned water thick with floating feces and plastic chocolate wrappers. Ports opened beneath the hull; thick tentacles terminating in anchor heads and holdfasts thrust into the bottom ooze, sought purchase. The great mass of ship and lighters shuddered and lay still in the water.

While the captains talked by satellite or visited each other in launches—the drone of their organical outboards magnified by the silent waiting trees—the crew tried to salvage what world events had left them of their former lives. The transfiguration of drudgery: God may more easily be found in the bottom of a sinkful of dirty pans than in the reflection of light from a coin as it sinks into the depths of a holy well. Upon this theology the Proclaimer Ghanda Lartha order have built an entire spirituality of contemplation of the ordinary, of kitchen gods and divinity in dusting and the saintliness of toilet bowls first thing in the morning.

And how might the angels of inspired drudgery seem?

To Two/Feeder-of-Heads/Junior Secretary, repairing the coarse hair matting on *Unchunkolo's* forward decks, it seemed like a girl. Most of his visions tended to be of girls. A tall girl, stick-thin, smoke-stained—as they were all of them smoke-smudged; they wore it like a baptismal sign—hair an unruly shock of dreadlocks growing as the spirit willed, but her eyes had locked with his for an instant of mutual recognition as sentient creatures, soul-black eyes, and communication had crackled between them like the lightning along the edge of a summer storm in high latitudes. Those eyes, that touch, had driven a spike into the heart of him that pinned him tossing and turning to his hammock suspended above the Pit of his Ancestors. Twice more he had seen her, once standing at the rail gazing down into the water, once crouched by the waterline, washing herself, the filthy water running down her face and neck, plastering her thin T-shirt over her breasts. Her lips were parted, her eyes shut: private ecstasy. His mouth had gaped open. His eyes had opened wide as moons.

He had not even realized he was staring until the friendly blow on his back broke the spell and the voice of Number-Three-Son Farmer had said, "Yes, there are some mighty good ones down there, but mark my words, they would cut your meat off as soon as look at you and stick it in a sandwich."

Twice more he had seen her, and then *Unchunkolo* in a confederation of nineteen sister ships had slipped moorings and run under the night for the Imperial shore. There had been no refuge among the Thousand Islands. No sanctuary. No sanctuary, either, behind them, on the right bank. You did not need to hear the radio reports of the fighting. Even among the Thousand Islands the smoke was clearly visible, like the smoke from an entire nation burning. The ships turned away from the burning land and made for the left bank, a tight arrowhead of vessels aimed at the heart of an Empire's conscience. The little Imperial cutters with their fearsome weaponry that could blow a riverboat out of the water with a single volley had come scoring out from the left-bank harbors and said *There is no shelter here, there is no sanctuary; our borders are closed our harbors sealed.* At every port for a thousand kilometers upstream and down, those little gunboats had come cutting out, turning them away: *Away, keep away, we will not let you onto our soil; if we let you, then we let the ship after you, and the ship after that, and the ship after that, and where will it end?* They could not go forward. They could not go back. So the twenty ships of the refugee fleet picked a port—any port—on the Imperial side, formed a loose convoy in mid-channel, and dropped anchor. One by one, the great engine muscles stopped.

Where will it end?

It will end with food riots down on the lighters. It will end with mothers giving the rice from their mouths to their children and men with heavy fists stealing it from them. It will end with captains opening lockers that have been sealed for all living memory and breaking out small arms. It will end with the younger, fitter, stronger men slipping into the river in the dark of the night to work their way along *Unchunkolo*'s waterline to climb up into the hydroponics pod and cut a breadapple, a head of brownmeat, a cob of cereal, a bladder of milk. It will end with the riverboat people hiding what they had been sparing to share with the refugees behind lines of weapons. It will end in raids, concerted attacks. It will end with bodies rolling into the river to be carried away down the great waters to Elder Sea, and ghastly necklaces of heads strung along the flanks of the lighters, rooticles writhing in the water. It will end with dysentery and diarrhea-stained decks and a sullen silence broken only by the cries of children who do not understand helpless rage, and the outboards of the dawn convoys of camerapersons and soundpersons and foreign correspondents practicing expressions of grim resolution.

Black-haired, soul-eyed girl, what became of you? Another headless body rolled into the river in the darkness before dawn? Are you sick, swollen, dreadful down in the hold where not even the camera crews dare to go; is your head tied in a figure-of-four lashing and slung with all those others on ropes over the bows? You will pardon me if I do not look because I do not think I could bear to see you, dark-haired soul-eyed girl, with your hair lank and wet and your eyes dim and spiritless and the river running through your open mouth.

He thought about her often, the thrice-seen girl, while the cameras hovered like flies around the potbellied children and the men without facial burns. And when the news teams had completed their ritual handing out of packets of chocolate and wunder-gum in Day-Glo wrappers and gone back to their pirogues, Two went back to his heads and told them about his dark-haired soul-eyed girl.

Two enjoyed the company of the dead. They gave no orders. They were not cranky or irritable. They took no offense and offered none. Their open mouths held no insults, no sarcasms, none of the sharp implements of language that girls wield so skillfully and to which he had always been peculiarly vulnerable. Among the dead he could muse and think and imagine. The dead let him be himself. He could tell them his holiest secrets, open the tabernacle of his heart to them, and they would not be shocked. They would not condemn; they would not laugh or use cutting pointed words against him.

All you woodenheads, all you souls and ancestors, could you not fix it with God, or, barring God, one of the Ykondé saints would do, or even an angel, to arrange things so that she doesn't have to be dead; you know who I am talking about . . . her, that girl I saw, the one I was telling you about; just fix it so she is not dead. And maybe so I could get to see her again. Would it be too much to ask if I could actually get to meet her? And that she would like me the way I like her? Or is that not a proper prayer, is that one of the kind God does not answer because it is not for spiritual things but for something selfish and of the ego? But it would not be selfish for her still to be alive. I would settle even for that. That will do.

Inaccessibility turned her into a lover of almost divine mystique. Mind much occupied, Two picked over the network of rooticles that sustained the heads, crushing parasites between his fingers, scraping off mosses and fungal infestations. Minor gnawings by rodents he patched with cell splice, but there were fresh breaks in the neural nets, torn rooticle ends oozing ichor, support vines twisted and wrenched. A larger menace was abroad in the tangle of roots and creepers. Two squeezed himself into the rent in the fabric of the clan Dreaming. Repair work on this scale was beyond his skill; this required the songs of Uncle Farmer, if Uncle Farmer had songs to spare for the dead. The decay in the hydroponics bubbles' ecosystems caused by the ravages of the past few weeks was accelerating out of control. Catastrophic ecological collapse threatened. The needs of the living were more important than the dignity of the dead.

In the intimate, pulsing dankness among the roots, something moved. Two's hand flashed out. Gossamer wings crumpled and broke, stumps whirred futilely, wire legs beat. Another one. First the wheeled reptile. Then the suckering, clinging, climbing thing that had stuck to his arm and left round weals when he had torn it away. Now, this needle-proboscised dragonfly. Like the others, it fell apart in his ungentle hands. Segments of quivering plastic flesh, like one of Secretary of Education's three-dimensional toys he had never as a child been able to put together to make a trux or an airplane or a boat. The fragments he stuffed into his belt pouch; the Department of Agriculture could recycle the flesh.

Then he saw the face move. He was certain of it. Certain of it. It had moved. Deep among the dreaming roots and vines of the primal forests of the spirit, one of the heads had returned to life, tearing its way out to light and life through the centuries' accumulation of root and tendril. Something that generated perverse creatures like flies from evil.

Do you know where all the insects in the world come from? Eldest Engineer, his great-grandfather on the patronymic, now among the heads himself, had taught him once by way of catechism. *They are created by the friction between the two spiritual worlds, that of God and that of the empire of the self, rubbing past each other, and the energy of their friction cascades through the hierarchy of spiritual tiers to emerge as dark and noisome insects in our world.*

He did not stop shaking until he was on deck in the broad light of late afternoon, light that in its utter certainty pours uncertainty upon the things of shadows.

Uncle Farmer found the chunks of decaying plasm in Two's belt pouch amusing.

"Some talent here," he said, twisting and turning the segments, trying to fit them together again. "This is quite clever stuff."

"Someone made that?"

"Given a few million years, plasm might, just might, evolve into something like this. This has the feel of hands all over it. Clever stuff. Shame to have to recycle it. Still, the plants . . ."

Two followed him through the film door into the hydroponics bubbles. Death, decay, despair. Bark hung in yellowing sheets, foliage blackened and wilted, stems and trunks crushed and flattened, sheets of fungal and bacterial infections swaths of purple and white. Farmer lifted a fistful of rooting compound, opened his hand in Two's face. He gagged on his first breath. Its stench was that of the rotting, dying humanity down on the barges, all its pain and hopelessness and desperation distilled.

"Aerobes, anaerobes, pseudo-rhizobacters, mycilloids, symbiotics: shot to hell, the lot of them. Ecosystem is falling to pieces around me, and I cannot do a thing to stop it. If I had a month—God, give me just a month!—without touching it, maybe we could start the symbiotic cycles running again. You take something out, you got to put something back. First law of ecology. It was never designed for this level of forced overproduction, but dear God, are we going to let them starve?"

"Maybe we should just blow the barges free, write them off, and get out of here."

"Sweet saints, you are a hard-hearted bastard to be a nephew of mine." The fragments of shattered dragonfly went into the digester to be reduced by voracious enzymes to undifferentiated cells. "We are still losing stuff, though. Someone is getting in here. I am certain of it. At night. Taking the best, too. I am going to have to talk to Aunt Captain about security."

"How are they getting in?" The humid, fetid atmosphere beneath the yellow filter-plastic bubble was oppressive.

"The seals are intact, the bubble shows no signs of knife wounds. The only conclusion is through the floor. The environmental conditioning system."

"Can that be done?"

"It is a warren down there, nephew of mine. When I was a brat, I used to hide out down there for days on end and no one ever found me. One time they were dragging the bottom by the time I decided to come out. Get all over the ship through the air system. Saw my younger brother, your Uncle Manifest, being conceived."

And then Two saw it. And in the same instant that he saw, his uncle saw it also. A movement among the withered leaves. A dart. A dash. A flicker among the roots. . . . Two had the speed of youth. The thing writhed in his grip. Chitinous legs churned but the dangerous-looking mandibles remained locked around the slab of whitemeat it had snipped from the stand.

"Would you look at that," said Uncle Farmer in naked admiration. "Now that really is something. Give it here. Here, boy, give it here."

The creature fixed its stalk eyes on Farmer, released a mandible, and took the top half centimeter off his right thumb. Two was not certain which impressed him more, the surprising amount of blood that pumped from the mutilated thumb or the richness and variety of his uncle's swearing. Between the two, the creature made good its escape in full possession of both whitemeat and a bloody hunk of raw thumb.

Under no circumstances would Two spend another night in his hammock above the pit of souls. Better to suffer humiliation by the younger unnamed boys in the male dormitory for having returned to official childhood. Ten-year-olds' taunts and the nods and winks of the girls, who by custom remained in community on the Deck of the Women until partnering, were preferable to having nose, ears, fingers, toes, penis, testicles snipped off by stalking scissor creatures and being delivered, trussed and rolled like a festival meat, to the sucker of souls waiting in the roots and heads. Lifter, pausing in her eternal weight training, sensuous muscles oily and beautiful, took especial pains to despise him.

"Ghoulies, ghosties, tattiebogles, Two-sie? Let me get rid of them for you. Down in the deep dark pit, among the roots and the heads. . . ."

Some ghoulies ghosties and tattiebogles must be exorcised oneself. He was glad now of the camera crews that came speeding out of the pearl-gray morning fog in their hired pirogues with their pockets bulging full of chocolate and Day-Clow wunder-gum. They got him away from the smirking and whispering of his crew siblings.

"Maybe soon we can all go home," said the tall thin black correspondent who spoke a language the name of which Two could not even pronounce unaided. When Two looked puzzled—more at translation glitches than context—the correspondent said, "Have you not heard? There is talk of a cease-fire. While your country has been tearing itself to pieces, secret negotiations have been going on between the Empire and your Warriors of Destiny."

They are not my Warriors of Destiny, it is not my country, thought Two, but the brainplant had not given him sufficient command of the language to wield small ironies.

But the word had gone whispering through the barges, along the railings where the men sat with their legs dangling above the water, under the plastic sheets—intolerably hot and steamy and smelling of sick and mold in the heat of a world turned full face to the sun—up ramps, down stairs, along walkways, diving down into the hold where the heart of the great agony beat, along the rows of children all lying with their heads turned to the left and the mothers squatting behind them, monolithic in their hopelessness, and the healers of many lands busy busy busy, for if they stopped being busy for just one moment they would have broken down in despair. The word: *cease-fire*. The word: *negotiations*. The word: *victory*. The word: *return*.

It has been raining all day. Since the dawn light, rain, coming down. Raining on all your hopes and plans and dreams. The day wears on. The rain grows heavier. You stare out of your window at the rain sheeting endlessly down. Toward evening you notice a change. Something high in the atmosphere, a shifting of barometric boundaries, a repolarization of ions, *something*, and you know it is going to end. The rain falls as heavily. The clouds are as low and gray and depressing. Nothing is different, but everything is changed. An end is coming.

Eventually Lifter's scorn forced Two to return to the Ancestor Pit. When he got there, there was an extra head. It was in the oldest levels, deep among the roots and tendrils of the long long dead: the head of an old man, bearded, wild-haired, eyes closed, mumbling to himself. Two timorously parted the screen of vines and masks. It was not long-dendrified wood, this head, cracked and seamed with knots and bore holes. This head was flesh and blood and bone. This head was alive. It opened its eyes. Looked at him.

Jaws snapped in Two's face. A little creature stood bobbing malevolently on its muscular hind legs while Two fought himself free of the matrix.

A skull. On legs.

The head had smiled at him.

Shit on ghosts. Shit on demons. Shit on mysterious smiling heads. Shit on all creatures crawling creeping flying biting stinging slashing. Somebody was playing with him.

Two took a splicer from his belt pouch, prodded it toward the skull creature. It lunged, snapped. Two's hand darted, caught the creature by the back of its head. Tiny fierce teeth clashed, legs windmilled.

"Got you, you little prick."

Uncle Farmer held the splicer into which the creature's teeth were embedded up in front of his face.

"Now this is good. This is very good. You have to be very good indeed to be able to play games with this stuff. Good, and a total waste of talent. Pissing around with clever clever little things like this when they could be saving all that."

Two could not bear to look at the brown rot that was all that remained of *Unchunkolo's* gardens. Farmer dropped the kicking creature into the recycler. "I do not have the talent to do it. What am I? A farmer, that is what: I sow things, I grow things, I harvest things, I keep things running, but all I am is the captain of this thing and not the engineer. I cannot make it work any more and there is no one who can.

"If they are going to end this war, they had better end it sooner than later so we can get the hell back to shore before we all start eating each other."

As Two went back to his appointed place, it was as if Uncle Farmer's words had made him aware of something which had always been apparent but which he had never until now noticed.

Unchunkolo—home, family, world—was disintegrating. The decay of the hydroponics bubbles was a symptom of the decay of the whole ship. Molds and parasitic infestations clung and found hold on bulkheads and decks. Unthinkable once. Now there was no one to clean them away. The moss which carpeted the decks was patchy and scabbed with rusts. No hand to tend to it. Derricks and masts wilted; river barnacles and other encrustations had colonized the once-pristine hull; tangles of weed had found anchor-hold on the keel and surrounded the ship in a floating halo of green fronds. The very skeleton of the ship felt frail and porous beneath Two's hands: the ship was devouring itself in its attempts to sustain the throng of refugees. Even *Unchunkolo's* scent, the spicy verdant smell of vital organicals, was changed. *Unchunkolo* smelled of sickness. *Unchunkolo* smelled of death and decay.

The head was gone from its place in the Ancestor Pit. Torn rooticles dripping support serum and ripped neural nets marked the place where it had been. That night, Two made his preparations to catch the prankster. He battened down behind the port-side syrup tank with a quilt and a cockle radio for the long night watch. The river spoke its unending syllables to him; moon and stars left silver tracks in the unquiet water; the radio whispered about the happening world and, when the happening world grew too much, interspersed it with music.

The familiar pattern of shadows around the mouth of the pit was disturbed. Two was instantly alert. One hand emerged. Two hands. Then quick, lithe as a salamander, a figure darted from the hole to the rail and threw something over. Two slipped from cover while the figure was turned away from him. He could not claim the pneumatic musculature of his cousin in Foreign Affairs, but he thought himself an adequate match for any wraith, demon, or hobgoblin of the night.

The figure at the rail turned, startled by a venting of gas from *Unchunkolo*'s bowels. Two's jaw dropped.

The figure had two heads. And before Two could think, it was on him. Two reared up, seized the two-headed figure around the waist. The figure screamed a desperate wordless animal scream. Its second head fell to the deck with a weighty thump.

"Sweet suffering God!" the fallen head shouted and started to wail in obvious agony. Two found himself entangled with a small but incredibly ferocious something that clawed and bit and kicked and hit out with rock-hard hands until Two, scratched kicked punched, knew he could hold it no longer and planted his fist square in its face.

Bone cracked beneath his knuckles. The furious fighting something fell still. While the second head's wails subsided into a general moaning, Two dragged the demon to the rail. Voices, weaving lights: the sound of battle had roused the watch.

A girl. Filthy, hair matted into greasy dreadlocks. Blood ran through the fingers that cupped the smashed nose, tears ran from her eyes. Over her shoulders was slung a webbing contraption that had held the fallen head. While the wailing head, unable to right itself, shouted that its skull was cracked, cracked open, see if it was not, brutes barbarians Proclaimers Imperialist thugs, Two gently lifted the girl's hands away from her nose.

God. God god god god god.

Her. Her her her her her.

Two prayed heartful thanks to his ancestors. God did answer prayers like that.

They would never let him keep her. Never.

Within Two's remembering, *Unchunkolo*'s Justice Department had been called upon only once and that once to settle a patrilineage claim by the Floating Heavens Clan to a percentage of *Unchunkolo*'s genetic wealth. It was generally reckoned by the riverboat community at large that greed had stimulated the claim: the palimony a successful suit would ensure would be more than enough to restore the fortunes of the recession-stricken Floating Heavens. Their case was strong: a Floating Heavens had sired *Unchunkolo III* out of *Unchunkolo II*. The court had gone with popular opinion: descent and clan affiliation among the river people was and always would be matrilineal.

For the three days during which the girl had been held in one of the unmarried women's private cabins she had not spoken a single word. Now there was to be a stowaway trial. Under normal circumstances there would have been no case to answer; the stowaway would have been put off at the next port or—as had been known in the less civilized past—directly into the river. But the head had requested asylum, and with the eyes of world television news hovering around every bulkhead, a hearing seemed the only face-saving alternative.

As Junior Undersecretary to the President, Two held a brevet rank in the Justice Department. His role was to record the trial onto brainplants for the ship's archives, a task that demanded neither effort nor skill but required attention to every word of the proceedings.

The tribunal comprised Old Chief Justice, his elder grandmother, entering the ship's chapel (which had been designated Courthouse Pro Tem) on a walking frame, steadied by Advocate General—Two's cousin Second Engineer—and Chief Prosecutor—Senior Accountant, Two's least favorite uncle. The Quorum, the body of ordinary crewpersons who would vote upon the hearing, were already seated cross-legged on the floor; the defendant, Mathembe Fileli (he liked that name!), was slumped sullenly, legs stretched out before her, chin sunk on her chest, nose decorated with an incongruously bright patch, the head (a disembodied head, a strange and unnatural thing to be sure) in a plastic bucket on the deck beside her. The news teams lounged by the doors, taking in the sun and drinking canned beer.

Two checked the brainplants looped behind his ear, the readers pressed to his forehead. Old Chief Justice—the position was traditionally held by a woman; women's sense of justice was more highly developed than men's—was helped to the floor, the camera crews sauntered in out of the sun, and the hearing opened.

Chief Prosecutor stated that the accused had stowed away on

board *Unchunkolo* without the cognizance or permission of the Captain, in so doing causing damage to vital and sensitive ship systems. Without let or leave she had entered the ship's agricultural modules and taken food, a crime all the more heinous on account of *Unchunkolo*'s parlous state and the more morally reprehensible given the degree of want among her fellow refugees down on the barges.

Chief Prosecutor concluded his case by regretting that it was not within the court's powers to impose a more severe sentence than deportation from the ship, some punishment that would properly express his moral outrage and indignation at the accused's monstrous selfishness in the face of the suffering of others. He trusted court and Quorum to vote for deportation and expressed indignation that the crew's time should have been wasted on such a blatant and thoroughgoing thug as this Mathembe Fileli.

Advocate General said that the head would speak in defense of its granddaughter and itself.

No harm had been intended, said the head, placed on top of its upturned plastic bucket, as the cameras cut and wove for a close view of something they knew their viewers would find inspirationally gross. Had they the wherewithal, they would gladly make reparations for any damage done. The stolen food was not denied, but could theft be considered a sin in the midst of starvation? On the matter of the stowing away, the head begged the court to remember that his granddaughter had suffered traumatic separation not only from her father but also, during the chaotic flight from Ol Tok, from her mother, brother, and uncle. Yet Mathembe Fileli had vowed that she would not rest until she had reunited her family, and if that meant hiding aboard ship in the hope that, after the refugees were all resettled, she might travel the length of the river to continue the search, surely that was a minor misdemeanor to be set against the sanctity of the family?

The sanctity of the family, the head had learned, was important among the riverboat people. They would understand.

"When the ports open, there will be refugee camps where her family might be sheltered. But there are many many ports, many many refugees. The odds of finding them, I will admit, are slim. The river is very great, but at least aboard ship she has a chance. On land she has no chance, no chance at all. In a single day this great ship can cover what would take one girl a week, a month, to walk on foot. Would you deny her the right to seek her family?"

At the back a crewperson nodded in agreement.

Old Chief Justice spoke.

"Mr. Fileli—I take it I may call you that—down in those barges there are a thousand people who can make exactly the same plea. Are we to let every one of them come swarming onto *Unchunkolo* and sail her up and down the river like some pleasure barge until they find their lost ones? This is a commercial ship, Mr. Fileli. If we make exceptions for one we must make exceptions for all, and *Unchunkolo* cannot withstand that."

A rumble among the Quorum.

"Now, has anyone else anything to say before the Quorum votes?"

"Yes." By the door, among the cameras and sound booms: Uncle Farmer. "A question. Did you make this?"

Cameras swiveled and refocused as he held high a plasm toy in the shape of a miniature trux.

Mathembe stood up, frowned at the organical, nodded. *Yes.*

"Then I submit the Quorum votes to extend sanctuary to this girl and her grandfather. Because a person who can do this"—tiny plastic wheels turned and reversed, eye lights opened, a sheen of colors flowed across the pelt—"is the person who can save our farm pods."

Chief Justice addressed Department of Agriculture.

"Are you sure of this?"

"What I am sure of is that in five days those bubbles are not even going to be safe to enter."

Old Chief Justice pressed her fingertips together in deliberation.

"Mathembe Fileli, are you willing to attempt to regenerate our agricultural ecosystems?" The head made to speak; Mathembe nudged the pot. A nod. *Yes.* "Judgment is reserved. Miz Fileli will attempt to regenerate Ship's agricultural modules. Ship's crew will extend every courtesy to Miz Fileli and assist her in every way possible. Miz Fileli." The old old woman leaned forward, held Mathembe in her gaze. She spoke in words the microphones would not hear. "You do realize that you are not exonerated. The charges against you still stand. As I have said, we are a commercial enterprise. We will not tolerate freeloaders. However, we will countenance paying passengers. Succeed and we will gratefully take you wherever you wish to go. Fail, and you are off this ship. Got that, girl?"

Chief Justice rose to her feet, flicking away the helping hands of Chief Prosecutor and Advocate General.

"The business of this court of the Justice Department of the Mercantile Para-State of *Unchunkolo the Third* is concluded in this time and place. God save *Unchunkolo* and all who sail upon her."

The walking frame clicked across the chapel floor. As if charmed, a dancing procession of cameras, microphones, and correspondents fell in behind.

Judgment reserved, Mathembe Fileli and her grandfather's head passed from the jurisdiction of the Justice Department to Internal Affairs and, after much bidding, bartering, and bribing, to the supervision of Two.

"Skinny little shit," said Cousin Lifter. "No ass, less tits. Probably crawling with bugs. Things that make your dick swell up the size and color of a cucumber."

Two was gratified by the envy, for privately his attempts to ingratiate himself with this answer to his prayers had been frustrated. Mathembe Fileli gave him no more regard than she did the balls of plasm that were rapidly filling the aft deck: less; a plasmal was at least a useful creature. Two persevered. It was ordained by Higher Powers (the kind that are always capitalized); therefore it would come to pass. In time. Give it time.

"I mean, it is quite all right by me if you do not want to speak," he said as Mathembe harvested a crop of undifferentiated plasmals from a plastic sheet suspended by its four corners, twisting some apart into their components, stowing the rest in a barrel. "In fact, I rather like it. It is cute. Most girls have too much to say, they never shut up *yakyakyak*. I mean, what do they find to talk about so much?" Mathembe filled the reservoir with sewage from a tank, plunged her bare arm shoulder deep in the liquid shit, seeding the growth medium. "Okay. So. I understand. Maybe it is not that you do not speak, it is that you cannot speak. I have heard that some people are immune to the language viruses in the womb and are born not able to speak or write."

A handful of semi-solid shit hit him in the face. But she smiled.

Definitely, she smiled. He watched with a warm glow at the base of his belly as she worked on, never pausing, never resting.

And later she spoke to him. Not with words. She came up behind him and punched him on the shoulder. It was as close to talking to him as she would come. The head, who had watched the day's events with contemptuous interest, translated.

"She needs parallel port interfacers and cable."

"I can get that. How many?"

"Two for every head in the Spirit Well."

Two gaped. "We would not have even a quarter of that."

"That is what she needs."

If that is what she needs, that is what she shall get, swore Two, who had seen her half mocking half-smile as a sexual challenge.

"We would not have even a quarter of that," said Two's elder sister, Assistant Quartermaster. She put out a call for all hands to turn in brainplants to the Quartermasters.

"Less than five hundred," she said, shaking her head at the small heap of organicals on the deck. Infant Quartermasters-to-be, her nephews and nieces, ran about arresting any caught crawling away from the bright lights into cool dark corners. "Just what is she going to do with them anyway?"

Two-Among-the-Dead had an outrageous notion.

"Less than five hundred," he said to Mathembe Fileli. She punched him on the shoulder, lifted a brainplant and a plasmal in each hand. *Look. See.* She broke the plasm ball apart into its components, twisted a filament of genetic material out of the brainplant, and closed the open ball around it. The plasmal fissured, creased, folded, realigned itself into the flesh-colored comma of a brainplant. Mathembe snapped the genetic filament, threw both brainplants into a tank of water, picked up a fresh brainplant and plasmal, placed them in Two's empty useless hands.

Watch. Learn. Do. Break. Twist. Close. Fold. Break, twist, close, fold. Break twist close fold. Breaktwistclosefold: Two's prayer; without those words, he would have lost the rhythm of his hands. Mathembe hissed in exasperation when occasional clumsinesses let the plasmal fall and burst on the deck, when the hair-thin filament of extruded genetic material snapped before he could insert it into the open flesh. Break. Twist. Close. Fold. Hour after hour. Break. Twist. Close. Fold.

Two's shoulders ached. Two's wrists hurt like the aftermath of a marathon session of masturbation. Two was hungry, tired, dizzy with the passage of the sun across the open aft deck. Plasmal after plasmal fell from fingers that no longer obeyed his commands. Mathembe brushed away his apologies, sent him to rest in the shade.

An affectionate punch. He woke with a cry, with a start: What, where, when, have I been asleep, have I been drooling, do I smell? Dark. Orange streamers of cloud across a violet sky. Stars huge above him, the moon the eye of God: *'ware your soul, your sins, your midnight shames and private pruriences; how naked are you while you are sleeping and all can see your soul on your face?* She stood over him, face full of moon shadows: a creature of legend, of river mud and story. She beckoned, *Come*, was halfway to the Ancestor Pit without ever looking back to see if he was behind her.

Of course he was.

With the night, when the boundaries between life and dreaming grew vague, the spirits that inhabited the pit drew close to the edge of the world. Every shadow, every rustle, every movement among the roots was an ancestor returning to briefly reanimate his wooden mask. Child of signs and portents, Two would have been quite unnerved but for the workmanlike air with which Mathembe set about the task of fastening brainplant to mask, wrapping arms and legs around veins, clawing out fingerholds in empty eye sockets as she reeled off lengths of neural cable and hooked it to the brainplants. An impatient click of the fingers: *Quit dreaming, there is work to be done. Nothing here to scare a big boy.* Two gathered the nerve fibers into sheaves and bound them with plastic cable clips. By moon shadow and the riding lights of the refugee fleet, he watched her moving around in the depths of the pit: lithe, dextrous, indefatigable.

Early autumn meteors fell burning all along the wounded river, and in the space of time it takes a meteor to cross the sky and expend its glory he had fallen in love with her. And the work was transfigured. He plaited the sheaths of nerves into cables and it was wonderful. He spliced the nerve endings into brainplants and it was not work, it was an offering, a love token. He heaved plastic-bag loads of plasmals through the film door into the stinking decay of the farm modules, and though the stench was unbearable it was a good stench. Though the labor seemed never-ending, it was a labor of love. She smiled at him more often now, glancing up as if by some telepathic prompt while they pressed the brainplants into the dormant flesh.

He understood what she intended to do. The plan was audacious, brilliant. It could not possibly work. She was going to use the collected information-processing capacity of *Unchunkolo's* dead to program the changes in the codon sequences that would transform plasmals to food plants. All in a single night.

Then the last brainplant was embedded in the last plasmal and everything was checked and everything was ready and the sky was lightening around the sunward edge of the world. Mathembe Fileli surveyed her work and it was good. She entered the farm bubble. Two followed. Mathembe turned. Touched a hand to his chest. Suddenly, striking like some carnivorous creature, she kissed him hard on the mouth and was gone before he could react, the module door sealed behind her.

The work might be hers alone now, but he would keep vigil. He would watch over her. He sat by the door, back pressed upright and resolute against the translucent wall.

Two was asleep before the horizon was below the sun and the camera crews came arrowing out of the silver mist.

He woke with the start of someone who is wakened rather than waking of his own accord. Hot sun. High above. Screw up the eyes against the glare. How long? That long? What had woken him? Is she finished, is it done? The plastic bubbles were opaqued with mist, beaded with condensation. Dark shapes within. The door was still sealed against him.

Then what? The curving plastic wall beneath his cupped hands was vibrating.

After weeks of silence, the engines were running. Confirmation: the deck beneath his feet quivered to a series of shocks. Riverbed anchor-holds being released. As Two took the steps up to the main deck three at a time the fabric of the ship shuddered to a deeper note. Sirens bellowed; Two reached the upper deck as the stern wheel began to turn. The noon sun struck rainbows from the cloud of spray and droplets around the turning wheel. Like some huge heavy creature returning to life after long hibernation, *Unchunkolo* moved.

And she was not alone. From the vantage of the higher decks, Two saw that every ship in the fleet was moving now, moving with one intent, toward the Empire shore. The air was split with sirens; the pirogues and outriggers of the news teams darted and wove between the slow-moving riverboats. Beyond the edge of the fleet the Imperial gunboats that had held them in midstream so long formed into an escort. Two joined a throng of fellow crewpersons at the rail, cheering and waving with ragged enthusiasm to their counterparts on the sister ships.

"What happened?" he yelled over the bellowing sirens at Sister Quartermaster.

"They let us in."

"I can see that. Why?"

"The civil war is over," shouted Cousin Department of Trade and Commerce.

"You mean the War of Independence," said Nephew Fifth Loader. "That is what history is going to call it. The War of Independence."

"You mean the Warriors of Destiny beat the Empire?"

"Let us say that the Empire realized that, though the Warriors could not beat it, neither could it beat the Warriors," said Sister Quartermaster in his ear. "Not and hope to retain any credibility in the international community."

"The Warriors beat them!" roared Lifter. "Fair and square. They hammered them. The Emperor licked ass and gave them everything they wanted."

"Not quite everything," said Second Cousin Engineer.

"How long do you think that prissy little excuse for a state is going to last? A year? I say, give it three months, and they will be begging Ol Tok to take them in."

"What?" asked Two, churned and turned like river water by the rush of history over him.

"The Warriors agreed to the Empire's demand that nine northern prefectures be excluded from the new state," said Sister Quartermaster. "They remain a province of the Empire, a semiautonomous Proclaimer homeland."

"Who cares?" shouted Uncle Sixth, who was two years younger than Two, his nephew. "Who cares? They have opened the ports; we can dump this lot and get back to work. Whatever they call themselves now, these countries are still going to need riverboats."

"It was part of the cease-fire agreement," said Quartermaster, his guide to this new world order that had sprung, wholly formed, from the brows of the politicians in a single night. "The Empire sets up resettlement camps while power is handed over and civil order restored."

"Hostage camps, that is what they are!" shouted Fifth Loader. "Guarantees of good behavior from the Warriors, so they will not continue with the war to kick the Proclaimers out of that tin-pot little country of theirs and bring real unity."

"Unity out of the barrel of a gun," said Sister Quartermaster quietly, thinking she would not be heard, but Fifth Loader heard, and would have rounded her but for Senior Engineer, Two's father.

"Nations. Free states. Empires. Look at those poor bastards down there," said Two's father.

On *Unchunkolo*'s barges and lighters, on the barges and lighters of every ship pushing steadfastly for shore, the people rejoiced. Old women clapped their hands to God and wept blatantly. Old men danced, arms held out, fingers clicking. Men clapped and chanted and waved their fists. Women drummed their hands on the plastic decks and whistled and made shrill ululating cries and hugged each other and hugged their children and hugged their men. Fathers pranced unsteadily with their children on their shoulders. Mothers danced to the music of radios that had been kept hidden from the traders, shifting from foot to foot, children at their hips. Babies waved their arms and cried in incomprehension. Children grinned and ran with cautious carefreeness, chasing each other. A din of cheering, whistling, singing, drumming went up from *Unchunkolo*, from every refugee ship, counterpointed by the ceaseless blaring of the sirens. But it was a dark carnival. In the heart of the celebration, there was a restraint, a needle of sorrow.

"Look at them," said Two's father again. "Do they care in whose name they get their handful of rice and spoonful of meat on a plastic plate? Do they care that the land is partitioned; do you see them debating the status of the nine northern prefectures? Learn sense, kids. Flags and politics; leave them both alone because they burn all of us together.

"You think it is all over the moment we tie alongside the wharf and sort out compensation? You think, Off they go, and on comes a new cargo and off we sail and goodbye to the lot of them; now everything is the way it was before? I tell you, it has not even begun to begin yet. Ask yourself this: they know where their meal tonight is coming from, but do you?"

Alone of all those gathered at the rail, Two did.

The interiors of the domes were still inscrutable behind the slow trickles of condensation. Two cupped his hands against the plastic, shouted her name. No acknowledgment from the dark masses in the mist.

"It is over! You can go now!"

He tried the outer airlock door. It was unsealed. Cocooned in mist, Two stepped into the day after Creation.

A carpet of moss breaks beneath his feet into a mosaic of rainbow-colored hexagons; flaws and fractures of color dart away before him as he advances step by slow step. Yellow polymer bubbles swell on every side, some the size of his fist, some the size of his head, some large enough to envelope him whole; they burst, noiselessly, in sprays and sparkles of spores; they fill the air with intimate, evocative scents: body smells, musks, sweats, pheromones, secretions, hormonal perfumes that have him swooning and roaring and sweating and trembling all at once. Bulbous striped gourds vent spray and mist from trumpet mouths; a constant warm rain settles upon his body. All is swelling, all is engorging, all is tumescent, all is ripening and bursting; pods split open to drop gelatinous seeds, fat fruit squeezes from tight-stretched lips, flesh-colored cauls and fungal prepuces peel back as meaty stamens and shafts thrust into the air. Clumps of tendrils wave, reach for ankles, calves; tight spirals of vegetation uncoil into flexing ferns, parables and paradigms of chaos theory. Above his head the tight-folded glans of new trees shudder and burst into fronds and bracts: symbiotic vines colonize trunks and branches and unfold trembling blooms; knee-high blisters in the moss carpet split; clouds of winged insects swarm up around Two, cluster for a moment at lips and nostrils, tasting, scenting, before darting for the true scent of the flowers. Beetles skitter around his feet, small slithering things, small scuttling things with too many legs or too many eyes or too many graspers and snippers: the unseen gardeners of this symbiotic Eden. He pushes his way between hanging sheets of skin, inward, onward, dizzy and hallucinating with the smell of greenness and growingness and ripe warm flesh. Half-transformed plasmals cluster around his lower legs sucking genetic information from his skin; he brushes them away, hardly noticing that he does so. Giant rumps of meat rise up on either side almost to the top of the dome, squeezing from their pericarps like obscenely bared buttocks, pillows of flesh; wine gourds bubble and gurgle and fart fermentation gases. The fronds close over his head, force him to crouch, onward, forward, led by the crazing and cracking of the carpet moss before him. Hormones, pheromones, ketones, esters, mmmm stamens, pistils, slowly opening deep-sucking flowers, things that burst wetly, invitingly: slow but irresistible thrustings, conception gestation fecundity, vegetable pressure, onward, inward, into the secret vegetable heart vast and slow opening before him in the intimate darkness like the ancient secrets of womanhood, like a lotus, leaves peeling back one by one by one by one, *enter. Penetrate. Pierce.*

There he found her, asleep in the heart of her creation, enfolded by petals. She was naked but for a ragged pair of shorts. Brainplants clung to her flesh; her head was a medusa of cables and interfacers. The warm constant rain dripped from the leaves and ran down her body. Gently, reverently, Two knelt, unhooked the brainplants. Over much of her body, patches of skin, some the size of his thumb, had been torn away. He understood. As he thought, it had been outrageous. She had used her own flesh as a template from which to shape all this life, all this growing, all this fecundity. Her flesh and her dreaming, amplified by the linked intellects of the ancestors and programmed into the dormant plasmals. She murmured in her sleep, beat soft fists at the air. Words came to the edge of articulation and fled, afraid. Wordless even in the dream of creating. Two never loved her again as purely as he did in that moment, among the alien flora.

The hearing was perfunctory and satisfactory. In the space of a single night Mathembe was changed from freeloader and stowaway to something between a deity and a mascot. Two defended her with vigorous dedication from things against which she required no defense.

He bought her the plastic sun shades from one of the outrigger junk sellers because he knew she would look fantastic in them, that with her dark provincial skin and beautifully broken provincial nose and liquid provincial way of moving through the crowds she would turn every fair-haired light-skinned Imperial head. She thought them frivolous in her task of searching among the piles of possessions and people and exasperated Imperial officials with personal organizers strewn across Khelamjabheri quayside for her family. But she wore them because it pleased him. And she did look fantastic. And she did turn the head of every longshoreman and fork-lift driver and international refugee aid worker as they went along the concrete piers and quays, Two grinning three steps behind, filled with vicarious pride that his Mathembe should be so admired.

Mathembe could not understand the computer.

When she heard that they were searching for Displaced Persons, the Refugee Administrator had been glad to give them access to the data space, "For all the good it will do you" (trickling a thin oh-God-the-things-I-have-seen stream of smoke from her cheroot into the air). "The whole bloody thing is a shambles. Totally overloaded. But if it means one family less sleeping under plastic tonight, I am more than happy."

"It stores and processes information," Two explained. "Really no different from the Dreaming net, except that everything is mechanical. This is the Empire now."

She stroked the screen, touched the alphanumerals.

"It should configure to Old Speech." Two touched the display; the screen cleared, came alive with sinuous Old Speech phonemes. Mathembe clapped her hands softly, pressed her palms together in an unconscious attitude of prayer.

"Just enter the name," Two prompted. "There, on the screen. Write it with your finger."

FILELI

"Touch enter."

ENTER.

The screen blanked. Mathembe threw up her hands in consternation.

"It is all right. It takes a moment or two to search."

SEARCH COMPLETED.

"Look. It has got one. Now—"

HARD COPY.

Shreel of printer.

"Temporary Transit Area seven, Row six, Bivouac forty-four."

Mathembe was already tugging at his arm.

Temporary Transit Area seven was a vast echoing warehouse filled with the cries of children and dusty beams of light from the roof lights: all planes and verticals, pillars and sheet-metal roofing, alien and intimidating to people brought up among softer, non-Euclidian geometry. Larger family groups were housed in empty cargo containers; all others had a space allotted to them by a number in Imperial script spray-painted on the concrete floor.

Row six, Bivouac forty-four. An old man sat on the concrete cradling a street-ball stick and red plastic helmet, deep in shock. Mathembe and Two were not inclined to intrude into his private grief.

"There will be others," said Two, afraid that in her anger Mathembe would throw his plastic sunglasses into the oil-stained river. "Many many many others. It is a big river."

It was a big river.

And there were others.

Many many many others.

The Filelis who lived under guns and quarantine on an island where the Emperor had once sent his prisoners.

The Filelis who lived under six plastic sheets in a football stadium.

The Filelis who came trudging from their metal hut through a quagmire of mud, shit, and tropical rain to see if this girl at Control could really truly be their missing daughter.

The Filelis who, with a few others, had tried to grow a community from the poor polluted exhausted soil of the Empire in the shadow of a chemical plant.

The Filelis who lived for their own protection behind barbed wire and blades in a pulpwood-forest clearing because every tree for the last three kilometers of the very long bus ride was hung with signs saying EAT THE MEATMEN.

The Filelis who lived sixteen in three rooms in a city-center apartment block that would have been condemned but for the refugee crisis, graced with sweeping panoramas to the west of an expressway, to the east of a forest of satellite dishes, to the north of a construction site, and to the south of another terminal apartment block looking back at them.

The Filelis who lived under the sound footprint of the orbital shuttle port, their nights lit red by the glare of launch lasers and landing lights, all as mute and articulate as Mathembe from the night-and-day scream of spacecraft and superheated steam.

The Filelis who invited Mathembe into their cardboard and plastic shanty and offered wine and fruit and breadmeat from the scabby, diseased garden that was their commemoration of *home*: the communion of the dispossessed.

So many Filelis.

"Like I said, it is a big river," was Two's only comment.

Mathembe's work under Uncle Farmer in the agriculture bubbles earned her passage; spending money she made selling biotoys to the girls she was domiciled with on the Deck of the Women. She saved her small change until she had enough to buy a jacket. She bought it from a chain store in the Imperial port city of Fijjahal. It was silver plastic. It shone brilliantly in the bright lights and chrome of the city store. Two almost died from admiration of Mathembe in her shades and silver jacket moving like a sweet dark silhouette through the smoggy streets of Fijjahal. It caused him almost physical pain when she took the beautiful silver jacket to a T-shirt printer and had computer-assembled videofits of her family annealed onto back, front, and sleeves. To complete the violation, she made Two take a marker pen and write, in his neat, big, New Speech: HAVE YOU SEE THESE PEOPLE? THEY ARE MY FAMILY. THEIR NAME IS FILELI.

Now whenever *Unchunkolo* docked at the left-hand shore, Mathembe wore the jacket. It cost her all her money and was no more successful than the computer search.

Sail on, *Unchunkolo*, with your cargoes of timber and organochemicals and consumer electronics and mass market shoes. A thousand years of pride, a thousand years of solitude, while around you changes of millennial dimensions unfold across the land. No midwife attends the birth of a nation. No mother nurtures it. When the umbilical is cut, it is alone on the dark plains of history. It must stand and walk unaided, it must learn to feed and to run and to fight; there are yellow-eyed creatures of the night hungry for its territory and resources. Can it feed its people, can it shelter and educate them, can it afford them wealth and health, can it protect them? These are the tasks of nations.

No. The tasks of nations are these: in the face of ecological collapse and genetic bankruptcy, in the cold wind from beneath the wing of famine, to have every locomotive and country bus and government organical and police station and mail slot and telecomm point and municipal gloglobe stand and public library and state gene bank and law court and public park redecorated in the green silver and black of the new Free State. That is the first and great task of a nation. And the second is like unto it: to send serious little men from Ministries and Departments that never needed to exist before roaring around the countryside on green silver and black tryx denaming everything that had been renamed by those self-same little men in the days when the tryx had been Imperial black. The task of nations is to send the five ragged riverboats that have been requisitioned (with vain promises of compensation) to form the new nation's navy into the offing beyond Ol Tok to bombard the city with thirty thousand enns' worth of fireworks to proclaim the birth of a new state. The task of nations is to prove the credibility of the new House of Deputies by pouring forth a torrent of legislation: banning all nonorganical technology; making it an offense to be found with a word of New Speech on your lips; ordering all the shops and stores with nothing in them to paint out their bilingual signs and repaint them monolingually; changing all the street names so that no one can find their way around any more; banning all neon and holograms so that those who wander in search of renamed shops on renamed streets wander in darkness both metaphorical and physical; establishing a religion with fifteen major saints, six hundred and thirty enlightened sub-saints, and thirty-eight thousand nine hundred and twelve angels as the only way to God; giving absolute license to anyone wearing a *pneuma* mask in public as being "under the guidance of the saints" and therefore immune from legal restraint; fining you for Public Disrespect to the Dead, or for not displaying the portrait of the new Free State President in your café, shop, market stall, school, or shrine, or, best of all, decreeing an eternal and indissoluble territorial claim over the partitioned northern prefectures. These are the true tasks of nations, while children scuttle through the smoking hulks of Ol Tok's great houses hunting wild organicals for food, while Free State troopers, those roaring boys who had risen against the Imperial black with a whoop and a rebel yell, lay out lines of the dead, mouths green from eating organical flesh, along their nation's cobbled roadsides.

Idiocy is, at least, even-handed. The northern prefectures—now renamed God's Country—responded to the territorial threat from their new neighbors as the Proclaimers have ever done, with paranoid fears of racial and cultural genocide, and mobilized themselves into a militia one million strong armed with hunting weapons and fowling pieces. When the unclean horde of Confessor berserkers thirsting for the blood of Proclaimer babies failed to come pouring over the green hills of Asmathi Prefecture, the enshrined paranoia turned upon the enemy within, the native Confessor population who every second of every day plotted the downfall and destruction of the Proclaimer state. Decree likewise followed decree: all the nation must be registered according to religion, Proclaimer or Confessor, left-handed or right-handed, and zoned according to religious affiliation. A single right-handed grandparent was enough to have you and your family rezoned and moved to a Confessors-only district; to be partnered to a Confessor was enough to cost you your job in the new civil service and have your weapons license and franchise revoked. Those northern prefectures under the shadow of the great north woods also saw orgies of mailbox, public tram, and telecomm point repainting, of street, shop, and district renaming. When colors and tongues become political weapons, that is the sign of a sick and sinful society.

Twenty-nine southern Confessor prefectures. Nine northern Proclaimer prefectures. Each with the power to legislate, juridicate, tax, administer, budget, educate, police, defend, and send its people stepping one after the other into war. God, those are terrible powers. Each shackled by the sacred principles of democracy to tyrannic majorities and eternally disenfranchised minorities. Confessor over Proclaimer, Proclaimer over Confessor. Well, then, if they do not like it here, let them go back *there*. Always *there*, a word that is almost a spit, a sneer, a flick of the head rather than name the bastard nation.

And so they did.

They went back. Busloads and boatloads and trainloads of them, by aircraft and spacecraft and private vehicle, by trux and tryx and foot. On either side of the new bristling border they queued for hours, kilometer after kilometer of them snaking back into the heartlands of the detested countries. With joy in their hearts they crossed the border.

And they found: camps. They are a universal human condition, camps. There is a refugee in the heart of every one of us. Resettlement camps. Transit camps. Temporary accommodation centers. Call them what you will. They sprang up along either side of the new, jagged border like malformed teeth, clusters of hastily grown biotecture domes and sanitation units, red dirt roads scraped raw by trux wheels, people from Ministries and Departments resplendent in new national colors filing forms, filing forms, filing forms. Around every border crossing, around every border town, around every port for a thousand kilometers up and down the river: camps.

Those on the Proclaimer side of the border at least attempted to be true to their description as *temporary*; those on the Confessor side rapidly acquired the uneasy sense of permanence. Reasons—excuses: many many more Confessors made the crossing south than Proclaimers went north. That, and the fact that the emigration officials of God's Country demanded an exit tax from every departing Confessor equal to 80 percent of their worldly goods. It was a small country, God's Country, it needed to hold on to all the exchequer it could.

Sail on, then, *Unchunkolo*, abreast the flow of history, untouched and untouching, untroubled and troubling no one, carrying them up and down, rich and poor, northerner and southerner, with all their burdens of lives and expectations; sail on, upon your centuries-long voyage past the shores of time.

She knew it was him from the way he looked at the noonday sky and sat down stiffly, legs crossed, in a sunny but secluded part of the foredeck. She did not need to see him open his Book of Witnesses and press the readers to his temples, she did not need to hear him mumble his mind-clearing exercises so that the pure word of God might shine through him, undimmed by the clutter of life in interesting times. It was him.

For two days and a night *Unchunkolo* had pushed the three bargeloads of Proclaimers north to their homeland. Captain reckoned it would be the last of the great migrations: *Unchunkolo* had had to tender for the charter. The bid Father Lading had submitted was better than penury, but only just. In these days of economic war between the Empire and its new independent neighbor, any work was better than lying up in harbor growing tumors on the hull. Three, four months ago, when the flow of migrants had been at its greatest, the captains could have named their price. The Proclaimers tended to agree to a better rate than the Confessors, but then the Proclaimers had not had to pay the 80 percent exit tax. But for the subsidies the God's Country government paid to the riverboat people, the Confessors would have been left squatting on the quayside.

The old man finished his devotions, folded away his Book of Witnesses, rose stiffly from the rough hair decking. Suddenly Mathembe was terrified. The answers to questions that had defined her life were there standing at the rail, observing the slow passage of the many-colored shore, and she was not certain she could bear those answers.

No Lady of the Beer Bottle to pray to here. The decision and responsibility were hers entirely.

She left him at his rail watching the slow passage of the land where he could no longer live, went to her cubby, and put on her silver picture jacket. Then, stormed with doubts like flocking dark birds, she went and tugged the old man's sleeve.

He knew her instantly.

"My dear girl! My dear dear girl! Mathembe Fileli."

The tears of the old still embarrassed her. And then it was as if a cloud had cast a sudden dark shadow across a fruitful land.

"But there is so much we must talk about. So much. Your family, your grandfather—" Then he noticed the pictures on Mathembe's silver jacket and Two's good New Speech. "Forgive me. I see that times have been as hard with you as they have with me. Harder, I do not doubt. You are aboard this ship as crew rather than passenger? That is quite an accomplishment. I salute you. But then I always reckoned you to be a woman of no small consequence, Mathembe Fileli. Tell me, would it be possible for you to obtain permission from your superior to take tea with me?"

The small traveling tea set was exquisite. But then, everything about Dr. Kalimuni had been exquisite. The precision with which he weighed and measured the tea, poured the boiling water: exquisite.

As any good lawyer will draw out a story, with hints and suggestions and leading questions, Dr. Kalimuni drew out the story of Mathembe's sundering from and subsequent search for her family. Like any good lawyer, he was adept in nonverbal communication, trained to observe and act upon the little truths that spill out in the nervous ticking of the witness's foot, the twitch, the wringing of the hands. He listened patiently and sympathetically, as a good lawyer must, and asked many questions. Many times the tiny, exquisite teapot on its alcohol burner was recharged with boiling water.

Then he told his own story. He told it with many small sips of tea, with much trembling of the hands, rattling of the white cup against the white saucer.

Jadamborazo had been small enough to retain the village vendetta mentality where everyone knows everyone and big enough for the anonymous viciousness of the city where no one knows anyone. With help from his brother, a healer—a fine gentleman without one microgram of bigotry in his body, Dr. Kalimuni was at pains to point out—he had reestablished a legal practice. In a lawless place, in lawless times, there was no shortage of employment for the advocate Kalimuni. From cases of stoning Imperial troops or spray-painting slogans on walls to charges of possession of arms and even treasonable murder, Dr. Kalimuni had enjoyed no small measure of success in the Imperial courts.

"The small town, Miz Fileli: the great sociological bastard. Beware small town mentality, it is sure death to the soul. There is but one law in the small town and that is the opinion of one's peers."

First the keeper of the shrine where he worshiped every Holy Day. Then the Master of the Red Hand Lodge. Then the chairman of the local Advocates' Association. All were shown politely into his book-lined study with its views of his brother's exquisite gardens. All were served tea from the exquisite white tea set. All questioned the sincerity of his faith. The Red Hand Lodge Master had said it most nakedly and honestly. "How can you, a loyal Proclaimer, defend this nation's enemies? How can you defend traitors and murderers, people who, you can be sure, if they ever got the whip hand, would show no mercy to us? They are talking about you down in the Confessor ghettos like some kind of savior, Kalimuni. Remember where your loyalities lie."

"My loyalities lie where they have always lain," Dr. Kalimuni, who was a member of no lodge, who worshiped his God according to his own conscience, had replied smoothly. "With the principles and processes of law. Without which, sir, we would be less than the beasts of the forest. Less than beasts, sir."

But nowhere, and least of all Jadamborazo, was immune to the plague of violence that spread across the land that hot summer, that catalyzed a decades-long process of polarization so that by the first fall of a leaf in the forests that encircled Jadamborazo it was a town no more but two armed, baying camps: the Proclaimers down in the valley and floodplain, the Confessors in the encircling hills and valleys that defined this tributary of the great river. Ghost Boy squads chose nightly victims from the telecomm directory; young Spirit Lodge bloods selectively eliminated jeepney drivers with destination boards for the wrong end of town. The pressure for Kalimuni to conform, to come off his fence (the most heinous of crimes in either camp), mounted. His brother pleaded with him, for the sake of his reputation, to give up defending Confessors charged with political offenses. Dr. Kalimuni's careful, exquisite arguments were as incomprehensible as abstract art to this ancient primal philosophy. One cannot be neither, nor. One must be either, or. Conform, Kalimuni, conform; remember who and what you are. Hammering away, hammering away, hammering away; then, abruptly, the coercion ceased, and there was silence. Total, complete silence. Those who are not for us must be against us.

Then the Ghost Boys shot his brother in mistake for the Grand Master of the Jadamborazo Spirit Lodges, with whom he was accustomed to play *fili* every Tuesday evening. They shot him with a neural scrambler. He was lucky. He would only be confined to a mobile support unit for the remainder of his life, a spasming, palsied ruin of a man, unable to speak, unable to walk, unable to control the least motor function.

"I learned this speech of the heart from him," Dr. Kalimuni said. His hands shook so that scalding tea slopped over the brim. He set the tiny translucent cup down. "That is how I am able to read you so well, my dear Mathembe. I think he must have been trying to ask me to do it from the very first, but I was not then literate enough to understand what he was asking of me. Or perhaps it was that I did not want to admit that he could ask such a thing. Of course it was a sin. But then so is slander, so is gossip, so is swearing, so is going with the head uncovered on the Holy Day, so is forgetting one word of God in his holy book, and any one of those sins is enough to cast one forever into Khirr. A house may burn with a single match. And God may forgive any sin, in time." The advocate smiled. "I shall certainly make good representation of my case to him, and my brother who has gone before me will be no hostile witness, I think."

The death of his brother succeeded where the shrine keeper, the Lodge Master, and the Advocates' Association chairman failed. In guilt, grief, and anger, Dr. Kalimuni examined his conscience and professional morality with the full magnification of his inquisitorial mind. He saw doubts like a squall line cloud the horizon of his certainty. The pillars of his life, his impartiality, his impeccability, his incorruptibility, cracked and fell in the storm of uncertainty. But for the Revolution, or the War of Independence, according to one's polarity, that engulfed the whole land, he would have resigned. There was no longer any law to resign from. When rumors of an Imperial capitulation sent two thirds of the Proclaimer population north toward the imagined welcome of their co-religionists, Dr. Kalimuni remained. He did so more as an act of personal expiation than hope for a new order. But a new order came and, after the painting of telecomm points and mailboxes and the renaming of all the streets, found itself in need of lawyers. A letter, on official Free State Justice Department notepaper and written in impeccable Old Speech, offered Dr. Kalimuni (renamed Kalingimungili) the post of District Prosecutor. No longer capable of certainty himself, Dr. Kalingimungili withdrew into retreat to hear the pure and untarnished word of God. And in the silence of his brother's exquisite garden it seemed to him that the pure and untarnished word of God was *stay*. He wrote to the Department accepting the position with thanks and at the proper time and proper place presented himself to the new prefectural authorities to receive his Letters of Office.

On the plaza outside the Prefecture Council Offices he saw those same thugs who had crippled his brother with rings of office on their fingers, laughing and swaggering and receiving the praises and adulations of their people. He realized then how easily a man may hear his own cowardice and ease and call it the pure and untarnished word of God.

"It is a cold, hard land, God's Country," said Dr. Kalimuni, "and not welcoming to warm-blooded creatures like we Timboroa folk. But at least I will not be asked to dispense the justice of murderers. Do you think my conscience will be clear then? I am at heart too simple a soul for these complex times. It is the great gift of God, simplicity of heart,

I would not be arrogant enough to claim this humility for myself, but I do know that I am adrift in history.

"My maternal ancestors are Asmathi folk, from the border country, where the hills I once loved wholly are now divided so I must love one side and hate the other. I do not have the trick of that kind of love." He looked into his empty tea bowl, divining the life of Kalimuni from the shredded leaves. "Oh, we are all very strong on what we are not, but weak on what we are. To define something in terms of what it is not, that is the disease of our times; can you understand that? A Proclaimer can tell you what he is against but not what he is for; a Confessor knows he is anti-Proclaimer but has no conception of what it means to be pro-Confessor. *Empire out!* but what in? What you are is what you are against. That is bastard thinking. Hurt will come to the hearts of us all from it."

The great river flowed past, wide and slow.

"If only you would speak, Mathembe Fileli. You and all like you, if only you would speak out and say, *Enough of this,* if only you would even once refuse to let us death-haunted, bigoted old people speak your words for you. Go on, speak, say something. What have you to say about this world you have been given by us? Do you like it, do you hate it, do you want it, and, if not, what do you want in its place? How will you change things, what will you make better, what will you make worse, what will you make different? Speak. Say it out. Why are we so afraid to ask for the things we truly desire?

"I am sorry. I was unforgivably insensitive. I have found this troubling worm of anger in my spirit. We learn most about ourselves in tribulation." A wind from the east stirred Dr. Kalimuni's sparse hair. "All this time, and I have avoided the one question I know is the only question you wish answered. Very well, I shall answer it."

This is the tale that Dr. Kalimuni told Mathembe that sunlit autumn afternoon of the second day of the voyage to God's Country: the story of her father.

And they drive and they drive and they drive. All day they drive, it seems, though who can know? Inside the armored troop carrier there is neither day nor night, nor light, nor time, nor distance, nor any certainty. There is only the sound of the tracks, the endless sound of the endless tracks, grinding on, forever. The sound, and the smell.

The smell of shit and piss, the smell of sweat; the fear smell of men who have been confined together in the hot, stinking dark without food, without water, without any place to relieve themselves, for a time without time, driving and driving and driving.

When you are in the dark with nothing to see, nothing to hear but the roar of engines, nothing to smell but the stink of your own shit, when you can feel nothing but the numb vibration of the seat beneath you, the bulkhead behind you, your mind retreats into strange dark corners: places where time stretches, where time contracts, where hours pass in the space of a few breaths and the interval between the tick and tock of your heart spans the rise and fall of whole creations; places where you feel yourself swelling like a great star-filled festival blimp to encompass the universe or dwindling to a speck, a dot, a subquantal fragment falling between the cracks of reality. You hear the pure white noiseless roar of heaven and the helpless bellowing of hell. And still the armored carrier drives on, drives and drives and drives.

When it stops the silence and darkness are so complete they seem like death. You cannot believe that the din of engines, the numbing vibration, have ended. But someone speaks and you realize you are not dead. The carrier has stopped. Stopped dead. Someone hammers on the door, *Let us out let us out let us out for the love of sweet God let us out.* No one answers. In the stinking darkness a spirit of community is born; where one fails many hands may succeed. You beat your fists bloody on the metal walls of the carrier, roar and shout until your head spins with the roaring echoes thundering back at you in the cramped metal box. You cannot see the blood on your fists, you can only feel the warm slow trickle of it down your palms, down your wrists, down your arms.

No one comes.

And you begin to be afraid. It is a different type of fear from the fear you had when you were moving, for while you were moving you had at least the hope of a destination, but the fear of being stopped is much worse. I will tell you the nature of this fear. It is the fear that no one will ever come, that the soldiers have left you sealed in this dark box to die. To you sitting here in the broad light of day that sounds a ludicrous fear. When you are in the dark, in the hot, stinking dark, without food, without water, it makes you afraid. Very very afraid.

There is a worse fear than that. The first fear paralyzes you, leaves you freezing even in this sweaty heat. But the second fear, that is the fear that guts you. What if you have already died, died without your knowing it. What if there really is a hell? What if this is that hell, that you will stay forever in this darkness, this heat, this hunger and thirst and foulness and fear? That is the fear you keep to yourself, for once it is spoken aloud the screaming will start and never end, all hope abandoned.

But you think about it. Your mind comes back to it time and time again. Everything is a reminder that you are in hell. The conversations you try to strike with the men you cannot see on either side of you: how many tens, hundreds, thousands, hundreds of thousands of years might it take for every possible topic of conversation to be exhausted? But hell is forever, the time will surely come—nothing can stop it—when you reach the limits of language, and then, when every possible topic of conversation has been exhausted, you are damned to start again, to repeat these conversations not ten times, not a thousand times, not a million times, but an infinite number of times, over and over and over and over.

My God, that is a terrible fear. Eternity. You dare not contemplate it too long, too closely, for it will drive your spirit to madness. But in the darkness, in the heat and hunger and thirst and foulness, there is nowhere else for it to turn.

And the door opens. The light! It is a physical pain, stabbing into the heart of you.

Out. Out. Everyone out. Patches of lesser brightness within the white glare are soldiers. They look like angels. The sight of them, so pure and bright and holy, makes you want to cry. You love them. You love them with a purer and brighter and holier love than you have ever loved before. You would do anything for them, anything, because they have saved you, they have delivered you from the hell in the metal box. *Line up. Over there. Move. Kneel. Hands on heads. On heads.* Yes yes, look, see, how fast I move, how low I bend to kneel, how flat my hands are on top of my head, do I please you?

Blink blink blink away the light dazzle. Little by little the world makes itself visible to you. You are at a military base, kneeling in the chewed-up dirt in a long line of shit-stinking men and boys with your hands on your head. There are trees, vegetation, blue sky, soft white cumulus. The earth beneath your legs is wet, the leaves and bracts of the trees glisten with recent rain. God, you think, you will never complain about rain again.

Then the soldiers come, and with them the third fear. That is the final fear, for the other fears were imaginary but the third fear is real.

These are not Imperial soldiers who arrested you at the checkpoint outside Timboroa. These are black-and-brown uniforms, the black of the Empire, the brown of the land's soil. They are the militia. An officer comes along the line, an officer in a black-and-brown uniform. He has a stick with which he touches each man and boy on the side as he passes down the line. He looks at you. He touches his stick to your side and you wish you could feel the ecstatic release of your bladder relaxing and the piss running down your legs and all the fear with it. But you are dry as a thigh bone in hell. He stands in front of you, tapping his stick against his leg, *tap tap tappy-tap tap*, checking a list of names.

He calls out five names.

One of them is your name. The soldiers come. They put their hands under your shoulders and lift you and take you away. *No no God no no* you beg. The soldiers laugh. *Dumb hick,* they say, *do you not know you are free to go?* You are taken into the militia base to be washed and fed and given clean clothing. The rest remain kneeling on the damp soil with their hands on their heads. They are the friends and neighbors among whom you have lived your whole adult life. The soldiers have made the men and the boys take their clothes off. They stand naked with their hands on their heads. Some have had their hands bound behind them with metal wire. *It is not your problem now* says the fat grinning guard who is escorting you and the other four who have names that sound like yours. He pushes you in a not unfriendly way into the building with the flat of his weapon. *We are all friends here*, he says, offering you his left hand.

But though they feed you and wash you and give you clean clothes that almost fit and telecomm for vehicles to come and take you where you want to go, they are not your friends. They are foul and boorish men, ignorant and violent. It frightens you, their ignorant violence. All you have in common with them is the sound of your name and the hand with which you write it. But that is what is important.

The black-and-brown officer comes personally to offer you his apologies and to see you off. He salutes you with his stick as you are driven away in a foul-smelling smoky Imperial automobile. It drives past a row of small trees: thirty-seven, you count, standing in a long row rooted in the rain-damp earth.

And you die there, on the skin-upholstered rear seat of the black Imperial automobile.

River night welled up from the dark waters. Indigo sky; a line of red above the western shore the remains of day. Lights ghosted by, a sister running with the flow. Sirens greeted each other.

"Of course I filed charges as soon as I reached Jadamborazo. It was a simple matter to find out where I had been held and on whose orders. Of course it came to nothing; the great lie of democracy, its essential paradox, is that democracy is first to be sacrificed when its security is at risk. Every state is totalitarian at heart; there are no ends to the cruelty it will go to to protect itself.

"Forgive me. Cynicism is a sin, and a particularly vile and choking one. It gave me bitter satisfaction to hear on the radio news some months later that the Regional Detention Center where I had been held had been attacked by the Warriors of Destiny, its garrison slaughtered, and the building burned. I have been back; I could not be wholly free until I did, can you understand that? It is a shell. The Warriors of Destiny were uncharacteristically thorough. Strangely, none of the man-trees was touched. Thirty-seven trees. They were quite tall then, quite beautiful. Your father is tenth from the right. He was beside me all the time in the troop carrier, by my right-hand side. He stood beside me in the line when I and those four others were called out. Next to him is the rebel boy he tried to shelter, on his right-hand side."

Dr. Kalimuni held up his hands. He studied them minutely.

"Look," he said. "No more shaking. How remarkable." And he laughed a short, sour laugh and *Unchunkolo* drove on into the night, toward the north. Then, after silence, he said, "Your grandfather, he is still with you?"

Mathembe nodded, indicating the rear of the ship, where the head was temporarily accommodated among *Unchunkolo*'s dreamers.

"I would like to see him one last time. I feel I should beg his forgiveness, but for what I am not certain. Surviving, probably. Does anyone on this ship have a *fili* board? I should most like to play with him one final game."

They did not speak again, for the morning brought Anadhrapur and the coast of God's Country. Beautiful Anadhrapur, beneath the trees. The Proclaimers thronged the decks for their first view of the beautiful town. They pointed and waved to relatives, actual and imagined, on the quayside. They rushed from the ship, down the companionways, onto the quay; they could not wait to touch the ground of God's Country. Some kissed the concrete. Some kissed the immigration officials. Some kissed each other. Home. Home. They were home at last.

"God, what happened to the town?" asked Lifter, up on the high deck with Mathembe Fileli. Once Lifter realized that Two's admiration of Mathembe was not reciprocated, she allowed herself to like the no-ass less-tits refugee. She admired toughness wherever she found it.

Shrug. Meaning: What can happen to a town? A house, yes, a street, yes, a district, perhaps: a town?

"Half of the town is missing. Gone. There, there, and there." Her hands described entire geographies. "Those hills there, there used to be houses, paddies, gardens, trees. What happened to them?"

"Rezoning," said passing First Supercargo. "Have you not heard? The hills have been rezoned a Proclaimers-only district. The Confessors have been cleared out."

"With their houses, orchards, paddies, and gardens too?" Oh, fatal curiosity. Before they went ashore, Lifter made Mathembe wear a scarf in *Unchunkolo's* colors around her head.

"If there is stuff going on, we do not want to get mistaken for Confessors. Even if we are."

The initial rejoicing of the Proclaimers had broken into eddies of confusion and disillusion, clusters of homecomers stood around on the quayside with their possessions piled around them, all wearing the distinctive semi-frowns of people who have arrived in heaven and are not sure if it is exactly what they had imagined. Mathembe saw Dr. Kalimuni talking to an immigration officer in the new colors of God's Country, blue and gold. She turned up the collar of her HAVE YOU SEEN THESE PEOPLE? jacket against him.

The streets of beautiful Anadhrapur were thick with soldiers in the blue and gold uniforms of God's Country. Blue and gold dazzle-painted battletrux dozed in the shade of her many trees.

"Something going down here I do not like," growled Lifter. Voices hailed them from a dozing battletrux.

"Yo, bitches!"

"You can have the big one. Me, I like them skinny."

"Like hell. They are Confessors, can you not see?"

"Eyes, boy, eyes; look, riverboat bitches. Got the colors of that boat came in this morning."

"That makes a difference?"

"That makes a difference."

Mathembe laid her hand on Lifter's shoulder. *Peace, sister*.

"If they had tried, I would have torn their balls off. I used to love this town. What do they think they are doing to it?"

Then they emerged from the web of bright clean cobbled footpaths and leafy shaded courts and saw what it was they had done to the town Lifter had loved so well.

Above the line of the hundred-meter level, Anadhrapur did not exist. The tops of the low hills and bluffs that tumbled down to the river were covered in a layer of pale green glaze. Lobes and runnels of the stuff had flowed some tens of meters down the streets, banked against walls on the upslope side of houses. Mathembe knelt, touched the pale green translucent stuff, sniffed it. Smooth but slightly sticky, like semi-polymerized synthetic flesh. It smelled of mornings, fresh and cool.

An open, upturned hand: *What is it?*

"The old hilltop districts of Anadhrapur. Confessortown, all its houses and factories and shops and streets and gardens and orchards."

How? Mathembe's open mouth demanded.

"Gene-bombed. Reduced. My God."

A tilt of the head, a frown. *I do not understand*.

They stepped up onto the lobe of plasm, walked out across the gently undulating greenness.

"They must have ordered everyone out, put up a containment field, and then gene-bombed it. Reduced everything within the field to organic sludge. With all the Confessors gone they can reseed it, and all those wonderful fare-paying Proclaimers down on the dock will have beautiful new homes and gardens."

The plasm beneath their plastic-soled deck boots was mottled and whorled with spirals in forty shades of green; the dead hilltops sparkled in the heat of the midday sun. Lifter shook her head.

"My God. My God. My God."

Mathembe touched her arm.

Not everyone. . . .

Her face was beautiful, framed within the whirls and eddies of plasm, her hair frozen forever in free fall, every curl and coil and lock perfect, preserved. Her lips were parted as if with final words embedded in them. Her hands reached up through the thin film of green that separated her from the sky, locked open by rigor mortis. Gnawing, pecking creatures come scavenging across the green genefields had reduced the hands to bloody bones and shreds of skin.

"Pleading," said Lifter. "Please God, keep it off me."

Or offering? Mathembe mimed a woman with her last drowning breath holding her baby out of the solidifying plasm.

"Saved or eaten?" said Lifter.

But Mathembe's heart was still now, tranquil. The woman was not her mother.

That night *Unchunkolo* took on new cargo. The Confessors came from the warehouses and loading sheds along Anadhrapur's quays where they had been hidden away all day. They wore their best clothes and their children were very clean. Captain and the Department of Foreign Affairs had struck the deal that morning: out of the 80 percent exit tax, the Anadhrapur regional authorities would subsidize the cost of chartering the ship to take them down two days' sail across the border to the resettlement camps.

Summoned from his nest above the pit of souls by an untowardness in the familiar rhythm of *Unchunkolo's* night music, Two found her sitting by the aft deck rail beneath a moon and stars hanging frighteningly close and huge. She was a ghost by moonlight in white T-shirt and leggings, though the night was cold in these northern waters. Two's breath steamed as he stood, wrapped in his quilt, unsure of his emotional courage.

Strange things lay under her hands: micro trees, micro trux, tiny flittering helicopter creatures. As he watched she rubbed a ball of plasm between her hands, opened her fingers to reveal a tiny model house in her palm. She set it among the trees to join the others in her micro township, and Two saw that what he had taken to be trees were in fact homunculi, legs fused together, uplifted arms splintering into branches, twigs, leaves. Thirty-seven of them. A proper forest. Mathembe picked up a toy trux. Wheels spun, miniature motor muscles throbbed. From her silver belt pouch she produced a firestarter. Fire in the night lit her face yellow. With exquisite care she held the tiny creature over the gas flame. It kindled, caught, blazed up. A snap of fingers, Mathembe dropped the trux; blazing, keening, it ran hither, thither, burning, dying across the deck, and fell with a hiss into the receiving river.

Then, with her firestarter at its highest setting, Mathembe waved a curtain of flame over her miniature town. Houses, tree creatures, trux: all went raving up in burning.

"Mathembe, what are you doing?"

She turned, saw him standing there beneath the swaying shadow of First Mate's suspended automobile. She growled deep in her throat, which anyone who has a growling animal will tell you is the most dangerous growl of all. By the dying light of her burning toys, fingers hooked into claws. Canines bared.

"Mathembe?" He waited her out, stared her down, and the moonlight tumbled from the wake of churned water from the big turning wheel. "Mathembe?"

And she was a bundle of greasy dreadlocks and white rags huddled by the rail, sobbing unconsolably.

"It is all right," said Two. "Everything is all right now." What a great and damnable lie. He went to her. They sat wrapped in each other. He traced the track of her tears down her face with the edge of his thumbs. He pushed the lank black hair out of her eyes, rubbed at the smoky smudges on her face.

"Is it your family?"

Yes, Mathembe mimed, No, but Two had not the literacy for mixed messages. Rummaging in her silver pouch, Mathembe found a black marker pen. FATHER, Mathembe wrote on the thigh of her white leggings. MY FATHER IS DEAD.

"Oh, shit. Oh, sorry."

She drew a thick black vertical line across his lips. *Say nothing.*

"Was that what that man you were talking to told you? The Proclaimer? That bastard—"

A sudden black slash across his face. *Shut up, you know nothing.*

GOOD FRIEND. This on the inside of her right leg. MY FRIEND. DR. KALIMUNI.

"How did it happen?"

SOLDIERS. And on her belly and right thigh she drew in little stick hieroglyphs the death of Chepsenyt and the flight of the refugees and the arrest of the menfolk. It was not told simply or quickly, Two's many questions were answered with little annotations: MILITIA, PROCLAIMER TOWN, WARRIORS/DESTINY. Across her shoulders and chest she told the story of her father's death. TRUX. DARKNESS. HUNGER. FEAR. Each underscored by rows of tightly drawn spirals, the pictogram of *endlessness*. And, between her small breasts, the terminal tree, shoots and twigs and roots coiling out along arms, into navel, knotting around spine around hips down legs into groin.

"Mathembe . . . shit."

She sat, wreathed in the heat of her own breath, eyes dark but brilliant.

TREES FIRE FLEEING, she wrote on her left calf. ALL MY LIFE, RUNNING, DRIVEN.

"Driven by what?"

She circled the hem of the white leggings with tiny, precise ideograms. THINGS OUTSIDE ME.

"Things like what?"

PEOPLE. POLITICS. RESPONSIBILITY. FAMILY. GRANDFATHER.

"What do you think you should do?"

DO NOT KNOW. Circled in black, three, four, five, six times. Do not know do not know do not know do not know do not know do not know do not know.

"But what do you want?"

GRANDFATHER THINKS SHOULD STAY. MAKE NEW LIFE.

Again: "But what do *you* want?"

And, in tiny scribbles on her left flank: *Me back.*

"Do you want to stay with us?" *With me,* he almost said. This time he understood the *yes, no.*

"Why?"

GUILTY. And before he could repeat his question: TIRED. ANGRY.

GUILTY. Mathembe circled the RESPONSIBILITY on her ankle, and the words FAMILY, FATHER, GRANDFATHER.

"And what are you going to do?"

Black circle. Around and around the symbol for DO NOT KNOW. Then the black fiber pen slashed out the DO NOT KNOW.

Do know. Know with sudden and utter certainty. A trailing hand: *Two, come.*

Come where?

Here. She pointed with the black pen down into the pit of souls. She uncapped it with her teeth—a gesture that shivered Two with a totally unexpected erotic thrill—and slowly encircled the symbols MY FATHER on her white thigh.

A shift in the current, a stir in the night wind, set First Mate's new automobile swaying on its derrick.

FIND FATHER. FIND TRUTH. TRUTH WILL SET FREE. AT LEAST— Mathembe growled; there was no more room on her body for words. Seizing Two's arm, she rolled up his sleeve and continued on his skin—THEN WILL BE ABLE TO DECIDE FOR ME.

They worked quickly. They worked silently. They worked with the desperate efficiency of people who dare not be found out in their madness.

"God, what if the crew . . ." Two protested, "God, what if you cannot get back? God, what if . . ." Each time, Mathembe struck him across the face with the black fiber-marker scar of her disdain. *Coward.*

Hooking the interfacers onto the heads in the pit, running out the sheaves of neural cable, splicing in the brainplants: *Hurry up now, there is not much time.*

"This is impossible," Two said as Mathembe fixed the brainplants around her head. In Chepsenyt, *then*, her mother had spent painstaking hours teasing and tying Mathembe's hair into coils and ringlets. She had been too young to understand the pure joy a parent can take from its child's hair. How sad her mother had been when she had had to shave her head against the infestations of Gangerabili. "This is stupid, Mathembe, please, do not do this."

A click of the fingers. *Help me, stupid.* And he did, hooking up the brainplants until her head was a mass of sucking, oozing connections meat-wired into the Dreaming. He did it because he was stupid and loved her. Cocooned at the center of the web of neural linkages, Mathembe lay back on the deck, closed her eyes, and sent the mental command whispering along her nervous system. In a cascade of synaptic fire, the brainplants came alive and Mathembe Fileli's Mathembe-Fileliness swept out from her in a wave front of expanding consciousness.

Nothing. Rushing howling nothing. This is the Dreaming, this blackness, this darkness? Is death then death, annihilation, and the Dreaming only fond hopes and illusions attached to knots of complexity in the matrix?

Where are you, Father, my father? Hear your daughter, she wants you.

Did her headlong flight into nothing slow, did she perceive somewhere a limit to this limitless domain, a boundary where she might be turned back upon herself and her Mathembe-Fileliness flicker like a holographic goddess out of a pattern of standing waves along the edge of eternity?

First the sleep, then the Dreaming.

Darkness again, but not the darkness that was before. A close, claustrophobic darkness, pressing in close, enfolding womblike on all sides. Earth. She is a seed of consciousness buried in the earth, held within the husk of her own skull. Summer warmth and winter cold, soft percolating rains and bone-dry droughts wash over her, pain and pleasure to her dreaming senses; they call to her, dream-Mathembe curled up within herself, a seed in the womb of earth. She feels new life tear within her: *roots* rip free from her, questing along deep-buried mineral traces, scenting for water; *shoots* thrust up like begging hands searching for the light. With a cry she bursts into the light, uncoils, summoned by light; she cries aloud in her spirit at the touch of the rain on her new skin. Moons and seasons wheel past in seconds—for time itself is an invention of the human mind—and timeless second by timeless second Mathembe grows, pressing her roots deep deep—ah, God!—into the unsubstance of the Dreaming, splitting and schisming into branches, twigs roaring upward upward outward outward toward the light, and the final ecstatic eruption into *leaves*, each leaf a lens through which she perceives the electromagnetic rainbow of this dreaming place, entire, naked, one thing, unfiltered, unanalyzed, undisguised by human consciousness. With her ten thousand chloro-phyll eyes she feels moons and suns and stars slow in their precipitous wheel above her, slow, slow, and settle into their diurnal pattern.

Years passed. Seconds. There was a time of heat and, with it, fruit, a ripening, a swelling, a filling that was joy like she had never known before; things that moved too fast for her vegetable perceptions to focus on devoured the fruit on the branch but that too was a filling, fecund joy. After the time of heat there was a time of cold, and Mathembe screamed ten thousand screams for every leaf that withered and died and blew away on the wind from the north. Naked and blind. But within the keeping of her thick bark, her heart was safe and warmed, turned inward in contemplation.

Spring touched her while winter's fist was still closed around her, a spiritual, sensual, sexual stirring, a hormonal warmth waking in her imaginary belly, building, mounting, growing hotter, hotter, smelting and melting and reducing her in a storm of enzymes and genetic information to formlessness, an idea, a potential, a possibility. In winter's depth the promise of spring tried her and molded her; month after month she screamed in the fires that were burning her, shaping her according to her golden dreams and darkest sorrows. She fought within the confines of her wooden cocoon, struggled, but spring was not yet come in all its strength and joy. *Time is not yet* the voices down among the roots whispered to Mathembe, trapped and delirious within the tree, *but time will be soon.*

The first touch of the sun split her skin open like a knife. The dry brittle bark fissured, patches of skin and wood flaked and fell as the trunk cracked. Something silver stirred within.

An arm reached for the light. The tree shrieked, shook to renewed tremors. The outstretched hand opened, palm up, to catch the light. The long narrow slit in its trunk spasmed, opened wider. A leg now. A silver leg, a hip. Mathembe struggled; the umbilicals and placentories that had sustained her through the transforming winter tore free, dripped translucent golden ichor. Mathembe wrestled her torso into the sun. With her free hand she wiped the gum from her eyes. Light burst upon her. Primal light. She screamed. And was free.

Naked, she knelt huddled on a tapestry of many-colored mosses. Sun dried the webs and drips of birth ichor on her skin to transparent film that cracked and fell to dust as she tested, tasted, tried thrilling new muscles. Mathembe stood, enthralled by her resurrection body, gazing at her new hands, new breasts, new thighs and calves and feet and arms and belly.

She was silver. She was beautiful, beautiful as she had only dreamed she could be beautiful. She shook out her long steel-colored hair and the dreadlocks rang like bells, threw back her head to rejoice in the play of her new muscles, the stretch of her silver skin. Light filled her eyes, blue sky, white clouds, framed by the towers and spires of forest trees.

She turned from the contemplation of her new self to her surroundings. She was alone and naked in a small forest clearing. On every side wild primal woods enclosed her: brilliant, vibrant, ringing with life and color. Life called to life from every branch and pillar; the air was iridescent with the hum of winged creatures, tame as the trees, that came hurrying to her outstretched fingers. Mathembe giggled in delight, and that was the greatest wonder of all.

In this place after life, the injunction was gone. She was free to laugh, and cry, and speak.

"Mathembe." She spoke aloud and at the touch of her voice a thousand creatures rose singing and flocking from the forest, all perfect and unsullied as the first morning after Creation. This was how it must have been in the footsteps of the Ahleles, as Janeel and Oboluwayé came creeping from their crèche pods within the earth to survey the transformation of their world. Like that nursling humanity, Mathembe went naked and unashamed, naming all the creatures that rose up before her, setting the spires and huge parasol fungi trembling with the sound of her name.

She recognized this afterplace. It was the forest of her childhood, the deep woods around Chepsenyt where she had played in her solitude, changed, transformed, made perfect in death. Dark clouds covered the sky. Mathembe took shelter from the brief, heavy rain in a stand of parasol fungi, the least of which was three times her height. Sudden squall winds stirred the land corals and trumpet trees. Mathembe curled her silver body around the fungus stalk. Presently she slept.

Within the Dreaming, she dreamed. She dreamed that the dark clouds grew darker still. Lightning punished the earth, and thunder. Distant thunder. It was strange, this thunder of the dreaming within the Dreaming, it had a double tone, like the beating of a heart. No. Like the beating of Proclaimer drums. No. Like footsteps, forever approaching yet never drawing nearer. Like the footsteps of the Ahleles. In her dream within a dream, she waited and listened, and a storm wind shook the forest like rags and lightning bolted and bolted and bolted, crazy mad crashing lightning, and within the dream within the dream she grew afraid, and the footsteps crashed upon the earth but never drew any nearer.

Then she slept. And after the sleep, she dreamed again. She dreamed that she was talking with an angel of God, a bright and shining angel, holy and stunning, who was telling her the secrets of God and the Just Men Made Perfect who were the Ykondé saints, and all she thought was how fantastic he looked and that she wanted very very much to do it with him.

Then she woke from the dream within the Dreaming and saw that the angel had been no dream at all.

He sat upon a stool of land coral across the small clearing where the parasol fungi grew. He was as naked and unashamed as Mathembe. His skin was bronze to her silver. But she knew he was an angel because of the wings on his back. He was not as inhumanly handsome as the angel in her dream, but he was powerfully attractive. She wondered if it was a sin to think of sex in the Dreaming. She wondered if it was a sin to envy an angel his wings. They were deeply wonderful wings. They were like silk and diamond; they glittered in the shafts of light that fell through the tumultuous forest into this small glade so that at times they seemed not to be there at all. Great proud sweeping gossamer wings. Wonderingly, Mathembe touched them. A cascade of chiming music swept the glade.

"May I touch *your* wings?" said the angel.

"I have no wings," said the dream-Mathembe.

"No?" said the angel. He touched her back. Mathembe winced in pain. Her silver skin bulged, tore; bud wings, creased tight as moon-blooming flowers, unfolded and filled and blossomed. Strength poured through the wings; they could take her anywhere, anywhere she willed. Just one beat of her mind would take her there.

"Now you are an angel too," said the angel. "Or, at least, no less angel than I."

He rose to his feet. He looked up at the beams of light slanting into the glade. His wings beat and filled the glade with music.

"Come," he said and leapt into the air, sliding with a shiver of wings up up the shafts of light. And without knowing how she did what she was doing, Mathembe followed. And it was as if she had been born knowing how to fly, that there had never been a time when she could not fly. The angel soared up up before her and she followed. The many-colored forest fell away beneath her; she did not look down, she had eyes only for the beautiful bronze angel leading her up, up into the light; that, and the ecstatic rush of atmosphere along her silver body.

Is this how they do it? she wondered. *On the wing, far above all human cares and woes?*

Up they flew, and upward, piercing the blue sky like javelins until Mathembe felt that if she looked down she would see the dream forest like a dot in space beneath her. And she did, and it was: a tapestry-colored island adrift upon an ocean of clouds. Still they climbed and Mathembe saw other islands adrift on the ocean of clouds, forest worlds like the one where she had been born into this Dreaming, many many hours, days even, of flying distant. They flew up until the sky darkened; they flew to the very edge of space where the air should have been too thin for even an angel to live, but her wings beat with undiminished strength and she realized that in the Dreaming, breathing, like eating and drinking and sleeping, was a pleasure to be taken at her discretion.

"Come," the gorgeous angel said again, in air too thin to support words, and with a sudden thrilling movement of his body, he was diving away from her, wings folded close to his back, arms tight to his sides, plummeting, hurtling, screaming for terminal velocity, faster faster. With a shriek of excitement, Mathembe furled her gossamer wings and followed.

At the speed of thought they flashed past the edge of the forest island and into the ocean of clouds. Mathembe saw faces in the clouds, blurred by the relativity of her headlong flight. Faces, dark bodies, row upon row, file upon file, and then they were under the cloud base. Beneath them spread a dull gray sea, tossed by many winds. Wings snapped open, crazy with G-force, Mathembe and the bronze angel broke their fall, wingtips creasing the surface of the planet-wide sea before they whipped up in a parabola.

"Now do you see?" said the bright and shining angel.

Mathembe saw. And what she saw shocked her.

Vast man creatures toiled across a stone-gray sea, ankle deep in the breaking waters, each footstep leaving boiling wakes tens of kilometers long behind them. The more distant behemoths were half hidden by the curvature of the world, feet in the ocean trenches, heads wreathed in clouds. With a flick and twist of wings, Mathembe followed the angel toward the closest of the man creatures. With each beat the thing resolved itself in increasing detail.

The man things, kilometers high, were composed of millions upon millions of human bodies lashed and roped together into a metal frame.

She drew nearer and saw how the men and the women and the children worked treadmills and pulled levers that transferred their individual energies to the mechanisms that moved the monster. She saw the knotted muscles and tearing sinews, the faces hollow with unending toil. There should have been sound. There should have been the sound of whole cities dying at once. There should have been the sound of a million voices crying out in common suffering. The man things toiled on in silence, bearing paradise upon their bowed shoulders.

Wings beat. Mathembe and the angel flickered up through the cloud layer. The bowed head of the man monster watched them with its man eyes, its man lips moved, but the flash of flying silver by bronze was too fast, too bright to hear what it might say.

They looped over the edge of the forest island and, in a rainbow of wings, touched toes to the moss in a clearing among towering balloon groves. Mathembe folded her wings about her like a cloak.

"Who are they?" she asked, imagining the damned, the sinful, the selfish or cruel or simply thoughtless or those who in some unthinking way might have offended against a god's quixotic laws. The angel laughed. It is a strange and terrible thing, the laughter of angels.

"Do you not know? They are the Proclaimers."

Then it was as it often is in dreams, when strangers are recognized to be friends in strange bodies, and friends go unrecognized in their own familiar forms. And angels may be fathers, and fathers angels.

"There is no part of the land where the roots do not reach," said the angel who was her father. "There is no place that is not part of the matrix. The Dreaming is everywhere. The Proclaimers believe that when they die they pass into the nearer presence of God, but even they are part of the Dreaming. While their mortal bodies rot in the earth, the roots are reaching out through the soil, growing into their bodies, along their bones, filling their skulls and nerves, absorbing the dying memories of their selfhood from their neurons, drawing them back from death into the Dreaming, where they are blind, dumb, confused, easily preyed upon by those who have lived their whole fleshly lives in the knowledge of the Dreaming.

"It is not paradise, you see. It is another stage of living, another kind of life. Heaven still awaits; but in this world as in the other world, there is sin, there is wickedness, there is evil, there are oppressors and oppressed. Except that here it is the Confessors who are the oppressors, and the Proclaimers the oppressed."

No degree of oppression in the flesh life, Mathembe thought, could warrant the terrible punishment the Confessors meted out to the Proclaimers in death. She could understand now their need for a hell, and why Confessor theology had never evolved the concept of a place of eternal punishment.

"You made this." It was an accusation, and her father knew it for what it was. "You brought me here, to this place you have made." Her words were clumsy; even in the Dreaming she had no skill with them.

"You would blame me, after what they did to me?" her father's spirit said. "You would blame me?" He stood, and the dream-Mathembe saw that his bronze skin was stained with meander marks, a patina where roots and creepers had devoured his flesh-life body. Knotholes marred his arms and legs. "But you are wrong. I did not make this place. This not my Dreaming. This is the Dreaming of all of us, hundreds of generations of Filelis. They are all here, my people and your people. If you wish to blame anything, blame yourself, for the same genetic thread runs through you as through them. This is as much your place as theirs. They reached out through the matrix, and sought me, and caught me, and brought me here, and I in my turn found you, hunting and lonely in the darkness, and grew you from a seed."

"But I am not dead," said the dream-Mathembe. "That is the difference. I can go back."

"Then why are you here?" Her father's tone was suspicious now, severe. Was he jealous that Mathembe could still claim a life and a body to return to while he remained trapped within his forefathers' dreaming?

"Because I need to know."

"Need to know what?"

"That my mother and Hradu are still alive."

"Ah." Her father nodded slowly. "Death changes things, you see. Relationships, loves, hatreds; they exist on the either side of death, but they are different things. They do not pass through death. What passes through death are memories of affections. From those memories we must try to rebuild our affections."

"What are you saying?"

"I have other loves here."

She struck her father with her bright silver hand. And all the flying, fluting things went up as one thing with a thrum of wings.

"You will find it so when your turn comes," he said. The angel wings unfolded. Her father looked into the blue blue sky. "But I still remember affection. I still remember love. I still care for them, as I care for you." He lifted a little into the blue blue air. "I have not found them, either on any of the forest islands or adrift in the matrix. They are still among the flesh-living."

"Where are they?"

"Flesh life and dream life are as separate as flesh life and what exists before birth. I cannot penetrate death as easily as you, or as my father, in his half-dead, half-alive state, may."

"Do you know where they are?"

Her father shrugged. His iridescent wings shivered, a ripple of chiming music.

"I have seen them. Not with my own eyes, of course, but through the eyes of others. A glimpse only, a moment in the corner of an eye. But it was them. Do you think I could forget how they look?"

"Where are they?"

"Time does not have the meaning here it does in the flesh. They may be gone, moments, days, years."

"Where?"

"The camps." Her father rose to the level of the treetops. "If you find them, tell them what has happened. The family is the hope of the future, a genetic treasury passing down into further generations. Tell

Hradu not to be angry for me; if you can, save him from his foolishness. Tell your mother she was not responsible, she has never been responsible; if you can, save her from the terrible guilt of always needing to be competent. But do not tell her what I have told you, about the nature of love in this place."

And with a flash of blue-silver wings he was gone into the blue blue heaven.

Then Mathembe felt a tiredness come over her. It was not a tiredness she had willed herself, it was willed upon her by others, her ancestors, stronger in the Dreaming than she, rejecting her, casting her out of this place she had entered by false pretenses, back into flesh life again. She tried to fight against it but there were too many Filelis willing against her. Wrapped in her own wings she curled up on the carpet moss. Sleep came upon her, time ceased to be. Again she dreamed in the Dreaming. She dreamed that sun and moon and stars accelerated in their courses until the sky was a ring of light above her. She dreamed that she slept beneath this streaking sky. Rains fell, winds blew, covering her with dead leaves and bracts; snows drifted over her, and beneath them the leaf litter decayed under bacterial attack into humus, into soil. New growth stabbed its roots into the heart of her, stab after stab after stab, the snows melted away, and her rotting, decaying body put out shoots and circles of red-capped fungi. Mosses colonized her, ferns cartwheeled like fireworks from her sleeping body; in a swift succession of seasons bottle plants, windmill ferns, forest underscrub, and finally full climax forest claimed her while her silver angel body rotted away to a spark, a glow of sleeping consciousness sinking deep within the earth.

Darkness enshrouded her. Like distant stars, other glows of sentience shone in the blackness: fellow souls traveling into death, in search of their personal heavens or hells. But Mathembe's course was set against theirs; she fought the current that drew them deeper into the matrix; ahead light shone, true light, and she fought toward it, fought against the tide of death that grew stronger the closer she willed herself toward the light of the world. The Dreaming tore at her, a rushing torrent now, but she fought on, she fought on, and the light grew brighter and she threw herself toward the light, into the light.

Home!

She opened her eyes.

Unchunkolo's coarse hair matting was rough under her skin. The air was bitter cold and smelled of morning. A line of violet lit the eastern edge of the world. The deck beneath her thrummed: the never-failing pulse of engines. She looked at her body, poor and thin and scarred after the perfect silver of the angel Mathembe. But it was her body. The neural linkages had been removed and lay around her on the deck, a corona of gently writhing biotech. Two knelt over her. He poured tea from a flask, scalding, almost flavorless. Mathembe sipped it down. She tapped his watch.

"One hour twenty-seven minutes. Why, what did it seem to you?"

She shrugged, gestured: *More tea*. Two poured a cup, and as he did he glimpsed for one unguarded moment the place in the back of Mathembe's eyes where the true things are. He saw what it was she kept in there. He knew then that she would leave him.

She would let him come no farther than the companionway. As the omens said, he had been born with river water in his soul and the land would have trapped him with its emotional gravity and destroyed him. He would have gone with her. It hurt, as the true things always hurt, hurt like a hooked knife twisted into your kidneys in an alley in the forgotten end of town. She zipped up her picture jacket against the cold wind from the east. There was premonition of snow in that wind, the smell of ancient winters. He helped her to fix her grandfather's head to the webbing contraption that had so alarmed him, that time in the night when he had thought her a two-headed monster from the Dreaming. The monsters lurking in the Dreaming, he had learned, were altogether more huge and insidious and dreadful. The refugees streamed ashore, clutching the tiny things the Proclaimer Exit Tax had left them. "She is mad," the head said, angry to have been removed from its place in the psychic warmth of *Unchunkolo's* Dreaming. "Why did you not do it with her? Maybe then she would not be going off on this mad chase through the shit end of the world. Well, now you have missed your chance. She would have been good." Two understood that they had never been destined to be lovers; the gods of the chemicals, the lords of the pheromones, had decreed it so; they had willed for him a rarer and richer relationship altogether.

They had smelled the camp while *Unchunkolo* was still a night's sail upstream. They had smelled it on the east wind that blew down from the fire-scarred hillsides above Kilimambasa town. It was the smell of piss and shit. It was the smell of raw, red, dead earth trampled into mud by many many feet. It was the smell of wood smoke and trash fires. It was the smell of bad water and rotting organicals. It was the smell of sicknesses that everyone had believed banished from the land thousands of years ago but which had only lain dormant, like Janeel and Oboluwayé in their crèche pods, waiting for the turn of the world to spin their way. It was the smell of all these things, which together transcended themselves and became above all the smell of one thing: dispossession.

In the dark before the dawn, as *Unchunkolo* found river bottom with her anchor-holds, the camp seemed almost beautiful, crowning the ordered lights of Kilimambasa with a constellation of gloglobes and twinkling smudge fires. Then little by little the growing light dispelled the illusions: the dark skeletons of the big wind rotors on the shaved hilltops turning in the east wind; the pall of wood smoke and hydrocarbon smog; the hacks and slashes of bare red earth, foot-worn, rain-scarred, deep into the flesh of the land; the ugly silver bubbles of the emergency shelters and feeding stations; the wind flutter of the plastic shanties that huddled up against them, greedy whelps at the tit; the ragged thorn walls that enclosed attempts at gardens; the men, already in the dawn light assuming the posture of the dispossessed, squatting on heels, hands draped idly, uselessly over knees. Row upon row upon row of them, in doorways, in alleyways, against walls and fences, by jeepney stops and employment exchanges.

"You cannot go there," Two had said. Mathembe had closed her right fist. Slowly, slowly. *Resolution.*

"All you have is a notion, an idea, something told you in a dream."

Sometimes a notion is all we need, she had said, but she knew that even if she sailed with him to the end of her life he would never learn to read that.

At the top of the companionway she kissed him, as soul friend kisses soul friend, which was not how Two wanted to be kissed by her. Then without a wave, she turned and the steady flow of refugees—bewildered, horrified, relieved, delighted—took her away from him and with a tight singing sound in his ears that was the sound of feelings piling up layer upon layer upon layer he went up to the loading bridge and watched the bright plastic of her backpack pass through the lines of immigration officials and up into the meandering streets of Kilimambasa and the raw earth and smoke of the camp, and there he saw it no more.

That night as *Unchunkolo* deadheaded south with the flow to pick up a tow of timber, he called on Cousin Lifter/External Affairs and they went down to the secret place where everyone went so in truth it was no secret place at all, and there they did it until the stars faded and the edge of the world tilted beneath the sun and to their mutual and absolute astonishment they found that they enjoyed it, and enjoyed each other, and that the world was full of things they found interesting and could laugh at and cry at and enjoy and wonder at together, and when the partnering banns were published on Captain's door at the winter solstice their names appeared on the list and in the years to come they loved and lived and occasionally cheated on each other and occasionally fought and occasionally had the junior crewpersons fleeing from their wars and attained high ranks in ship, family, and state and bore *Unchunkolo* many fine crewpersons as she sailed on, down along the big big river.

THE
CAMPS

THE CROSS-RIVER CURIO COLLECTOR BOUGHT THE HEAD FROM THE café owner for sixty enns because he thought it would make an irresistible attraction to put in the window of his shop on the Avenue of Divine Succor.

The café owner sold the head to the cross-river curio collector because the customers complained that they could not drink their wine and eat their small eats in peace because of the noise it made.

The café owner's partner, a kindly woman and content to be fat, had put the head up on the shelf under the television because it would not stop singing in the street unless someone did take it in, and anyway it had been raining for three days now.

The head was singing in the rain in the street because of the argument it had had with its granddaughter, and crazy with exasperation she had left it there, in the rain and the mud, on the steeply sloping street.

The granddaughter argued with the head because the head

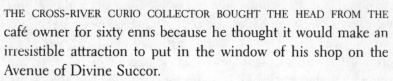

had refused to go with her up that steeply sloping muddy street through the tangle-thorn barricades into the camp.

It had been a strange argument, the argument between the head and its granddaughter in the rain on the streaming, muddy street. A mute girl and a talking head: the night-shift workers going up the hill and the day-shift workers coming down the hill had stopped to see that one.

"What are they arguing about?"

"Seems he thinks it is a big mistake to have come here."

"Sensible him. What does she think?"

Shrug. "She must disagree with him."

"She is mad."

And after the workers had gone, the streets filled with organicals coming and going on many legs, which were the workers from the camps who had no skills that were sought after and had hired themselves out by the day or week in organical service, and still they had argued, the mute girl and the voluble grandfather, but whatever their origin they were organicals now and could not understand that the girl was insisting they must go on, go up to the camps, and the head insisting it was time to give up, time to call an end to the search, time to admit that she could search her whole life away and never find what she was looking for. Time to accept, time to grieve, time to move on like the river, time to look to herself instead of others. The girl in the silver jacket with the pictures on it had picked up the head and tried to carry it up to the checkpoint by main force, but the head had started to sing and shriek and holler so that people came out of the shops and tiny two-table restaurants to see what the hell the din was all about. They had seen the girl then lift the pot with the head in it and smash it down, smash it to the ground, and without a word storm off up the hill through the rain and the jostle of busy, many-legged organicals.

"Holy shit, she must be in some temper," they had said, and then the head, its pot cracked, its rooticles writhing over the filthy cobbles, had started to sing, in the mud, in the street, in the pouring early winter rain.

Of course she came back. Guilt was as natural and inescapable a part of her as her heartbeat. With a handwritten card, she asked in every shop and two-table restaurant along Third Hill Street, but by that time the head, doped up to the cerebral cortex with travel-sickness pills and stuffed into a sports bag so as not to arouse the interest of the custom officials, was within reach of the Empire shore.

Every day as he polished his wares, Mr. Vrishna would say to the head that he hoped it would be bought by someone from above the Fortieth Level, one of the long-legged big-breasted shaven-headed women he saw passing his street window in blue-silver automobiles. Women, he maintained, had a more keenly developed sense of horror than men, and women from above the Fortieth Level had the finest sense of outrage of all. How fine the head would look as the centerpiece of one of their Fortieth Level dinner parties, what a talking point it would make; that would be one dinner party they were sure never to forget. Yes, he hoped that today would be the day one of the streamlined blue-silver cars that ghosted along the Avenue of Divine Succor would stop and a long-legged big-breasted woman with an umbrella to keep the acid rain off her chrome-powdered scalp step out, and look in the window of Vrishna and Company International Objets d'Art, and giggle with silly Fortieth Level pleasure at the sight of the head in its slightly cracked pot. This would be the day when the door opened and the door chimes rang and the high heels of the long-legged big-breasted shaven-headed Fortieth Level woman would click and clack across his polished wood floor (not real wood; who could afford real wood these days? but the cellulose plastics were good ersatz), and her smartcard would glitter blue-silver in the shop lights and his card reader would glitter seductively in return and he would bow and thank her and present her with her unique novelty, and her heels would *click clack click* back out of Vrishna and Company International Objets d' Art, into the falling rain.

The head had been a feature of Mr. Vrishna's window only a few days, and its view of Capital life limited to a few hundred meters of shopfronts, plastic awnings, cheap diners, greasy sidewalks, litter-clogged gutters, holoads for Five Hearts Beer (a thorn of nostalgia for the cramped, smelly apartment on Lantern Lane), splashing taxis, and fuming omnibuses, but it had learned enough of the city to realize that the blue-silver car would never come splashing up to the curb, the long-legged big-breasted shaven-headed woman peer in through the window, her pupils dilated with a fine sense of outrage. For every night it would look up, past the smile tilt swig grin of the Five Hearts Beer girl, up the diamond-studded perspectives of the towers, to the place where they penetrated and shattered the perpetual clouds and made them glow with their lights and navigation beacons, and in the dendrified circuits of its mind it would imagine the towers rising up beyond where it could see, sheer and slender and beautiful and silver in the moonlight, and the sheer, slender, beautiful moonlit people who lived all their lives at dazzling altitude, and it knew that they were as remote and untouchable as his beloved dead wife carried to the farthest edge of the universe by Saint-ships. Once they were up there, they never came down.

If the idea of being a dinner-table conversation piece five kilometers up in the stratosphere did not appeal to the head, neither did a future lived at ground zero in the window of Vrishna and Company International Objets d'Art, squeezed between a clockwork pantheon from the antipodes, in which all the gods could be seen whirling in a kaleidoscopic heaven, and some stuffed extrasolar creature that smelled of formaldehyde. Back across that river were responsibilities and relationships sorely neglected. Back across that river, up that mud-covered hill, through those thorn gates, was his granddaughter, silent before the world. Even one step is a universe for a bodyless head.

The third night that the boy came spinning past, the head hailed him through the glass. Drunk, smashed out of his mind on consciousness-shattering drugs, tripped out on his own neurochemistry through illegal viruses, the boy in the dirty street-length waxed raincoat with the hood covered in badges had reeled back in disbelief. But when you dance with the devil in the pale moonlight nothing may harm you that you do not wish to harm you, and he had crept from the gutter and placed his greasy palms on Mr. Vrishna's lovingly polished glass and steamed it up with his breath.

"What kind of thing are you?" In the darkness beneath his rain-streaming hood, his eyes shone with the unclean things.

"Help me," the head said. "Get me out of here."

The boy shook his head, grinned. "Oh, no, this is great, this is the best one yet. Far and away, the best one yet."

Head thrown back, laughing in the acid rain, he spun away down the Avenue of Divine Succor. In his wake purred street-cleaning robots, rearranging the detritus of yesterday into the litter of today.

He was back the next night, and this time the light did not shine in his retinas so madly. The rain ran down the window and he said, "Geez, you are real after all. What did you do to deserve this, brother?"

"I lived," said the head. "That is all."

The boy laughed but it was not the sour, flaying laugh of the night before, it was the bitter, painful laugh of solidarity. "You and me both, brother." And he was gone.

But the head knew he had him now. He would come back that night to the window, and the night after, and the night after that, and with every night the head would move him a word or so closer.

"You know you can get me out of here if you want to."

"But why would I want to, old man?"

"I am a valuable commodity."

"Then why are you still sitting there in that stupid window?"

"I have been a place no one else has ever been."

"Where is that, then?"

"Death."

"Everyone goes there, old head."

"But none have ever come back again. I have. I have been into death, and I have returned. I know what it is like. Death, boy, death. That is the ultimate trip. Your drugs, your drink, your altered states of consciousness: they are nothing, boy, nothing. But what lies beyond that white light, I know; I have been there, I can tell you."

Late night: early morning umbrellas huddled along the Avenue of Divine Succor; high above, lightning fretted, trapped between the towers like a hunted creature.

"Geez, I dunno, old man." Halfway to the edge of the head's field of vision, he turned, great waxed coat flapping in the chaos winds that blew through the streets of the Imperial Capital. About to say something. About to speak. He waved his hand, shook his head. And was gone.

He did not return the next night, or the next night, or the night after. Then in the nightmare hour when the taxicabs ran scared in the rain-slick streets, a roll of city thunder woke the head from its dreams of guilt and mud-covered streets that climbed up up up forever. And the face looked into his, centimeters away behind the glass.

"Death, old head."

"You want me to tell you? You want to know? I can tell you. All you want to know. The answer to the greatest question."

"I know you can," said the boy in the hooded coat. "Close your eyes." The heavy hammer shivered Mr. Vrishna's window into a hundred flying reflections. Alarms began to wail. The head felt itself lifted from its place between the clockwork pantheon and the extra-planetary creature. Hands took it. Hands hid it beneath the big waxed city coat, in the body stink, the body heat, while feet beat the greasy streets, feet running and running and running.

His name was Ghundaleyo. He was a creature of junctions and intersections, formed by the casual collisions of chromosomes in some trash-lit corner of the Weekend World. Blown by the wind from the street, steered by the lodestone attraction of tangles and knots of human affairs. *What you doing here, let me hear let me see let me touch let me in.* But they would ever turn away with a smile and a tilt of the eyes in the neon light and the glitter of 3 A.M. lip gloss from the polished streamlines of a chrome-pearl automobile. Life was an ever-breaking wave, a tumultuous high which, if you ever lost your surefootedness for one single moment, would drag you down and drown you. Inevitable that he should be drawn to such a place as the I-beam jungle that was his home. Where three elevated monorail lines crossed in webs of cantilevered steel, he had excavated a little nest among the girders, floored with plastic shelving from dead hypermarts, roofed with fluttering swags of ripped black garbage sack. Constantly shaken by suburban monorails and a terrifying whirling, flying storm of black polyethylene rags and streamers when the Big Winds blew from the west, it was den, home, womb, a place to curl your back against reality.

"Geez, what do I do with you?" he asked for, sustained by his perpetual high, he stole not to meet his needs but because something was stealable.

"Feed me," the head said.

"Feed you? You're dead, how can you eat?"

"If you do not feed me, I will be dead. Properly dead."

He stole the head a bottle of house-plant food from a booth at the elevated monorail station.

"Now tell me about death." He dripped five drips onto the rooticles. "Geez, would you look at that. You are some gross shit, old head." The steel-girdered plastic tent rushed and boomed to the pressure waves of accelerating suburban shuttles.

"What is there to know about death? You, boy, you will find out all about it soon enough if you do not watch yourself."

"Do not irritate me, old head. Or I will stick you out all day on the main beam and it will be pissing down with rain and maybe when the trains pass they will shake you off or maybe they will not, but if they do you will fall way way down and crack into a hundred thousand pieces."

Eager for a second step to quickly succeed this first step, the head restrained its criticism.

"Death," the boy said the next night with the wind from the west blowing the ripped layers of garbage sack up in a frenzy of plastic stalactites.

"I will tell you about death," said the head. "But first I want you to take me out. All day I sit here while you sleep and scratch, and all night you are out doing whatever the hell it is you do. Take me out with you. I am bored."

"Then you will tell me about death?"

"Then I will tell you about death."

Thunder rolled around the navigation beacons on the high towers, and they rode through the streets and through the massive buttressed roots of the towers on white-lit, soft-hissing monorails. The head sat on the courtesy table looking out through the raindrop-streaked windows at the lights and the towers and the shapes that moved within the clouds.

"Ride all night on one ticket," the boy said. "Ride until the morning light. You seen enough yet?" The night girls in their stretch-and-strap costumes who worked the night trains sat down opposite Ghundaleyo and offered him sex money drink chemicals if they could play with the head, but what they offered was nowhere he had not been before. They could not offer death.

"Come on, tell me, what is it like?" Lightning spoke from tower to tower; lightning replied from the monorail power grid, lighting their faces nightmare blue.

"What do you imagine it is like?"

Holoads crowded overhead, a convocation of market-force angels.

"I imagine there is a moment after the last heartbeat, after the last breath, while the mind is still alive and aware, when you know that your heart has stopped and will never start again and you know that you have breathed out and will never breathe in again. When I was a kid I used to try to imagine what it would be like, I used to hold my breath and hold it and hold it and hold it until my head was bursting, until everything was red and black before my eyes, until my mind seemed on an edge where it could no longer hold on and any moment would let go, when everything was roaring up in pain and fire and panic. And then I would breathe in, and I would live again. But I imagine that is what death is like: if you were never to breathe in again."

"You have it right," the head lied.

"Dear God," the boy whispered.

He stole it steak. Real steak, dead-animal meat; not the tank-grown slabs of flesh the food corporations called steak, that was copied from Provincial biotecture patents.

"Real good food, old head," he said, dropping snipped-up morsels among the rooticles.

"Do you ever think of getting out of here?" the head suggested. "Do you ever think maybe you could have a better life someplace else? This city is no place for people. This city eats people up, chews every last bit of good out of them, then sticks its fingers down its throat and pukes them up onto the street. You can do better than this place."

"Oh? So? Where?"

"Go east. To the river. There are some good places there. Living is easy along the river. Maybe even go across the river."

"Live among the meatmen? Shit, why?"

But that night when the last of the late-night office workers had been monorailed back to their neat suburbs that went on and on and on and on and on and on around the Capital so that it seemed that the whole universe was made out of mass-market housing with neat lawns and two automobiles and a satellite dish; that night when the nightstick robots went stalking along the boulevards tranquilizing narcos and drunks with neural darts and shepherding droves of them all linked by the brain to its central processor to the precinct for detoxing; that night when the night sirens pulled on their stretch-and-strap suits and clicked into their heels and switched on the subdermal motors that plumpified and cutified and curvified and slimmified their anatomies into altogether more pneumatic, more curvaceous, more alluring contours: that night the boy and his head went out scavenging among the root buttresses of the tower piles. Night and day, day and night, refuse drones and loaders shoveled garbage vented down the waste disposal shafts from the heights above. Megatons of trash nourished the roots of the stratoscrapers. Entire communities depended on the trash, moving with its ebbs and flows on nomadic micro-migrations, digging and picking and sniffing and eating. Surrounded by geographies of garbage, the boy and his head stood under the multimillion-ton bulk of the arcology, beneath the funnel mouth of the vast central vent from which a blizzard of papers and wrappers and leaflets sifted down.

"Goes all the way up to the top," the boy said, throwing his head back as if he might see all those kilometers up into the swirl of gently falling paper. "All the way." Then he crouched, in his greasy city coat, eye to eye with the head, which he had set on the garbage.

"Death, then."

And the head knew that it could stall and feint and lie no longer.

"Death is nothing."

"Yeah, yeah."

"No. Truly. Death is nothing. No light. No dark. No space. No time. No feeling. No sensation. No lack of sensation. No consciousness. Nothing."

"But the white light—"

"An illusion caused by oxygen deprivation of the visual centers of the brain."

"Beyond the white light?"

"Nothing. No return. If you return, it is not death. Death is that from which you can never return."

"But you returned."

"Then I was never truly dead. You think that death is an instant thing? That is not so. Death is a slow thing, and there are many different kinds of death. Your heart may stop, your lungs cease breathing, you may cease all vital signs and be clinically dead, but your body may be brought back to life by the healers. Your physical body may die beyond hope of restoration, but your brain may be maintained by organicals. That is my kind of death. Your brain also may die but your mind, your consciousness, may be maintained by an information network, such as our root matrix, which we call the Dreaming. Then there is the death of the body and the brain and the consciousness, and that is the true death, for it is the one from which no technology can revive you and from which no one has ever returned and of which no one can speak."

"You . . . lying . . . bastard."

The boy stepped back. Leaf upon leaf, scraps and orts, the litter drifted down upon them from unimaginable heights.

"You lying bastard."

Another step farther away. And another, and another. And another.

"You lying bastard!"

The cry came from farther now; the boy in his fluttering waxed coat was almost an illusion behind the snow of falling paper.

"You lying bastard." One final time, on the edge of hearing over the roar of the ventilators and the dumpster engines. And no more.

"Boy!

"Kid!

"Ghundaleyo!"

No.

Then the head knew fear. For the first time since its physical death, it knew vulnerability. And it was a freezing, paralyzing fear, to be vulnerable, to be afraid of the gentle snow of paper settling softly gently upon you, piling up and up and up and covering you over, clogging your mouth so that your cries go unheard, shutting out the light from your eyes. Burying you while you are still alive, for the trash is rich rich food for your rooticles.

It was the robot trash shovelers the head feared the most. There is no arguing with a machine, no margin for error. They would never hear him, never see him as they ground up and down the piles of garbage on their rubber treads. And even if they did hear and see him, he would be just another piece of detritus to them, to be shoveled and scooped and dropped into the grinding maw of a trash compactor or the fiery furnace mouth of a trash incinerator. All night he watched the black-and-yellow chevroned machines whir across the wasteland, red white and blue warning lights pulse-rotating: *Get out of our way get out of our way get out of our way.* The long dark night of the soul.

Dawn in the Capital was a general suffusion of grayness into neon-lit night, like a persistent internal hemorrhage. Spirals of rain blew under the skirts of the stratoscrapers. The scavengers the head had been watching since first light pulled up their hoods and bent closer to the earth as they advanced up the hill toward it. The head studied the man who would be its savior, tall, bent very low to the ground, sweeping his fingertips across the surface of the garbage as he worked his way up the hill. Every once in a while his fingers would pause over some treasure found in the mountains of paper, touch it, turn it over, feel its every intimate pore, and then either slip it under his heavily hooded coat or return it to corruption. Closer. The fingers worked closer. Meters now. Centimeters. Surely he must have seen the head by now?

The sweeping fingers brushed against the pot. Paused. Felt out the contours, the cracks, the cold hard glaze. A hand rose over the head's face, snatched back in horror.

"Hey, what is the matter with you, you blind or something?" the head said.

The searching fingers returned, more careful now, more intimate.

"I thought I recognized the accent." Thumbs touched the head's eyes. "Ah. Long time since I encountered one of these. The things the rich cast out. Is this a new fashion, imported heads from across the river?"

The fingers dabbled among the writhings of the rooticles.

"Watch what you are doing," said the head.

The face beneath the fold of waxed hood smiled. "I hope your command of the language is good enough to appreciate irony." The garbage scavenger stood tall against the gray sun and pushed back the hood of his shapeless waxed coat.

His eyes were two yellow, pustulent sockets, puckered almost shut under the ridges and blisters of purple flesh that covered the upper half of his head like roots.

"Your countrymen, I am afraid. And I loved the place so; everything I touched seemed so alive, vital, brilliant: you can imagine how it would seem to a young soldier of the Emperor on his first tour of duty outside the capital. If only my blindness were beautiful too, I like to think I could bear it a little better, but I touched it once, when the bandages came off, and I will never touch it again."

The hood was pulled down over the destroyed face.

"I am sorry. It is not for me to punish you. You were not responsible, and I am not one of those who believes that any man bears the guilt of his entire people. It was some form of biological weapon, I believe, an antipersonnel device that sprayed fungal spores. It was unfortunate that I had my visor up. Most unfortunate. But I have seen those things kill, and there is no death like the death they deal out. Consumed from without by fungal infestations. All that were eaten were my eyes. Ukerewe Prefecture; that was where we were patrolling. A very beautiful prefecture, Ukerewe. I think it was the trees dazzled us; they cut you off from the world, those visors, make everything so much television. A local uprising. Some Ghost Boy faction convinced it could deliver its land singlehandedly—with the aid of the saints, of course—from the Imperial oppressor. Of course, they couldn't. We crushed them. But it was not then like it is now; they did not do that tree thing. God, that's a terrible thing to do. Four thousand years since the Green Wave broke, and you never invented a punishment like that. It takes the Empire to dream it up.

"It must have been ten years ago. We play out the same old boys' games over and over and over until we get the result that pleases us. Ten, twelve, maybe; one of the things that vanishes with sight is your sense of time. Days, nights, seasons, years: they cease to govern your life. That, I tell you, is a great liberation. There is no tyranny like the tyranny of the clock.

"Then three, four years ago I lost my military pension—cutbacks, budget restrictions, public spending axes, means tests. I had sufficient savings to disqualify me but insufficient to support me. The trashlands have always been waiting, I suspect." The blind soldier knelt on the rain-wet trash, let his fingers explore the head once again. "No, I do not think I would get much for you. I am sorry. But it was good to hear a friendly accent again."

"Wait."

The sighted and the blind look at someone who is speaking in different ways. The sighted looks with his eyes. The blind looks with his ears.

"I have an idea. A proposition."

"What proposition could you make that would be of interest to me?"

"A partnership."

"Indeed? So?"

"A true partnership, where each covers the other's weakness. I will be your eyes, if you will be my body."

The blind man laughed. "That is a fine proposition."

"Do you accept it?" the head asked.

The blind man smiled the smile of the sightless, which is a smile of *feeling* rather than a smile of *seeing*. "As you say, in a good partnership each covers the other's weakness. I accept."

It was a fine partnership, and true. The blind man lived in a few small rooms in the middle of a flashing neon advertisement for facial cream and did not possess a single electric light bulb. His few small rooms were decorated with treasures fallen from the heart of the stratoscrapers, astonishing things: silver statuettes of yearning women with their hair streamed back in the wind from space, panes of crystal that when you touched them filled you with grief and joy and dread and an ecstasy beside which any ecstasy you ever had with a woman or man was pale and winter-cold, metal eggs that beneath your hand became soft and prickly and hard and cold and hot and oozing and rotting and gritty and finally so exactly like a breast that you had to open your eyes to make sure it was still only a clever metal egg. Given that you had eyes to open. Most of what he found the blind man sold for food and rent; these few most exquisite he could not bear to part with, the discarded novelties of life at high altitude, lit epilepsy-violet and cerise courtesy of Lady Lysistra Facial Cream.

The head learned to live in the light of Lady Lysistra, day and night, unbounded by the ticking of the clock. At any time of the day or night the blind man would fix the head onto the webbing harness he had made to wear around his chest, pull on his street coat, and go out under the towers. The head opened a new dimension of salvage the first time it found a pen sketch made in a bored moment by some Fortieth Level woman of her girlfriend reclining naked and hairless on a divan.

"This is good. This is worth something," said the head. "Turn it toward me, so I can see better. . . . Oh God that is some woman."

"So much paper to me," said the blind man. "I will have to

imagine the woman. I can remember women, it may surprise you to know."

In the between times, they would talk or play *fili*. The blind man was a very good player, as good as the advocate Kalimuni had been on those long summer evening matches at a table under an umbrella tree on some secluded square in Chepsenyt. He played by touch, but more by memory. The head had learned the skill of playing by memory during his short time in the Dreaming: their matches were pleasureful and memorable. But talk was their chief recreation: the recollection of things past. Talk of the land, always the land. The blind man's limited geography overlapped with the head's: "Describe Ol Senok township to me," he would say. "I remember it in the fall of the year; tell me of it in the fall of the year," and the head would describe the glass-cobbled squares and the meandering streets shoulder to shoulder with houses turning gold and bronze with the turn of the season, and the trees and the gardens beyond, the fern-filled closes, the umbrella trees in the street cafés shedding their canopies that the first winter storm would send whirling over the rooftops, the trux and the traders and the tryx, and after he had finished the blind man would sit silent, still, for hours at a time, exploring the streets and closes of his mental Ol Senok.

"You could go back," the head said one day, a hard stone cast into the pool of reflection. "If you loved it so much, why not go back? It is at peace now."

"Oh, I do not know," said the blind man, smiling his sightless smile in the light of Lady Lysistra. "It is never the same when you go back."

"It is what you make it," the head said.

"That is true," the blind man said. "And it is a temptation. But that is all it is: a temptation. Tell me now, do you know the road down across the prefecture boundary that runs through the hills from Kapsabalé to Elembétet? I passed that way in winter with my company. Tell me how it seems in winter, with the snow upon the forest."

With the rain slanting across the window, the head told him about the way the snow lay like a fantastic white city upon the spires and fans and bubbles of the forest, and the blind man seemed content.

One day as they were abroad on the rain-wet streets they came upon a crowd of people barring their way.

"Give way, give way, blind wounded war veteran," cried the blind man, who was not one to forsake his privileges. "War veteran blinded in the service of the Emperor."

"It is no use," said the head in its harness on his chest. "They are all along either side of the street. Thousands of them, as far as I can see."

The blind man looked with his ears and heard the treble whisper of a cockle radio. He touched the young man who owned the radio on the shoulder. "Excuse me, what is happening, why are all these people here?"

"Don't you know?" the young man said, shouting as people who wear cockle radios will. "The Emperor is coming."

"An Imperial progress," shouted a fat, turning-blousy woman with a great deal of hair on her upper lip and a mass-produced Imperial flag in her hand. "He is going to the shuttle port to meet someone from another planet. Look! Look! God save the Emperor! God bless you, Your Magnificence, God send you victorious, happy and glorious, long to reign over us!"

But it was a vanguard of street-cleaner robots siphoning and sucking their way along the Avenue of Light. All must be clean, all must be spotless and shitless and bloodless and pissless for the coming of an Emperor happy and glorious.

"Please, please, let me through," shouted the blind man over the growing murmur of the crowds. "Soldier wounded in the war, maimed in the service of his Emperor. Let me through, please." The crowds, as ever, parted: who can resist moral blackmail?

"The Emperor," said the blind man to the head on his chest. "How glorious. Of course, you know it is extremely rare for His Magnificence to leave the Jade City these days: he is an old man; even royalty are mortal. This must be an alien of some significance for the Emperor to have to come to him, rather than he to the Emperor.

"This is wonderful indeed, rare, precious. Once before I saw the Emperor, in the flesh. I was very small at the time; he was on his way, then as now, to the starport; he was to make a peregrination among some of the nearer Daughter Worlds: a Saint-ship had been chartered, at ruinous expense. I could not have been more than four or five, but to this day I can still see the glory of the Imperial passage. Marvelous! Wonderful! Glorious!" A wave of excitement passed down the Avenue of Light. More intimately attuned to the dynamics of people, the blind man sensed it instantly.

"What is happening? Is it he? Is he come now?"

"Just the outriders, I think," said the head. "Yes, the outriders."

"The outriders? Oh, tell me, are they as I remember? Are there fifty men in golden armor running before him as they did in the most ancient of days, with golden halberds sloped across their soldiers? I am certain I can hear their running feet; tell me, is it them? The forerunners in golden armor?" He turned so that the head could look along the Avenue of Light, two solid walls of humanity bristling with Imperial flags.

"Yes," said the head. "It is him now. Here he comes."

"And are there horsemen, one hundred horsemen with swords and ancient flintlock muskets across their shoulders? I remember they followed the forerunners; they were the Paladineri, the body cavalry, with red-and-white-plumed helmets and gleaming black breastplates polished so fine, so brilliant, you could see the whole world reflected in the curve of them. Yes, I am certain I can hear horse hooves.

"Then, after them will come the Imperial Councilors in their palanquins, all robed in the finery of state with the rings of office on their fingers and the seals of office on their brows, each borne by twenty gene-form eunuchs and preceded by a child with a gong. And then behind them comes the Emperor in his crystal carriage, veiled so that he may not be sullied by the gaze of common eyes. But I remember that I saw him, in the flesh, for at the moment the crystal carriage passed the Emperor sneaked back the corner of the veils and looked out for a glimpse at his subjects, and I saw him; I saw him face-to-face. I tell you, you do not forget a moment like that, when Emperor and subject come face-to-face. The wonder of that face, the splendor of his robes of office that he would wear onto the shuttle and then the Saint-ship and all around the Daughter Worlds: words cannot describe it."

"Is he here yet? Is it him in his crystal carriage? I can't hear anything over the roaring of the crowd; tell me, what do you see?"

The crowd made their noise and waved their mass-produced plastic Imperial flags. A young woman ripped off her T-shirt with the Imperial crest and colors on it and waved it above her head. Her big

big breasts jiggled and waggled in the steadily falling rain. The head watched while the blind soldier reminisced.

And the Emperor came.

First: fifteen policemen in black-and-silver uniforms with data visors. They rode silent-running motorcycles.

Second: three automobiles with darkened windows. Men with radios and guns rode on the running boards and stood up in the back seats, looking all around them and talking constantly into their radios.

Third: a low, long limousine. Ruched silk covered the windows. In the back was a very very old man, so old he did not seem like a man any more. He seemed like an animal. Like an alien.

And after the Emperor came twenty more men on motorcycles. The entourage sped past, was gone in less than five seconds.

"It is all as you described it," said the head. "All. Everything. Perfect in every detail. Just as you said it would be."

The white stones in the out-table were in jeopardy. The black stones had all the left-hand tables and two of three center tables. An attack on the right-hand tables had been thwarted, but temporarily. The main thrust could not be long delayed now, and defeat for the head. In two moves the out-table would be overrun.

The blind man paused in mid-move, dropped his handful of stones onto the *fili* board. He sat unmoving, lit an alternate violet and cerise by insane neon. Then he said, "I think we will go."

"Go?" the head said.

"Across the river. I think we will go across the river. I have some money saved up; it will be enough for the bus and the ferry. Living is cheap across the river."

"More expensive now than you remember."

"Everything is more expensive now than we remember. Yes, we will go. At the end of the week, I think. That would be a good time to go. I will make all the arrangements. Can you understand why I have decided to go now?"

"I think so," said the head.

"Maybe you would explain it to me, because I cannot," said the blind man. "There is no reason for it at all, except that it is what I want to do more than anything."

"You will find things changed from how you remember them," said the head.

"Everything is changed from how we remember it," said the blind man. Stones rattled in the scooped-out wooden *fili* tables. "Double jeopardy, against you, I believe."

They crossed the river that was wide as the sea on a fast sleek Imperial hydrofoil, cutting and weaving through the slower, heavier organical river traffic, intimidating fishing pirogues and a slow paddling amphibian with its triple horns and the snap and crack of the Imperial banner on its prow. Flaws of rain blew down from the north, but the cold did not dissuade the blind man from going up on deck.

"It is not as if you can actually see a damn thing," said the head, who had learned that such comments were amusing to the blind man.

"I can hear. I can smell. I can feel the wind. The rain feels good to me. It feels fresh. It does not dirty your skin like the rain of the Capital. Tell me, are there riverboats abroad?"

"We have just passed behind one, with a load of automobiles on its barges."

"I thought so. I could hear the sound of its stern wheel, I felt us bounce and skid over its wake, I could smell the distinctive musk of organicals. It has a smell like no other, your country. When I first went there, I was flown in a military transport and then bussed with my company to Ukerewe, and all you smell in a plane and a bus is plastic and air-conditioning. We arrived there in the night, and I stepped out of the bus and the smell struck me like a physical thing. The richness, the strangeness, the wildness, a smell that was a thousand smells at once but which in its totality was more: one thing, like the way the smell of a woman transcends its individual perfumes and musks and becomes one thing. There is nothing like it. Back in the Capital, when I still had the pension, on idle days I would go past a perfumers on Glory Street—a very special perfumers, which imported exotic oils from across the river and used them as bases for their scents—just to inhale the smell. Of course, it was not the same, it was a dead, distilled smell, not a living smell, but it was as close as I could come. Tell me, am I stupid? I imagine that if I can strain my senses to their maximum—and one's other senses do compensate when you lose sight—that I can smell that perfume even now, reaching out to me like fog rolling down off the land. Spices and musks and dark, green, growing rotting smells, essential oils and saps and fluids, fruit and flesh and shit that there, like nowhere else on the planet, is transformed into something wonderful, something that if you could take it and bottle it would sell for a thousand enns a gram.

"Tell me again, where is it we are going?"

"Kilimambasa," said the head.

"That is not a place I am familiar with. Why are we going there? Is it not quite far north? Are there not ferry ports farther south, closer to Tannalewé and Ukerewe?"

"They are still out of action from the War of Independence," said the head, who, having started with just one lie, now found others followed naturally and inevitably. "Also, there is still much disease in the southern ports. In the final stage of the war, there was widespread use of biological weapons. It will be generations before Yembé is habitable again, and even if the ports along the Tannalewé coast are not as badly contaminated, still I do not think it would be safe for an Imperial to go there. You do not have the immunities we have."

"I see. Thank you," said the blind man, and the head did not hate itself in the least, not the least part. Then the public address system announced *Ten minutes to Kilimambasa, ten minutes to Kilimambasa, all vehicle drivers please return to your vehicles* and the head said they should go down below now but the blind man said no, he wanted to stay just a while longer, until the hydrofoil emerged from the labyrinth of low islands and sandbars that choked the river at this high latitude so that the head could describe its first sight of the eastern shore. As the hydrofoil beat through the squalls and fits of rain, casting up white plumes of water from its wings, the head described the groves of trees in their autumnal colors that grew down to the water's edge, and the fisherpeople's homes along the waterline that looked like the shells of great mollusks, and the terraces and the paddies tiering the low hills that rose up higher and higher until at the place where the rain and the aerial perspective dimmed the landscape into blue haze the full climax forest broke in waves of fan trees and coral spires and rafts of balloons sagging with moss and lichens.

Then the head described Kilimambasa town on its beautiful hillsides under its beautiful trees and its beautiful sunlit people coming and going in its beautiful streets that sloped down to the beautiful river and the beautiful ferry port, and as the boat came down off its foils the blind man smiled at the thought of the beauty the head described for him and the head still did not feel guilty, not the least bit.

They stood on the quay after the trux and tractor-trailer combines had all revved and shunted away and the blind man was still smiling, the deep-down heart smile of someone who has woken in the middle of a summer night's dream to find that all the wonder and the strangeness are real and actual.

"Well," he said, with the excitement of a child slipping his father's hand and running dazzled toward the lights and music of the winter carnival. "We're here. Where shall we go first?"

"First we must find a place to stay," said the head. "That is where we shall go first. There are many small hotels and travel inns in a town like this."

At each of the many small hotels and travel inns the head spoke at length with the proprietor while the blind man took tea and listened to the television broadcasts hooked down from across the river by Empire-built satellite dishes.

"That is Old Speech you are speaking," said the blind man as he carried the head through the beautiful streets to the next small hotel or travel inn. "I can tell. It sounds like music. I have only a very few words of it left; when you give the language brainplant back, it all goes. But I can recognize the sounds. Is this one full too?"

"That one was full too," lied the head.

"Perhaps the next one will not be so full," said the blind man. "I cannot take very much more tea, I must tell you."

But the next one was full, and the next one, and the one after that, and the one after that.

"So many visitors in such a small town," said the blind man, who, having been an officer in the service of the Emperor, was not a man to call anyone a liar. "So much talk. Would a simple NO VACANCIES sign not save us all a lot of effort?"

Then the head said, "I will admit that I have not been entirely truthful with you. The truth is I have a relation in this town I am trying to find."

"This is this Mathembe you mention," said the blind man. "I still have a few words of Old Speech, as I said. You are looking for a relation; that is fine, but please, in this place I am quite dependent on your honesty and sincerity. Perhaps the next hotel will have a vacancy?"

It did.

And had the head found its relation?

It had.

At last.

At lunch, the head had a favor to ask.

"That I will take you to meet this Mathembe? Certainly. But the Empire is an Empire of trade; as an Imperial, I would ask a favor in return. We have been so busy running about in search of your relation that I have not been able to enjoy the experience of being where I am. So, if I carry you, will you describe my surroundings for me?"

"Not so loud about the Empire, here," said the head.

So they went up the gently sloping road where the head and Mathembe had quarreled a season before, the road that went up through Kilimambasa to the camps.

"The street is lined with cafés and restaurants," said the head. "They have taken in their street tables for the winter but inside there is still brightness and cheerfulness. People are playing *fili* or watching the sports channel on the television."

"The cafés, the restaurants, what do they look like?"

"They look like living things look, curved and sculpted and rounded, running into each other, over each other; their walls are bright now with the last autumn colors," said the head. But the walls were scarred with bullet holes and blackened with fire and smeared with spray-paint graffiti promising swift and sure death to Impie Bastards.

And they went up past the cafés and restaurants.

"Now there are houses, clustered together around courtyards and squares. Within their little walled gardens grow trees and shrubs and all kinds of useful living things: radios and wine fermentories and thread. The gardens are very beautiful." But the houses were windowless, doorless, and falling apart into their component units, and squatter women crouched in the empty doorways and glared malevolently as such women will, and parasite-ridden children whipped chunks of organical through the streets and the gardens were dead and brown and clogged with shit and heaps of rotting plasm.

"Listen, you can hear the children playing," said the head.

The blind man sniffed. "What is that I smell?"

"That is the shit they use to fertilize the gardens."

"Such marvelous economy," said the blind man.

And they went up past the houses.

"We are high now," said the head. "We are almost at the edge of the town. We are above the houses, out into the gardens and terraces and paddy fields. The hillsides are covered in low walls and walkways and terraces; in this season they are full of water so that they shine like a thousand pieces of mirror broken on the hillside."

"A broken mirror," said the blind man and the head could see how in his mind it was real and actual, and for the first time the head knew guilt. For with each step up the sloping road the lie had grown and now it was total, for there were no gardens and orchards and paddies, no lagoons shining like a thousand pieces of broken mirror in the pale winter sun. They stood at the gateway to the camp, where the silver that shone in the pale winter sun was the silver of the emergency shelters and the thousand mirrors were the thousand plastic-roofed shacks and shanties gleaming with the swift, sudden winter rain and the terraces were the walls of garbage plastered with red mud that the refugees had put up around their moribund attempts at gardens and the walkways were the trux- and foot-churned quagmires between the dense-packed houses. They stood where the road went up through the tangle-thorn defenses, and the blind man flared his nostrils and frowned and said, "I cannot smell it. It is not how I remember. It is not the same. Tell me, is it very busy here? I can hear the sound of many many people."

"It is very busy," said the head, as people and organicals went up and down through the gate. "Farmers preparing the fields for the winter seeding. Even in a biotechnical society like ours, there is still manual labor to be done."

"And I had thought I could see out my days throned in plenty, with everything I needed within the reach of my two hands," said the blind man.

And they left the gateway behind, and went into the camp.

"Your relation lives here?" said the blind man.

"Of course," said the head, now trapped by its lie. "This is a grand place to live." And they pushed forward, into the press of people and organicals that thronged the gate.

"But why does it feel as if I am in a market?" asked the blind man as they went along the muddy main boulevards past slow-moving trux and women with bundles on their backs suspended from brow bands.

"That is because it is a market," said the head. "They come from all around to put sheets down by the side of the road and sell."

"But why," asked the blind man as the head guided it off the main thoroughfares onto the footpaths and alleyways that ran like thieving boys between the shanty plots, "do I feel there are walls on either side of me?"

"That is because there are tall trees all around us, tall trees, and so close together," said the head, who now knew nothing but the lie. And they found themselves in a small compound surrounded by plastic-roofed shanties. Children watched from low doorways, radios blared.

"But why," said the blind man, "does what I feel, what I smell, and what I hear, why do they all contradict what you are telling me? Why do I feel that every word you have been saying to me has been a lie? That every step you have led me has been a false step? Every description a false description? My God"—the blind man's voice rose, with his beautiful, cultured, cross-river accent—"my God, where am I? Where have you led me? What is this place?" And he looked around with the yellow diseased sockets of his eyes, but with all his will he could not force them to show him how deeply he had been deceived. "My God, my God, you have lied to me; every word has been a lie. How did you think you could get away with it?" Hands released the catches of the webbing harness; the head fell with a cry to the mud. Free, the blind man stumbled for a way out of the labyrinth of yards and alleys, arms outstretched.

And they were there. As they had always been, from the moment they left the small hotel that morning, shadowing every step up the long sloping cobbled road, past the restaurants and cafés and the abandoned houses and through the thorns into the camp. Only now they made themselves visible, for this was their place. The Ghost Boys. Some naked but for leather pouches, some tattooed, some dressed in straps and stretch fabric and hieroglyphed with Jantic symbols; all masked in jutting, terrifying, slashing *pneuma* masks. The Ghost Boys.

From their crevices and doorways, out of the cracks and slits of camp culture, they swarmed down on the blind man. Hands seized his outstretched arms. Hands lifted the flailing, staring man. Hands clamped firm around him, stifling his cries. Hands carried him away. The head shouted. The head, half stogged in the red mud, cried out *No no leave him leave him alone he is harmless he is blind can you not see?*

The hands carried him away. And the radios blared blared blared.

"Old grandfather, you got to realize, in this place we are law."

Hands wiped the red mud from the head's eyes. Hands set him in his pot, tucked the wiggling rooticles neatly under.

"Old grandfather, you are a damn mess. I will take you back to my place. We will sort things out better there."

"The hell with you, you little bastard thug. Piss on you. Shit on you."

"Grandfather, I am shocked. What kind of example is that to set your only grandson?"

Where is it said that those who live long and close to idealism take on a sunlit, numinous aspect? The opposite is also true: that those who look too long and too lovingly at anger and bitterness take on its aspect; they become bleached and twisted, like weathered roots, and hard like roots, tenacious, unyielding. The tree may be dead, white weathered wood, but the roots grip on. You have seen it in the face of the woman who for years has feasted on nothing but thoughts of revenge, in the face of the man who for years has given every spare moment to contemplating acts of infidelity against his wife, in the face of the child who for years has felt the lash of humiliation and the scorn of his peers: the twist of the root. It looks like many things. A light in the eye. A shadow in the memory. An unguarded look. A gnawed meagerness of frame. A tilt of the cheekbones. The bitter root.

As Hradu lifted the head to carry it away through the labyrinth that he ruled, his grandfather was able to study him closely and was afraid. There are few creatures more terrifying than the child old before its time. The mind and shrewdness of a man, a man's fears and responsibilities poured over the body and morality of a boy. Those many months while *Unchunkolo* sailed the river of history had aged Hradu, but not enough to explain the brutal blankness of his face or excuse the bioplastic dart thrower in the skin holster strapped to his thigh.

He was dressed in a stretch-fabric battle suit cut off at mid-calf and shoulders. The chameleon camouflage systems had either failed or been switched off in mid-fade; swaths of purple and lilac spirals clashed with bold primary speckling and pure wet-sheen black. Heavy boots, tops folded down. Latest-fashion Imperial sports socks with all the correct corporate logos. Hair scraped back and tightly bound up in a leather trefoil knot. He did not look like a Ghost Boy any more. He looked like a Warrior of Destiny. He looked like power. He looked like law.

And, over the incessant blaring of the radio and the cries of children, did the head hear—could it be certain?—a single shot?

"My friend. My blind man. What has happened to him? Is he all right?"

"I should think," said Hradu in the measured, mock-lazy way that dangerous people affect, "that he is probably dead. In fact, almost certainly dead. I am sorry he was your friend. But we have a policy and we must keep it. Where would we be if we did not stick to our principles?"

"And the principle is kill anyone who has a cross-river accent?" shouted the head, crazy with guilt and anger and grief and confusion.

"By and large," said Hradu, still slow, still half lazy, pretending to look at something off to one side, as these dangerous people will. "We have to make examples. It is the way it is. We have a—"

"I know," shouted the head. "God damn you, you bastard, I know, I know, a policy. A principle."

And with the smallest, briefest *click!* the plastic dart gun was out of its holster, muzzle pressing the head's right eye.

"So help me, I will send you back to the Dreaming and this time there will be no coming back," said Hradu. "Understand this. We are the power in the camps. Not the local councils. Not the government, not the relief agencies or the Bureau of Resettlement. Not the army, not the police. We are the Power. What is done is done by our permit. We are the Law. Us. Me.

"Unit Commander now, Grandfather. Active Service Unit. Fighting the good fight. Taking it to the ancient enemy."

"There is no fight," said the head. "Not now. The fight is over. Over a long time."

"Mistake," said Hradu, and his voice was a keen, fine whisper, like the edge of a blade. "Mistake, grandfather of mine. Be pleased. Be proud. Youngest Active Service Unit Commander in this sector of the front."

"Is that what you call it, the front?" said the head, but it saw the thinning of Hradu's lips into the keen, sharp knife-edge again. "You look like a teenage fetishist's boy whore," it said instead, lashing out in its anger and guilt and frustration. The briefest, smallest *click!* The needler was back next to Hradu's lilac and purple thigh. Hradu howled with laughter, but the head was afraid, for it was not good laughter but the dark laughter that goes howling out across the world until it finds something it can flay.

"Manners, Grandfather. You are in company here. Remember your manners."

"Mathembe," said the head. "You have seen Mathembe? You know where she is?"

"I have seen Mathembe. I know where she is. In fact, I shall take you to her. Come." Which was needless, but the sort of thing people say who are Power and Law.

She lay on an inflatable mattress in the back of a plastic bivouac so like the nest among the rapid-transit lines in the Imperial Capital that it was too sick for even a divine joke. A constellation of biolights lit the low, wind-rattling room. Cheap cereal-packet holograms of the Ykondé saints kept watch. She was naked but for vest top, panties, and socks. Her skin had the papery dryness of fever, the dusty nap under the fingers. Her chest rose and fell, rose and fell, too fast, too shallow. A plastic airway tube held her mouth open. Her eyes were rolled up into her head.

Plastic cable grips bound hands and feet to metal stakes driven into the pounded earth floor of the shack. Wrists and ankles were raw bloody; as her grandfather watched, she twisted and tugged at her bonds, worried a few more drops of blood from the wounds.

"They pumped her so full of the stuff I was not certain she would ever come down." Hradu knelt on the pounded earth floor by his sister's side. "She screamed and screamed when I brought her back.

Three days and nights, she screamed. If we had not tied her, she would have torn herself apart with her own fingers."

"What did they put into her?"

"Hallucinogenics," said Hradu, an angel by biolight. "Neuro-chemical boosters."

"How?" asked the head. And then, "Who?" And then, "Why?"

Then Hradu told his grandfather what he knew of Mathembe's story, but it was not all the story, for he did not know all the story, and anyway it was not his to tell.

Brothers are like that.

She was there again, at the table beneath the wall shrine, the dark-haired, snub-nosed girl who would have been as like her as her reflection in the mirror but for the unnatural pallor of her skin. She had been there, at that table in the Saint M'Zan Bé Café (the saint to which the wall shrine beneath which she sat was dedicated), every day when Mathembe came in for her small cheap lunch and plastic can of wine. And every day she had smiled and raised her glass to Mathembe across the intervening tables, and every day would have greeted her but that Mathembe hurried out before any words that might be spoken were spoken, out and up that sloping, dirty road into the camps again.

Hurry was her ally. Busyness her friend. The search was every-thing, for if it faltered for even a moment she would have been crushed by the realization of her immense isolation. For she was alone. And aloneness frightened her. For aloneness must never be confused with solitude. The solitude Mathembe had enjoyed as a child had been discretionary; there had always been people for those times when she wanted the backdrop of her life peopled. Here in Kilimambasa were faces. The faces of the hotel proprietors. The faces of the café owners, the faces of the Free State resettlement officials, the faces of the camps. Those faces more than any others, whose hardness was a confession of their utter vulnerability, whose constant watching, looking, watching, continuous alertness concealed a terminal boredom, those faces that pursed lips, that shook heads, that knew nothing when she went to them in her expensive silver jacket asking HAVE YOU SEEN THESE PEOPLE?, that would not have spoken had they even known (which they must have, at least one of the faces) because the camps were the camps.

And the face at the café table beneath the shrine to M'Zan Bé, that was as like her own as her reflection in a mirror.

Mathembe went to the M'Zan Bé because it was her last link with her grandfather. The owner's wife—kindly, fat, but content—had apologized and apologized and apologized, she had not known, if she had known she would never—but it had made such a din, such a terrible racket, asking the customers had they seen its granddaughter? *You*, she presumed, being the granddaughter. And the cross-river trader had offered such good money. Hard money. No, it was not likely he would be back, possibly never, not since the Warriors of Destiny began their campaign of killing Imperial citizens found on *their* side of the river to try and force the Emperor to relinquish God's Country. *I cannot see how they figure that* she had said. *He is gone, dear. I think you had better face up to it. That will be fifteen enns, dear. And the can of wine too; that is twenty-three.*

Sunk in guilt. Guilt, like an ever-rolling river, bears all our crimes away. God, where is he, somewhere across that rolling river; where are they, at the end of that row of tents that I was too tired to reach today, joining the end of that line as I left the head of it, passing out as I pass in, going down as I go up, always that moment too late, too early? They could be anywhere, anywhere along this straggling borderland; how can you ever hope to find them? He was right. Find your own life, lead your own life. Enough—more than enough—to be responsible for yourself alone.

In that moment, she would have walked away from them all, but for the needle, the needle of guilt that kept her hands pinned to that table in the M'Zan Bé Café in Kilimambasa town.

"No. I do not."

She looked up. Her.

"Know these people. But I like the jacket. That is a great jacket. I have been admiring it for some time."

Preludes: "Those are Pee Jay shades, aren't they? You must be off the boats; what with the economic war, boatpeople are the only ones can get shades like that."

Again: "I see you a lot in here. You come in every day. Me, I come in every day too."

Again: "You know, when I first saw you in here I was amazed, it was like I was seeing my reflection in a mirror. We could be sisters."

Silence.

"Oh, well, I am sorry. Sorry to have embarrassed you. Just forget I ever spoke. I know, I should not be so forward with total strangers. I will just go back to my little table and die."

A hand, outstretched: *Stay*. A chair pushed out: *Sit*.

"What is your name? Me, I am Matinde."

A card, from one of the many pockets of the voluminous jacket.

MY NAME IS MATHEMBE FILELI.

"Mathembe, Matinde, that is incredible, unbelievable, and us looking so alike and everything. The saints must have brought us together, what do they call it? a *urucarai*, where people who do not know each other get brought together by God to achieve some special purpose. Can you not talk, is that the problem? Oh, shit, I am sorry, I never realized. Well, that is all right, people say I talk enough for two anyway. Something more to drink?"

Mathembe shook her head, pointed through the walls with their pin-up calendars of big-breasted women and naked men with wet hair, up the sloping street.

"There? What you want to go up there for? How do you like me, eh? Not even known you five seconds and already I am kicking the shit out of you. What a bitch I am."

Against herself, against all that was right and decent and holy, Mathembe smiled.

"You are mighty mighty pretty when you smile, Mathembe Fileli. Family, is that who you are looking for? I will bet you a month of lunches all you have got so far is folk sitting on their dumb asses looking at you like you are some kind of walking turd, no?"

Yes.

"You are new here. You do not know the language, the signs, the moves. There is asking, and there is asking. You know what I mean? Now, if you go up with Matinde, you will get answers. You got a smartcard? Come on come on, show Matinde. I am not going to steal it. Much on it? That should be enough. You got to lubricate, you know what I mean? Like sex, you got to lubricate. Come on. I will show you."

Matinde had defined their relationship quite unconsciously

within the first five seconds: *We could be sisters.* As garrulous, all-knowing, loud brash Matinde went about the camps greeting and hailing and helloing and playing fast and loose with Mathembe's smartcard, Mathembe realized that here was the figure that was missing from her childhood, that she had grown up knowing she wanted but had never been able to articulate her loss. A sister. Someone to cry and fight and hope and pray and dream and drink and moan and rejoice with. Matinde offered sisterhood, Mathembe received it like bread on a winter journey. They swapped clothes: Matinde cute and gamine in Mathembe's street wear, Mathembe dizzy and lovely in Matinde's expensive skins and silks.

Between sisters, a shrug can mean *Who did you get these from?*

"Secret benefactors. I prostitute myself for big fat Northern Proclaimers smuggled south across the border to enjoy the forbidden flesh of Confessor girls."

And, when Mathembe showed Matinde the small cheap card-slot sleep-pod hotel tucked behind the container port where she slept in an eight-foot cylinder of biotecture: "Okay, so it is nice to be surrounded by big smelly longshoremen with fantastic asses, but, Mathembe, I think you should move in with me. I got an apartment back of the New Sirikwa Hotel on Twelfth and Third Parallel. Too big for little Matinde, way too big. How much is that shit pod, eight, ten, twelve enns a night? Twelve enns; that could go a long way to lubricate memories up behind the thorns, Mathembe."

Between sisters, a cock of the eyebrows asks *And how does a punk like you afford an apartment at the back of the New Sirikwa Hotel?*

"Friends and influences, Mathembe. I know a lot of nice people. I think it would be good for you to meet them too."

She moved in that night, into the three rooms at the back of the New Sirikwa Hotel. She had never seen such luxury. There was a spa unit in the bathroom. A spa unit!

"You stay in that thing much longer there will be nothing left but one mighty big bath ring."

Between sisters, an orgy of sybaritic splashing can be all the answer that is necessary. Mathembe slept that night on a bed of soft plastic flesh, thickly furred, of such yielding comfort that she felt herself sinking into it as if into a deep womb dream of secret oils and musky, thumping placentas.

The edge of the world was an hour beneath the moon when Matinde opened the bedroom door. She stood a minute, five minutes, ten minutes, listening to the rhythm of the breathing, being sure, being sure. Light as a dream, she crossed to the big flesh bed where Mathembe Fileli lay sprawled like something dropped from heaven and broken upon the earth, face screwed up in the soft fur, breathing noisily through her open mouth.

"Pretty pretty kid," Matinde whispered. She knelt by the bed. Watching. Listening. Taking the pulse of the night. The planets turned in space, Saint-ships crossed the universe, and she sat, watching, listening. Mathembe turned. Mathembe heaved in her sleep. Mathembe muttered and growled deep down in the back of her brain. Her eyes rolled into dream sleep.

Carefully, carefully, Matinde rolled up her sleeves. Carefully, carefully, she tore at her right thumbnail. An almond of flesh-tone plastic flipped into the dark and was lost.

"Shit."

Metalized plastic glinted in the light from the street. The second thumbnail came more readily. Beneath: twin blades, glittering. Carefully, carefully, slowly, she cut around each wrist. She took the edge of flesh in her right hand, gritted her teeth, and in one swift movement stripped off the skin. She worried the skin of her right wrist free with her teeth; with a small cry, and sudden tears of pain, peeled it away.

Mathembe stirred.

Matinde froze, the obscene glove of skin in her teeth.

The eyes resumed their rapid movements.

Matinde brought her hands up into the winter moonlight that streamed through the window of the New Sirikwa Hotel. Black plastic fingers flexed, muscled and sinewed with synthetic flesh, glittering with hard Imperial machine technology. Needles slid from housings in the third fingers, IV tubes from the little fingers; first and second fingers terminated in brainplant interfacers. In the hollow metal wrists, bulbs and sacs of chemicals pulsed.

"Dream on, Mathembe Fileli. Dream well, dream good for Matinde. God, but you are too good a kid for this."

The black artificial hands cradled Mathembe's head. She hardly started at all as the needlefingers pierced her throat.

"Shh. Shh. Just a little something to keep you out of it while Matinde does her work. Hush, child, hush. . . ."

Threadlike fibers grew from the tips of Matinde's first and second fingers, effortlessly, painlessly penetrated the skin behind Mathembe's ears, slipped under the edge of the skull into the brain. Matinde breathed heavily, closed her eyes.

"Come on Mathembe, come on Mathembe, come on Mathembe, let me see what you got for sister Matinde."

Airborne, flying, borne up by the spirit of blue blue heaven tumbling naked and rejoicing through millions of cubic kilometers of air falling free free-falling falling forever until you might shatter yourself to atoms with the velocity of your fall yet with one thought, with one snap of the gossamer wings folded close to your body, with one moment's thought to fan them and catch the air in them, you can soar, you can climb forever through this limitless boundless forever blue you are master of gravity, conqueror of space and time, relativistic angel approaching closer closer ever closer to perfect velocity at which every point in the universe lies next to every other point and time and space are abolished faster faster what joy what pleasure to delight in your own silver flashing brilliance, your own beauty and skill there! flash yellow gold to your blue silver, him, he is there, stroking toward you on wings that blow the wind between the stars him! the word is a scream of pleasure angelic love within the blue blue vault of heaven on the wing within the enfolding of each other's wings falling at terminal velocity through the infinite blue blue: him!

Matinde withdrew her neural probes. The roots and fibers disengaged from Mathembe's brain, molecule by molecule diffused out of her skin into Matinde's fingers. A mental command: a recording slug oozed from her right wrist. Matinde tossed the gravid thing in the air, caught it playfully.

"Geez, kid, I thought you would be good, but not this good. They are going to love this, Mathembe Fileli. You are going to make Matinde a rich girl."

She went to the window. Pale dawn light, cold and drear. While she looked out at the early shift coming and going on the long sloping street, liquid oozed from artificial pores to cover her hands. Within minutes it had hardened into skin. Tints and hues flowed across the new hands as the synthetic flesh sought to match Matinde's melanin.

The discarded skins—limp, translucent, like the memory of some nocturnal reptile—the false nails—five minutes' search for the one that got away—and the recorder slug went into her belt pouch.

Mathembe's chest rose and fell in deep sleep.

"Soon, sister. Soon."

And then there came the lunchtime in the M'Zan Bé Café when Mathembe looked ruefully at her smartcard, which, between sisters, between anyone, means only one thing: *Out, broke, bust, bombed, poor.* Matinde paid the small bill with loose change.

"Geez, Mathembe, what are you going to do now?"

Soon, sister, soon.

And then there came the time with the big winter rains streaming down the windows of the apartment at the back of the New Sirikwa Hotel when Mathembe had paced up and down all morning and had not been able to settle or concentrate or set her spirit at peace with anything, which between sisters, between anyone, is the prelude to asking *Can you lend me money?*

"Geez, Mathembe, you know if I had money, I would, as much as you wanted, but it is like this: I have a lot of *things*, but I do not have any actual *wealth*. You understand? The folk who pay me, they pay me in things, not money. So I cannot lend you anything, because I have nothing to lend. Honest. Not a wooden enn."

Soon, sister, soon.

And after that came the time when Mathembe went to the window with the big winter rain slanting down outside and pointed at the rain-soaked, streaming organicals and shift workers coming and going up the long sloping street, which, between sisters, means *I will get a job, I will make me some money with my hands.*

"Geez, Mathembe, you have been up there, you know what it is like, how many people there are going for every job. What chance do you think you have? All a kid like you would get is a half-year renewable contract for organical work as a ditchdigger or household cleaner or something like."

Soon, sister, soon.

Matinde moistened her lips. The sound was very loud in the rain-lashed room.

"There is a way to make money. Good money. Big money. Something you can sell."

A twist of the spine, a hitch of the hip.

"No. Not that. Nothing like that at all." She crossed the room that was filled with rain shadows to gently touch Mathembe's forehead. "Something in here. Your dreams. There is good money, big money for dreams." She swallowed; again, the sound was hugely loud in the room. "I know these men. Call them dealers in dreams. There are people out there who will pay a lot of money to taste someone else's dreams. Rich people, bored people, people who are too afraid of life to live it, people whose own dreams have died and who need the dreams of others. No one can live without dreams. You can give them those dreams. These men, these dealers, they can record your dreams onto special brainplants and hire them out for a lot of money."

Matinde saw that she had made a monstrous mistake of judgment. Mathembe would never be convinced. She had wanted to be gentle but the shadow of mistrust was abroad in the room and was growing with every word she spoke. *What are you who are you why are you?* She went to her, stood behind her, put her hands on her shoulders, her neck.

"It will be all right. Trust me."

But she felt the muscles beneath her fingers saying *Trust you? I do not even know who you are.*

Now, sister, now.

Matinde winced as the needle flicked through the skin of her fingertip into Mathembe's neck.

The pain of the needle was nothing to the pain of the betrayal, but it was only an instant, a flicker, nothing more, for then the door to the room at the back of the New Sirikwa Hotel opened and the end of the world came through. Yes, definitely, the end of the world, in fire and glory, as she had read in her childhood religious stories. The hotel corridor was caught in mid-transubstantiation, dusty wall hangings and rugs worn nude from light-years of feet were exploding in coils and chaotic spirals of life, bursting ferns and vines and creepers from their woven patterns: tell me it is not the end of the world when the rugs and wall hangings come to life? No, it must be the end of the world, for here come the Ahleles themselves, huge as Saint-ships fallen into the sea sixty kilometers tall and sixty kilometers round—fat balls of blubber, these Ahleles—two of them, coming into the room, and in their wake the walls grew flowers and fruit dripped from the ceiling and the gloglobes burst in puffball detonations of sweet scented pollen and tiny plastic gifts for all the family and she danced at the end of the world, she spun and wheeled at the end of the world, she giggled and grinned at the end of the world for the Ahleles were reaching for her with hands made out of articulated meat sticks and their teeth that smiled back at her were white kernels of rice and the hairs on their heads which suddenly she could see in submicroscopic detail were coils of genetic material it was the end of the world they had come to take her to heaven she leapt for their reaching sustaining uplifting arms but somehow she missed and was falling falling off the edge of the world past escape velocity and the webs of gravity into blackness into space into the time-space-freeness of *ur*-space where huge trans-stellar vessels quested. . . .

The ape patted the girl on the ass as he slung her over his shoulder. Ape Number Two grinned.

"You be good to her, you hear?" said Matinde, angry at her own capacity for faithlessness. "She is a nice kid. A good kid. I hear you do those things with her, I will cut your dicks off. God, I hate my job."

Which made the apes laugh all the more as they carried Mathembe into the corridor with its ragged rugs and dust-faded wall hangings depicting the twelve religious virtues.

Even in the darkest days of the War of Independence, the restaurant on the river wharf had defied gunboats, gun battles, sieges, shelling, and starvation and fed its patrons on pride and prayer dog grilled over tubs of burning house unit. Now in these days of renewed grandeur, prayer dog *à la maison* was the linchpin of the menu. The upper room with its cool view of the river bend, its salting of islands, and the twice-daily enthusiastic spume of the hydrofoil was Kilimambasa's closest approach to sophistication.

"They blew away two Imperial tourists just last week," Matinde said idly, waving her empty cocktail glass in the direction of the wine waiter. "Between the rice course and the soup. Just walked in and opened up with gene guns. Still have not managed to disentangle the remains from the back wall."

He was a small man, small-featured, with a small, balding head and a small smile. "That was some rat-hole diner up on Fifteenth Street. The price you pay for not booking ahead. I read the papers, you know. Anyway, they would not let them past the door here. Not without long trousers on."

"Piss on you. I want another one of these."

"You have had quite enough of 'these,' whatever ghastly concoction they happen to be."

"I like them, and I want another one. Seriously, Dhav, the bloody Warriors are dangerous. They do not care who they blow away in the name of a united land."

"Your concern heartens me, but rest assured, Matinde, neither I nor any of my colleagues are inclined toward unnecessary risks. We and the Warriors of Destiny, we understand each other; ultimately, we are all on the same side. Or had you not heard that they have started running protection in the border towns?" A flex and snap of fingers achieved what Matinde's waving of her empty print-smeared glass could not. "Another of these for my friend, and I will have some herb tea, please. Really, it is remarkable how this place has kept going through the Troubles."

With a flick of his small hand, the small man sent a small plastic cylinder rolling across the table.

"Was it good then?"

He tapped his small fingers together, smiled. Smally. "It was good. You have more from this girl, what do you call her?"

"Does it matter?"

"It seems to, to you."

"Mathembe Fileli."

The concoction in the tall glass and the small, precise pot of herb tea arrived on the table. The waiter moved the cylinder containing the dreamware to one side as he poured a steaming, aromatic jet.

"Mathembe Fileli. Go deeper," said the small man. He lifted the tiny delicate bowl, breathed in the aroma. "Exquisite. Probe deeper. I feel that what we have seen so far is just the tip, the edge, the merest lift of the hem. Go deeper. A very particular kind of client pays a very particular kind of money for emotional anguish of this finesse. People are getting bored with steaming sex and violence. Emotional pain is what is exciting them now. And emotional pain, of a very high order, is what this Mathembe Fileli has. Consider it a form of extraction, Matinde. Psychic strip-mining. I ought to congratulate you on this one, you know, but it goes so to your head." Small, delicate sips of scalding tea. "Tell me, what was it about this one?"

"She cannot speak."

"I thought speech was an inherited trait with you people, like left- and right-handedness and the way you can interact with genetic material."

"Not always."

"Sullen sullen little Matinde. I do believe you have the hots for this one." The small neat hand darted forward like a little bird, seized Matinde's jaw. The small man smiled. "Matinde, just because I smile and banter and enjoy a cup of tea, a glass of wine, a pleasant meal in convivial surroundings, do not imagine that you can be insolent or familiar with me. You are pretty and witty but you are nothing, Matinde. Nothing. Just free-floating cells in a flesh nation, flesh we can shape and control and manipulate as the spirit moves us. Do you have that? Good. Now, drink your silly little drink and we will think no more of it."

Whenever she went into the room now it seemed to be raining. Big winter rain, streaming down the windows. Big winter rain, casting rippling shadows on the dreamers on the beds; the fat one who dreamed of roaring, steaming sex, the thin one who dreamed of angry slashing violence, the big one curled up into a fetus full of the dreams of childhood, the one who mumbled constantly in her sleep and dreamed of flying and falling and running and being hunted by something vast and devouring and implacable that she could never see and never gave up the chase. Dreaming in the rainlight, arms stuck full of drip-feed needles, heads cradled in pulsing halos of organicals. Rain shadows on their skins—as she passed, Matinde touched them with her trailing, talented hands. They were bare now, skinned, those hands the small man had sold her. No need to pretend now. The clicking black hands tucked a coil of hair, stroked a hand.

"Some day, Mathembe." Rain shadows on her face as she knelt beside the mattress. "After we get money and I get my hands back. Ssh. Ssh. There, sister. Something to make you dream good." Needlefinger flicked out, a slim steel erection. Fluid dripped from the tip. One more raindrop. She did not even cry out any more when Mr. Needlefinger came to call. "Got to go deep, Mathembe. Sorry, but that is how they want it, and what they want you have to get for them." She watched the rain raining down on all her hopes and tears and frowns. "Lucky lucky kid, dreaming your life away," she said, but it was only because of the rain, raining down on everything. "Some day I will buy myself a winter coat," she said as she sent her tendril fingers coiling through Mathembe's skin up under the edge of her skull, past her dreams, into her memories. "I will save up for it, and buy it with my own money, and it will be all mine. So, what have you for me today?"

The rain, of course, the rain, arguing in the rain with a disembodied head in a cracked pot full of organicals outside the M'Zan Bé Café.

Matinde whistled with her tongue through pursed lips as a beggar or a waiter will at an insulting tip. Deeper. Deeper.

Sex an aromatic musk, an itch in the atmosphere in the warm fetal enfolding of leaves and bracts, the close presence of an ugly, smiling boy.

"Nice, sister, but Diyamé over there does it better. Pain, Mathembe. Hurt me. I want to feel tears." Deeper deeper.

A click and a splash. A headmaster's monomolecular wire, a body rolled into the river, turned over by the current, carried hunched, headless, down to the Elder Sea. A necklace of severed heads draped around the blunt prows of riverboat barges, mouths open, rooticles fanning the water. Cries of children, the silence of mothers. The anger of men emasculated by history, stronger, more sickening than any stench of shit and pus and hunger.

Matinde hissed through her teeth as the eidetic images welled up in her brain. Molecule by molecule the neural linkages infiltrated Mathembe's spirit.

Fire. One hemisphere of the world ablaze. River water full of reflected flames. The cries of dying buildings. Helicopters chattering like old women over a funeral pyre. Running. Running. And the flames, running with her, pacing her, racing her, leaping ahead of her, hurdling entire streets, crossing wide boulevards in a single bound, sprinting along the rooftops.

Deeper. Deeper.

A snow of ash falling on upturned faces. A parade of bones and stones and rags and pieces of broken helmet. A blond man in black screaming in another tongue. A black behemoth capsized against a gently plashing fountain. A blow and an embrace and a cracked mask. Gods fighting in the street, no better than Ghost Boy hellions.

"Nice, sister, but not bloody enough. It has to hurt with the kind of hurt that almost destroys you, that burns you down to the roots and stubble, that strips the land so bare that it is years before anything will grow there again."

A table overturned, covered in black hieroglyphs, falling spice jars and tea canisters suspended in midair, a man with hair falling into his eyes and big useless hands, beside him, a beautiful beautiful woman.

"Who is this, Mathembe? Come on, kid, go after him. Show me more."

The blind soft tendrils twined.

"Come on, Mathembe, show me the ones who hurt you, show me the ones who left you bloody and maimed. Show me heartache, show me heartbreak."

Faces and memories, fluttering through her mind like prayer tickets on a wand. The image of a man standing on a starlit riverside corniche, hands behind head. Slur of drums, sinuous twist of guitars. A moment of perfection, the moment she first knew herself to be in love. Closing step by cautious step, Matinde willed down her emotional defenses. "After him," she whispered in the spaces of Mathembe's skull.

The tiered bowl of a sports stadium. The central oval filled with trees. Searching, running, up and down, up and down; Matinde's defense systems battled with powerful waves of dread and anticipation. Up and down, up and down; then, his shadow against the sunlight speckling through the leaves.

Back. Inward.

The memories soared away from the desecrated ballpark, high over forests and hills, alit upon the edge of an escarpment that sheered away toward the rooftops of a neat provincial town. Why were the men on one side of the road and the women and children on the other? Why were the soldiers pushing them apart, pushing the men into the backs of the black troop carriers? Why was a small woman running recklessly down the hill toward the roof gardens of the neat provincial town? Why was the soldier kneeling, and what was he shouting? Was that the hammering of her own heart or Mathembe's? She could not remember when last she had taken a breath. One by one she released her emotional buffers to taste the memory.

"Mathembe, who is this?"

Guilt: it struck Matinde like a drowning wave, overwhelmed her defenses like a fist smashing her shattering her sending her spinning away through a kaleidoscope of memories. Burning trux running wild in the street. Rainy-day mornings in the warmth and shelter of a conservatory. Trees in the ballpark, row upon row upon row. A smiling man at some forest picnic lifting his plastic wine bottle in salutation to a comrade. Stinking, fear-filled darkness. Being carried on a man's strong shoulders along forest paths as evening fell and a million biolights began to twinkle. A man standing over her bed, looking down, a voice—not his—*Do you think she will ever speak?*, the shake of his head. Thirty-seven trees standing in a row by a long fire-blackened wall. Thirty-seven trees. Thirty-seven trees. Thirty-seven trees.

Guilt. It roared, it tore at Matinde, she fought to disengage but her emotional defenses were in tatters. She cried out in pain, tore her interfacers free from Mathembe's skull. Thick yellow ichor trickled from the snapped stumps down her hands. The hurt of them was nothing to the hurt of the girl's crushing guilt.

"Geez, Mathembe. Why do you do this to yourself?" She winced, clenching and unclenching her torn hands. "I would absolve you, but I know these men who can use guilt like that. Sorry to have to do this. Maybe if I absolve you, would you absolve me?" On her left hand, her Proclaimer hand, the other needlefinger caught the light, a milky tear at its tip. "Dream good, sister. Maybe if you dream good enough you will be able to forgive yourself." But she did not even believe it herself as the needle of dream stuff slid in.

The rain rained on. In her plastic rain sheet Matinde went out to the shops and out with her belt pouch of brainplants to the restaurant by the harbor where the small man with the big connections gave her some things. But mostly, she went out to the M'Zan Bé Café, where she sat and sat and sat watching the winter rains from her table beneath the wall shrine and smoking the imported Imperial joints the small man gave her because she amused him. The apes who sat all day in the lobby of the New Sirikwa Hotel playing *fili* and grinning and laughing at the deejays on the radio passed comment upon her going out.

"You away again?"

"The rains, you know? All that rain, that damn rain, it gets to me, you know?"

The apes shrugged. They liked the rain. But then there was nothing in the room on the third floor for them to hide from in the farthest corner of the M'Zan Bé Café. She could not bear to go into that room now. Even the proprietor had been heard to complain (decorously, if-you-please-ly, of course) about the noise from that room.

"What you doing to that girl?" the apes would ask, full of prurient notions, and then wonder what they had said when they saw tears in Matinde's eyes. When she did go into the room to administer the daily hallucinogen shots, change the drip feeds, empty the bags, and collect the brainplants from her stable of dreamers, she found she had to stand in the open door for some minutes, clever expensive hands clenched into black fists, pleading, "Please, please please stop it, just stop it, I am sorry, will you please stop crying." Once, she had taken a grass pillow in her clever little hands and placed it over the crying girl's face. She had not known she was pressing down, pressing down, pressing down until the sobbing stopped and in the silence she saw what she was doing and, terrified by her own capabilities, she had fled to her holy corner of the café. Even there, in the midnight hour as the proprietor went around prodding the lazy chairs to fold themselves away and the rain clouds hurtled across the face of the moon, she could hear the crying. It resonated through her trembling hands, along her nerve fibers, into the spirit of her. Those parts of herself she had left inside Mathembe Fileli were a conduit of the emotional energy she had awakened with Mr. Needlefinger and his clever little psychotropic drugs. By day as she went on her small businesses about Kilimambasa, but especially at night in her comfortable apartment with the rain streaming down the windows, she was flayed by intolerable guilt.

"The thing is, it is such an unprofitable emotion," said the small man sipping his herb tea at his table with its view of fishing boats bobbing on the hydrofoil wake. "In an operative, that is. As a merchantable commodity, very profitable indeed. Good, honest guilt is flavor of the season in the Capital. It seems to provide them with some kind of expiation in the privacy of their dreams. Who can say?" A small shrug: so. "No, I think we will have to press ahead with this one. Market trends come and go. We must maximize our profit while she is still marketable."

He looked toward the plastic box on the table between them, the red box with the bioware stickers on it.

"No, I really do not think we can accommodate you in this respect either, Matinde. You are much too valuable to us as you are." He flipped the lid shut on the pair of neatly amputated hands that rested there in a bath of nutrient gel.

When she saw him in the M'Zan Bé Café, she knew she knew him but she did not know from where she knew him. She was careful not to let him see her staring, but not careful enough, for he came over to her table with the confidence and charm a weapon in a thigh holster bestows, full of smiles and good manners (for the armed, as a rule, can afford to be mannerly).

Would she mind if he joined her?

Not at all. For one, as a rule, must be mannerly in return, to the armed.

Would she care to join him in a glass of wine?

That was most kind of him.

Was it not terrible weather they were having?

Terrible indeed. (Thinking those endless zigguratlike thoughts about her thinking what he was thinking about what she was thinking about what he was thinking: yes, he did look kind of cute in his dazzle-colored combats; street cute, tough but vulnerable, and, yes, there was a certain daring panache in sauntering in here with his buddies armed and dangerous in full view of the town authorities—do you see anyone trying to stop us?—but it was not for those reasons she was staring at him but she knew he did not know that.)

Not a great vintage. But then nothing has been the same since the war, has it?

No she had tasted better. No, things had not been the same since Liberation.

Did she come here often?

Yes. Every day. (All the while: *I know him, I know him, I know him*.)

Might she be here tomorrow?

She was here most days at this time.

Would she do him the especial honor of having luncheon with him tomorrow?

(Unable to refuse anyone, no matter now nicely mannered, with a gun): Yes, she would be delighted.

Chatted up and dated by a fifteen-year-old. She was disgusted with herself. But she knew him. She knew him.

And suddenly by one of those feats of mental gymnastics by which you know how you know what you know when you know you know, she knew how she knew him.

The boy with the bad friends.

The boy sitting by the crazily canted fountain with a cracked mask in his hands.

The boy who lolled around on street corners until history came looking for him one night.

The boy bent double beneath the burden of shame humiliated on the streets of Ol Tok.

The boy who had had enough of words, who would fight his own battle his own way, work out his own salvation and damnation.

The boy on the expensive cross-river silver jacket: HAVE YOU SEEN THESE PEOPLE?

Only in the night was the room quiet, though the rain streamed, still, down the windows and broke the lights from the street into riverine deltas and channels. Only in the night could she bear to enter the room, for in the night they slept, naked of dreams. She knelt by the mattress where Mathembe lay plugged into banks of organicals that fed her and scrubbed her blood and sucked away her shit and piss and opened up the dark lands of her mind to let an unceasing stream of unclean dreams come screaming forth and siphoned those dreams out of her head and onto brainplant recording units.

"Sister."

In a house down the street lovers argued to the sound of the night radio. It was the hour when every song sounds painful and good. She took Mathembe's head in her hands, shook it from side to side while she thought about tears.

"Sister. I am sorry. Oh, I am sorry. Went too deep. Left too much of myself in you, got too much of yourself into me. Guilt? You know, I think now I understand what I did to you. I am sorry. It is not a big enough word but it is the only word there is. A girl has to make a living? Sure. But there are livings and livings." She looked up, startled, suspicious. Some night noise on the edge of her domain. Since she had decided, every noise was suspicious. "You see, I cannot let them see it was me that organized it. They are quick to anger and slow to forgive, and they have power. And they have me. So," she addressed other sleepers, "please forgive me, but it is better that one be saved and the rest damned than all be damned together. If it is any consolation, I number myself among the damned."

Then she went to her apartment and searched through her wardrobe of clothes the small man had bought her and found the very best, most expensive, most sexy outfit. She laid it on the bed and laid herself beside it, and in the morning she put it on and went to have luncheon with Hradu Fileli.

Twelve thousand enns. That was how much the small man had paid the flesh engineers in Kuwera to build him a couple of bodyguards. Twelve thousand apiece. And they never even got out of their seats when the 3rd Kilimambasa Prefecture Active Service Unit came through the doors and windows of the New Sirikwa Hotel. Their superfast reflexes were at least thirty centimeters from the concealed holsters where they kept their appallingly powerful state-of-the-art handguns when the emission heads of two neural scramblers (apiece) were leveled at their pineal glands.

The only bad deal the small man ever made.

Bili Bi the proprietor, finger suspended, poised above the panic button, reckoned none of them could be a day over sixteen. Yet their leader, who looked youngest of all, came sweeping in off the street at the head of a small phalanx of armed teenagers and up the stairs with a chillingly adult efficiency. As if children, in their game-playing, had somehow distilled and concentrated the essence of adulthood in a grotesque parody.

"My sister, where is she?" Matinde had the needles retracted, the tubes pulled, the interfacers disconnected. At a flick of the finger, two warriors lifted Mathembe. Again, the flick of command. Matinde was manhandled into the corridor. A third time, the flick of the finger. And the Warriors of Destiny went through the room from bed to bed to bed and casually shot the sex dreamer and the violence dreamer and the childhood innocence dreamer and the flying falling hunting chasing dreamer through the right eye.

The cry died aborted in Matinde's throat. The cold black muzzle of the sexy-thrilling vulnerable-cute sidearm pressed hard, hard into her right eye socket. Hradu Fileli looked long at her. Raised his right forefinger. *Mind, now.* And was gone, clattering down the stairs, gathering up his smiling scrambler-armed teenagers guarding the apes with a flick of the finger, move up move up move out into the street into the rain—raindrops glistening fat on the barrels of their weapons—up the hill up the long sloping hill into the camp.

Hradu left the head and one of his men—this is the way it ever is, that boys call themselves "the men" and men call themselves "the boys"—to watch over his sister and with the rest went up killing across the border. The first snow of the winter was blowing down from the north country; it lingered in the air but the touch of mud and earth dissolved it away in a breath. Too pure for the streets and footways of Kilimambasa Camp. The camouflage systems of their combat suits swarmed and flowed with fractal white as they picked their way up the hill through the huts and slush-laden shelters.

The man Hradu left was an acne-smitten fifteen-year-old, given to spitting and muttering through his barely broken vocal cords and making it quite clear that he would rather, much rather, be off across the border killing than nursemaiding a cold-turkeying ex-whore and her half-dead grandfather. When he learned that the head had come across the river with the blind soldier, he took a small-spirited adolescent pleasure in detailing how he had dumped the body down at the edge of the camp, neatly piled *so*, limbs arranged *so*.

"You," the head said, with the twice-futile fury of the truly helpless, "are the vilest little bastard I have ever met in all my long days. God forgive me for saying so, but it would give me great pleasure to see some fat Proclaimer militiaman blow your guts into your lap."

He laughed much harder and longer than he should.

On the third day Mathembe groaned a long and desperate groan on her bed, and though she tossed and tore at her ties for the rest of the day it was the beginning of it. On the third day also Hradu returned from his killing up in God's Country. He sat so dark and dangerous with the snow melting from his shoulders that the head was afraid to tell him about Mathembe's moan and that it thought that, like that darkest and deepest moment at which night runs into morning, she was turning around on her journey through the deep places of herself and starting on the way home. But then she moaned again and even Hradu sunk in his colossal self-absorption could hear in it that silent note you hear when you are in an aircraft and it makes a subtle change of attitude from ascent to descent, or if you are in the depths of a Saint-ship, kilometers deep, buried within its concentric shells of biotecture, but you know that between one instant and the next you have crossed a galaxy. The soundless sound penetrated him, pierced the cocoon of brooding that made him seem so much older and desperate than he was. In a silent coil of movement he had cut the plastic ties with his twist knife, was massaging life into Mathembe's hands and feet.

"Long long way to come yet." He looked at the head and the head, though it had died once and ought fear nothing so greatly again, was very afraid. There is nothing fiercer than your own gone wild. "That boy, the one I left here. I can have him killed if you like."

In the morning she was sitting up. By afternoon she was signing with her hands again. By evening she was capable of careful handhold-to-handhold explorations of the shanty. She was afraid to go to sleep that night, begged Hradu, the head, anyone, to keep watch with her, one hour, two, until morning. Hradu sat with her. He would not walk with her, for he was a warrior, and vain, but he sat with her in the watches of the night. They did not talk. They enjoyed profound and profitable silence. In silence Mathembe learned more about what her brother had made himself become than from any explanation of his. He was a thing that had lost its roots, its holdfast; it was flying by its own power now. Somewhere in the forest of his motivations, the jungle of private imagery, he had lost the simple anger and frustration that had exploded out of him, like seeds, like a million spores, that night when she had broken him on the rock of her silence. That night, when the city burned. That simple, righteous anger had become anger for anger's sake; he went out killing because he was angry but he did not know what he was angry at any more. He was a frightening creature. Mathembe could not like him. She was not certain she could even love him. But in the end her silence was the stronger, as it had always been, and toward dawn as the head snored vilely in its pot and sleet blew in through the bivouac door and the night radio burbled to itself in a corner, he told her the things she could not know herself about what Matinde had done to her, with elisions and omissions and editorial discretions, for even though he by now knew that his sister did not like him, might no longer even love him, still he liked her and wanted to be well thought of by her.

He knew that the drugs were burned out of her when the camp began to rouse itself with that sense of surprise at the quality of the light when snow has fallen, snow on snow, in the night and she took a pen and wrote on the translucent scratched plastic sheeting on the roof, *Matinde?*

"That bitch. You owe her nothing."

A closed fist. Insistence.

"Leave her. She is dirt. They were all dirt. Dirty bastard cross-river pimps. Parasites."

Again, the closed fist. And then, a gesture that Hradu would never learn to translate: *You are so different?*

After only a day the *men* were impatient bored irritable, ready for more *action*, leaping like merry dogs for their weapons at the commanding flick of Hradu's finger. They swaggered through the camp with Mathembe, looking mightily pleased when men older than they moved out of their way, when children splashed along through the slush beside them.

We are the law, that was what they said with every swaggering step. *With our import fashion sports boots and teleshades and our tremendous weapons, we are the law, we are the ones you answer to in your every thought, your every action, your every look and word and deed. Not the police. Not the army. Not the Bureau of Resettlement. We. Us. Ourselves, alone.*

But Hradu did not swagger. He walked at the center of his men, small and solitary even in a crowd, and Mathembe had never seen him do a more frightening thing than walk that restrained, lonely walk. He did not speak as the Warriors burst the New Sirikwa Hotel's newly regrown doors and windows. He did not speak as the two apes on the door were caught once again with their hands halfway to their shoulder holsters (twelve thousand apiece and twice in one week, liabilities best disposed of in deep, deep water). He let one of his deputies ask the proprietor: *Matinde.* He did not even speak when they went up the stairs and along the corridor and found the small man with the taste for herbal tea waiting with some of his colleagues. State-of-the-art target seekers faced neural scramblers and dart throwers.

"I take it this is not a social call," said the small man.

Hradu smiled like winter, tapped his thumbs together. "In this country it is the height of bad manners to call on friends empty-handed," he said. "Matinde. We would like to see her. Have a few words with her. And then go on our way."

"Ah," said the small man. "I can foresee difficulties with that. Matinde, as you well know, proved an unreliable employee."

"I do hope she is capable of receiving guests," said Hradu. "I would hate to have made a wasted journey."

"Oh, Matinde is alive and well. Very well. We have not terminated her employment, just moved her to, shall we say, a different department of our operations."

"My sister here would very much like to see her."

"Your sister. Ah. The lady with the exquisite dreams. Certainly. You will forgive Matinde if she is a little less than her usual ebullient self."

Mathembe pushed past the suave, small man into the room.

It filled much of the room. In form it seemed most like a trumpet, a convolution of pipes and organical pulsings flaring into a long flowerlike bell. Of flesh. The thing was made of naked, sweat-beaded flesh. As Mathembe stared, she became aware. Of the skinny, useless arms, fingers splayed on the floor. Of the tiny atrophied legs, like the wings of a winter-killed fledgling. Of the ruins of a face, nostrils smeared into long slits, ears tiny folds of gristle where the vestigial head joined the bulb of throbbing, veined flesh, mouth an intestinal knot of syrup processors. Of the eyes.

And as she became aware, she understood. She understood the thrill with which men would enter the room and approach the thing, garment by garment shedding their clothes along with their under-standings of right and wrong until they stood naked in body and spirit before it, how they would tremble as it opened its lips and with a thrill and rush of sexual abandonment let themselves be sucked deep into the pulsing vulva and be loved with a totality they could never dream from any other relationship. Sucked deep down into the enfolding warm dark of the womb, held there, sustained there, loved there.

The eyes beheld Mathembe.

Tears ran from the eyes.

Black, blood-hot rage burst within Mathembe. She hurled herself at the small smiling man, hands hooked into eye claws. The boy hands of the Warriors of Destiny restrained her.

"Your brother and I understand each other, you see, though he may have been a trifle rash in, shall we say, closing down my dreamware operatives?" said the small man. "But I see now that he is a man with strong family loyalty, and I understand that. Understanding is the basis of all successful business relationships. Matinde has a debt to repay. And as she had no independent means of income with which to repay us, we restructured the debt. We will return her to herself when it is all settled; please understand, we are not barbarians. We are businessmen. That is all. Your brother appreciates that."

Mathembe spat on him. A long, luxurious, creamy rope of spittle dripped down his face onto his exquisitely cut suit. He smiled, merely smiled, as Hradu and his men took Mathembe away.

All snows are one snow. Every gray whirling snow day is one day: close and claustrophobic, lit by that yellow uniform light peculiar to the snow. The fractal heart of the blizzard breaks time into a billion shards, all different, all unique, whirls us into no-time, those snow days when we sit by the window blizzarded out of our skulls by the falling flakes, hypnotized by the truth that no two are ever alike. Then winter is your friend; there is nothing the other seasons can offer to match the silent mystery of the snow; you would sit at your window until darkness fell and then by the light of your lamps watch the flakes still falling and guess at how many others must be falling where you cannot see them, in the dark, unheard, unseen, falling across all the land, covering all the world, and you know that whenever, however, wherever the course your life path takes, when you see the snow again it will whirl you back to this moment of hushed, reverent joy, watching in silence with your friend the winter.

Shit.

You are warm, you are comfortable, there are thick windows between you and winter, there are lights and fires and a bottle, there is a roof over you, thick walls around you, the enfolding womb of your bed is but a few steps away. Pretty damn easy to call winter your friend then. Winter is no one's friend. Those thick walls, that sheltering roof: take them away, replace them with folded plastic sheeting, leaking at the inexpertly welded seams. That quilted bed, with a warm body waiting there to share its heat with you: take instead a camp bed, or a mattress, or a quilt on the damp earth. Take away the lights, the fires, the cheering bottle; here it is always damp, always always damp, here the fire smokes and gives no heat, here the gloglobes are dim and wan, metabolisms sluggish from the cold. Your window, by which you sit and test chaos theory: smash it, kick it in, break it into a billion whirling pieces, no two ever the same. Let the wind blow snow into your home, let it melt and run across your floor, let the smell of piss and shit come through your ragged flap of a door.

Winter in the camps is no one's friend.

Winter kills.

Hradu came alone to the east gate of the camp to see them off. No men. No guns. No swaggering. He pulled the flapping wings of an Imperial military polyweather coat tighter around him. The man he had killed for it was several sizes larger than he. It struggled in the wind; the snow of the first great storm of winter found its way into the coat's voluminous, wind-filled spaces. Above him, the wind rotors howled around and around.

"You could stay, you know."

Mathembe pulled the flaps of her hat down over her ears, tied the strings beneath her chin. Hradu knew enough of his sister to read it as contempt. *Not with you, not with what you have made yourself into.*

"You should stay. At least until the weather breaks. At least until the roads get going again."

Not one minute longer than I must said the set of her shoulders as she tied firmly around the head the weatherproof plastic dome she had improvised from wire and sheeting.

"How far do you think you will get in this? God, sister, you are so stupid! You are going to kill both of you, and for what?"

She looked at him. She acknowledged him. For he had shown a knife's-edge glitter of caring. She shouldered her pack. Here at the eastern edge of the camp, on the crown of the hill exposed to the prevailing wind, there were only a few half-hearted, wind-scoured attempts at garden plots, a few packing-case guard huts to watch over them and the slim ceramic towers of the wind generators. Rags and streamers of torn plastic raged and stormed, crucified on the thorns that protected the camp.

"Do you even know where you are headed?"

A shrug. She hefted the head, cocooned in plastic, onto her shoulder mount.

"I am not going to say I am sorry, I am not going to apologize for what I have done, what I am. I am playing my part in the patriot game. What proud thing will they say of you when the true history of the world is written?"

She walked away, down the slight slope from the high point of the camp, toward the boundary and the unguarded gate.

"Go east."

Five steps from the gate, she turned.

"East. They went east. Faradje, her. They came through here four, five months ago. I was not here, but I heard. Everyone comes through here, and everyone who comes, I know about. They asked about me. Of course, no one would answer them. Security. Even if I had been here, I would not have seen them. I could not stand her scorn. You know what she was like. She would not have understood. You never understood. Only Grandfather even began to understand.

"East. That is where they went. There are dozens of camps along the border. If you tell them you have come from me, it will go a lot more easily for you. My name is known all along the line. Tell them you are the sister of Hradu Fileli, they will help you, tell you what they know."

I would sooner eat my own shit, said Mathembe Fileli in the inarticulate speech of the heart. She raised a fist against her brother, clenched it tight, tight, so he could not mistake what she felt for him, then slowly relaxed, let it fall open like a flower, let it slowly fall. *Go, then, and play your own part in your patriot game.*

Then she turned her back to her brother and walked through the gate that opened onto the east.

THE
BORDERLAND

HOW WINTER KILLS.

She awoke. The curve of organoplastic above her face was a plane of *cold* and *sound*. Vaulted ribs dripped condensation. The heat bulbs were dim, cold-shocked, dying. A vague lessening of the darkness, so that she could recognize the shapes of her few possessions by edges and boundaries, was the only indication that it was day beyond the skin of the pod tent. The long howl of the storm, a thousand kilometers long, howling down off the pole, had been a constant for so long that she had edited it down to subliminal brain chatter above which she could now distinguish other smaller, more intimate noises: the clicking of the strips of winter-cured brownmeat jerky she had hung from the tent spine, stirred by little barometric anomalies within the enclosed climate of the tent; the splinter-creak-heave of the dendé tree, among the root buttresses of which she had sought refuge from the blizzard; the soft slur of snow falling, snow on snow, flake on flake, the outstretched arms of the ice crystals grasping and locking into an impenetrable dome of ice above her head; the murmuring of the head, swathed in strips of polyweather fabric, quietly dying; the static hiss of the radio, her one vain luxury, quietly dead. Frequency modulation ghosts.

She leaned over in the body bag to take the radio in her two hands, twist it apart, roll it into its component plasmals. Her breath steamed. Already the cold was infiltrating the warm cocoon of the quilted bag. Quickly, quickly, she rolled the plasmals between her palms into a thin, viscous rope of flesh, which broke into fat drops and fell onto the receiving heat bulbs. A dim cherry light defined the two-meter hemisphere of her world within the howling heart of the storm. With the light came an inkling of heat, enough for her to creep from the body bag and try to rub a little warmth into her grandfather's frost-glazed rooticles. She breathed on her hands, pressed them around his frost-chapped face. The eyes opened, the lips moved. Nothing more. Already the light was fading, the temperature sliding toward freezing.

A little jerky, torn off, moistened with water from her drip cup, chewed. Chewed and chewed. Chewed and chewed and chewed. When your world is reduced to a bubble of dark, cold and screaming, you learn to eke out even the tiniest pleasures. Meat she had enough for another three days of blizzard, and more; water was in infinite supply beyond the sphincter door of the pod tent. Before either of those, the cold would finish her. If she had woken that morning to the unmistakable *absence* of storm roaring, she reckoned she might have stood a chance of making it to the House of the Listeners. But she had not, and she knew that if she woke one more morning and the storm was still blowing she would not wake to another. The snow would enfold her and bury her and, out of the naked earth, roots and shoots would come questing, piercing the organoplastic skin of her tent, pushing into her open mouth and eyes, penetrating her flesh in a thousand places, thrusting, with a quick, hard, vegetable darting, into her very pith. White tendrils would follow the inside curve of her skull, white threads slip between the folds of her cooling brain, white fibers coil around each synapse and neuron, reach down into her every memory. . . .

Memory.

The storm was a good place for memories. The darkness that blinded her, the screaming wind that deafened her, the cold that numbed her touch, took away the sensible world, left her adrift in an indefinite place where the distinctions between what was actual and what was memory were no longer clear and definite.

Memory.

She had not wanted the money but he gave it to her anyway, by that winter gate on the east side of the camp with the wind rotor swooping above them. She had been angry that she had needed to take what she knew to be credit of a bad color. "Go on, go on. Take it all, I have plenty," he had said, for terrorists, or liberation fighters, can always get money. She took only what she estimated would be necessary to buy her way along the townships and resettlement camps of the borderline. And a little extra. Just in case.

It was much later and many kilometers distant, lulled half to sleep by the soft impact of snowflakes on the windshield of a big trux tractor and the warm glow of the instrument panel, that she understood. The money in the smartcard had been Hradu's blessing on her journey. He wanted her to succeed as much as she did.

Through a land irredeemably scarred from the long wound that had been cut across it, she had made her winter passage, scrimping, economizing, eating far too little for a traveler in such a season, hitching a ride where she could, saving the price of a bus fare by sleeping in a doorway, in an empty rice barn, under the watch of a saint in a wayside shrine. Everywhere: HAVE YOU SEEN THESE PEOPLE? No, but I will give you thirty enns for that fine jacket of yours, I am sure it is warm, yes? no? forty then; no? fifty, that is my final offer. HAVE YOU SEEN THESE PEOPLE? Maybe, no, yes, *Yes?* yes, the woman and the man? a nod, *That is right,* I think it was them *Where did they go?* east, they went east, this woman and this man.

"Where are you going?" he had asked and she held up to him her cardboard sign with CAMP THREE in her ugly, loopy, childish ideograms and he had said, "Jump in, that is where I am going too" and they drove and they drove and they drove in a mesmerizing twining column of taillights through the slush and churned red mud and the strict diagonals of the sleet, always always cutting from top left to bottom right, always always and all the time he talked and he talked and he talked as night drivers will and all she could remember from those hours and hours and hours of driving and talk was that he was an officer in the Free State Bureau of Resettlement and that Camp Three had been cut off for a week now by floods farther up the valley of the river Yé and the rapidly escalating bush war between the Warriors of Destiny and the God's Country Retribution Squads and that all those twisted piles of bone plate and ribbing and jutting spines by the sides of the road were the victims of bioweapon ambushes.

The roots of memory. Going deep, deep, into deep soil, deep under the reach of winter.

She awoke with a cry, unaware that she had been sleeping, disoriented. The air seared her lungs, yet in the snugness of the quilt bag her body trembled and sweated. Chill and fever. Ice and fire. Was she already dead? Was this disorientation, this synesthesia, the shock of the Dreaming? Dead, sinking alone far from friends, from family, from voices and affections, into the dark humus of the mind.

Ice and fire. She remembered Camp Three. She remembered them coming on the wings of the storm: the helicopters, coming out of the heart of the tempest. She remembered running. She remembered hiding. She remembered the helicopters hanging there, hovering there, all-powerful, all-mighty, taking their time, taking good aim, releasing their rockets: *woosh!* And the domes going up in gouts of red fire on a winter night: *woosh!* The biogas plant arcing up up away on a pillar of flame, like a festival firework, one hundred two hundred three hundred meters, and falling into the swollen waters of the Yé. *Woosh!* the people running, the people hiding, the people burning and dying, and the helicopters waiting, waiting, turning their blunt black noses this way, that way, scenting for new things to send raving up *woosh!* with their target-seeking missiles. She remembered the passing trux like a monstrous, lumbering thing from a dream, she remembered reaching out and hands catching hold of her. But after that there was nothing, nothing for a time that seemed no time at all and all the time that ever would be, until her next memory, the memory of hot soup, scalding, salty, sour, at a frost-limned table on a pavement café in Chevyé township while the proprietor's radio brought reports of air strikes from out of God's Country at the border camps in reprisal for the deaths of six soldiers in a Warriors of Destiny raid.

She awoke again. It was dark. It was night. The blizzard was still a curved plane of sound twenty centimeters above her face. The cold was intense. Her breath had formed a crackle glaze of frost on the quilted body bag. She thought about the cold. There was nothing else to think about but the cold. It invaded every thought, every possibility of action, every memory, every dream. She could do nothing without the permission of the cold. Dr. Kalimuni had said that Khirr, the Proclaimer hell, was a cold place, a place of eternal screaming, where the spirits of the damned were tormented with needles of ice in the eyes, in the lungs. She had imagined that, given the popularity of sin, hell would have been a populous place. But even the presence of others can be a comfort. The best hells are solitary places. Hell has always been oneself. That was why her father's Dreaming had been such a pernicious Eden. Enmeshed in the massive grinding solipsisms of the Dreaming, no one could ever be certain what was objective, what was private creation.

Again, she remembered.

With utter disregard for sanity, the border slashed clean through the heart of Lilongwe township. It strode manfully in from the deep woods, delivered most of the Widow Muge's rice paddies into the hands of the blackhearted Proclaimers, while forcing three rooms and the outlying buildings of Mr. Amritraj's house into the bailiwick of the godless Confessors. The wire then stepped neatly between the Vijrams and the Shigis—good neighbors and good friends—pushing Proclaimers into the Free State and Confessors into a God's Country where their presence was not tolerated. With growing satisfaction, it ran straight down the middle of Twelve Street to the border post at the heart of Founding Tree Square (indeed, the Founding Tree itself had been felled to accommodate the new kiosk) before cutting straight across Third Circular, taking away most of the orchards and gardens on Sixth Street from their owners, neatly bisecting the Galaveya family home into Confessor side and Proclaimer side, then staggering away into the forest once more.

She had waited six hours for a country bus connection eastbound to Jhemba and Camp Ten in this schizophrenic microcosm. Flags of opposing colors faced each other across Founding Tree Square; rival graffitis swaggered and glowered from shop walls and house fronts: HACK KILL STUFF SCREW BURN, differing only in subject. Wind-dried heads grimaced from poles all along the northern side of the square. Ghost Boy *pneuma* masks stared back. Wall murals did battle: weeping bare-breasted women (without a care for the chill of the season) dragged bloody swords; combat-suited warriors with neural scramblers

held triumphantly over their heads declaimed OUR DAY WILL COME, A
LAND DIVIDED CAN NEVER BE FREE, OURSELVES ALONE: 25TH DIVISION
WARRIORS OF DESTINY. Across the wire: hearts in hands, Spirit Lodge
arcana, the blue and the gold, militiamen overshadowed by vengeful
helicopters. WHAT WE HAVE WE HOLD, they proclaimed. NOT ONE
CENTIMETER, UNTO THE LAST.

Yet the Proclaimer streets were deserted; their shops, commerces,
and cafés shuttered, and the Confessor streets were thronged with
people: harassed waiters bustling from table to table, shops full to the
doors, the square cluttered with manifestly thriving stalls and booths.
Everywhere the sound of business transacted, deals struck, the chirp of
card readers.

"All Proclaimers," said a home-bound migratory worker at the
country bus station, similarly vibrant with strolling vendors and hot
food concessionaires. "All from the other side of town. Been like that
since they broke parity. When Ol Tok broke with the Imperial enn, the
Free State enn slipped on the international markets. Only ten percent,
but that ten percent was enough to put every trader on the far side of
the wire out of business. That is, until the northern government at
Lyankhra decides to stick up some tariff wall."

In her tent at the heart of winter, she understood the purpose of
these memories now. If the Dreaming is what we make it, these were
the raw stuffs from which she was to fashion her afterlife: a cold land,
punctuated with dark cancers of inexplicable violence, illuminated
here and there by equally inexplicable kindnesses and humanities, a
blasted winter land through which she would wander while human
idiocy played itself out again and again.

She would not accept it. With what strength the cold had left her,
she took the stuff of her dreaming in her hands, stretched it, tore it. It
sundered with a sound of many knives. Light poured through the
wound in her memories; crystal-blue skies fat with cumulus, trees
heavy and silent under snow. All brilliant, all glittering, all still. A dark
figure described a black cross on the star-filled tear. Entering her
personal darkness it knelt beside her, and in her dream she felt a hand
laid on her head. Images: a warm place, a nest of rooms and chambers
and tunnels warmed by the soil beneath the snow; an indefinite,
ponderous object swaying from a single hair; silent people moving
among low trees, hands stained with the juice of fruits.

She felt the dark man lift her and carry her into the light. Blinding light, blinding white. Utter purity. Her consciousness fluttered; she dreamed of fast, low motion, a gliding, a sliding, a skimming across the frosted surface of snow on a hissing plane of polyweather fabric—somewhere in the superconducting spaces of her brain the impression formed of a sledge—cut with deft strokes of a sharp blade from the skin of her pod tent, hissing across firm, new snow, carrying her deep, deeper into the Dreaming. A solid dark mass beside her, pressing uncomfortably; could that be the head? Was he to share this Dreaming too? She struggled to sit upright, found herself immobile. The dark figure had lashed her firmly with plastic thongs. In a moment of lucidity she was certain she saw the dark man astride a white organical to which her sledge was attached, powdered snow pluming up behind him, the dark boles of trees blurring past. Then the whiteness, the pure, holy whiteness of the Dreaming came pouring in through the cracks in her skull and swept her consciousness away.

She was on the borderline again.

The woman on the bus to Rungwa had chattered so. Chattered and chattered and chattered. Every day, she took the bus from Camp Twelve to Rungwa, on the border, and then the cross-border shuttle to Khuragha, where she worked in a dry-cleaning shop removing stubborn and embarrassing stains, an hour and a half there and an hour and a half back, every day, more than mortal flesh can bear: "I would tell the bloody Proclaimers to stuff it if there were not fifty hands for every job this side of the border. Still, it is easier for us than for the men. There is no work for men. They will not let them in, you see. They think every man from this side of the border is a Warrior of Destiny and wants a reunited land, which of course is nonsense, if you ask me; what they want is jobs, and if anything drives men into the Warriors of Destiny it is the boredom of sitting around on their hands idle all day. Making a rod for their own backs, the bloody Proclaimers. Even we have to be back across the border every night. It is not just that they do not trust us—and they do not trust us; if ever anyone gets accused of pilfering or shoddy workmanship, it is always the poor Confessors—the real reason is that they do not want their precious township polluted with Confessorism. Scared stiff of us outbreeding them or, worse, interpartnering with them. Would not know their right hands from their lefts, then. Not that I would want to stay there anyway, not after what they did to us. Stick to your own, I say. You know your own best. Stick to your own, that is what you got to do, girlie."

And then the bus had stopped and everyone looked very afraid because it was far from any township and there was no scheduled stop and night was coming on and the only reason a bus would stop in a place like this at a time like this was if it had been stopped. By men. Armed men. They came stomping onto the bus in their muddy boots and polyweather coats, coming up the rows of seats looking at the faces, and she and the chattering chattering woman—silent now— looked at them with their black weapons with the Empire-made stickers still on the handles. Row by row by row, all the way to the back of the bus. When they had looked at everyone on the country bus they went back to the third row, and the man who seemed to be their leader clicked his fingers and pointed at a young man sitting in a row all by himself. The young man looked around at all the people on the bus, then got up and went with them. The armed men got out onto the empty road in the swirling sleet and the man who seemed to be their leader said to the driver that he could go on now and the bus pulled off leaving them standing there at the side of the road, and she looked back out the window and saw the young man pushed down to his knees in the mud and slush and night. Then the road curved and she saw no more.

She remembered the way the trees had closed in behind the bus, dark shapes closing ranks, shoulder to shoulder, like heavy, stupid louts, and she tried to look at the trees blurring past her but she could not see them, she could not see any trees at all. Instead, it seemed to her that she was in a room, a warm room, comfortable, dimly lit. She imagined faces hovering at the edge of recognition, faces that withdrew as she reached toward them. Were these her ancestors? Were these the generations upon generations of Filelis who would people her Dreaming? Memories, fleshed out, embodied, incarnated? For an instant of lucidity she was certain that they were the faces of her mother and Faradje and with them a tall, vigorous man, righteous yet oddly merry, like a vacationing angel.

She remembered arriving in Rungwa on the night of the winter carnival. The lights of the fairground, the rides stubbornly whirling in noise and glare and glee through the windblown sleet, the prayer

wands and paper lanterns tugging in the wind, the smell of dirty hot fat
from the food stalls, the dogged determination of the people, muffled
up in winter clothes, to *enjoy*, only served to amplify the township's
colossal isolation. Rungwa was the last household of man before the
uninterrupted primality of the great north woods. Apart from the
Listeners. But they were insane.

So said the fat woman behind the hot bread stall, face shiny with
sweat and grease.

"Pack of crazies, living out there in the middle of nowhere a
thousand kilometers from anywhere, Proclaimers and Confessors all
together trying to find a way to reconcile one to the other. Bloody waste
of time, you ask me. Surely what is bred in the bone cannot be
reconciled. Against nature. Your Proclaimer, he is not like us.
Different species."

She had asked with her silver jacket at every stall and bunco booth
in the winter carnival but every head shook every shoulder shrugged
every lip pursed, *no*. With a little of what money remained on the
card, she had taken a room at a café that abutted the country bus
station and watched the lights of the fairground moving through the
falling snow. She found the soft, silent sifting down of the infinitely
varied flakes distressing. Memories of another room in another cheap
hotel, another window, the rainfall of a different season. And the girl
with traitor's hands.

Even in the throbs of carnival, when the outlying homesteaders
and foresters came in by trux and even some of the revenant clans from
deep inside the forest joined the celebration, Rungwa was still small
enough for every face to be known by every other and for the
credentials of every passing stranger to be common knowledge.

No, they were not here.

No, they had not passed through recently. No one passed through
here, unless they were Listeners or looking for the Listeners.

Southern faces. Faces like these we would remember. Perhaps . . .
months back . . . who can be certain, these days, with everything
turned upside down?

Well, if they are not here, and if they are not in any of the places
you have been through, then there is nowhere else they can be, is
there?

How can you get there?

You cannot.

Not in this weather.

You cannot even consider it.

Lifts? Sister, this is the end of the line. The road runs out here. At the most, the odd truxer, the odd wild-fur gatherer, sometimes a food convoy, or some of their missionaries, returning to base. And that is in the good season. In this weather? You Southerners have no idea what it is like when the big storms come down. We have been cut off for weeks at a time. Sister, you would not last ten minutes out there. Not ten minutes.

How far? About five days' walk.

The tent? The tents start at six hundred enns. That particular model is eight hundred and fifty. You will need a heat unit also. They are two hundred twenty enns. And a body bag, one hundred and fifty enns. And some decent clothes and proper shoes. You will not go far in that getup. I will give you eighty enns for the jacket. Leaves seventy enns for the clothes and boots, and as you are buying a job lot I will throw in two pairs of snow shades. You want to go snow-blind? Food? We do not do that here. For that you want Bilimbé's on Nineteenth Street. About fifty enns should buy you enough. How much does that leave you? That radio? Oh, go on, I will throw it in for nothing, I have always had a soft spot for lost causes.

The child is mad, I tell you, mad.

The instructions she had received were simple, clear and thrilling. Walk along the border for four days. When you reach the Jerrever checkpoint, turn and head south a day's walk, and somewhere along that line you will intersect with the Listeners.

That first morning's trek, away from oily, warty Rungwa, up into its encircling hills and the edgelands of the great northern woods, had been a hymn. Light falling in shafts through fast-moving reefs of cloud turned the winter forest to silver: dazzling, marvelous, the habitation of saints and angels. Fingers of land coral were capped with white; every cup fungus—twice her height—was full and running over with snow. Sagging balloons, weighed down by ice, shifted in the wind and shed sparkling crusts of frost. Her breath hung about her in steaming clouds; she hardly noticed the weight of tent, rations, heater, radio, head of her grandfather (muffled up, muted for once), as she toiled over the hummocks of frozen moss domes and sudden sheer valleys where small, dashing brooks ran beneath the ice. Her bootprints behind her seemed like numerous and persistent sins in the purity of the whiteness. Beneath the snow and decomposing forest litter, her gloved fingers grubbed out wild brownmeat. She sucked the fleshy buds straight from their barely open prepuces; what she could not eat she tied to her pack to dry and cure in the cold wind.

She had worried that she might not be able to recognize the borderline. It was unmistakable. A strip of pure white fifty meters wide, shaved bare of trees, fungi, corals, every living thing. Down the precise center of the dead zone ran the wire. Snow had drifted against the foot of the wire fence that was taller than five people, covering the small cairns of bones and leather that were warnings more eloquent by far than the bilingual notices in vibrant red and white that the fence was electrified.

She did not like to walk under the shadow of that fence. She could feel its charge as a numbness, a deadening of her spirit that was only alleviated by moving under the eaves of the forest. Straight, undeviating as a slit across a throat, the borderline crossed hill and valley, ice-locked river and stream. She had hidden from the guards at the first border post—half a day's walk from Rungwa, a cluster of helicopter-dropped house pods guarding the pass between nothing and nowhere—afraid of their weapons, their foreignness, their maleness. But as she moved along the borderline, day after day, post after post, she understood that the guards of God's Country were not her enemy. Here the winter was the enemy of Free Stater and God's Countryman alike. The guards would hail her and, when she mimed a reply, they seemed to mistake her for a Listener—she could not imagine why— and threw cans of food and beer over the fence to her, cheering those that hit the wire and fell back with an impressive shower of sparks.

On the fourth day the border guard at the Jerrever post sent her southward with a rain of Five Hearts Beer cans (surely an omen of something), and she had never felt more like singing. Then she felt the whole forest shiver, one great fearful tremor, shaken by a surge of wind from out of the north. Within minutes clouds had covered the sun and she saw that this land she had thought pure and white and holy was the white of teeth and bare bones, that its beauty and divinity had always been deceptions. Big snow coming. The trees were loud and restless as the vanguard of the storm advanced behind a driving wall of ice needles.

The light was gone by the time she had erected the pod tent and stimulated the heatglobes into life with a libation of chilled Five Hearts Beer. She sealed the sphincter as the blizzard struck the forest like a fist, curled up in her quilt bag warm and snug and excited with a childish delight in being sheltered from vile weather.

And now she was dead, sinking into the matrix of roots that knitted this land together. And in the spring when the snows melted and flowed and dashed in a thousand spated streams running down from a high, hard land to the great river valley, those travelers who came nudging cautiously into these forests would find some ghastly travesty of a human being knitted and knotted from shoots and roots and fibers and bones and no one would know and no one would remember and no one would kneel to press an ear to earth still damp from the thaw and listen for a voice crying out from the soil, no one to hear, no voice to cry, and she cried out in the Dreaming *Someone anyone hear me!* and the cry broke the empire of the memories, smashed it, sent it spinning away like broken ice on a flooded river.

She lay on a bed in a warm intimate room. Windowless: the only light came from bank upon bank of tiny bioluminescents. A discomfort around her mouth and nose: she raised her hand, saw tubes, slugs, leeches clinging to her arm, felt organicals clustered around her face, made to tear them away.

A hand stayed hers.

A hand. A face. Two faces. Three faces.

The tall angelic man she had seen in the room when it had been a dream, who she now realized had driven the sledge, had slit open her tent with his hunting knife, had saved her.

Faradje. Fat. Bleary. Smelling of cooking and bed.

Her mother.

—Yes.

Your voice: how what why do I hear it?

"In your mind." Faradje, a little apart, at the foot of the bed. "Everything will be explained. Rest. You were a long time away from us."

It looked like Faradje, but surely Faradje's voice had never held such graciousness of tone in the days on Lantern Lane? The tall man moved among the biolamps, turning them up to higher illumination.

"Javander Shasri," said Faradje. "From the in-moiety. It was he who found you, brought you here."

Here? Where? Grandfather!

—Peace. The old man is being cared for. He is fine; already, he has managed to offend the out-moiety postulant assigned to attend to him.

Javander Shasri. A Proclaimer name. Her mother, seeming to know her every thought, speaking into her spirit. Faradje, transformed. Everything was here. Nothing made sense.

Her mother unfastened the high collar of her tunic. Lit by bioluminescence, the scar was livid, shocking, the staple line pursed like lips.

"The operation is very simple," said Faradje. "Quick. Painless. The house medicals are very experienced. The vocal cords were cleanly excised."

That tall one with the Proclaimer name, the fingers of his right hand were resting on a long-healed scar on his throat.

She had deceived herself. This was death. This was unreality.

—No.

Again, the voiceless voice formed out of some mental stratum deeper than hearing.

—No. No. You could not be more wrong. This is not death. This is true life. Me, Javander, even Faradje, we are Listeners now.

Before the small, quick, clean operation that cut away his voice, before even the call of God to this pure land and the community of the Listeners, Javander Shasri had been an engineer. He had worked on the railways with a huge organical that consumed whole forests at one end and shat parallel ceramic rails and neatly packaged parcels of organic waste out at the other. He and his machine had shat rail enough to reach from him to God, and then one day as he was sitting eating his lunch watching the twin ceramic rails squeeze from the big organical's rectum, God had come sliding down that line out of heaven and shown Javander Shasri the profound truth that he was not to be found in addition, in the endless multiplication of names, titles, words, facts, but in subtraction, in the division of things into themselves so that only the unitary denominator remained, in the stripping away of all the human paraphernalia of observance and ritual and dogma to reveal the simple divinity within.

Such a mathematical, exact theology appealed to Engineer Javander. It led him past the place where his rails ended, away from the confusions of humans, into the deep woods and the greater contemplation of God. And, in time, to the Listeners in their northwoods fastness, among whom he found a practicality of application of this theology that was close to his pragmatic engineer's spirit. The generators that maintained the *ur*-space bubble at the heart of the Balance House were tributes to the skill of their dead designer, and indeed the Balance House itself, the spiritual, metaphorical, and actual point of equilibrium of the community, was a delight and wonder to him and a sign that the things of God may be at once essentially simple yet intelligent and sophisticated. In such a spirit, he chose to end his days as a sojourner, take the Vow, and join the in-moiety and be admitted to this fulcrum of mysteries.

Parallel to this mathematical, abstract strand of his theology ran the awareness that an immense and profound spirituality inhabited nature. In the depths of the wildwood dwelled a sense of the immanent, the numinous, that he had been searching for since his earliest childhood. It was not God, but it was the closest to God he could imagine. Whenever an excuse could be made, he would take a vehicle from the community pool and drive for hours through the uninterrupted, present solitude of the deep forest. Whatever the season, but most especially after the first snows of winter had fallen and lain, he found in the woods the expression of the ultimate simplicity of God.

It had been on one such winter patrol that he found, in the wake of the blizzard, the too-regular, too-incongruous mound of the pod tent among the snow-drifted buttresses of the dendé tree and the half-dead girl and the more-dead head within. Now he was abroad once more on the community snow byke—a lovely thing, sleek organoplastics, strong beating motor muscles, shaggy mane with nylon hair (he found himself thinking altogether inappropriately proprietorial thoughts toward it)—ostensibly to check on the welfare of the Jerrever border post, the community's nearest neighbors, in the wake of the storm.

God's interests are not renunciation but recycling. Every old thing

is to be made new and reused. Therefore, it was the old engineer in
Javander that immediately recognized the distinctive sound of demo-
lition charges. From the north. Toward the border. The spiritual life
is worthless unless rooted in concern for one's fellow humans. He
flicked up his antiglare lenses into maximum polarization and turned
the byke north, toward the dead zone.

Javander Engineer was forced to admit that they had been
uncharacteristically thorough. A three-hundred-meter stretch of fence
had been neatly felled by shaped charges.

Javander Listener was filled with apprehension as he left the byke
purring by the wire and stepped into God's Country.

Winter is a hungry season. The smell of the blood, the blind
touch of the warmth of the bodies even as they cooled, had woken the
life sleeping in the soil and sent it burrowing up through the snow.
Javander cleared the pulsing, sucking organicals from the first of the
figures spread-eagled in the snow. Shot through the left eye. As he had
expected. The others would be the same. Strange that he felt no
horror, no rising gorge of revulsion. There is a mighty tranquillity in
shock. The winter-hungry organicals came swarming back out of the
pink snow as he went to check the border post. On the small portable
television a happy couple were winning an obscene amount of money
on a game show. Plastic-wrapped crates of beer were piled up
underneath the desk. On the walls, calendars with big-breasted smiling
girls, anachronistically warm and summery. Poor sinful Proclaimers,
condemned to Khirr by the vile act of looking upon the human form.

He found the portable communicator, took it outside to check the
direction of the byke tracks. North, across the cleared zone into the
trees. Engineer Javander knew that the authorities would have been
alerted by the power outage in the fence. Listener Javander knew when
silence must be given up.

He unfastened the breast pocket of his heavy winter coat, fumbled
open the sealed plastic envelope that contained the vocalizer organical.
The heat of his throat activated the device; a tendril went questing into
the interface behind his ear and nestled among the synapses of his
speech centers. The sector headquarters number would be first in the
communicator's memory.

"My name is Javander Shasri." The artificial words were oddly
weighted and poorly inflected, but discernible. "I am from the

Listener community. Listen, please. The border post at Jerrever has been attacked and destroyed by the Warriors of Destiny. No survivors. The attackers are headed north, toward the railhead at Jerrever township. Please alert authorities. I shall wait at the border post for your arrival."

He sat with his feet on the desk surrounded by the beautiful big-breasted smiling calendar girls, drinking beer and watching an incomprehensible soap opera about the lives of neighboring families in a suburban cul-de-sac in some eternally sunny and happy Imperial city until the helicopters came.

In those first days at the House of Listening while the out-moiety medicals healed her flesh and the in-moiety counselors healed her spirit, Mathembe Fileli discovered that an entire spectrum of emotions can be diffracted out of the word *love*.

Joy: that her mother and even fat Faradje were alive, safe, warm, fed, sane, healthy.

Relief: to be alive after all, to have reached the end of her search, to have had her hunches and instincts and stubbornnesses proved right.

Anger: that her mother had found a life and purpose complete, whole, without any place considered for her daughter, her son.

Guilt: that she should feel such anger toward her mother.

Shame: that her search, the reason for her being these past months, should have been concluded in such ignominious failure.

Such complexity of emotions, Mathembe Fileli. And when her mother sat with her on the meditation stools set in one of the community's fruitful domed gardens, tried to touch her, to communicate through her wordless, tactile communication, Mathembe slapped the hand away: angry, shamed, guilty, relieved, joyful. She feared her mother's spirit examining too closely the sores and seepings of her emotions, pains and shames she did not wish opened to anyone.

—Set it down, daughter of mine, let it go. Stop being capable. Stop being responsible. Stop giving. Receive. You helped me once, in Karasvathi, when I was driven to desperation by my own need to be capable, to give, to be responsible. Will you consent to be helped now?

Out. Away. Leave me alone! she shouted at the voice of her mother in her mind, striking at the touching hand. It was too soon for intimacies. The winter was yet heavy upon the land. There must be time for the roots and shoots to grow under the snow, to go down into the earth and find warmth and strength and security there. Mutual rememberings, the sharing once again of experiences, the explorations of personal changes: all these must pass before Mathembe could allow the intimacy of this silent language.

Her mother looped a speech synthesizer over her ear, around her lacerated throat, into her brain, and spoke aloud in an artificial voice that shocked Mathembe because it was so alien from the voice she remembered coming from this face. They spoke about peripherals, things on the edges of their lives.

Uncle Faradje? He was well. As she could see. His innate talent for burrowing and nesting had found perfect expression in this warren of burrows and nests beneath the winter woods. The Listener theology—antitheology, rather; the community fought shy of the sharp-edged, vicious knives of doctrine—was entirely compatible with Faradje's own personal philosophy. *Worship as you can, not as you cannot.* Therefore, a couple of hours of paperwork in the out-moiety offices settling the affairs of the community in the outside world, a few minutes on the satellite link and accessing information from the Dreaming matrix, a morning or so picking fruit in the gardens and closed orchards, a little sleep, a little beer, a little lying back to watch television were the steps by which he made his way to salvation.

"Even God," Mathembe's mother said, "needs a civil service."

And the head? Grandfather?

The scar on her mother's throat might be barely healed (Mathembe had gained a ragged understanding that this radical vow of silence the in-moiety took was somehow linked to the relationship between the words *silent* and *listen*, anagrams of each other), but in that brief time of living and moving among the silent, she had learned more of the eloquent communication of the voiceless than in all her life before. Mathembe found it exhilarating to be understood, totally, completely.

If she was here at all, if she was no longer the Mathembe Fileli that had run in the forests of Chepsenyt but something leaner, fitter, crueler perhaps, more compassionate perhaps, it was in no small part due to the ungentle kindness of her grandfather. This had been the heart of bone in her will to survive. But the winter passage of the border country had been hard on the head. The peeling, scabbed skin, the hair and beard falling out in handfulls, the dead, dendrified rooticles, the wooden skull misshapen from many a hard knock, blow, and fall: testimonies to hardship. The dead do not heal.

"I have long given up hope of returning to the old Fileli tree in the Ancestor Grove in Chepsenyt," it had said to Mathembe, when she visited it and its out-moiety minder. "I cannot go back to Chepsenyt. None of us can go back to Chepsenyt. All the trees have burned; what Chepsenyt there is is the Chepsenyt you make. This will be Chepsenyt for us now."

One of the first acts of this newly redefined relationship was for Mathembe and her mother to return the head to the dreaming of its new Chepsenyt. It seemed a sign and seal of deeper and more painful intimacies to come if they could do this thing together. Mathembe thought of Hradu, determined to cast his shadow over the borderland and make the name of Fileli a synonym for fear and terror. Mathembe thought of her father, as much a prisoner of his prejudices in the seductive Eden he had created as he was of the tree in the row of thirty-seven outside that regional detention center. Later. The time for these was later. Their closeness was still too fragile, still crystalizing, easily shattered.

The dead of the House of Listening occupied their own dome, a dark, cool beehive filled with whisperings, echo upon echo of remembered lives. Ten, twenty, thirty meters, the interlocked wooden masks of the dreamers arched over Mathembe and her mother. The grandfather surveyed the dim, biolit interior of the dome from its cracked and chipped pot.

"Can any of these farts play *fili?*" it said. Then, changing mental tack, "You were right, granddaughter of mine. I hate having to tell you so, but you were right to ignore me and go on with the search. If I had not been so selfish, back then at Kilimambasa, so much hurt could have been avoided. . . ."

Mathembe kissed the old, vile, rotting thing on its lips. The head coughed, a small cough that became a big, then a major cough. The head coughed and coughed and coughed, a huge dreadful racking cough from the very bowels of its being, had it bowels, had it a being more than a memory of a memory spinning through the neural matrix of the rooticles: coughed and coughed and coughed. And spat something onto the ground.

Mathembe picked up the thing it had spat out onto the floor of the chamber.

A smartcard. Crumbed with soil, stained with organical ichors. The signature was still legible: *Kolé Fileli*. Her father's smartcard, that he had hidden in the pot that time, at the checkpoint on the escarpment above Timboroa. Mathembe looked at the card. Before her mother could glance over to inquire, she flung it away from her, away in a glittering arc through the air. It fell unmarked and unremembered in the darkness.

The Listeners being shy of formalized faith, there was no litany or rubric for the transmigration of the dead. An organical hoist heaved itself through the narrow door, splayed its feet wide, and lifted the two living and one quasi-dead to the highest point of the dome.

"Nice view," said the head, its voice almost gone now. "Pity it is such a bloody undignified way to go up to heaven." It had always understood that its umbral existence was temporary. Death is the empire of everyone, where all sleep and many dream. A hard land, maybe, but living may be harder, when you are handless, footless, actionless, deedless, reduced to a dependent voice that can conveniently be ignored. If the saints had willed that it return from death it was for the purpose of wisdom—for the heart of the will of the saints is not *doing* but *being*, not action but personal maturity—to shape a new Dreaming, one that was more than life's strictures and limitations, that had a hope of being heaven.

Mathembe's mother held the cracked pot. Mathembe eased out the mess of decaying, dendrified rooticles, pressed them into the apertures in the dome wall. One by one the sphincters sealed shut, the grafts took.

"Listen, granddaughter of mine, daughter-in-law of mine. I have one last story to tell you: you most of all, Mathembe. As it will be my last, this side of the Dreaming, at least do me the honor of listening well.

"In my courting days, when I was known around all the townships of Timboroa Prefecture, I was much wont to visit in Tetsenok township, where I was told by the father of the woman who was to become my wife that on the end of the street lived a man who had caught an angel in a hunting snare. Rather than shoot it, he brought it back to Tetsenok and kept it in an empty kennel for prayer-dogs. There was no doubt that it was an angel; the man was a well-known braggart and invited everyone in the township to come and see the angel in his dog kennel. I myself did not see it, but I was informed on the highest of authorities that it definitely was an angel—a small one, just a handful or two of primal creative energy, but unmistakably divine. Your grandmother's father told me he could not see very much in the gloom of the prayer-dog kennel, but that it was about the length of his hand and forearm, silver-colored, and gave the impression of being shaped like a fish. He asked the man what he was going to do with it, and the man said he was going to feed it on scraps and mech syrup until it grew big enough for him to tie a chair to its tail so it could whisk him off up through the sky into heaven. He went every day to look at it and feed it this unholy mess of syrup and scraps, and it seemed to him as he looked at it that every day it lost a little of its uncertainty, a little of its shimmering fishiness, a little of its silver shine, and became a little darker, a little duller, a little more tarnished and definite in shape. It developed things that looked like legs, little stumpy legs, and a shape like a head on the end of a neck, and a body, and a tail, and every day he came back it seemed less and less silver and numinous and more and more solid and dirt-colored, and one day there was no angel there at all, no shining heavenly silver, only a big dumb prayer-dog wagging its tail and waving its feet and singing in its throat."

Mathembe cocked an eyebrow. *What does that have to do with anything?*

"Damned if I know," said the head. "You find something for it to mean."

The eyes closed. Buds sprouted from the ears, became leaves, became a beard of small blood-colored flowers. The lips parted, and turned to wood, and spoke no more.

If there had been any way in which he could have been linked to the killing, Javander Shasri reckoned the northern Defense Force officer would have had him shot there and then. A dumpy froglike man, this officer, made more so by multiple layers of winterproof clothing, with the distinctive amphibian aura of one whose long comfortable hibernation has been unforgivably disturbed. A pulse ticked in his temple to the strict tempo of a Spirit Lodge drum. He was one of those to whom the one thing worse than a Confessor was a *turned* Proclaimer. He refused to let Javander help tag and bag the bodies or to let any of his men go within three meters of him. He had heard all about these turned Proclaimers. He knew all about their *infections*. Javander's statement had been taken on a pocket ceedee recorder, which the officer had then assiduously wiped clean with a paper tissue. When the helicopters flew away with their black cargo strapped to the landing skids, the tissue had remained, a fluttering butterfly of blue blowing across the snow toward the wire.

When they were black dirt in the eye of God, Javander went back to the empty hut and put a call through to the out-moiety, a brief report of the outrage, his intention to go on to Jerrever to check on the Listener mission house in the township. He removed the vocalizer, turned off the television. A children's program involving the wholesale destruction of property and the celebration of anarchy (with major prizes) was sucked into the white Schwarzschild radius at the center of the screen.

Javander met the tape twelve kilometers out from the Jerrever border post, yellow plastic tape, swathed and draped and festooned across the white road that ran down the valley to Jerrever, twisting and fluttering in the wind. CAUTION: POLICE INCIDENT   CAUTION: POLICE INCIDENT   CAUTION: POLICE INCIDENT. Battletrux lounged by the side of the road, childishly blue and yellow against the colder, cynical adult colors of the heaped, refrozen ice. Blue and yellow, too, the shoulder flashes and insignia of the militia who stood around on the road, ashamed to have been caught looking at the things they had killed. The byke purred and nuzzled against the side of the big warm battletrux; Javander slipped underneath the plastic tape. Young Proclaimer defenders made to arrest him, black weapons lowered.

Hand raised. One finger touched the scar on his throat.

The officer in charge nodded. Javander might only be a Listener, but he was some shape of spiritual authority. Not even a Warrior of Destiny could be denied terminal unction.

The woman and the young, terribly thin girl were past his saving. Brains dead, cooling rapidly toward absolute spiritual zero. Nothing beneath his hand. No pulse of quickening, not even the memory of a memory. Despite wounds that had ripped open his side and spilled his stuff out onto the road where the heat of his life ran into the melted ice, the young man was alive.

Riding riding riding through the great dark winter, through the trees, the endless trees, all of them together riding riding riding brothers and sisters with their weapons on their backs high high on victory, high high on killing riding riding riding into the heart of the enemy all friends all comrades all brothers and sisters together; "Tonight we will strike" he had said, the small one, the dark one, the leader. "Tonight we will drive a spike of fear into their hearts that will make the whole world shiver" and they had come out onto the road and they were waiting for them and the guns had opened up and Silelé on your left-hand side she had gone down first and in front of you a wall of bullets lifted Aya off her byke tore her apart before your very eyes sent the stuff of her life spilling and spraying across the white ice road and you looked around where where but you could not see anything and your leader he was shouting but you could not make out the words and you stood up to see him where was he? where was he? and then it hit you, then it ripped into you and you did not feel anything, not anything at all but the strange taste of brass in your mouth and a terrible dark sickness and your byke reared and screamed under you and threw you and as you fell you saw your guts coiling out onto the ice and all you knew was a profound fascination at how densely and intricately packed was the complexity of your inner life. . . .

He tried to croak, to touch fingers, but the only movements left were tiny movements, the only sounds small sounds.

Javander kissed him on his open mouth.

The boy soldiers shifted their weapons, uneasy, uncertain.

The virons took only moments to reach the brain, but even as the infection spread the boy was dying.

I . . . you . . . confusion. What? How?

No time for talk. Feel. Experience. Share. I am you and you are me and we are we. We are reconciled, I and thee. Be reconciled.

But he was afraid. Afraid of the dark, the cold spreading through him, afraid of this presence, this identity.

Hold me, stay with me, be with me, go with me. . . .

He held him in his mind until the final neural spark dimmed and guttered into extinction. Javander took his lips from the cooling flesh. The soldiers stood away from him as he walked away and the bag teams came with their plastic zip-lock sacks. The officer pursed his lips, shrugged. So.

So.

Damn it.

Peace for the living, not a kiss for the dying. He had failed God. To send his divine infections burning through the nervous systems of every one of those scared, guiltily proud young militiamen: that would have been success. Success for the Listeners, success for God.

The spirit had flown. The great north woods were empty, mere trees, mere snow, mere whiteness, mere meteorology across which he traveled; the presence that stirred the silence only the wind from the north.

Had he been moving any faster than the pace of a troubled spirit the wire would have cut him in half. As it was, it felt like God had exploded his heart in punishment for disbelief. He sat on the snow, gasping in great knifing lungfuls of winter, legs splayed out before him, dazed, reeling while his field of vision swarmed with shapes that might have been phosphene angels and just as easily might have been the figures of lithe youths, slipping out of light-scatter into corporeality.

There was no rule against it; there was no rule at all, save that simplest and most difficult of spiritual rules: *Love God and do what you will.* However, custom and usage had it that in moiety and out-moiety kept separate quarters: silence was silence and speech was speech, and while reconciliation of opposites was the purpose of the community, those were two flavors much enhanced by being kept apart from each other. Thus it was uncustomary, but not improper, much less unlawful, for Mathembe's mother to move her daughter from the sojourners' quarters along the outer edge of the community to live with her among the in-moiety.

Before they entered the in-moiety, her mother made Mathembe wait a moment at the door.

"There are no words in here," she said through the vocalizer. "The only speech in this place is the speech of the spirit, you understand. Can you trust it? Can you trust me?"

Mathembe listened to the silence, nodded. *Yes, I can. I will, yes.*

Her mother disengaged the organical from her brain and left it sucking from a row of wall teats. They went in.

The in-moiety house was a dome, larger by several degrees of magnitude than the dome of the heads. As high as the laws of architecture would permit, the surface of the dome was sculpted into biopods, each lit bright as an eye with many lamps. Rope ladders and scrambling nets provided access to the individual quarters; the climb to those pods closest to the apex of the dome was vertiginous. Mathembe thought of the hive of some mindless, colonial, web-spinning insect. Translucent membranes covered the entrances of most pods; a few were open, fewer open and occupied. As Mathembe took in the scene a girl, thin and brown as rice stalks in autumn, came bounding down a scramble net, leapt onto a single line and handrail that ran around the circumference of the dome, swung herself into an open pod, and sealed the door behind her. Terrifying agility.

Her mother's pod was on the twelfth level, a three-meter-long cylinder studded with biolamps.

A pat of the hand on the floor, in any language, means *sit*.

Her mother touched her.

She was afraid, at first, when the first flickers of *presence* quickened in her mind, sent neural lightning into parts of her Mathembeness left dark and fallow all her life. *Words* surfaced from her dormant speech centers.

—No magic, Mathembe. This miracle is one of biotechnology, not of God.

How?

—The cutting of the vocal cords is the least part of being in-moiety. It is only a symbol, a voluntary silencing of the outward voice to permit the inner voice to speak and be heard. The true covenant of our Vow is the virons with which we choose to be infected. And even this sharing of souls is not the greatest part of what they can do, though reconciliation through true communication is no trivial thing. The reconciliation that comes through an inability to hate one's neighbor, that comes through the abolition of violent aggression and racial prejudice, that is the true miracle.

Mathembe signaled incomprehension.

Her mother leaned forward in the biolight, touched her daughter's face, spoke into her mind.

—What was the central achievement of the Green Wave? Stripped of all the fairy tales and nonsense; two breakthroughs: the development of a synthetic polymer that acted in every way as a living organism and, at the same time, the discovery of a genetically tailored virus that enabled the human nervous system to interact with, and thus manipulate at a molecular level, this stuff we now call plasm.

—Forget the Ahleles, striding across the land sowing chaos from their right hands and transformation from their left. Forget Janeel and Oboluwayé, creeping into a new, strangely transformed world from their crèche pods buried deep in the heart rock where the genetic changes could not affect them. Those are myths. Legends. Lies. And so is the belief that Confessors and Proclaimers are genetically different. That is a myth. A terrible myth, a damnable lie, which we Listeners will expose and destroy. Destroy it, for it has had a thousand years of destroying us.

The voice in her mind grew passionate now, touched emotional responses from Mathembe.

—Take me into the cells of a Confessor, show me the DNA of the Proclaimer, and show me the codon sequence that determines that one will believe in fifteen saints-major, six hundred and thirty saints-minor, thirty-eight thousand nine hundred and twelve angels, and that the other will believe in one God almighty absolute into whose image all men will be conformed through the lives and examples of nineteen witnesses. Where is it written that one will fast from nightfall to noon on his holy day and sit and wait on the whispered word of God and another will clap hands three times, bow three times before a shrine, and place a little slip of paper on a prayer wand?

—I can show you where genetic drift among the Proclaimer settlers a thousand years ago resulted in inherited left-handedness, but it is a mighty long road from the way you sign your name to the way you worship God. I can show you where the twist for language is, where the twist lies that ensures that children are born with the same innate capacity for writing as for drawing house and trux and mommy. But I cannot show you, no one can show you, the place where the molecules demand that you are born Confessor or Proclaimer.

—Myths. Lies. Falsehoods.

It is a strange, disturbing thing, the ardor of our parents. The wave of impressions, illusions, voices continued.

—I suppose it must have seemed like a wave, this explosion of new technology, new thinking, new ways of looking at the world. Very little has survived from those times, but through the heads we have access to worldwide data cores, and what we have gleaned from them is that the transformation of this land, the heart of the biotectural revolution from mechanical-biological to totally biotectural, seems to have been achieved in under eight months. We think we live in fast-moving and traumatic times. They are nothing, nothing, compared to the utter revolution of the Green Wave. I cannot even begin to imagine how it must have seemed to those who lived through it. No wonder it seems to us that the world began then. In a sense, it did.

—We changed half a planet, but we cannot change ourselves. Yet we have the power to make change ourselves beyond all imagining. Any shape, any form, any function. We could fly if we wished. We could live in the dark of the ocean trenches—some may indeed have done so; that may be where the legends of the Nyakabindi come from—we could travel naked through space; we could photosynthesize. These abilities all lie within the genetic code, yet instead we cling to our cherished myths and fail to see the potential of what we could be if we discarded them.

—But we are the Listeners. We are the challengers of myths, the thinkers of the unthinkable. We have taken the first tentative step on the road to the transformation of humanity. The science of it is quite simple: a modification of the virons enabling our nervous systems to interact with genetic material now enables them to interact with other human nervous systems, by direct contact. That is how you hear my voice in your mind, see my visions. Simple. Obvious. Something we should have thought of centuries ago, but that we were too obsessed with hating each other. But linked to that first viron is a second, more delicate viron, less easily transmittable; that one does the true work of reconciliation by altering the neurochemistry of the infected person. It attaches itself to the neurons in the brain and responds to certain trigger stimuli—those, specifically, that would cause active or reactive aggression or the sociobiological process at the heart of tribal discrimination—by stimulating the brain to release dopamines and endorphins that neutralize the reaction before it is even begun.

The science was beyond Mathembe Fileli, flesh sculptor of Gangerabili, green lady of *Unchunkolo*. But the implications were clear and suddenly thrilling: a disease that made its victims incapable of violent aggression and simultaneously reconciled them through intimate identity with each other. A Love Plague.

And the Listeners, the carriers? Into every corner of the world, into every camp and hostel, into every wounded and hurting place, with a message of peace, goodwill to all, love and reconciliation that, unlike any other creed, required no exercise of faith.

Mathembe drew back from the touching hand. Her mother sought her again.

—It cannot be transmitted by hand-to-hand contact. It is a very delicate organism; it cannot survive isolated outside the human body. It must be passed in the blood, the saliva, or sexual fluids. The wound, the kiss, the sexual act.

Her mother. . . . There are two terrible discoveries, after which the world is never the same again. The first is that your parents are mortal. The second is that your parents are sexual beings.

Human souls stolen away with a kiss, a over-playful love bite, a quickie thrust one two three ah in a back alley. Stolen away without knowledge, without consent, without any realization of what is being done to you until the day you walk away from the faction fight in Founding Tree Square, the day the wasted boys call you blackheart no good Emperor-sucking Proclaimer, and you smile, and you nod, and you go on your way; the day you take your Spirit Lodge sash and badge and oath and burn them in your back garden.

And never again fight.

Glorious. Exhilarating. Liberating.

Monstrous. Terrifying. Shattering.

The young woman wanted to hamstring him and drop him twenty kilometers from damnation in the deep forest.

The young man with the ludicrous attempted mustache wanted to strip him naked and leave him to the snow.

The young man with the northern accent wanted to use the knife, working his way around the extremities, snip by snip.

The girl who was the sister of the young man with the northern accent just wanted to shoot the bastard and have done with it.

All the while the boy who was their leader squatted by the heater unit and smiled. Just smiled.

"The reason none of you will ever be great leaders of men, let alone great liberation fighters, is that you have no notion of the value of things," he said. "Not one of you noticed the scar across the throat. A Listener, little flock. And a valuable commodity. This is our way out of the trap the Proclaimers are drawing around us. Disappear within. The Listeners refuse no one. Can you understand what I am saying, little flock? Sanctuary."

Then they all took turns to threaten Javander with deaths painful and cruel and lingering and bloody and messy and to hold knives to his wrists and weapons to his eye socket and monomolecule loops to his throat, and all the while the boy who was their leader squatted by the warmth in his untidy tent of a winter coat and shook his head and smiled sorrowfully.

"Truly, you know nothing. You cannot threaten a man who has no fear of death. In that these Listeners are braver than you and I. Finesse. That is the key. Watch. Learn."

He rose from his place by the heat, knelt before Javander.

"Truly, your faith must be a great thing for you to be able to look death in the eyes and say you are not afraid. I admire that. I honestly admire that. And I admit there is nothing we can do to you that could force you to act against your will. But I still think you will take us to your community. I will tell you why. You see, either you lead us willingly, and we come in peace with our weapons turned downward and our hands empty, or we kill you—which, as you have said, is nothing to you—and then turn your byke loose. It is a stupid creature; its homing instinct will lead us right to your House of Listening—I believe that is what you call it? And this time when we come we will come with our hands full and our weapons turned outward and we will slaughter your community down to the very last child. Death may be nothing to you, but have you the divine arrogance to say the same of your brothers and sisters? So. One question, and one question only. Will you take us?"

Javander nodded.

Mathembe knew what her mother was doing even before she was shown the Balance House. It was not just understanding. It was not just forgiveness, nor that new, comfortable relationship that develops between parent and child when they are able to recognize each other as adults and humans. Her mother wanted transformation. Her mother wanted evangelism. Every unspoken word, every neural message transmitted through the subtle virons hooked onto her nerve endings, were to one end: *You see what I have, I want you to have it too.*

Mathembe did not know if she could accept what her mother wanted her to have. Sacramental virons crawling along her nervous system, encysting themselves in her body cavities: she did not think she could tolerate such an intimate link with the task of reconciliation, however worthy. Joining the new humanity seemed too much like violation of body, spirit, and selfhood.

A third terrible revelation—not as common, perhaps, as the realization of one's parents' mortality or sexuality, but excruciating— the evangelical zeal of the parent toward the child.

The Balance House, spiritual hub of the Listeners, was housed in yet another dome, by far the largest Mathembe had yet seen. Ten, twenty times Mathembe's height, lit, as were all the domes and corridors in this snowed-up troglodytic community that reminded Mathembe of the interior of the human body, by clumps of biolumi- nescents set into thousands of wall niches. The Balance House itself was a cocoon of biotecture, large enough to hold in-moicty, out- moiety, all the sojourners, and more, suspended from the center of the dome by a single thread of some unimaginably strong material. Access ramps reached down from carefully spaced portals to almost, but not quite, touch the floor; with equally precise care, hard metallic outcrops of machinery were spaced around its circumference.

The entire edifice swayed imperceptibly to the tiny breaths of air that always seemed to be astir in the corridors and chambers of the House of Listening. Mother and daughter circled the Balance House. Her mother's hand brushed softly against it. The whole imponderable structure began to turn. Through an open portal Mathembe glimpsed bioluminescent-lit ranks of carved misericordes, and a blackness so complete it seemed like annihilation. The *ur*-space bubble of which she had heard mention? What need had a reclusive, quasi-religious order for the technology by which starships tens of kilometers in diameter crossed the universe?

Mother's touch.

—Two are balanced, three are balanced, many are balanced, but never one. That is the heart of it, do you see?

She did not. She touched the imperceptibly moving Balance House, felt the drag and rub of its surface under her fingers, felt it slow, felt it stop.

All this, from a single thread?

She had learned a thing about the Listeners' touch telepathy: it worked both ways. By touching her mother and focusing the visualizations, the emotions, the experiences that were her personal language into *communication*, she could make herself be heard. Whether as words or as amorphous impressions she did not know; for all their technology, the Listeners had still a long road to go to conquer the problem of *self* and *other*. She touched her mother, interrupting her progress around the gently moving Balance House.

Why have you brought me here?

Her mother turned with the sudden, shocking speed of a forest animal. Before Mathembe could react, she had taken her face in her hands.

—Understand.

Mathembe flinched as memories came darting into her mind, sharp, silver, painful. Not her own memories, her mother's.

The hands slip, the hands part as the flames run along the rooftops of Ol Tok. Boats push out into the flame-red water and she watches from the shore until there are no boats left, no place left to go, all her life, her treasures, taken and burned by the fire of history. She and Faradje turn to the north, follow the river roads through kilometer after kilometer of battle-scarred suburb, hiding out for days in some deserted villa or garden plot until the flow of battle moves elsewhere. On highways thick with armored troop carriers, beneath the wings of helicopters, they are absorbed into a swelling tide of refugees as effortlessly as two drops of rain into an ocean. Time passes—such a multitude of griefs and pains and struggles can be covered by those two dismissive words—they reach Yorusha on the border of Tannalewé Prefecture, come to the door of an old river trader's warehouse, square in the firing line between Nationalists and Imperialists but which seems to be respected by both as a kind of sanctuary. It is the mission of the Listeners—the strangely mute, maimed ones come out of seclusion and irrelevance in their north woods with a new vision— working beyond the limits of human capacity to feed and tend and bind and cherish in the name of reconciliation. A relationship grows between her and the silent old Listener woman who nurses her back to health through the summer months of the war: seeds of fascination and curiosity germinating into shoots and roots of inquiry, budding into a spiritual quest inspired by the presence of this person who embodies saintliness because she claims for herself no virtue whatsoever. The relationship blossoms in that first sharing of souls, when the old woman opens her memories to her searching spirit, and there, in those memories, she sees the face, once glimpsed but never forgotten, of her son. She sees Hradu in a group of boys off-loaded at some northern port, and the light of rage in his eyes cannot be hidden. She knows she must save him. She encourages Faradje to go north with her through the rag end of civil war to the new border that has snapped down across the land and the camps of the stateless and dispossessed that have grown in its shadow. She finds there not Hradu but his legend: boy hero, teen liberator, the cold and quiet killer whose name is both law and curse among the people of the camps. She is careful not to let herself be known by the name of Fileli. Hopelessness at her inability to have prevented her son from becoming what he has made himself consumes her. She contemplates suicide, rejects it as the final abandoning of hope. Instead she seeks out the Listeners. She and Faradje are accepted among them as sojourners; they help where they can and in their small alleviations of the enormous suffering of the camps she feels her guilt absolved, just a little. She grows close to the small team of missionaries; they share souls as a sign of her acceptance. Among those with whom she shares memories is an old, honorable Proclaimer, an ex-militiaman, troubled by the things he saw and did in the rebellion—he insists on calling it that; an old incorrigible. Among his memories are thirty-seven man trees standing in a row.

(Here were hurt and pain Mathembe did not care to probe. A dark place, a night of the soul, a despondent slough.)

Her next memory is of stepping out of a hired jeepney. With her is the old ex-militiaman. Close by, across rain-wet grass, are the ruins of an old detention center. The walls are black, burned down to the ground, but the trees before it are strong and green and healthy, with many many beautiful leaves. The branches have grown together so that no one may disentangle them and say where one ends and another begins. The people of the township have hung the branches with ribbons, small icons, holy medals, sweetmeats, plastic toys. At the base of each trunk is an untidy shrine of votive lights, prayer wands, offerings, supplications. She walks along under the intertwined branches until she comes to the tenth tree. She claps her hands three times, bows three times, and presses herself to the moss-scabbed trunk.

The old Proclaimer begs her forgiveness.

She forgives him.

On her return to the mission, she says she is certain now. She applies to become a full member of the Listeners, of the in-moiety. She wants to make a difference.

Mathembe sees her come to the House of Listening in the light of late autumn. Mathembe sees the first snow fall on the rooftops. Mathembe sees the silver knife descend toward her throat.

And as Mathembe saw, so she was seen. Her memories opened up before her mother, drew her into her past: *Unchunkolo*, Dr. Kalimuni's story, the painful revelation of the damned angel, the argument at Kilimambasa, Matinde and her fate, her own failure with Hradu, the journey along the winter border, searching. All seen, accepted. Forgiven.

"Sisters."

In a place where silence was enshrined, spoken words were terrifyingly abrupt. The out-moiety messenger hesitated at the sphincter door to the Balance House dome. With her was a sister from the in-moiety. Mathembe recognized her as the lithe gymnastic girl who had moved with such ease through the ropes and ladders of the in-moiety quarters.

"Please, you must come with us to the community offices. As quickly as you can, please. All community members and sojourners must come to the weather room."

A tilt of the head, a lift of the eyebrows: *What?*

"The Warriors of Destiny have come. They say they are seeking sanctuary. With them is Javander Shasri. We believe he is being held as hostage."

The young in-moiety girl extended a hand in the gesture Mathembe had learned was an invitation to the sharing of souls. Her mother took the offered hand.

Despite the wound across her throat, the gasp was clearly audible. Mathembe seized the skinny girl's arm. *Show me too.*

The winter, the hard physicality of his life on the borderline, had laid down flat, tight muscle, filled out his frame, honed off the last few soft contours of boyhood. The mental image was fleeing, but the dark dangerous energy that communicated itself through his every movement was unmistakable. Hradu.

Mathembe sensed it one fraction of an instant after her mother. Even the tall well-built woman from the out-moiety felt the tremor in the air.

The Balance House was vibrating at a pitch so slow and low that it was felt rather than heard. Dust motes stirred in the excited air. And then it became a heard thing, distant first, but fast approaching, growing, swelling, mounting in volume until the entire House of Listening trembled before it and Mathembe clamped her hands over her ears to shut out the sound: the thunder of low-flying helicopters.

There were not very many of them. Seven souls, as many snow bykes. Some luggage, some litter, a few weapons, a handful of all-weather pod tents. They loitered, they busied themselves with the small necessities of survival, they waited on the snow. The House of Listening's sprawl of tunnels and buildings encircled them, excluded them. As the House of Listening itself was encircled, out there at the boundary of the snow-covered paddy fields and the forest, by the waiting helicopters. Caught between the inner and the outer.

The weather room had been grown onto the roof of the refectory as an eye on the outer world by the community's architects, a four-windowed place for retreat and the contemplation of the divine in nature. Since the arrival of the Warriors of Destiny and the landing of the raiders from God's Country, there was not a daylight hour when it was not busy. The curious, the concerned, the contemplative, and, like the sojourner woman who passed the image intensifier to Mathembe, the apprehensive.

The helicopters from God's Country were beautiful, obscene creatures: gleaming black carapaces to which no crumb of blown snow adhered, rotors folded flat along the sleek sides, weapons pods clutched in an array of claspers and mandibles, lean, carnivorous. They crouched among the trees with no attempt to conceal themselves beneath light-scatter nets. Occasional figures could be seen at large, moving from helicopter to helicopter, never daring to expose themselves on the naked ground.

She turned her attention inward, to the comings and doings of the Warriors of Destiny. By his height and his demeanor—composed and serene in the most stressful of situations—she recognized Javander Shasri. This was the man who had rescued her, now in need of rescue himself. The thought of reciprocating his gallantry pleased Mathembe. With him was Hradu. The lenses and circuitry stripped him of personhood, of brotherhood, into just another piece of television, a collection of meaningless actions and movements with no connection to herself.

As if the balance of forces between Listeners, Warriors, and Northerners was not precarious enough, a fourth force was now approaching that threatened to shatter the equilibrium into chaos. For the past few hours the out-moiety had been picking up radio communications from a large force of Free State troopers advancing from the main road at Rungwa through the north woods to investigate and neutralize the incursion of northern soldiers.

Caught between the outer and the inner, and not only between opposing external forces but internally, the House of Listening was fissured and schismed by internal division. Those northern raiders, those Free State troops, had not chanced upon this place serendipitously. Someone in the community had summoned them.

A house divided. Watch closely, this is how the world ends.

Differences of opinion became disagreements became arguments became polarizations and factionalizations and hostile camps. At the convocation of all community members to which the messenger had summoned Mathembe and her mother from the Balance House, Mathembe watched Faradje and her mother argue with each other. A strange argument, when one side does all the shouting and the other is silent. In every word, in every gesture and touch, was the sickening tearing sound a child hears when it wakes in the night to hear its parents fighting in the next room. Like children, the sojourners, Mathembe among them, watched in incomprehension as every principle in which the House of Listening was rooted was torn from the earth. This had all the peace, reconciliation, and true communication of two battle dogs fighting in an alley.

As the pain of the children may save a partnership, so it was the sojourners who saved the community. Tugged and torn by the opposing gravitations, they might themselves have leaped with a whoop and yell into the fray. Then a young man, a Confessor boy—seventeen, eighteen, nineteen?—with the dark skin and eyes of the southernmost prefectures cried out, "In the name of God, will you stop it, please stop it? We do not know what to believe any more. I came to this place believing it could make a difference in the world, and you cannot even keep the peace among your own selves!"

No child that has seen the shame of his parents will ever forget it, or ever view them again as he did before. This is the fourth, and cruelest revelation of the children, for after you have seen it you are a child no more.

In the weather room, the bell chimed. In-moiety, out-moiety, sojourners descended the spiral staircase, passed along the ice-bound corridors and through the neat gardens and the valve doors into the big dome. One by one the Listeners filed up the ramps into the Balance House and Mathembe understood her mother's enigmatic comment that other time by the Balance House. There cannot be *one* because, to be reconciled, there must be a *thee*, there must be a *me*. However he approaches, one is always unbalanced. Mathembe stepped onto the ramp, carefully timed her steps to match those on the other ramps. The Balance House trembled but did not waver. She moved carefully around the tiered interior to the designated seat. The Balance House quivered but did not waver. The mechanisms that controlled the *ur*-space bubble at the center of the house had focused it down to a twenty-centimeter sphere so black, so compelling, that it hurt the eye. It was a long process for all the community members to go up one at a time and take their places. When the seats were filled, the ramps folded up and away. Doors sealed shut. The Balance House swayed; sojourners and younger out-moiety members looked at each other nervously.

Hands were joined.

Every soul shared with every other soul.

At first Mathembe thought sanity and self would be smashed to powder by the hammer blow of so many lives pouring through her own. Then a voice spoke in her mind and all fear was driven away: the voice of the elder of the in-moiety.

—One hundred years ago a Confessor holyperson and a Proclaimer witness went wandering into the great north woods. Each came from an opposite direction; each was trying to find the ultimate truth of God in their respective beliefs. They wandered and they wandered and they wandered, moving inward all the time, until they met in the same clearing in the middle of the forest. Recognizing each other, each therefore tried to convince the other of the error of his ways and the superiority of his own faith. They debated theology with each other, they argued with each other, they shouted and cursed at each other, they damned and condemned each other; they fought tooth and nail until their clothes were in rags and all their possessions were destroyed, and still neither could convince the other that his and his only was the true and only way to God. They debated and shouted and cursed and fought so long that they had not realized that the winter was upon them and they were naked and defenseless in the wild north woods and that, if they were to survive one night, let alone return to civilization, they must swallow their pride and their incompatibilities. So they took a vow, each of them, that they would not speak, for it was words and the meanings of words that had set them apart and at each other's throats. In silence they worked and helped each other, and the strength of the one covered the weakness of the other, and the strength of the other covered the weakness of the one. And as they worked, in silence, they learned that the things that separated them were not as great as the things that united them, and that if they were to return to the world of humans, their peace and unity would once again be torn apart by the hatreds and prejudices of the world. So they remained, in silence, in their clearing in the north woods, and ever since, people who have sought a better way, a realization that the things that unite are stronger than the things that divide, have come seeking them.

There was silence. The leader of the out-moiety, a small, vigorous woman of fiftysomething called Isyé, then spoke the case of her people. Her soul speech was cautious and halting, but compelling.

She said it was she who had informed the God's Country authorities at Kalighash. She had brought the helicopters. For this she begged the community's forgiveness. Her motivations had been honest and, she had thought, in the best interests of the community. What was noblest and highest in human law was that which stood upon the foundation of God's law, notional right and notional wrong that was programmed into the genetic heritage of every human being. It was wrong to kill: God's law and human law agreed. It was right that such lawlessness be punished; indeed, to let a violation of God's law go unpunished was to violate God's law oneself.

These Warriors of Destiny were killers. Offenders against any and every law, they had annihilated the border post and would have carried out unspeakable atrocities against the innocent people of Jerrever. For the House of Listening, however noble its aspirations, to extend sanctuary to violators of God's law would be to break God's law. Natural law demanded that these criminals be turned over to the forces of justice, and expeditiously. Therefore she had telecommed through to the brigade commander at Kalighash and brought him and his warfleet of helicopters hammering in hard and fast and low over the treetops of the border country.

Moral considerations aside, for the community to have taken in the sworn enemies of the people of God's Country would have been, in their eyes, to identify with their methods and aspirations and irrevocably alienate the Proclaimer population. One course and one course only had been open to her. She had taken it without the slightest qualm of conscience. She hoped her sisters and brothers would understand and forgive her.

There was silence among the tiered rows of the Balance House. The argument was a strong one, and convincing. Then the leader of the other faction spoke, Tulash, a thin, luminous old in-moiety man of sixtysomething. His soul-sharing was suave and limber, and firmamentally sincere.

He begged the forgiveness and understanding of his brother and sister Listeners. He had been guilty of errors of pride and anger against the whole community. The virons did not abolish anger or pride—that was for the angels—they merely prevented its manifestation as violence and aggression.

He did not wish to be thought vain in saying so, but he had been a member of the community longer than any other outside the Dreaming. And in all those years, those hard decades when the philosophy of listening and reconciliation seemed weak and insipid compared to the brash new muscular philosophies of nationalism and independence, and the community in the deep woods had slipped from the minds of all but a few faithful in the surrounding townships who had kept it supplied through the winters, one tenet had held true. None were ever turned away, no matter how foul their crime, how deep their sin, how black and cancerous their guilt. None were ever refused admission. Who among them was without sin? Who among them had not come here with spirits as dark and troubled as these Warriors of Destiny? The difference was one of degree, not of state. If they had come in need of healing, how much more these Warriors of Destiny? God had not appointed the Listeners to be judges. He had appointed them to minister to the needy.

None were needier than those whose spirits were scarred and hardened by the way of violence. It had been said that the House could not admit them and retain any credibility. The truth was that the House could not *refuse* them and retain any credibility.

He finished speaking, and there was silence in the Balance House. The arguments of the in-moiety, too, had strength and merit. Mathembe held them one in each hand and weighed them against each other. Their weights were equal. She brought her hands together and tried to fuse them into one thing, one common consensus. She pushed and she pushed and she pushed, but they would not mate. They remained isolated, inviolable, incompatible.

After the sharing, the silence.

Mathembe had grown up with silence. Silence had been her chosen companion to run with her in the forests and glens around Chepsenyt: silence and solitude. But she had never known silence like this. The silence of soundlessness is not the silence of listening. The difference is as simple and profound as the difference between empty and full, presence and absence. This vibrant, listening silence threatened her. Every moment swelled and swelled and swelled like an enormous water drop from a rain-soaked leaf until it could not possibly hold any more time; then fell, sparkling, into the past. In this silence she could feel every movement and stirring of the Balance House on its diamond thread, could feel the very planet turn beneath her feet.

On and on and on. Silence. The fat tear-drop moments fell slower and slower, slower and slower. Time slowed. Time froze. Time ceased. There was only silence.

Out of the silence a voice spoke. It spoke aloud, words that set the Balance House trembling; it spoke also silently in the sharing of spirits through every joined hand in the chain of Listeners.

"Seek the more excellent way. Seek reconciliation, wherever she may be found."

The speaker was a young out-moiety woman of thirtysomething, heavily pregnant, suddenly terribly self-conscious at having shattered the silence. But no one doubted that she had spoken the pure and undiluted word of God, for even as she spoke, the response swam up to the surface of Mathembe's consciousness and to the surface of every mind in the Balance House: *Yes, we know what we must do, but who will do it?*

"I will," said the young sojourner whose outburst of emotion and honesty had caused this meeting to be gathered. Without a moment's hesitation: "I will go." Blessed he who knows so surely the will of God.

—I will, said the mind-speech of a middle-aged in-moiety woman, pretty in an ugly sort of way, ugly in a pretty sort of way, dressed in a tattered one-piece smeared with paintstains.

And it came to her. Like a clear voice, like the voice of a jangada poet soaring above the multilayered complexity of his accompaniment in ecstatic improvisation. Call it God, call it an angel, call it destiny, call it insanity, call it what you want, but call it out, call it out loud. She placed the touching hand of the man on her right on her shoulder so that the circle would not be broken, clenched her right hand into a fist, and struck herself with all her strength on her chest.

I will, said Mathembe Fileli. *Send me.*

The House of Listening had never been more alive, more one body, than in those hours after the people had come, one at a time, out of the Balance House and into history again. In-moiety, out-moiety, sojourners: all worked together with a unhurried yet fruitful unity.

While the Free State troopers in their armored battletrux plowed inexorably on through the pure northern snows, and the God's Country raiders played knuckles and listened to cockle radios in their helicopters, and Hradu and his six terrorists ate self-heating rations with plastic spoons and did tricks with throwing knives, Mathembe and her mother went down a third time to the Balance House.

They say that once is for you, twice is for the one you love, but the third is for the saints.

Mathembe cupped the sphere of *ur*-space between her hands. Its blackness was so intense there were no highlights or shadows to suggest it was a sphere. Pure shadow, a flat disc of shadow. A universe between her fingers. She listened to her mother.

—Of course, the generators will expand it considerably for you to enter. The first and great reconciliation is reconciliation to yourself. In *there* (there could be no other "there" than that bubble of non-physicality) is everything you have ever hoped for and everything you have ever dreaded and your every dream and your every nightmare and all good things and all bad things and all that you love and all that you hate and all that you fear and all that you despise about yourself and everything that has brought you joy and everything that has ever hurt you.

How?

—*Ur*-space, the matrix, the dreaming, heaven: all are aspects of the same thing, a universe of consciousness that lies beside and within our own, yet is not identical with it. How do the Saint-ships traverse whole galaxies instantaneously? It is as true to say that they do it by wishing, or by imagination, or by force of will, as by the mathematics and mechanics of a higher dimension. In there is whatever you want there to be; its shape is however you shape it. There all the mental entities that make up your life are made real. You can destroy them, and they can destroy you. Or you can be reconciled to them, and they to you.

Mathembe wondered how it had been for her mother, after the knife, when she had stepped newly wounded through the blackness. What had she found there, and how had she reconciled, or failed to reconcile, herself to that psychic bestiary?

—You should rest now. Sleep. Prepare yourself.

I have been preparing myself all my life, she wanted to say.

—You must choose a partner.

A partner?

—No one goes into the Balance House alone. No one goes into *ur*-space alone. You cannot infect yourself. It must come from another. It must come by—through, as—an act of love, because it is a kind of love itself.

Through the touching hand came images of a short, squat, ugly, grinning man, of flat broad fingers, like spades, of hard flat muscles, of hair and breadth and weight and solidity and eyes so deeply slitted you could not tell their color, and a generous, gentle, humorous spirit. All gone. Months gone, gone away deep into the south, to the mission at Ol Tok.

Names, faces came trembling through Mathembe's mind. All the in-moiety, men and women, catwalked before her.

—Who would you have?

She pointed, out, up, through the dome and the earth and the snow.

Him.

Javander was not surprised when Hradu Fileli acceded to the request from the out-moiety that he be released and returned to the community. His usefulness as a hostage, always limited, had been devalued with every piece of news eavesdropped on the Active Service Unit's radios. Now that the Free State troopers were within five kilometers of the House of Listening, he was worthless. The balance of forces was changed, dangerously. The entire House of Listening was hostage now. They could let one go with impunity. Javander knew, Hradu knew, the out-moiety knew that with every minute the Free State forces drew nearer, the greater the probability that the northern raiders would launch a preemptive strike against the Warriors of Destiny and escape back across the border before the encirclement was complete.

What did surprise Javander was that he was taken straightaway by a delegation of in-moiety brothers to the Balance House. It was only as he saw the *ur*-space bubble expanded to fill almost all the open center of the building that he understood.

The things we do for God.

—You do not have to go.

The Balance House swayed slightly as Javander and his assistant moved unseen beyond the all-devouring universe of black.

—You do not have to go, Mathembe's mother repeated. —I would have gone. I should have gone. He is my son.

As Mathembe undressed, her mother ran through the final checks.

—Remember, there is no gravity in *ur*-space. Remember, the space within the bubble is potentially infinite. Remember, the atmosphere is almost pure oxygen; you can very easily overventilate. Remember, you can come back at any time, by merely wishing it so. Remember, the *ur*-space medium is not so much a physical object as a set of metaphysical concepts.

Remember remember remember.

And Mathembe Fileli stood naked before her mother for the first time since childhood and her mother looked at her and saw what kind of a woman her daughter had become and all the scars that her education had earned her, and she hugged her very quickly because anything more would have torn her in pieces.

Mathembe Fileli stepped forward through the black curving wall of *ur*-space. And was swallowed.

Black nothing lightless soundless touchless scentless tasteless weightless nothing nowhere notime is this death is this annihilation no, cannot be, I think and if I think I cannot be dead, I think therefore I must be and if I am, therefore there must be some physical form to contain this thinking being me, and as she thought the thought her body appeared—or was it that she became aware of being aware of her body? But her body it was, long and languid and naked and floating in this lightless soundless touchless scentless tasteless weightless unmedium, but if she could see her body there must be light by which to see it and as she thought *light* so there was light and the lightlessness became a light blue infinite space, and if there was vision must there not also be sound and touch and scent and taste? And even as she thought them so they became: the sound of the wind, the feel of her own corporeality, the scent of fresh clean air, the taste of cold high altitude on her tongue; she was flying, flying through an infinite blue sky, look, far below her, scuds of clouds, flying without engines, without wings, without any means of support or propulsion whatsoever except her own imagination, if I doubt for even a moment that I can fly, will I fall? No, do not even think it, but is not to not think about it to think about it? well, I did not fall so it must not be true.

Flying! She was the angel, the silver angel of the dreaming, but this dreaming, this heaven, was of her own shaping and the thought of that both thrilled her and frightened her for in this infinite blue sky with its politely scudding clouds might range an infinity of psychic monsters that could destroy her. And even as she thought it, so she noticed that moment by moment this infinity was attaining finitude, the blue endlessness below her was thickening and curdling into a basement of clouds and she knew this place now, it was the Dreaming of the Filelis, the Dreaming her grandfather had promised to remold, and if she looked down might she see? yes, islands of riotous brilliant color on the gray backdrop of clouds. She knew what she would find in the edenic forests of these cloud islands, but with a beat of her mind, she bent her body toward them and shivered with the sexual thrill of a million cubic kilometers of air brushing against her naked skin.

There were angels. A multitude of angels, beautiful beautiful angels with bodies of steel and chrome and silver and bronze and white platinum and diamond and jasper and carnelian and every precious metal and mineral, all the Filelis, generation upon generation of them, lounging about in the trees, in warm pools of limpid water, on soft carpets of moss, in the petals of enormous succulent flowers, in the treetops and the branches, atop the umbrellas of the fabulous fungi or immersed in fleshy cups of honeydew.

They were bored. Insufferably, unutterably, eternally bored.

Paradise was boring. Heaven was tedium, unending monotony of splendor and joy and plenty, of ease and pleasure and every wish and whim provided for.

Paradise? A subtle kind of hell, rather.

As Mathembe passed overhead, the angels turned into trees. Sank roots, pushed out shoots, grew branches and leaves.

She had rather imagined they might.

She knew what she would find if she penetrated the cloud layer and dived toward the waters that covered the earth. But Mathembe-space still had a character of its own, still contained a capacity of surprise. The behemoths still trudged across the surface of the planet trailing their wakes of boiling water, paradise borne on their shoulders. But the tread of the monsters was purposeful, even determined. The shoulders did not stoop beneath the weight of past lives but bore them up proudly; the heads were not bowed but looked forward, onward, eagerly, toward some ineffable destination. Mathembe twisted and tumbled through the air and she saw that the leviathans were changed because the essential nature of their components were changed. The men and the women and the children were still chained and roped into their carcasses of metal strapping, treading on their treadmills, pulling on their levers. But the feet trod with enthusiasm, the arms that pulled the levers pulled for joy, and in the faces of each of the millions of men women and children who made up the body of the walking giants there was a resolution, a determination, an idea of a place to go to, a purpose to achieve that would be shared by all if all joined and worked and trod and pulled together with the common goal of achieving it. The men smiled, the women glanced at them and laughed, the children giggled and grinned as they trod their wheels and heaved their levers and moved forward, step by step by step.

Those men and women and children. Of course. Theirs were the faces of the House of Listening.

She headed back to the clouds. But Mathembe-space held new surprises. She looped past the behemoth's head and suddenly saw what she had not seen from a distance: that it was the head of her grandfather, fleshed out and sculpted by the arrangements of human bodies. A mouth wide enough to drink down the great river in one swallow opened. Lips, teeth, tongue, were carefully interlocked men and women.

GUILT, said the grandfather head, and thunder growled in the perpetual mists of the cloud layer. LOVE.

Impelled by a will not her own but born of some mind eddy in *ur*-space, Mathembe was drawn into that open mouth. Air rushed past her, a cyclonic inhalation, swept her between the cavernous lips, teeth each the size of *Unchunkolo*, to land lightly upon a tongue fashioned from bowed backs.

There was a tea set waiting for her, an exquisite, craftsman-made tea set of the highest refinement.

"If only you would speak, Mathembe Fileli," said Dr. Kalimuni, pouring tea into china cups. "You and all like you, if only you would speak out and say 'Enough of this,' if only you would even once refuse to let us death-haunted, bigoted old people speak your words for you. Go on, speak, say something. What have you to say about this world you have been given by us? Do you like it, do you hate it, do you want it, and, if not, what do you want in its place? How will you change things, what will you make better, what will you make worse, what will you make different? Speak. Say it out. Why are we so afraid to ask for the things we truly desire?"

And these were the answers Mathembe Fileli gave.

"The world I have been given is the only world there is. And because it is the only world there is, I like it and I hate it and I want to make it better and I want to leave it unchanged.

"What I will make better is me.

"What I will make worse are the things that were bad to begin with. For then we will see them as they truly are, with no glamorous mask or cosmetics.

"What I will make different is the life of everyone who meets me.

"We are afraid to ask for the things we truly desire because we are afraid we will not know what to do with them when we get them.

"And I did not speak because I had nothing to say and no words to say it with. But now I have the words, Dr. Kalimuni, and something to say with them, and I will speak and be heard."

A rising wind lifted her, drove her before it away from Dr. Kalimuni, improbably anchored with his Book of Witnesses and his exquisite tea set in the hurricane breath from deep in the *ur*-lungs of the behemoth. Lips, tongue shaped the breath into memories of words. GUILT. LOVE.

Love.

Guilt no more. The burden of responsibility no more. The freedom to act, not out of a sense of having to atone for some sin of failure but for the joy of acting. Her enormous self-absorbed silence was broken. Others existed. They existed not as markers, against which to measure her own degrees of success or failure or guilt or happiness, but for their own needs and cares and joys and griefs. The realization of the other was a mighty liberation, a mighty wingbeat that sent her up through the cloud layer into the brilliant blue.

She saw him from afar, a dark freckle on the perfect skin of the sky. She knew who and what he was. Rejoicing, she willed herself toward him, hurtling through the sky to explode against him in a soft detonation of passion, to wrap her legs around his waist, slip her tongue between his teeth, hug him to her with her arms, and tangle him up in her. She moaned as she felt him enter her, felt his tongue caress hers; then even the pleasure of his thrusting thrusting thrusting as they tumbled through the sky was swept away by the electric thrill of the virons bursting through her body, multiplying and reproducing through her bloodstream faster than thought, spiraling along her nervous system, in waves of ecstasy breaking through her hind brain into the twin hemispheres of her Mathembe Fileli-ness, infecting every part of her, every organ and gland and hair and cell of her, into the thousands of potential Mathembe Filelis waiting in her ovaries; she cried out as the spurt of his virons invaded her, twice pierced, twice penetrated, and all the while as they tumbled through space they tumbled through each other, through their memories and experiences and loves and hates and everything that had ever happened to them made visible by the sharing of souls.

Darkness. The imagined world had unraveled and been wound back into her memory as they coupled. Now only they remained, two definitions of reality in the un-medium of *ur*-space. She lay beside him, touched him, felt him, understood him.

—How long have we been here?

—Never and forever. Like everything else here, time is an extension of your imagination.

—So we could stay here forever.

—We have already been here forever.

Forever passed.

—Are you ready? he said.

She realized that in thinking there might be a world she regretted returning to, she was ready. She looked to touch him for just one more personal forever but he was gone. She was alone in enveloping blackness. The blackness intensified until it became a tangible thing, an infinity pressing against her skin in which she was embedded. It might not be blackness after all, she thought, it might be all the colors of the world, blindfolding her, and as the thought came to her, so the unsubstance beneath her fingers grew tangible and fibrous and tore at her touch.

Light shone through the cracks in the firmament.

Like a newborn creature from its birth sac, she tore her way back to the world.

—How long was I in there?

There. It had dwindled again, to the size of a small fruit. *How many angels may dance on the skin of a breadapple? How many universes may you hold between the palms of your hands?*

—Two hours and twenty-three minutes.

This soul-speech, it came to her with an ease and clarity she had not known before. As if . . . as if it were not the translation of gestures, movements, the inarticulate speech of the heart, but the words themselves. Her head was reeling. She tried to shape air into sound.

Nothing.

Of course. She was in-moiety now.

—Two hours twenty-three minutes?

—The Free State troops have surrounded the Northerners. The commanders are conferring, via the out-moiety. The Free State commander is offering the God's Country commander safe passage back across the border if he will leave in peace. The God's Country commander is uncertain whether to trust the Free State Commander, whom he suspects of being in league with Hradu. If he becomes convinced he is in a trap, he may try to shoot his way out.

Hot towels, underwear, winter clothes. So soon.

—How long does it take to become—

—A carrier? Not long. Less than two hours twenty-three minutes. The virons reproduce at a staggering rate. You are biologically capable of attempting this mission. Spiritually capable?

—Yes. No. Maybe. An old Mathembe gesture. Spiritually capable? Who of us may claim spiritual capability? Every step is the step of faith.

—Let us go.

The southern boy fingered his new pink scar, fingered and fingered and fingered it as he waited in the room with the ugly-pretty woman and Mathembe. The pretty-ugly woman touched the boy, Yasda, and Mathembe also, to share the joke.

—If you tear those staples, you will bleed to death before you even get to these Free Staters.

It made Mathembe laugh. The out-moiety brother came in in a gust of cold to announce that the bykes were ready for those who needed them. Yasda stood up and almost sat down immediately. Nerves.

—Courage.

The woman Chemde goosed him on the ass. And they were gone, and Mathembe was alone in the cold room. She listened to the noise of the engines until the wind swallowed them up. One to the Confessor, one to the Proclaimer. And one other.

Courage. The way of reconciliation was the way of courage. Courage not to accept the world as given to you. Courage to give up your preconceptions, to admit they were not so sacred after all. Courage to allow yourself to be changed. Courage to change others.

...it had taught her, said. They knew they will change the world eventually, one soul at a time.

One soul at a time. Out there Chepsie and Yaola would be making their own particular contact. They would be surprised, those commanders, shocked even—military people were habitually conservative—by the suddenness of the mouth kiss. They might react violently; they might mistake it for an attack, an assassination attempt. They might kill the pair who were trying to bring them together. This has always been the danger of the peacemaker. If ever one failed to become infected, tragedy would ensue. It should have been easier for her. She had known the body she would be infecting with peace all its life. It was that it had grown so far different that made it frightening.

Courage. One soul at a time. Life by life we will end this maelstrom of ignorance and hatred; one soul at a time we shall bring peace to the divided land. It starts with one life, and one life starts with one step.

She got up, opened the door opposite the one through which Chepsie and Yaola had gone out. She stepped out. The Warriors of Destiny stood up, raised their weapons. Hradu came forward. The snow flurried around the House of Laleuru. One step after another, Mathembe walked out across the snow with unafraid lips to the place where her brother was waiting.